feathers

Haim Be'er

feathers

Translated from the Hebrew by

HILLEL HALKIN

BRANDEIS UNIVERSITY PRESS

Waltham, Massachusetts

Published by University Press of New England

Hanover and London

BRANDEIS UNIVERSITY PRESS
Published by University Press of New England
One Court Street, Lebanon, NH 03766
www.upne.com

Printed in the United States of America
5 4 3 2 1

Published by arrangement with the Institute for the Translation of Hebrew Literature

Originally published in Hebrew as *Notsot* by Am Oved Publishers Ltd., Tel Aviv, 1980

Published with the support of the Jacob and Libby Goodman Institute for the Study of Zionism and Israel, and with support from the National Endowment for the Arts

Library of Congress Cataloging-in-Publication Data

Be'er, Haim.
[Notsot. English]
Feathers / Haim Be'er ; translated from the Hebrew and with a foreword by Hillel Halkin.
p. cm.—(The Tauber Institute for the Study of European Jewry series)
ISBN 1-58465-371-X
I. Halkin, Hillel, 1939– II. Title. III. Tauber Institute for the Study of European Jewry series (Unnumbered)
PJ5054.B374N613 2004
892.4'36—dc22 2003026808

THE TAUBER INSTITUTE
FOR THE STUDY OF
EUROPEAN JEWRY SERIES

The Tauber Institute for the Study of European Jewry, established by a gift to Brandeis University from Dr. Laszlo N. Tauber, is dedicated to the memory of the victims of Nazi persecutions between 1933 and 1945. The Institute seeks to study the history and culture of European Jewry in the modern period. The Institute has a special interest in studying the causes, nature, and consequences of the European Jewish catastrophe within the contexts of modern European diplomatic, intellectual, political, and social history.

The Jacob and Libby Goodman Institute for the Study of Zionism and Israel was founded through a gift to Brandeis University by Mrs. Libby Goodman and is organized under the auspices of the Tauber Institute. The Goodman Institute seeks to promote an understanding of the historical and ideological development of the Zionist movement, and the history, society, and culture of the State of Israel.

Gerhard L. Weinberg, 1981
World in the Balance: Behind the Scenes of World War II

Richard Cobb, 1983
French and Germans, Germans and French: A Personal Interpretation of France under Two Occupations, 1914–1918/1940–1944

Eberhard Jäckel, 1984
Hitler in History

Frances Malino and Bernard Wasserstein, editors, 1985
The Jews in Modern France

Jehuda Reinharz and Walter Schatzberg, editors, 1985
The Jewish Response to German Culture: From the Enlightenment to the Second World War

Jacob Katz, 1986
The Darker Side of Genius: Richard Wagner's Anti-Semitism

Jehuda Reinharz, editor, 1987
Living with Antisemitism: Modern Jewish Responses

Michael R. Marrus, 1987
The Holocaust in History

Paul Mendes-Flohr, editor, 1987
The Philosophy of Franz Rosenzweig

Joan G. Roland, 1989
Jews in British India: Identity in a Colonial Era

Yisrael Gutman, Ezra Mendelsohn, Jehuda Reinharz, and Chone Shmeruk, editors, 1989
The Jews of Poland Between Two World Wars

Avraham Barkai, 1989
From Boycott to Annihilation: The Economic Struggle of German Jews, 1933–1943

Alexander Altmann, 1991
The Meaning of Jewish Existence: Theological Essays 1930–1939

Magdalena Opalski and Israel Bartal, 1992
Poles and Jews: A Failed Brotherhood

Richard Breitman, 1992
The Architect of Genocide: Himmler and the Final Solution

George L. Mosse, 1993
Confronting the Nation: Jewish and Western Nationalism

Daniel Carpi, 1994
Between Mussolini and Hitler: The Jews and the Italian Authorities in France and Tunisia

Walter Laqueur and Richard Breitman, 1994
Breaking the Silence: The German Who Exposed the Final Solution

Ismar Schorsch, 1994
From Text to Context: The Turn to History in Modern Judaism

Jacob Katz, 1995
With My Own Eyes: The Autobiography of an Historian

Gideon Shimoni, 1995
The Zionist Ideology

Moshe Prywes and Haim Chertok, 1996
Prisoner of Hope

János Nyiri, 1997
Battlefields and Playgrounds

Alan Mintz, editor, 1997
The Boom in Contemporary Israeli Fiction

Samuel Bak, paintings
Lawrence L. Langer, essay and commentary, 1997
Landscapes of Jewish Experience

Jeffrey Shandler and Beth S. Wenger, editors, 1997
Encounters with the "Holy Land": Place, Past and Future in American Jewish Culture

Simon Rawidowicz, 1998
State of Israel, Diaspora, and Jewish Continuity: Essays on the "Ever-Dying People"

Jacob Katz, 1998
A House Divided: Orthodoxy and Schism in Nineteenth-Century Central European Jewry

Elisheva Carlebach, John M. Efron, and David N. Myers, editors, 1998
Jewish History and Jewish Memory: Essays in Honor of Yosef Hayim Yerushalmi

Shmuel Almog, Jehuda Reinharz, and Anita Shapira, editors, 1998
Zionism and Religion

Ben Halpern and Jehuda Reinharz, 2000
Zionism and the Creation of a New Society

Walter Laqueur, 2001
Generation Exodus: The Fate of Young Jewish Refugees from Nazi Germany

Yigal Schwartz, 2001
Aharon Appelfeld: From Individual Lament to Tribal Eternity

Renée Poznanski, 2001
Jews in France during World War II

Jehuda Reinharz, 2001
Chaim Weizmann: The Making of a Zionist Leader

Jehuda Reinharz, 2001
Chaim Weizmann: The Making of a Statesman

ChaeRan Y. Freeze, 2002
Jewish Marriage and Divorce in Imperial Russia

Mark A. Raider and Miriam B. Raider-Roth, 2002
The Plough Woman: Records of the Pioneer Women of Palestine

Ezra Mendelsohn, 2002
Painting a People: Maurycy Gottlieb and Jewish Art

Alan Mintz, editor, 2002
Reading Hebrew Literature: Critical Discussions of Six Modern Texts

Haim Be'er, 2002
The Pure Element of Time

Yehudit Hendel, 2002
Small Change: A Collection of Stories

Thomas C. Hubka, 2003
Resplendent Synagogue: Architecture and Worship in an Eighteenth-Century Polish Community

Uzi Rebhun and Chaim I. Waxman, 2003
Jews in Israel: Contemporary Social and Cultural Patterns

Gideon Shimoni, 2003
Community and Conscience: The Jews in Apartheid South Africa

Iris Parush, 2004
Reading Jewish Women: Marginality and Modernization in Eastern European Jewish Society

Haim Be'er, 2004
Feathers

In this city, staunch in its solitude,

the vast past takes the form of follyhood.

—Noah Stern, "Letter for Now"

Foreword

by Hillel Halkin

I am doubly happy to write this foreword to Haim Be'er's *Feathers*—in the first place, because it is already a classic of modern Israeli literature, and in the second place, because having translated it into English over twenty years ago, soon after its appearance in Hebrew in 1979, I had long despaired of seeing my translation in print. Why the English *Feathers* needed to make the rounds of so many publishers before Brandeis University Press had the wisdom to put it out, I can only guess.

Perhaps readers at some publishing houses found Haim Be'er's novel hard to follow in its kaleidoscopic jumps in time, back and forth in the narrator's memories from his boyhood in the 1950s to his service in an Israeli army burial unit in the 1973 Yom Kippur War. Perhaps others found its preoccupation with death, funerals, and physical dissolution morbid. Or suspected its humor, it sometimes being the fate of funny books, as it is of funny people, to make us think they can't be serious. Perhaps it was difficult to decide whether this humor was dark or light.

Feathers are light. But they are subject to gravity. When the winged Daedalus scans the skies for his son Icarus, who has flown too near the sun (the ancient Greek myth is alluded to in this novel), all he sees are scattered feathers on the waves below.

High-flying dreams that crash are a central theme of *Feathers*. They not only motivate the book's main character, the eccentric Mordecai Leder, whose mad ambition it is to found a utopia based on the theories of the nineteenth-century Viennese Jewish thinker Karl Popper-Lynkeus. They also inspire the family of the narrator, who, as a Jerusalem schoolboy, becomes Leder's only disciple. Or rather, they inspire his male ancestors, strictly Orthodox Jews with impractical minds and adventurous souls: his father, who periodically disappears from home on botanical expeditions meant to prove that the willow tree of Scripture is in fact the Australian eucalyptus; his grandfather, the indefatigable pursuer of "true biblical blue"; and his great-grandfather, famous for "stalking the Dragon of Time" in the mountains of Jerusalem.

The women in the novel fight back. Cynical and angry, they campaign tooth-and-nail to protect their lives, homes, and children from the havoc wreaked by male fantasies. This places *Feathers* in a long line of comic literature about the two subspecies of the human race, one of which keeps its feet on the ground even as the other has its head in the clouds.

Moreover, within a traditional Jewish context the comedy is even grander, for while Judaism, which circumscribes its men even more than its women with endless obligations, does not encourage solo male flights to far horizons, there is one exception to this rule. Although no traditionally raised Orthodox Jewish boy could reasonably dream of growing up to be a sea captain or an Arctic explorer, he could always legitimately aspire to find ways of hastening the coming of the Messiah. Jewish folklore is full of messianic dreamers, such as the legendary kabbalist Joseph de la Reina—who, having literally gone through Hell and high water to capture the archdemon Samael, fails at the last moment to bring about the Redemption because he offers the Fiend a restorative whiff of incense. How tragicomically Jewish to take Satan captive and then feel sorry for him! It is no wonder that, in the often weird annals of utopianism, Jews keep cropping up.

In the not so weird annals, too. Those of twentieth-century revolutionary socialism, for example. Or of Zionism, an exclusively Jewish project that has also been associated with powerful messianic and utopian impulses.

And now nota bene. Karl Popper-Lynkeus (1838–1921) is today a forgotten figure, although he was well known in his day as a scientist and social theorist. Besides having anticipated Einstein by hypothesizing the mutual convertibility of mass and energy, he published, in 1912, *Die allgemeine Naehrpflicht als Loesung der Sozialen Frage*, "The General Duty of Nutrition As a Solution to the Social Question"—the Bible of Mordecai Leder's "Nutrition Army."

Yet why should an Israeli author like Haim Be'er, in plotting his first novel, have chosen to make its main character a devotee of the forgotten Popper-Lynkeus? If Be'er wanted to evoke the cosmopolitan and decadent atmosphere of late nineteenth- and early twentieth-century Vienna, couldn't he have chosen a more famous Viennese Jew?

Sigmund Freud, for instance.

Freud, though, was no utopian. His theories would not have been relevant to the concerns of *Feathers*, except insofar as he pointed out that people, when burdened by unconscious thoughts or feelings about others, often displace these onto still others having similar characteristics.

Or Theodor Herzl.

Herzl!

Herzl's utopian work *Altneuland*, "Oldnewland," set in an imaginary Jewish state of the future, appeared in 1902, ten years before Popper-Lynkeus' *Allgemeine Naehrpflicht*. Can Popper-Lynkeus, in *Feathers*, be a symbolic displacement of Herzl? Can the real subject of this wonderfully comic but death-obsessed novel that begins and ends with the trauma of the Yom Kippur War be not the Lynkean but the Zionist dream? Can the story of Mordecai Leder be a subtle parable of this dream?

But I fear that I have already given away too many secrets. The rest are yours to find.

feathers

Chapter One

1.

As with most human endeavors, the beginnings of this story lie shrouded in a dream.

Months after I had finished my long stint of reserve duty along the western shores of the Great Bitter Lake, I still saw Fanara in my dreams.

In those days right after the Yom Kippur War I belonged to a small detachment whose job it was to find what was left of the Israeli soldiers who had been killed in the battle for the Egyptian naval base there. Every morning at dawn we left our little room, which was attached to the morgue at Faid, and drove south on the road that led to the "Nasser Works" that were visible in the distance, and beyond them, to the port of Adabia on the outskirts of the town of Suez.

There were three of us in the cabin of the truck. Mintz sat lost in thought while playing with his graying beard, his lips moving inaudibly. At least once a week, he told me, he made sure to re-read the text of Nachmanides' famous epistle to his son in Catalonia. He turned the pages of his prayer book and declared that this seven-hundred-year-old letter was just the thing to restore me—and the sooner, the better—to the true faith.

Our captured Egyptian truck kept bouncing on the badly paved road, which made it hard to read the small, blurred print. When I came to the part where Nachmanides writes, "Always remember whence you have come, and whither you go, and that you are a home for worms and maggots in your lifetime, as you are in your death," I shut the book and said that I knew it all already and would rather not strain my eyes.

Mintz went on murmuring to himself, while the driver, who had taken no part in the conversation, tried getting the army station on the radio. Yet the halting voice of the announcer of the Cairo Hebrew-language program came in strongly instead, masking the distant voices beamed from Israel. "What a place!" said the driver, switching off the receiver. After a while he pointed out the range of

the Genifa that rose to the right of us. The shitty bastards, he added, were close by on its other side.

Soon, at a point where the military police had erected a hastily written, corrugated-tin road sign on which was drawn a red arrow, we turned left for Fanara. There Mintz roused himself, spread open a map, and decided where to search that day. So, day by day, we patiently combed the area, which was heavily mined.

Mintz was good at his work. The tail of a jacket sticking out from a bush, a button, or the even swarm of an anthill was enough to guide him to the crumpled shape beneath it that was already merging with the earth.

The road was fenced with barbed wire and marked with red triangles on either side. In the afternoon, after we had found that day's dead, soldiers from the engineering corps came to clear a path to them through the mines.

For months after I was home again, even though I washed my hands every day with strong soap, I was afraid to touch my own children and I dreamed of Fanara all the time.

I dreamed that Mintz and I were walking along an abandoned road, through whose cracked pavement the weeds sprouted, carefully making our way toward the jetty in the lake. While Mintz went about his business I scanned the mine-strewn lake shore through my binoculars. More than one reservist, I knew from a soldier on patrol, had been killed going down to the water to bathe or wash his clothes.

I trained the binoculars on five ships that were huddled like frightened sheep in the middle of the lake. They were perfectly still, without a sign of life, and only their red-and-white buoys bobbed gently up and down on the waves. Then, very slowly, I turned to look at the ruined houses in the open space to my left.

They seemed so close that I could almost reach out and touch them. There was a tin-surfaced military mosque painted with Egyptian camouflage colors, a chinked British bungalow, and a house whose four walls had collapsed to reveal a floor with Arab tiles, a table, a chair, and a branch of bougainvillea—a fiercely flowering, painfully purplish-red branch that had grown into the house through a fallen window. Several feet beyond it stood a solitary wall, all that was left of another house, on which, in shades of brown, burnt sienna, and oriental blue, were drawn a donkey and a fiery dragon. Suddenly there appeared from behind the wall a cleanly shaven figure dressed in a white colonial suit and waving with gloved hands to a dark, prettily curled boy who stood with shut eyes among the myrtles far below.

"Reb Dovid, what are you doing here?" I called out in my dream and began walking toward him.

But Mintz, who still sat engrossed in his map on a rise among the ruins, came to life and shouted:

"Do you want to be sent home in a Formica box? You're nothing but a child, you!"

2.

I never saw Reb Dovid Leder, who made his exit from the world before I entered it. I once briefly did see a photograph of him, however, some twenty years before all this, when his son Mordecai Leder, the little alms collector for the School for the Blind, tried convincing me to join the Nutrition Army.

It all started one faraway Jerusalem afternoon while I was returning home from school past the houses of Nahalat Shiv'a. When I reached Ben-Yehuda Street I saw him, standing in the doorway of the Russian bookstore in the Sansour Building. He was looking at a picture of Stalin that stood, surrounded by red-bound volumes and festooned with carnations and asparagus leaves, in the middle of the display window. "Those Communists," he said, nodding when he saw me, "will never last. You'll live to see it yourself." And he asked me whether I had ever heard of Popper-Lynkeus.

"Is he the brother of Doctor Propper from Hadassah Hospital?" I asked.

Leder laughed quietly. "Not Propper, Popper." He opened one of the books that he had been holding under his arm and showed me a portrait of the man. "A great man," he said. "Twenty years before Deprez he knew all about conducting an electric current through copper wire."

He paused for a moment to regard the high-foreheaded face that bore a resemblance to Einstein's and the stylish signature beneath it, then suggested that we go to the Café Vienna. It was my first time ever in a café.

Leder was in high spirits. He told me how the Bolshie bookseller had frowned at him sternly when asked if he wished to acquire books by Popper-Lynkeus. He had pushed away the volumes that Leder showed him and said that it was pointless, especially in times like these, to read such obsolete stuff. It went without saying, he had added, that it had never been translated into Russian, nor was there any reason why it should be.

Leder pushed his hat back on his head and declared that, God willing, we would live to see the day when the olives and cheese in my parents' and Mr. Rachlevski's grocery stores would be wrapped in the writings of Lenin and Stalin. And in fact, to my astonishment, several years later this prediction came true, as will be related further on.

When a waitress appeared, Leder ordered two glasses of *aqua distillata* and some grated coconut and requested that the glasses be properly washed, since he did not wish to drink from anything bearing the marks of some streetwalker's lipstick. While the waitress gaped at him, he inquired unblinkingly whether she too was from Vienna like the name of the café, and, upon hearing that she was, he asked if she had ever eaten there in the vegetarian restaurant across the street from the university.

"When would that have been?" the waitress asked.

"In 1919."

"I beg your pardon," she said, offended. "In 1919 I was only a child."

"What of it?" asked Leder, pushing the paper napkin holder toward me. "Children eat out too."

"Only in Palestine," the waitress objected, taking out a cigarette to light.

Leder looked straight at her and said through pursed lips that in Vienna, at least, the restaurants were civilized enough to forbid smoking.

"Perhaps some *café au lait* and today's strudel," the waitress suggested coldly, smoothing her pressed apron with one hand.

Leder considered this and remarked that it was a pity that Mr. Pravrov had closed his vegetarian restaurant near the bus station. Resignedly he ordered two glasses of boiled water and some organic honey.

The waitress departed and Leder informed me that for an entire year in Vienna he had met regularly in a restaurant with the members of the Cocoberry Society.

"The Cocoberry Society," he repeated, noticing the wonder in my eyes. The members of the society, he explained, had believed the coconut to be the natural food of mankind and had intended to settle on an island in the South Seas, put civilization behind them, and live in a perfect state of nature.

"Would they have climbed naked on the trees like monkeys?" I couldn't help asking.

"What's wrong with monkeys?" countered Leder and cut short the discussion by declaring that we must be realistic and avoid nostalgia and inconsequential theological arguments. Taking out his Parker pen he began slowly and precisely to write on a paper napkin that bore the logo of the café: "Popper-Lynkeus' minimum social program." When he was done he glanced up and asked whether I thought that economic liberalism had solved the problem of starvation.

"Who has won the race, the plow or the stork?" he grinned at me, a look of triumph on his face.

Inasmuch as I had not yet heard at the time of David Ricardo and John Stuart Mill, or for that matter of Popper-Lynkeus himself, I went on looking fascinatedly at the curious emblem stuck into the lapel of Leder's jacket, whose meaning I could not make out. It consisted of an amateurish drawing of a sailboat with an eye at the top of its mast, from whose pupil rays of light streamed in all directions like sunbeams.

Having seemingly interpreted my silence as a plea of no contest, Leder inquired whether I thought that the Beveridge Report had managed to decrease in the slightest the number of old men and women dying of hunger and neglect throughout the United Kingdom—all the elderly souls who lay for days in their rooms with only their dogs to stand faithfully over them and howl stubbornly into their lifeless faces.

"And who can begin to count the number of those driven so mad by the sheer fear of starvation and indigence that they have been locked up in asylums with goons standing over them day and night to keep them from taking their own lives?" he mused, lapsing into thought.

3.

Several years after this, I was the youngest in a small group of people clustered in the yard of Avihayil Hospital, behind the municipal courthouse, waiting for Leder's funeral. I was standing next to the manicured grounds of the Russian nuns next door, scuffing the gravel surface of the narrow yard with my shoe, when suddenly I grew aware of Riklin. The old undertaker put an arm on my shoulder and drew a wide arc in the air with his free hand. "Everyone dies in the end, *mayn kind*," he said, his glance idly surveying the faces of those present until it fell on that of the curly-headed seamstress who stood not far from us fingering a branch of rosemary. "Everyone dies in the end," he repeated so loudly that I was sure someone would hear him.

He took a stealthy bite from a bar of diabetic chocolate and added with a heavenward roll of his eyes:

"But we get them in small doses, day by day. He knows that we can't possibly bury them all at once."

I asked Riklin how Leder had died. He looked at me sternly and replied that a boy who had just been bar-mitzvahed a few years ago was not supposed to ask such questions. "In general," he said, "it's the opinion of most mothers, especially yours, that boys your age don't belong at funerals."

The curly-headed seamstress approached us with small steps. "Would you like a piece of chocolate, Miss Schecter?" Riklin asked. Behira Schecter tossed her head and said that it was disgraceful to eat at funerals. Riklin burst out laughing and rejoined that were he to take her advice, he would perish of hunger in no time.

A man with rolled-up sleeves appeared in the entrance to the ablution room and Riklin clapped me on the shoulder and vanished through the door. Soon Leder was carried out wrapped in a prayer shawl. His belly had swollen into a little mound, so that for a moment it didn't seem to be him, since he had always been so scrawny.

The yellow prayer shawl revealed the contours of the corpse beneath it. I looked the other way, even though I wanted to see the face. Years later, enveloped day and night by that sweetish odor, surrounded by undraped faces spattered with vomit and blood, I still felt a wave of nausea whenever I thought of Leder's faintly outlined corpse on that afternoon in the Russian Compound in Jerusalem.

A stir ran through the crowd and a dignified-looking gentleman, dressed half like an ultra-Orthodox Jerusalem Jew and half like a modern seminarian, stepped forward with gingerly self-importance. This was Rabbi Tsipper, whose piety my Aunt Tsivya had more than once called into question. "The lowlife!" she used to say. "In London he drank five-o'clock tea *mit englishe dammes* and here he's best friends with the angels in heaven." She had known him as a young man and told us that he had such a passion for smoking that he had filled bottles with tobacco smoke every Friday so that he might drink from them on the Sabbath, when it was forbidden to light a cigarette.

Rabbi Tsipper cleared his throat and began in a low voice with a quote from the Book of Esther:

"*And Mordecai went forth from before the king.* The excellent man who lies here deceased, Reb Mordecai Leder, now goes forth before the King of the Un-ey-verse. In the tractate of *Kelim* it is written . . ."

4.

But I am getting ahead of myself and must return to that sleepy afternoon in the Café Vienna when the basis of my friendship with Leder—the core of this story—was formed.

The odd alms collector had already disposed of economic liberalism and was making short shrift of Marxism when the waitress interrupted his harangue. She placed two glasses of water and two small bowls of honey on the table and slipped away before Leder had a chance to taste them and make a sour face.

He poured the honey into the water while declaring that any society that considered itself a just one must attend to the minimum needs of life more than to strudel. Sipping the beverage, he announced that the time had come to found the Nutrition Army.

"The army," said Leder, "will supply minimum food to the population, both cooked and uncooked. Whoever wishes will take it home and eat it there; whoever prefers to eat in caféterias, as we are doing now, will do so—but with the difference that it will all be under public supervision. These aging Viennese bitches will listen to what they're told."

The water in my own glass was still clear and Leder urged me to copy his concoction. A blue inkstain had begun to spread on the green-checked tablecloth where his pen had lain. He noticed it and covered it with an ashtray while remarking that the little details of things must never get in our way. As soon as a youngster finished his army service, he said with a smile, he would be free to do as he wished and live the rest of his life where he pleased.

I fidgeted in my seat. I was afraid that my worried mother would begin searching for me in the streets and I started to rise. Leder ordered me to sit down and asked whether I didn't think that his plan was in some measure coercive. He seemed prepared for my nod. "And your Israeli army, your army isn't?" he shot back. "No one bothers to think things through to the end."

He drank from his mead and declared that there was no possibility of error. "We're standing with our feet on solid ground." The problem was simply to gather at least twenty realists sensible enough to establish the Popper-Lynkean state.

Here Leder stared at me and said that although he would not keep me any longer, the day was not far off when he would be the director of the "Biomaintenance Bureau"—"Commander of the Nutrition Army," as the press would undoubtedly refer to him—the highest authority dealing with the production and distribution of minimum needs. Despite my youth, he added, it had already been decided in the appropriate circles that I would be commissioned "Distributor First-Class" as soon as I joined the ranks.

"Think about it," he said, the stub of a smile appearing on his bloodless lips. He burrowed through his leather briefcase, which was crammed with receipts and collection boxes from the School for the Blind, and came up with a book wrapped in newspaper.

"Here. Read this book of Donion's and the forewords by Freud and Einstein. Yes, Professor Albert Einstein. You'll see for yourself the kind of man that Popper-Lynkeus was."

Refusing to let me thumb through it on the spot, he took my schoolbag, which was lying on a chair between us, inserted into it

The Lynkean State—A Program for a New and More Humane Regime of Life, and said that instead of running to the kiosk during recess to eat candy bars and drink soda pop sweetened with sewage, I should sit under a tree in the schoolyard and read the book.

He rose from his seat. Before turning to go, he asked me what school I attended.

5·

Leder was not liked in our home.

Every other month he turned up to take down from the wall a yellow alms box with a picture of an uncombed girl and a boy wearing a beret, both blind.

Once, while emptying the box onto the table, where he piled the coins in little towers, he asked my mother whether her sister, who had gone off to Zud Afrika thirty years before, was still as sweet as a sugar sifter.

My mother made a face and walked out of the room, leaving him to sweep the coins into his bulging cloth bag with the remark that whoever had not seen the world knew nothing about life.

At her friend Ahuva's house that evening, my mother couldn't resist repeating Leder's words. Ahuva responded that he had a dirty mind, and that even the sheep and goats had better watch out for him. It was no accident that he worked at an institution for the blind. Sometimes he crawled into the rooms there on all fours and fondled the legs and other parts of the unfortunate girls who had never seen the light of day.

My mother drew me close and mimed to Ahuva not to say such things in front of me.

"The apple didn't fall far from the tree," Ahuva said, her cheeks flushing red.

During World War I, Leder's father, Reb Dovid, had been a purveyor for the Turks, and Haim Segal, Ahuva's first husband, had been his right-hand man. The Turkish army had planned to block the Suez Canal with thousands of sandbags and the two men went among the starving, plague-stricken inhabitants of Palestine buying up their clothing for a song and reselling it at a good price to the Turks, who then sewed bags out of it.

At a time when Jews were stripping the silver crowns from Torah scrolls in the synagogues and selling them by the pound to scrap dealers, old clothes could not have been worth much, yet forty years later Ahuva was still convinced that Leder's father had swindled poor people and bewitched them into stark nakedness. She wiped away a tear and whispered that he had bewitched her own Haim, too, to say nothing of the well-known merchant Mr. Perlman and the benighted Turks themselves, who had never imagined that all those rags would rot in the waters of the Suez Canal.

That winter, which I spent along the shores of the Great Bitter Lake, crossing back and forth across the canal near Dursewar, I couldn't help smiling at the sight of the foul enemy corpses that were dredged from the bottom of it, their uniforms hopelessly rotted, though they had been made of superior cloth.

After the war Haim Segal had continued to work hand-in-glove with Leder, who fell in with the ultra-Orthodox Jews of Jerusalem. Strictly among themselves, Ahuva claimed, the Orthodox rabbis mocked the old fool; yet in the public announcements that they plastered over the city's walls they referred to him as "our distinguished spokesman," since his knowledge of English enabled him to phrase their memoranda to the British High Commissioner, to serve as their contact with the government and with the colonial office in London, and to correspond with various members of Parliament and with newspaper editors overseas. It was in meetings with the High Commissioner himself that Reb Dovid Leder was especially indispensable.

In the sole surviving photograph of him from those days, which I later glimpsed during a brief visit to his son's apartment, Leder, Haim Segal, and Dr. De Haan, who was murdered by the Zionists several months later, could be seen leaving Government House. De Haan stood unsmilingly in the center, a conspicuous bulge in his tightly knotted tie, his head covered by a large skullcap and his face ringed by a bristly beard. On his right was a clean-shaven Reb Dovid Leder, dressed in a white suit and waving with his gloves to an Arab gendarme. Haim Segal stood shunted off to the other side, a worn briefcase in one hand and Leder's overcoat draped over an arm.

Now and then Reb Dovid Leder journeyed to London and Vienna, or to Orthodox congresses in Marienbad, where he spent the days talking Torah with yeshiva heads and scholars, and the nights—this Ahuva revealed in a whisper—in cabarets. Her own Haim, on the other hand, never got any further from Jerusalem than Lower Motsa a few kilometers away, where he went on foot to draw well water for the baking of Passover matzah and to cut willow branches for the feast of Sukkot.

In the 1940s Segal was beaten to a pulp by hoodlums while standing outside the polls at Zionist elections, which he was urging the public to boycott. Three years after his death Ahuva married Binyamin Haris, who was now standing in this kitchen cooking milk and garlic, in the belief—so Father said—that they were a proven aphrodisiac.

My mother and Ahuva were talking in whispers when Binyamin, who must have sensed that the ghost of his precursor was stalking the house, appeared in the kitchen doorway.

"Churchill is a Jew," he announced, banging a milk-crusted spoon against the side of the door.

My mother objected that everyone knew that Churchill was a born-and-bred Englishman, but Binyamin clung to his opinion that only a Jew would name his daughter Sarah.

"Look what's become of my hands," Ahuva grieved, ordering her husband back into the kitchen, to make sure that his milk didn't boil over onto the kerosene stove. Since the day Binyamin had begun his pharmaceutical experiments, she complained, she had been forced to scrub the stove with cleaning fluid so many times that her hands were honeycombed with stains.

When Binyamin had vanished into the kitchen again, my mother remarked that, if only she had the talent, she would write a book about Leder. Ahuva sneered that the lives and times of the Leders hardly merited a book and deserved at most a few installments in a Yiddish weekly. Yet she took advantage of the opportunity to ask my mother, who was several years her elder, why the old hypocrite's son had left for Vienna soon after the British had come.

My mother was amazed at her friend's weak memory and replied that all Jerusalem knew that young Leder had fallen for two Chinese women.

“The Chineizerkes were in the empty lot behind the Alliance School,” said Mother, “pulling out little worms from the eyes of the girls from the Christian mission. No, not with tweezers, with glass chopsticks. Leder spent the whole day there, smoking English cigarettes and talking to them in German. The next week he set out for Beirut.”

6.

This episode from his distant past was mentioned to me by Leder himself about a year later, on our way back from the central post office at the far end of Jaffa Road—to which, he complained, he had been forced to drag himself because the mail clerks in the local Me'ah She'arim branch did not know enough of either the Latin alphabet or geography to prevent a letter addressed to Lambarene from being sent to Africa via Rio de Janeiro. The clerks at the central post office, on the other hand, had some command of English and would show proper respect for an envelope that bore the name of Dr. Albert Schweitzer.

In his letter, which was three pages long, Leder told me, he had sought to persuade the elderly healer to accept the august and well-merited position of supreme ruler of Lynkeania. He had not the slightest doubt, he added, that the man who had served humanity with such a deep and abiding reverence for life would agree to his offer.

Leder continued to shower praises on the renowned physician. Yet as we passed the missionary literature in the window of the Zion Bookstore on the corner of Prophets and Monboz Streets, he remarked that the clerical parties would almost certainly oppose the nomination of a Christian doctor and propose some famous rabbi instead.

“Missionaries are fine people,” he observed, and told me how, as a young man, he had made the acquaintance of two nuns from China who saved many patients from death until they themselves succumbed to a serious eye disease, went blind, and retired for the rest of their lives to a small convent in Italy.

He lapsed into thought, adding only when we reached Strauss Street, near Bikkur Holim Hospital, that we need not fear the religious extremists and would cross that bridge when we came to it—after which he inquired whether I would walk him as far as Press Street, where he had an appointment with the seamstress who was making uniforms for the Nutrition Army.

Behira Schechter, the seamstress, was notoriously good-hearted. "She can consider herself lucky," my father used to say two or three times a year, "that she's as ugly as she is," while on at least two of these occasions my mother quickly hushed him. After Behira had spent a long, hard day sewing in our apartment, my father would regard the skirt she had made from a discarded American suit, the pants she had cut out for me from a discarded dress of my mother's, or the sheets she had stitched from some sacks of French sugar, and remark that in Russia she would be sent straight to Siberia for such work.

I would play with the wooden spindles of thread, coloring the eyes of the smiling whale on the label with an indelible pencil, while the kettle boiled in the kitchen and my father whispered to my mother as he poured her tea that he was sure that Behira must like rubbing her legs together while working the treadle of the sewing machine. There was no other reason for her to slave like that from morning to night, he would go on, until Mother angrily told him to stop talking nonsense and reminded him that it was time to close the shutters for the night.

Now Leder knocked on a door with a green enamel sign, a red "S" in the middle of which contained the figure of a woman bent over a Singer sewing machine. Beneath it a skilled hand had written in fancy white letters like a Torah scribe's, "Behira Schechter, Certified Seamstress."

Miss Schechter opened the door a crack and announced as soon as she saw Leder that she was busy taking measurements for a client. If it was important, he could wait for her in the kitchen. Then she caught sight of me and exclaimed:

"*Yingele, tayrer yingele*, your mother is here."

Mother, in nothing but an undergarment, peered out in alarm from the large room at the end of the hall.

"What happened to your father?" she practically screamed.

"It's nothing," Behira explained. "He came with Leder."

"We've measured enough," said my mother.

A minute later, hurriedly dressed, she emerged from the room. She didn't say a word or even look at me all the way home. She simply held my hand tight and kept humming a children's song that began

Lo, the cranes fly high
And the bees buzz by.

Twenty years later, on the shores of the Great Bitter Lake, where I dreamed of Leder's father waving with white gloves to the dark-haired boy rising with shut eyes from the depths, I saw—whooping, screeching, yea, zealous for war, to borrow a phrase from Isaiah—my first flight of cranes.

Chapter Two

1.

My father and Riklin were sitting in the living room, drinking tea, sucking rock candy, and conjuring the dead.

My mother stopped to give them a sideways look as we passed the door in the hallway. Their two heads were bent over an oaktag sheet spread out before them and divided into tiny squares like a crossword puzzle. Books, rolled-up maps, and thick pads of paper whose colored tips made patterns like the wings of exotic birds were scattered over the table.

My father and Riklin continued to whisper without paying us any attention. My mother's lips curled contentiously. From the bedroom door she snapped that she did not understand how a diabetic of Riklin's age was unable to control his base appetites and went on gobbling candy like a boy.

Riklin pushed his eyeglasses up from his nose to his forehead and dismissed her rebuke with a wave of his hand and a smile on his beet-red, clean-shaven face. The slam of the door drowned out my father's reply. My mother did not stop talking to me as she began to fold the pile of clean laundry on the bed.

She was fed up with the friendship between my father and the old undertaker. In her opinion, Reb Elya was a humbug. "Every day he gets a tray of fresh eggs from the dairy," she hissed between her teeth. "But instead of washing the heads of the dead with them as he's supposed to, he gives them to his grandchildren for breakfast and dinner, while other children are eating powdered eggs and mashed potatoes."

My father had already warned her not to be foolish, since it was only abroad that Jews washed the deceased with eggs, whereas the custom in the Land of Israel was to use plain soap. He advised her to pay heed to her brother, who rubbed shoulders every day with advocates and judges in the course of his work as a court clerk and was certainly nobody's fool.

Indeed, the previous Sabbath, when the subject of Riklin came up, Uncle Tsodek had told us how once Reb Elya had stopped the sun in its tracks. Glancing at a picture on the wall of my grandmother holding me in her arms, my mother's brother declared that this had happened years before I was born, when Rabbi Hannales, the old kabbalist from Minsk, had been found dead one day in a field on the outskirts of the neighborhood of Bet-Yisra'el. Since it was a Friday, and the Sabbath was soon due to begin, the funeral had to be performed quickly. Ten men, led by Reb Elya, who was still a young lad at the time, hurried with the stretcher to the Mount of Olives. Yet the sun went down before the Arab laborers could finish digging the grave in the hard, stony soil, and it seemed that they, gentiles though they were, would have to inter the old Jew by themselves. Just then Reb Elya came to life. Pulling out of his jacket a heavy packet of brown wrapping paper that was covered on both sides with crowded script, he waved it menacingly at the heavens and shouted, "Is it the reward of this holy man, who wrote his books, as Moses did his commandments, in black fire on white fire, to be buried in the end by Ishmaelites?" At that exact moment, the sun rose in the west and began to shine again.

My mother scoffed that Reb Elya was not another Isaiah, who had turned back the shadow on the sundial in the days of King Hezekiah. How was it possible, she went on, her voice growing sharper, that her own brother, who gathered pearls of wisdom at the feet of Judges Heshin and Frumkin and even read secular books, did not understand that the sun had simply come out from behind the clouds that had temporarily hidden it?

Every day at about one o'clock, soon after my father had shut the grocery store and come home to rest, Riklin would arrive and join him at the table where he sat eating by himself. As soon as my father said the grace after meals, Reb Elya would rise and urge him to clear the dishes quickly so that they might get down to work.

Riklin's first visit to our home took place about a month after the raid by the Rationing Bureau.

"These bandits from the government have made a shambles of your house," Mrs. Adler shouted to us as we returned home one afternoon from a visit to my mother's friend Ahuva. Although the eyes of our neighbor, who was polishing her windows, seemed to pop from their sockets as she talked, my mother remarked confidently that people with thyroid conditions were known to be queer in the head, and that Mrs. Adler was simply looking for attention.

Among wide-open closets and mountains of clothing and pictures scattered on the floor, my father sat staring at a half-drunk cup of tea and the crumbs of a honey cake.

My mother froze. "It's like the Slonims, like Eliezer Dan Slonim's house in Hebron," she murmured, referring to the 1929 Arab riots, while she wandered aimlessly among beds piled high with household objects and finally collapsed upon one of them and buried her face in her hands. A flicker of fear passed over me.

Only once had I ever dared look at the memorial book for the victims of these riots, which lay hidden, to keep me from being traumatized by the sight of it, in a corner of our storeroom behind a photograph of my father's first wife. Yet the face of the one-year-old Shlomo Slonim, who alone of all his family survived the butchery, still burned in my memory. It resembled the face of my father, who sat forsakenly now by the window, his head and shoulders striped with strange, delicate shadows cast by the bars outside.

Atop a pile of clothing lay a blue-and-white sailor suit that must have belonged to a boy of about three. Two rows of gold buttons with little anchors on them ran down its front.

"Whose is that?" I asked, my curiosity getting the better of my fear. To the best of my memory, I had never owned such a suit myself.

My mother regarded me as though through a crack in a wall, pulled herself together, and rose without a word to put the little suit on a hanger. She draped three dresses that she had stopped wearing long ago over it and stuck it in an empty closet.

Two hours later all traces of the raid were gone from the house.

"What did those bastards take?" asked my mother, breaking the silence.

"The almonds," answered my father, as though in his sleep. The setting sun lit his face where he sat.

Half a year later, after my father's acquittal in court, a bailiff knocked on our door with a red tin box, on which were two Chinamen with long, narrow mustaches that descended to the collars of their shirts, each carrying teacups on a tray. My mother broke open

the court seal, which was stamped in brown wax at the point where the lid and box met. The almonds were full of worms.

Twelve years later, when father had been dead for exactly a month, the little sailor suit turned up again while my mother and I were packing away his few clothes in order to give them to the sexton of the Charitable Aid Society in Mahaneh Yehuda.

By then I already knew that the suit was the one remaining relic of my older brother, who passed away three years before I was born. Until my father's dying day my mother never mentioned him to me. But once, in an intimate moment, my Uncle Tsodek's son Shalom had told me about him, adding how dreadful he remembered Mother having looked as she walked by herself up Strauss Street after an all-night vigil at Bikkur Holim Hospital, pushing an empty baby carriage ahead of her.

About a week after the Rationing Bureau raid the fresh scent of willow twigs and the sharp though muffled fragrance of eucalyptus shoots that had long filled our house were replaced by a sour smell of rotting wood. The branches wilted on top of the chest-of-drawers and the closet, while the water that my father had changed every day turned green in its vases and jars.

Which was the end of his last—and to the best of my knowledge, only—attempt to rebel.

2.

In the beginning was the trip to Petach-Tikva.

But I must go back quite a few years before that. One stormy Jerusalem winter day in the 1940s an electric short circuit caused a fire that destroyed the fourth and upper story of the Zohorei Hama Synagogue in Mahaneh Yehuda. This top floor, which was shaped like a turret and stood out by virtue of its prominent formula against the Evil Eye, taken from Jacob's blessing in the Bible, that ran in huge letters all around it, had served for years as an observation post for pious Jews who wished to see the beauty of Jerusalem from on high but refused to climb the even taller tower of the Young Men's Christian Association.

The fire also ruined a set of sundials that had been used, in keeping with ancient custom, to determine the exact hour for morning and evening prayers, as well as two regular clocks employed for the same purpose on sunless winter days, one set by Greenwich and one by local Arab time.

The mechanical clocks were quickly repaired, but years went by without anyone being found to fix the sundials, whose arms, which had cast their precise shadows on the arched, numbered surface beneath them, were given for safekeeping to Perl Grevier, the daughter of the American tailor Reb Shmuel Levi, who had founded the Zohorei Hama Synagogue and its Charitable Aid Society.

My father, who for years had worshipped in the Zohorei Hama Synagogue as a regular member of its early prayer quorum, and had never ceased grieving for the damaged sundial, set out for Petach-Tikva right after the holiday of Purim.

Upon returning he reported that the sundial expert refused to meet with strangers. One of his relatives, to whom father's investigations had led him, revealed that the old horologer lived in constant fear of the lordly Jerusalem sheikh, Nimr Effendi, and that all attempts to convince him that the Arab half of the Holy City was now safely in the hands of King Abdullah, and was in any case totally cut off from the Jewish half, fell on deaf ears. He stubbornly kept insisting that the Arabs were out to get him because of his refusal, many years before, to install a sundial on the Temple Mount, between the Dome of the Rock and the El-Aksa Mosque.

This incident, to be sure, had taken place at the turn of the century, but the old man was convinced that the Moslem holy men of Jerusalem still meant to kill him in revenge for it. In those days a fierce dispute had broken out among them concerning the correct time for the afternoon prayer, and Sheikh Nimr Effendi had been of the opinion that a sundial like the one in Mahaneh Yehuda was needed to end the quarrel and restore peace to the elders of Islam. Yet because the pious sundial maker refused to contravene the rabbinical ban on Jews ascending to the Temple Mount, the purpose of which was to prevent them from treading with unclean feet on the destroyed Holy of Holies, he was forced to spurn the enticements of the kadis, who sought to persuade him of the golden opportunity that had come his way to bring Ishmael and Israel together, let alone to earn the thirty thousand gold napoleons that they proposed as his reward. When finally they threatened to do away with him, he secretly left Jerusalem and moved to Petach-Tikva, never to set foot in the Holy City again.

Though my father came back from Petach-Tikva empty-handed, he did tell us how, while walking through the streets of the town in search of the horologist's house, he had seen the eucalyptus trees planted along them and had been struck by the sudden and incontrovertible brainstorm that for generations Jews had been living in error, since the "willow of the brook" that the Book of Leviticus enjoined them to cut as one of the four plants used to celebrate the holiday of Sukkot, the Feast of Tabernacles, was not, as had always been thought, the lowly salix bush, but rather the stately eucalyptus.

My mother placed a plate of barley grits and a bowl of stewed prunes on the table before him and said nothing. When my father vanished a month later, however, in early spring, she told the investigating policeman that she had been sure at the time that he was merely dazed from fatigue and the long journey to an unfamiliar place and that, upon awakening refreshed in the morning, he would forget the whole thing as one forgets a bad dream.

Late on the third day of his disappearance, my father came home. He was red from exposure to the wind and sun, and in his suitcase, wrapped in wet burlap, were branches of salix and eucalyptus.

He described for us a land of artesian springs, of fruit trees planted in long rows, and of magnificent, towering eucalyptuses with flesh-colored bark and swarms of hornets and bees buzzing around them, pointing as proof of his account to his shoes caked with dried mud.

My mother sat glued to her seat, as embarrassed as she was helpless at the change taking place in her husband before her very eyes.

"Human beings are strange creatures," she muttered to herself, adding after a moment's silence that she would go tell the police to call off their search, though she hadn't the foggiest notion how to explain things to the desk sergeant.

When she had left my father remarked that the police were in any case too busy hunting down black-market profiteers to care whether a single stray sheep had returned to the fold.

A distracted smile played over his lips as he told me that he now had definite proof of his discovery and asked me to bring him from the shelf the Talmudic tractate of *Sukkah*.

"Which is the willow and which is the poplar?" chanted my father, his fingers running along the lines. "The willow leaf is red-stemmed, elongated, and smooth-tipped; the poplar leaf is white-stemmed, rounded, and sickle-tipped."

He laid the volume on the sofa, produced two branches from his suitcase, and asked me to tell him which was the willow and which was the poplar.

A cry of triumph came from him when I answered. It was as clear as the light of day, he declared; even a child could tell the difference easily. The first thing tomorrow, right after morning prayers, he would go to Rabbi Isar Zalman Meltzer of the Etz-Hayim Yeshiva to report his sensational find.

3.

When he came home the next day before noon his face was flame-red and he did not stop maligning the *paskudstver* rabbi. My mother, who was busy with the store, ordered him to put on his apron and warned him with a tap of her sandal to watch what he said before strangers.

As soon as the store emptied out my father related how, since Rabbi Meltzer was not at the yeshiva, he had decided to see Rabbi Boiml in Sha'arei Hesed instead.

On reaching the rabbi's house, he found him pondering a question put to him by an old woman, herself the widow of a Talmudic master who had passed away some years before. The door to Rabbi Boiml's room was open, so that he should not be suspected, God forbid, of closeting himself with a member of the other sex, and my father could hear the old woman asking whether a drop of water left hanging from the spout of a tea kettle was subject to the rabbinic interdiction on drinking liquids left uncovered overnight. The rabbi laboriously leafed through the books on his desk and even climbed a ladder to take down from its shelf a special volume of responsa, before advising her, though only after long thought, to let a little of the kettle's contents run off before pouring from it again. As he ushered her out he congratulated her on her query, adding that many great scholars in their holy books had criticized the widespread but inexcusable laxness in observing this prohibition, since a snake or other creeping thing might come to drink from such liquid and endanger human life with its venom.

When the old woman had left, Rabbi Boiml extended a moist, delicate hand to my father and asked what had made him seek the counsel of a rabbi. Perhaps he had a slaughtered chicken up his sleeve and wished to know whether it was kosher or not?

My father smiled while spreading willow and eucalyptus branches on the rabbi's desk and announced that he had come on business of far greater importance for the Jewish people than a chicken. Then he proceeded to explain his discovery.

The rabbi's patience soon gave out, and after listening for a few minutes he declared that Maimonides himself had written that the identity of all four plants used on Sukkot had been personally revealed to Moses by God, and that since time immemorial Jews had prayed with the same willow branches on the holiday that they prayed with today. Furthermore, he queried, upon seeing that my father remained unmoved since the eucalyptus leaf, once broken, had in fact a most pungent aroma, how could one possibly square his theory with the exegetical text that stated that the four plants of Sukkot symbolized four types of Jews, and that the willow, which had neither taste nor smell, stood for the ne'er-do-wells who neither studied the Law nor kept its commandments?

On the contrary, my father replied, this simply strengthened his case. Indeed, only his theory could reveal the text's true profundity, since even the ne'er-do-wells, who had neither knowledge nor works, were, once broken open, good Jews beneath their facade of disbelief. Why, he himself knew of persons who had perfunctorily gone once a year to synagogue to hear the Kol Nidrei prayer on Yom Kippur, had had an inner change of heart there, and had become paragons of piety in the end!

Rabbi Boiml cut my father short and advised him to waste no more time on such foolishness and to stop keeping a scholar from his books, lest they both be found guilty of profanation.

My father declared to us that Rabbi Boiml, which meant olive oil in Yiddish, was as slippery as his name. Even when he went to the toilet, my father mocked, the product was pure virgin oil. The man to see was Rabbi Tsipper, who had studied at the rabbinical seminary in Vienna, where he had been a pupil of Rabbi Doctor Tsvi Peretz Hayut, and was of a far more promising caliber.

4.

At the crack of noon we went to pay a call on Rabbi Tsipper.

We strolled down David Yellin Street while my father told me of beautiful birds with sky-blue wings, white breasts, and red beaks that dived suddenly into the water to spear fish and crabs; of great oleander bushes growing along stream beds, whose white flowers were bad for the eyes; and of the eucalyptus tree, which was called by the Arabs "the tree of the Jews."

To our surprise, at the corner of S'fat Emet and Yehosef Schwartz Streets, near a little courtyard fenced in by blackening boards that hid the grave of the Hasidic Gerer Rebbe—who, at the time of his death during the battle for Jerusalem, had asked that he be interred on the grounds of his yeshiva until the day when the road to the cemetery on the Mount of Olives was opened again—we ran into Rabbi Tsipper's wife. Dressed in flounces and frills, she was followed by a tall, thin woman who rattled a white collection box on which was pictured a bright sun shining down on calm blue waves. Around it, as though on a ribbon, was written "The Ritual Bath Fund." Father stopped to say hello, and Rabbi Tsipper's wife urged him to contribute generously to the annual fund drive on behalf of cleanliness and godliness.

My father dropped a coin in the box and asked if Rabbi Tsipper was at home.

The rabbi's wife nodded and answered that at this hour her husband was toiling heroically over the Law, although, if my father's business was urgent, it would be permissible to interrupt him. Although the rabbi, she added, lived entirely in the upper spheres and was deaf and blind to worldly things, a child of the neighbors, a gifted and excellent lad, kept house while she was gone and would let us in.

In his most sanctimonious fashion, as was his habit when talking to the very Orthodox, my father declared that it was better to trust in the Lord than in the wiles of man, especially if the man in question was only a boy. He who watched over us as we came and went would watch over the rabbi, might he live to a ripe old age, and shelter him under His wings.

Rabbi Tsipper's wife adjusted the kerchief on her head and replied that it was common knowledge that a scholar of Law needed tending and must not be left alone for a moment.

We took our leave of her and began to climb the steep stairway that led from a broad courtyard to the top floor of the building in which Rabbi Tsipper lived. At the top of the stairs we passed along a roofed gallery, from which fleeting glimpses could be caught of the insides of the neighbors' apartments.

The door of Rabbi Tsipper's apartment was locked. Muffled giggles, however, sounded from within.

My father knocked once and then again. Only after the third knock did we hear a shuffle of feet on the other side of the door and the rabbi's voice calling, "*A minut, a minut.*"

Presently the door opened and Rabbi Tsipper stood in the doorway, his jacket awry on his shoulders, his clothes disarrayed, and barely hidden alarm in his queer, watery eyes. A smell of books, cinammon, and Valencia oranges pervaded the house, whose windows were closed. Rabbi Tsipper led my father into a large room, while I lingered behind in the foyer, whose walls were painted an oily, bright brown colorstreaked with dark veins. These divided the wall into slabs so that in the dim light it seemed made of natural stone. Suddenly, something stirred in the rabbi's bedroom. A girlish-faced boy in a red-and-blue polo shirt slipped out of it like a cat and through the front door.

A bad taste filled my mouth. I wanted to return to the sunlit gallery outside, but just then my father called me to his side.

Rabbi Tsipper was ensconced in his chair, his fingers drumming on the table. His eyes were lowered and his slicked, shiny hair that fell in tresses down his neck resembled the fibrous roots of the strange tree that hung on the wall behind him—a tree whose crooked boughs were as tangled as the great oak's in which Absalom was caught on his mule, and whose every leaf was covered with tiny, medieval script in which were written the names of Rabbi Tsipper's illustrious scholarly forebearers.

My father broke off his lecture to ask me to stop biting my nails. Rabbi Tsipper roused himself and said that I was a wise boy with fine eyes, God be praised, and that it was wrong to scold me so harshly for a weakness of the flesh that the spirit could not control.

He pretended to listen to my father with interest, and remarked when he was done that one must keep in mind that the eucalyptus tree was brought to the Land of Israel only recently from Australia, and that furthermore, it and the willow were members of two entirely different, and not even closely related, species. The willow belonged to the salixes, while the eucalyptus was a myrtus; indeed, even a passing acquaintance with them showed that the former lost its leaves in winter and bore its seeds in spring, while the latter was green all year round and produced seed in autumn.

My father deferentially replied that he did not for a moment wish to impugn the rabbi's learning, but since truth was dearer to him than honor, he could not allow himself to keep silent. In the first place, the Australian origins of the tree were no serious obstacle, since the Torah was eternal and valid for all times and places, so that the eucalyptus, which bore the three identifying marks listed by the rabbis, was already fit for ritual use on the third day of Creation, when the earth put forth vegetation and trees yielding fruit after their kind. And secondly, and even more inexplicably in his eyes, how could Rabbi Tsipper possibly rely on the classification of Linneaus, who was hardly an authority any more and whose work had been discredited by more than one renowned botanist?

Rabbi Tsipper smiled and remarked that it was clear from such a detailed and learned rebuttal that my father was no novice to the subject, and that therefore he requested two or three days to look more deeply into the matter, after which my father might send me one afternoon to pick up his written opinion.

Once we had left my father remarked that there was nothing to be gained from the rabbis, neither from the Talmudists like Rabbi Boiml who could thread a needle with an Indian elephant, nor from the intellectuals like Rabbi Tsipper, who remained a dunce even if he was Docktor Rabbiner from Vienna. They were all cowards and doubters, and in a place where no one stood up like a man one must stand up like a man oneself, as it said in *The Ethics of the Fathers.*

All summer long Father pored over his books and even talked in his sleep. On the morning of the first day of Sukkot, my mother and I stood at the window and worriedly watched him set out for synagogue, clutching tightly in one hand a young palm branch, a cluster of myrtle leaves, and several fine shoots of fresh eucalyptus.

That morning his fellow worshippers gave him the name of "Calypta," which stuck to him until his dying day.

"Many a man who set the pace has had to live in plain disgrace," was the motto he took to citing to my mother (having read it no doubt in one of the afternoon papers or on the calendar that hung in our kitchen) before setting out from time to time on another one of his expeditions, upon his return from which our whole house smelled like a tabernacle.

5.

While searching for his will thirteen years later on the day of his departure from the world, my mother and I found a thick notebook that was yellowed with age among the pages of the tractate of *Sukkah*. On the first page of it was printed in elegant scribal letters, "The Willow Way," and underneath this was written, in rabbinical calligraphy, "In Search of the True Willow."

The notebook was filled with dense writing in my father's hand that contained, as far as I could make out, numerous references to the Talmud and its commentaries, as well as to botanical journals and books. Here and there it was accompanied by amateurish drawings and bits of dried willow and eucalyptus leaves that crumbled at the touch. About halfway through it broke off, and my mother, who had been looking with glazed eyes over my shoulder, sighed that here the heartless Rationing Bureau inspectors had put an end to my father's labor of love. On that brief and bitter winter day he had lost his will to live and begun to fall under the sway of Riklin, thus commencing his slow journey to the world of no return.

The will did not turn up.

That evening Riklin appeared for the first time since my mother had banished him from our house and told him to leave my father alone. He entered without knocking on the door, which was open a crack, and sat down in the chair that had been his in those faraway times when he had visited us daily. Without bothering to look up my mother murmered into her tear-soaked handkerchief that, now that the bridegroom had finally arrived, the wedding could begin. Riklin, who was accustomed to mourners venting their gall on him, pretended not to hear and informed us that he had been entrusted with my father's will.

"Did you bring it with you, Reb Elya?" my mother asked, in surprise, glancing at him with a softness in her voice.

Riklin handed her a long airmail envelope and said that he would see to it that my father's last wishes were carried out.

Mother read the will carefully and asked when she was done whether my father, might he rest in peace, had written it back in the days when the two men had conjured the dead together.

Riklin smiled sorrowfully, the thick lenses of his glasses misting over.

He recalled how, ever since the 1948 war, my father had gone every year, on the anniversary of my brother's death, to the tomb of King David on Mount Zion, climbing to the roof in order to get a glimpse of the cemetery on the Mount of Olives, which had fallen into Jordanian hands. Equipped with binoculars and aided by landmarks that he knew by heart, such as a stretch of stone wall, a solitary tree, or a fragment of road descending toward Jericho, he would begin to recite the kaddish as soon as he caught sight of my brother's grave, to which everyone present answered amen.

On one of those occasions—whose date, my mother now calculated, must have fallen about a month-and-a-half before that of the Rationing Bureau raid—my father failed to find his son's grave despite the landmarks. The little tombs in the children's section of the cemetery had been plowed up and were gone. Had it not been for two American tourists who happened by just then, my father might have toppled over the guardrail and plunged to his death among the stones of the Christian graveyard at the foot of the pine trees on the steep slope beneath the Church of the Dormition.

Though my father, Riklin told us, decided to keep the news a secret from my mother so as not to cause her more anguish, he subsequently made up his mind to compile an exact map of the Mount of Olives cemetery, in the hope that one day, when Jews would be able to visit it again, the desecrated graves might be restored.

Riklin related how painstakingly my father had labored at this task, and how he had accumulated one by one the slim volumes of the work called "The Lawgiver's Plot," in whose pages the pious scholar, Asher Leid Brisk, enumerated the graves in the Jewish cemeteries of Jerusalem by section and row.

Reb Elya removed his glasses, wiped them with a corner of the tablecloth, and told us that Brisk's mother was Rochke Lippalehs, the saintly woman who had lived in the cellar of the Bet-Ya'akov Synagogue in the Jewish Quarter of the Old City and was herself the daughter of the famous Lippaleh, whose well-known book of devotions was a favorite among Jewish women all over the world.

My mother, momentarily distracted from her grief, smiled and asked Riklin whether this was the same hapless woman whose husband had disappeared without a trace, leaving her undivorced and unable to remarry, and who used to go on foot every month in her wooden clogs, on the eve of the New Moon, to pray at the tomb of Mother Rachel near Bethlehem.

Riklin nodded and observed that one must never judge by appearances. My father, he said to me, had spared neither money nor health in his pursuit of Asher Leib Brisk's slim volumes, which were unavailable in a complete set and almost unobtainable singly, until he had found them all. Together, the old undertaker said, they had spent days and nights reconstructing the grave sites. Yet in the end the work had proved to be too much for two sickly and elderly men like themselves, especially as they only met with ridicule for their efforts, most of all from the members of their own families, so that their pamphlets, manuscripts, and maps were eventually consigned to the offices of the Burial Society, where they lay gathering dust to this day.

Reb Elya rose to go. In the hallway, before leaving, he said that he would wait for us in the morning in the courtyard of Bikkur Holim Hospital, from where my father's funeral would set out. In the meantime, he declared, it would be best if my mother covered the mirror with a piece of cloth, so that my father's soul, which was still at loose in the house, should not see its reflection there and grow weak from fright.

Riklin left and my mother threw herself on the bed, clutching at the long envelope and murmuring my father's name over and over, her voice soft and loving as it had never been while he lived.

6.

Yet on that distant afternoon in the early 1950s, my mother could not stop abusing my father and Riklin, her hand fluttering like a dove as it expertly sprinkled water on the bedclothes before ironing them.

When she was done ironing, she opened the bedroom door and announced in a chilly voice that it was time to re-open the store.

The old undertaker looked up from his oaktage sheet ruled into little squares and declared that my mother and I made him think of the impatient pupils in the Passover Haggadah who interrupted the five sages in the middle of the story of the exodus to remind them of the far less important duty of reciting their morning prayers.

My mother ignored him. A man's first duty, she declared to my father, was the education of his children, especially when his only son was keeping company with shady characters like Leder from the School for the Blind.

My father muttered something inaudible, but Riklin—who had nursed a grudge against Leder ever since the latter had let him down at the Ringels, as will be related in due course—remarked that the little alms collector had lately gone off the deep end, to which he added, as though revealing a dark secret, that already years ago, while passing the Patt Café at night on his way home from his office on Hasolel Street, he had often seen Leder in its garden pavilion with two Russian Orthodox nuns known to him by sight from the Mount of Olives, chatting with them as freely as if they were old friends.

My mother replied that, although Leder's life had been littered with nuns from the outset, this failed to explain how a man with no knowledge of Russian could converse with two Muscovites. Despite her skepticism, though, she was glad to find Riklin on her side, and she told my father that, if only he would pay heed to Reb Elya's words, he might finally understand what irreparable damage Leder could do to the sensitive soul of a boy like me. Who was to say if under such an influence I wouldn't grow up to be like the mad Holtzman from Rehovot, who went halfway around the world chasing wild ostriches and ended up losing his last penny on the vain mirage of marketing their feathers?

Riklin interrupted her and observed that, his profession notwithstanding, he knew something about live human beings too, and was convinced that they were far stronger and less fragile than they seemed—while as for my mother's objection to his story, the two sisters, although Russian Orthodox, happened to speak perfect English. This he knew from an official in the Polish consulate who was

on good terms with both, and who told him that one of them, Miss Mary Auchinleck, the sister of General Auchinleck, had come to Jerusalem many years ago on a honeymoon with her husband, a noted businessman and member of Parliament. To the latter's consternation, however, she became a different woman from the moment she set foot in the Holy City, for whose blandishments, she announced, she was leaving him. After vainly seeking to woo her back, the cuckold returned to Albion, while Miss Mary built a house for herself on the slopes of the Mount of Olives. Eventually she took orders in the Church of Mary Magdalene above Gethsemane and opened a religious school for girls with her own money in Tur-Malka.

The second nun, Sister Tamara, the mother superior at Tur-Malka, was in fact, Riklin continued, none other than Tatiana Romanov, the cousin of Czar Nikolai, who, miraculously saved from the vengeful hand of the revolutionaries, had fled with her family to England, where her daughter married the British diplomat Charles Johnstone, later governor of Aden.

It was no use for Mother to try to appear unimpressed by Riklin's knowledge of life in the Russian Colony of Jerusalem. Yet seeing me in the doorway of the bedroom, which reminded her again of my sinful liason with Leder, made her scoff that such goings-on must have been what the prophets had in mind when they predicted that the nations would flock to Jerusalem, their mistake having been their failure to foresee that this would happen because of a crucified Jew—of whom Leder too, her heart told her, was a secret devoté.

Riklin said nothing. He patted my head with his dry, arthritic hand and offered me a round, unusually red orange from his briefcase.

"Have you ever eaten a blood orange, *mayn kind?*"

My father came out of his trance to protest that eating blood was forbidden even to the gentiles, let alone to a Jewish boy like me. How could I be asked to eat such a fruit, which was crisscrossed with living capillaries?

My mother burst out laughing and forgot her anger for a moment. She remembered, she said, how my grandmother, might she rest in peace, had been gullible enough to believe that a blood orange was a cross between a tomato and a sweet lemon. But that my Father, who had spent an entire winter of his life doing advanced research in botany, should say something so ridiculous—that was beyond her wildest imaginings!

My father shut his eyes and a thin smile crossed his lips like the smile that was to cross them on that far-off day when the swift bird of his soul winged home to its heavenly nest.

Chapter Three

1.

As soon as Riklin left, my father slipped out of doors to stick the knife with which our guest had peeled the blood orange into the loose earth. Mrs. Adler, who was polishing her window, stopped work for a second, ran her fingers through her thin, uncombed hair, and inquired whether he was intending to open a knife nursery in the yard. My father tried not to smile and replied without glancing up at our goitrous neighbor that one might think a rabbi's daughter would know what must be done with a dairy knife that had come in contact with meat.

Unaccustomedly, my mother was waiting for him at the door when he returned. She touched him lightly on the shoulder and whispered that the two of them had better do something about me before it was too late and I fell like a ripe fruit into Leder's hands. My father, who hadn't heard a kind word from her since the summer, sensed the change at once and promised that he would come straight home from synagogue that evening without staying for Reb Simcha Zissel's Talmud lessson.

It had been ages since the two of them had last sat down to eat together. Through the half-shut kitchen door I could hear them talking in muted voices. After about half an hour my mother opened the door wide and signaled me to come in and wait while my father finished the grace after meals.

My father sat at the head of the little table, his lips moving inaudibly while he ran the back of a knife over the hearts-and-tendrils pattern of the oilcloth. My mother donned her apron and remarked, leaning over the sink, that she had thought she would turn gray at

Behira Schechter's today when she had seen me traipse in with that degenerate. If she didn't insist on getting answers right now to all the questions that were torturing her, it was only because she was afraid they might snap her heartstrings in two.

"You're not the first one in this family to fall in love with some bum," she said to me, glancing over her shoulder at my father, who kept crumbing the table while staring steadfastly at the flame of the memorial candle on the window sill. "Why don't you," she went on, pointing with a soap hand at the candle, "tell your darling son what the *alter bochur* did in Vienna?"

My father gritted his teeth angrily, ignoring her request, and asked me why Mr. Rachlevski's son Haim never came to visit anymore. He spoke highly of my fellow classmate and said that he was a model boy whose poems and compositions appeared in children's magazines and whose drawings were hung for all to see next to the principal's office in the lobby of my school. It would be good for me to spend more time with him and other boys my age instead of associating with undesirables.

My mother, however, refused to change the subject. My father's first wife, she announced, the anniversary of whose death was tonight, had known Leder well during his days in Vienna. If I were to hear even a fraction of what she had had to say about him, I would awake at once from his spell.

"Don't. Why bring up all that dirt now?" my father practically begged, adding in Yiddish, while playing with the knife among the pile of bread crumbs, that silence was golden for all things olden. Yet my mother persisted and declared that on the day Leder died, he deserved to be buried with his rear end up so all should know what he had lived from. There wasn't a house of shame in Vienna he hadn't been in. Why should my father want to sweep it under a rug that he had debauched Abbale Tsipper and snatched him from the arms of his young wife, who had never gotten over the disgrace?

"Enough, enough," murmured my father, burying his face in his hands. "Do you want the boy to lose all respect for his teachers?" Neither he nor my mother knew, though, that Leder himself had already mentioned those days to me during my second meeting with him, about a year before this scene took place.

2.

A week after my encounter with him at the Sansour Building, Leder was waiting for me in the schoolyard. I spied him during Bible class, while our teacher, Miss Schlank, was relating to us how Balak ben Tsippor, king of Moab, whose father bore the name of the birds, had performed witchcraft with the aid of them. Her puffed sleeves billowed as she talked, demonstrating for us with her strong, stubby fingers, which had something of the delicate mystery of talons, how the king would pluck a thrashing bird from the bush, release it into the air, retrieve it, cage it, and burn incense before it until it began to utter oracles.

Our notebooks lay closed on our desks as her voice, resonant with pathos, told of the day in Rosh Pe'or when Balak's bird took flight for the last time.

Miss Schlank rose from her seat, shook bits of chalk from her skirt, and described, with a sweeping gesture of her hand toward the open window, how the Moabite ruler had grieved when he saw the feathered thing spread its wings above the wilderness, climbing higher and higher while tongues of flame licked it from behind.

The after-rain sky was clear and high with a streak of gray smoke on the horizon above the Hill of Evil Counsel to the Southeast. Down in the yard Leder walked back and forth among puddles of water, tracing something in the wet earth with his umbrella tip.

Sitting down again, our teacher continued that Balak, a clever but unscrupulous man, had found the way to Balaam's heart, for, while the latter was the greatest prophet ever granted to the gentiles, he was a wild and unruly youth in thrall to the king of Moab, who could hex a bird from the sky as it flew.

And yet I was able to keep my mind neither on Miss Schlank's words nor on the ballerinas in cyclamen-colored crinolines that Tehiya Rappaport, who sat next to me, was drawing on the cover of her Bible book.

At recess time, when we raced out into the sun-flooded yard, Leder was standing under a pomegranate tree, shading his eyes as he scanned the clusters of children. As soon as he spotted me, he walked quickly toward me and called out:

"You, Reka!"

He shook my hand and assured me that he realized that Reka was not my family name, it being common knowledge that Eureka, which meant "I have found it" in Greek, was the word exclaimed by Archimedes when he discovered specific gravity.

"You still have a lot to learn," he observed paternally and asked me who my teacher was.

"Miss Schlank," I replied.

"Cecilia Schlank?"

"No," I corrected. "Tsila Schlank."

Leder swallowed an oath and informed me that my teacher was indeed called Schlank, as was her whole family of hornets and vipers, but that her first name had once been Cecilia and was Hebraized only after her marriage to Rabbi Tsipper in Vienna—a marriage, he went on, that had lasted no more than a year and a half, her moral standards not having been of the highest.

He laid a hand on my shoulder and steered me gently toward the old Moslem cemetery in the park near my school, while telling me that he had met the two lovebirds in the early twenties in Vienna. While Abbale Tsipper, whom he had known as a boy in Jerusalem, was immersed in his studies at the rabbinical seminary, where he sat at the feet of Rabbi Tsvi Peretz Hayut, Cecilia Schlank, the Fraulein from Lemberg, was turning the heads of the left-wing Zionists, whom she tagged after wherever they went.

His eyes hazed as he told me how he first met her at the Alt-theater at a performance of the Vilna Yiddish troupe. He was sitting way up in the gallery, watching the unforgettable acting of Alexander Granach, when suddenly his glance strayed from the stage to a prominent box in which the Zionist leaders Zalman Rubashov and Berl Locker were sitting with their wives. Other young socialists from Palestine—who had come to get a whiff of Europe, and had managed to empty their party's coffers in the process—sat around them. Leder was particularly struck by a red-headed girl playing with her long braids and stealing frequent looks at the infamous skirt-chaser Yisra'el Shochet, who was sitting in another box nearby.

During the intermission Leder went down to the Zionist box and was greeted loudly by Rubashov, who pronounced with a smack of his lips, "*A groysser yiddisher kinstler, der doziker Granach,*" and added that whoever had failed to see the great artist play Shylock in Her-mine Keerner's Berlin ensemble did not know what real theater was. Why, the very walls had trembled when this Galician merchant of Venice snarled, "Send the deed after me, and I will sign it!"

The young lady, who was introduced to Leder as Cecilia Schlank, commented that she had first seen Granach with the legendary Moissi in Schiller's *Robbers*, where he had played the part of Spiegelberg. Yet though the men continued to lavish praise on the Jewish Barrymore, she did not remain in their company for long. As the intermission was ending, Leder told me, he saw her beneath a gas lamp in the lobby, exchanging intimacies with a raven-tressed young dandy whose face he did not see.

Four months later, while standing on the sidewalk in front of the Austrian parliament and watching massed columns of workers marching by in the May Day parade, he saw her again, the red heifer, waving a red rag behind Rubashov. She beckoned to him to join her, which he—though astonished that she had remembered him from their brief encounter in the dimly lit Alttheater—declined to do, causing her to face front again and break into loud proletarian song.

"And now that viper, who carried on in the streets when she was already a married woman, teaches boys like you in a religious school that a woman's place is in the kitchen," Leder snapped, sitting down on one of the crumbling tombstones of the Moslem cemetery and regarding a pack of yellow dogs playing by the edge of Mamilla Pool below.

3.

Leder often reminisced to me about his years in the imperial capital. On one such occasion, we had walked as far as the train station at the beginning of the Valley of Refaim when he interrupted a formal lecture on the importance of Esperanto in the future Lynkean state to announce that he wished to rest for a while beneath one of the shaded branches in the square outside the station.

He took off his sandals and stretched out his legs, and for the first time I noticed how swollen his feet were and how the sandals themselves were unusually broad.

He had always, Leder told me, surveying the little Jerusalem station, imagined Vienna in the most regal colors. Yet the first color he saw when he stepped off the train there was the faded one of the great railroad terminal—a dirty sort of hue, halfway between bright brown and orange, which was the trademark, he soon learned, of all the public buildings in the former Austro-Hungarian monarchy.

It was cold that winter in Vienna. In the dead of the night, many of the city's inhabitants, famous men and high court justices among them, stole into its public gardens and broad streets to cut down trees with which to warm their freezing flesh. For next to nothing, Leder and Abbale Tsipper rented a large room in the students' quarter of town. Rosy-cheeked cherubs fluttered in the corner of its blue ceiling. Their landlady, an old and infirm widow who was too weak to chop wood, lit her fireplace with copies of the *Neue Freie Presse* that her late husband had painstakingly collected over the years.

On one such night, the blanket slipped off Leder's feet while he slept and his toes froze solid. They would have had to be amputated had it not been for Abbale Tsipper, who hastened to heat water on the alcohol burner and kept them covered with warm compresses until morning.

To the south we heard the whistle of the Jerusalem train as it cut through the mountains. Leder drew his feet in, shut his eyes, and inhaled the heady odor of the railway ties, which smelled sharply of creosote. The sleepy station began to stir. A young man and young woman, kibbutzniks by appearance, sat down on the bench beside us. The man read a newspaper while the woman lullabied a baby in her lap.

Leder appeared to listen. He opened his eyes, put his sandals back on, and said that the smell of the creosote reawakened in him the wanderlust that had gone unsated for years. As we left the station, he remarked, apropos of the kibbutzniks, that during his years abroad he had known many peasants. He had spent hours traveling with them in trains and had even visited them in their mountain homes, ignorant, uneducated country folk who could not so much as read a daily paper; yet never once had he heard anything so imbecilic from them as the Hebrew song, "In the quarry fell your father / Gone his soul forever." He raised the palm of his hand and declared that hair would grow on it before we in Israel would succeed in raising a race of genuine peasants like the farmers of the Tyrol.

A second whistle sounded sharper than the first and the train

pulled into the station. Leder regarded the handful of passengers descending from the cars and declared that when he first arrived in Vienna, he had cut a comic and pathetic figure. In typical Levantine fashion, he was wearing a white summer suit, bought in Alexandria before boarding the ship for Trieste, that had turned black en route from the smoke of the locomotives. Yet it wasn't the soot on his jacket that had made the ladies laugh pityingly into their fans when he entered a café in the Ring to order refreshment. Weeks went by before he was informed by Abbale Tsipper and Luba Ettinger, whom he met while wandering through the rooms of the Schonbrunn Museum, that only waiters wore white jackets in Vienna, and that even they wore black trousers like everyone else.

"Luba Ettinger?" I asked, surprised.

Leder fell silent, his thin lips twisting uneasily. He plucked an olive branch from a silvery tree by the road, stuck it in his mouth, and declared that one day the artists of the future would portray him as a dove of peace bringing the glad tidings of Popper-Lynkeus. He said no more about my father's first wife or meeting her in Vienna.

4.

Just like the large photograph of her, which was removed from the wall on the day my father married my mother and was put away in the back of the storeroom, the figure of my father's first wife had receded deep into the murky depths of the family unconscious. My father never mentioned her or kept in touch with her few relations. Only once, when he and Mr. Rachlevski were sitting by themselves in the yard on a dusky summer evening and eating muscatel grapes, did the memory of her come alive.

Our neighbor was talking slowly into the night, recollecting how he had returned from the Manchurian front after the Russo-Japanese War, a well-mannered young man from the 8th Rifle Brigade in a tightly cut Czarist army tunic who wandered about his native town at the far ends of Volhynia with a walking stick in one hand, as was the fashion in those days, and regarded with amazement the Progress Photo Studio that had been opened in his absence ("Bad Weather's No Hindrance to Progress") and the royal tomb from the time of King Oleg that had been visited by Nikolai II. Only a slight slump in one shoulder, where it had borne a rifle too long, bore witness to the endless movements of troops and the nights of unprofitable sleep snatched on the floors of God-forsaken train stations that smelled of wet dogs and sweaty puttees. And in the mysterious light of the vast Russian landscape little Luba Ettinger had laid her head in his lap and fingered his copper buttons with their double-headed imperial eagle, her purple hands sticky with mulberries.

"Yes," said my father as he listened to Rachlevski, who had been his first wife's childhood friend. "She liked mulberries." His voice cracked when he spoke.

Her hands, which were clothed in elegant lace gloves, extended forward with aristocratic care and rested, one on top of the other, on the arm of the chair where the photographer had put them, while her proud, sad glance drifted off into inner rooms. A woman magnificent in her longing, averting her face so as not to see the hulks of the abandoned workshops on the slopes of Tel Arza with clumps of Jerusalem buttercups beyond them, gathering dust and cobwebs in a corner of the storeroom, her features growing dimmer with the seasons.

When I returned home from the Six Day War, her faded picture that was crumbling at the edges stood next to my father's on the bookshelf. Noticing my surprise, Mother explained that, now that the road to the Mount of Olives was open again, we had a duty to restore not only my brother's but Luba's grave as well, which was what my father, might he rest in peace, would have wanted.

In those days she visited Riklin frequently in the offices of the Burial Society and, once the desecrated graves were located, and repairs upon them commenced, she even took a good part of her savings, which she had been keeping, so she said, for a rainy day, and entrusted them to a stone carver. In late summer of that year, on the eve of the new moon of Elul, I accompanied her on her pilgrimage to the Mount of Olives to pay her first homage to the restored graves.

Numerous clusters of people were scattered about the cemetery, which ran down the slope of the mount and along the Jericho road. Under a hastily erected canopy in the courtyard of an unfinished Moslem mosque, we found Riklin bent over a folding table laden with notebooks and maps, trying to help the grave-hunters who turned to him. As soon as he saw me and my mother, he hurried toward us with a notebook in my father's writing held out in one hand; pointing with his other hand at the graveyard, which was humming with visitors, he put an arm around my shoulder and said, "What a shame that your father could not live to see this!" Then he turned to my mother and, embellishing on Jeremiah, chanted in the plainsong of the Prophets: "Refrain thy voice from weeping, *mayn libe fraynt*, for the work of thy husband shall be rewarded, saith the Lord."

He jotted down the exact location of the graves on a piece of paper, which he handed to a yeshiva student huddling with his confreres in a corner of the makeshift structure, and asked him to take us first to the children's section, and from there to the very top of the mount, below the Intercontinental Hotel.

My mother stood quietly by my brother's grave, mouthing the brief inscription carved on her eldest son's little tomb and gently running a hand over the grayish stone. When she pulled herself away at last, she said to me in a whisper, while glancing straight up at the cloudless sky, so that our guide should not hear: "I'll never forgive Him for it until the day I die."

The yeshiva boy climbed quickly along the path between the graves, lifting the hem of his black frock to avoid getting snagged on the thornbushes, while we followed slowly behind him. Up this same path, my mother told me, she and my father had walked on the morning of their wedding day. My father had wished to part from his first wife before taking another in her place, and my mother went with him, stepping by his side and divining the unconsolable heart of the woman she had never met who had sometimes dozed for whole days by the window, stunned by the brutal sun, dreaming of the running brooks and the lost mulberry trees of her childhood.

The student stood waiting for us impatiently by her grave. He murmured something in my mother's ear and, receiving his tip from her, galloped quickly back down the slope like a mountain goat. When he was gone my mother said with a smile on her chapped lips that in Paradise, as I well knew, where neither lust nor envy held sway, the rabbinical ban on polygamy no longer applied, so that she, my father, and my father's first wife would all sit together in a pavilion made of Leviathan's skin and eat of the delicate flesh of the Cosmic Wild Ox.

She shaded her eyes, looking eastward toward the whitening peaks of the Wilderness of Judea, and recalled that on the day of their honeymoon she and my father had taken a trip to Jericho and its surroundings. It was the only trip she had ever taken in her married life. She spoke of having seen a purplish-blue bird with a chestnut spot on its wing that had looped acrobatically over the canyons and sung in a sweet, poignant, melancholy voice; of the harshly squeaking, ornamented peacocks that met them with a showy dance in the portico of a Greek monastery that clung to the side of a cliff; and of an old monk, his hair knotted at the back of his head, who had plastered the dome of the church with whitewash the color of bluing and told them that the peacock's flesh never rotted, since the bird had drunk from the chalice of everlasting life.

My mother laid a pebble on Luba's grave and said that if I wasn't in a hurry, she would like to return via the Vale of Jehosephat, in which she hadn't been for many years. The way down to it was hard, and I had to give her my hand to keep her from stumbling on the broken bits of tombstone that lay scattered in the narrow aisles between the graves.

Her hand was bony without the plump warmth that I remembered from the mornings when she had sat stroking my face on my bed before I woke, her fingers redolent of the etheric fragrance of the orange that she scored for me with a kitchen knife so that I could peel it more easily at school for my ten o'clock snack.

"You were so embarassed to hold my hand in the street," she whispered, and I could hear her sad, distant voice as it sang:

Lo, the cranes fly high
And the bees buzz by,
The storks fly high, high in the sky.

She recounted all she had suffered, though she had borne it without complaint, while trying to give me a proper education and raise me to be a decent person. She told how she had humiliated herself in the corridors of the municipal department of education, determined at all costs to rescue me from that stable of Mr. Friedman's that I attended because it was my district school; how she had tried to enroll me at the far better school downtown, whose pupils were the sons of teachers and government officials rather than street urchins; how she had not spared herself walking me there and back twice a day because of the dangerous streets that I had to cross on the way; and how she had even carried my briefcase and my lunch-bag in her hands. With bitten, tear-swollen lips she reminded me how my schoolmates had thought that she was my nanny and how she had never bothered to correct them for fear they might make fun of me if they knew . . . And yet along had come Leder in the end and ruined all her best-laid plans.

"Can you feel how that serpent," she asked, practically hissing the word, "is still crawling right under our feet?"

When she had calmed down, she went on:

"Now that you are a father yourself, how can you rationally explain such craziness?" How a boy who lacked nothing, whose teachers were men of such stature that some eventually became university lecturers, whose friends came from the very best of houses—how such a boy could have fallen for a shiftless low-life Leder was more than she could comprehend.

Since the conversation annoyed me, I replied that no one, not even I, could know what had gone on in my mind and soul as a child. Nevertheless, I added, I believed that Leder was in his own fashion a philosopher, though an autodidact of course, and that my imagination had been fired by the world of utopian thought he opened up to me.

My mother sarcastically repeated my big words and declared that even though she had no schooling and had never even been able to attend the Saturday night lectures at the community center, she knew enough to understand the difference between Leder and a philosopher.

"We're both adults now," she went on as we crossed the busy Jerusalem-Jericho road, "and it won't hurt you to hear the truth for once." She blamed Leder for my having dropped out of school. "You went to college thinking that a philosophy department was a lot of wise men sitting around with laurel wreathes on their heads and discussing Kant and Spinoza while solving the problems of the universe with hot air."

She was convinced—not entirely without reason—that it was Leder who had developed in me a taste for the bizarre. "That's why you can't even read a book from beginning to end. You never get past the introductions and acknowledgements, and you only look for what's odd or grotesque. That's why you don't have your degree to this day. You think you can go through life as though it were some kind of joke book."

No less cruelly, she insisted that my friendship with Leder had left its mark on all my relationships, especially in my preference for older men. "Father and I could never understand what you saw in them, how you could spend so many hours talking to them. One might have thought you had grown up swimming in the same river with them, or come to this country on the same boat."

She was sure I had been drawn to them because it had become second nature for me to seek easy ways of getting attention. Whereas with boys my own age I would have had to struggle for recognition, older people were ready to laud me for nothing more than my gaping mouth and the ears that I lent to their maxims.

And in the same tone, as though observing my life from the sidelines, she said that before long, because time was cruel and stood still for no man, I myself would be old and lonely and would look for some precocious youth to befriend, to whose sophomoric stammerings about the existence of God, or the reality of good and evil, I would listen with a wise look on my face. "But my one hope is that what little education your father and I managed to give you will help you find your way in life."

To our right, in the channel of the dry Brook of Kidron, Absalom's Tomb appeared in its full glory. My mother took off her sunglassses and stepped spryly up to its raised platform hewn out of the rock. She circled the massive mausoleum, feeling the reddish veins of its stone and looking up at the lotus flower carved at the top of its conical roof.

Afterward, while we sat on the stone steps leading down to Jehosephat's Cave, recovering from the heat in the fusty coolness coming from the burial chamber within, Mother recalled how in her childhood the lower half of the tomb had been covered by mounds of debris. She described its derelict state, her memories like a distant dream lit by a yellowish light that was clear and cloudy at once. Suddenly she leaped up and cried:

"Don't you see how that snake is following us everywhere?" Back in those days, she explained, a band of angry yeshiva students, of whom young Mordecai Leder was one, had assembed at a point near her house to protest the plans of a British expedition to uncover the base of the tomb. The students' wrath waxed sevenfold when they discovered, upon reaching the site itself, that the archeologists had already dug down to the bottom of the monumental tomb's columns and caused the collapse of a number of old graves whose bones had been sacrilegiously scattered to the winds. Their leader, Reb Yona Tsyebner—so the students, bruised and beaten, related upon their return—had commanded them to throw themselves bodily upon the debris, from which they retreated only when a detachment of Turkish soldiers appeared and pummeled them soundly.

The archeologists backed down, nor did they try again until the seventh year of the British conquest of Jerusalem. Once more the local zealots, led this time by Reb Dovid Leder, girded up their loins and sallied forth to the Brook of Kidron. Leder junior, however, was not present on this occasion, all trace of him having vanished since the day he ran off with the two Chinese nuns to Beirut. This second dig, my mother continued, was directed by Professor Nachum Sluscsz and Yitzhak Ben-Tsvi, the future president of the state of Israel. The two men enlisted the aid of a left-wing work brigade lodging at the Ratisbon Monastery, which fell on the rabbis and yeshiva students so savagely that it broke Reb Dovid Leder's right arm. Rabbi Eliahu Klatzkin, the Gaon of Lublin, who came to pay Reb Dovid a convalescent call, told him and his family that his injury was a case of divine measure for measure, to which Rabbi Yekutiel Vinograd, the old man's valet and authorized commentator, added by way of explanation that the master was referring to the ancient custom in Jerusalem of fathers bringing their mutinous sons to Absalom's Tomb and publicly thrashing them there, so that all should witness and know what lay in store for young malcontents. Because Reb Dovid Leder had soft-heartedly spared the rod with his own son, thus encouraging him in his sinful ways, Providence had allowed a profligate young man to strike him that very place.

5.

Leder himself mentioned this incident to me briefly during our second meeting, adding that had he not arrived in Vienna at an impressionable age when he was still young enough to learn, he too would have lived out his life in darkness among the tombstones of the Mount of Olives, the mountain peaks around Jerusalem forming the horizons of his world.

In Vienna, Leder told me, he had learned to love and appreciate the infinite variety of human culture. Despite hunger, cold, and swollen feet, he had spent long hours exploring the museums, especially the Liechtenstein Gallery, where he liked to linger before a Rubens portrait of a woman in a fur coat; had contemplated with emotion the exciting collection of shells, fossils, and sea animals in the Museum of Natural History; and had been enthralled above all by the Near-Eastern archaeological exhibit on display in the Schonbrun Palace. It was only there, thousands of miles from the cradle of civilization itself, that he had learned for the first time about the history of Jericho, where he had never been in his life, and discovered to his amazement that the prayer shawl immemorially donned by Jews was descended from the Bedouin *abbaye*, just as the Jewish phylacteries were a metamorphosis of the desert *akal.* In this fashion he grew aware of many truths about his people's and country's past that no cultivated man could deny.

And yet after a while he began to understand that all these things were mere bagatelles. The realization struck him like a lightning bolt one day when, passing through a village on the outskirts of Vienna, he was surprised to discover a grand piano inside a tumbledown shack. Wedges of cheese and strips of bacon were piled on top of the instrument, on whose keys a small, almost albino-skinned girl pounded away with pudgy fingers. In response to Leder's query, her father related that some wealthy man from Vienna had traded the piano to him during the great hunger in exchange for a few days' supply of food.

The previous night's rains had slicked down the dirt path that curved among the Moslem graves in Mamilla Park. Leder rose and began to inscribe with the tip of his umbrella a series of numbers in the wet earth. As he wrote he read each one out loud:

"1, 2, 4, 8, 16, 32, 64, 128, 256, 512."

Under the first row he inscribed a second row which he read for me too:

"1, 2, 3, 4, 5, 6, 7, 8, 9."

Then he asked if I could see what he was driving at.

I smiled uncertainly. He shook off the dirt clinging to the umbrella tip and remarked that ordinary soldiers in the Nutrition Army would carry out the precepts of Lynkean theory without being expected to grasp their philosophical basis.

"But you," he said, "who have the brilliant career of a high officer ahead of you, will have to study seriously." The two rows of numbers, he added, were the key to understanding Malthus' Law of Population Growth.

In somber words Leder described the apocalypse according to Malthus. Humankind sprang by the hundreds of thousands from the inexhaustible womb of a libidinous mountain of female flesh, between whose spread legs that reached to the ends of the earth it poured forth in ceaseless droves that could obliterate in no time all edible animal and vegetable life. He pointed to the top row of figures with his umbrella and said that the numbers in the geometric progression represented the incredibly rapid increase of human population, which doubled itself every generation, while the bottom row, whose numbers progressed arithmetically, stood for the far slower growth of the means of subsistence.

Within a few dozen years, explained Leder, surveying the crumbling graves of the Moslem Cemetery that were being reclaimed by wild undergrowth, mothers would be reduced to eating their own young were it not for the waves of wars and plagues that swept over the globe and held mankind in check by means of the Angel of Death's swift sword. Yet even then, in a society such as ours that consumed far more than its real needs and artificially prolonged the life of the elderly and infirm, catastrophe was approaching with giant strides.

Not far from us, behind a Mameluke burial dome on the other side of the pool, a young man suddenly rose from the ground and embarrassedly zipped up his pants. When he noticed us watching he turned away and, leaping over the cemetery wall, disappeared on the run towards Princess Mary Street. Leder's nostrils quivered. A sour smell rose from the earth. The bushes stirred again and a half-girlish, half-womanish figure now stood up, too. Her green skirt was hoisted over her knees and stripes of sunlight fell on her face and red blouse. Yawning, she stretched out her arms and began walking defiantly toward us. She passed very close to us, playing with the hair of her armpit and singing an Arabic song.

Leder lay a hand on my knee and observed, though without mentioning the whore and the strong smell of eau-de-cologne she gave off, that Malthus' disciples, who were more consistent and less timid than the retiring English parson himself, had taken his theories to their logical extreme by arguing that prostitution was a blessing in disguise, since it alone could reconcile the sex drive with the fear of a world of hungry mouths. Indeed, during the great famine in Vienna, he said, the city was flooded by a veritable deluge of streetwalkers.

"It's no accident that such harlots like to ply their trade in graveyards and have turned them into carnal fairgrounds," he declared, adding that death and sex went hand in glove together.

He gazed at the greenish waters of the pool and asked whether I knew that King Herod—who must have strode up and down in this very place while supervising the excavation of the reservoir below us—had embalmed the corpse of his wife Marianne in a sarcophagus filled with honey, from which he periodically removed her for the next seven years whenever he felt the animal urge.

Leder rested his chin on the round yellow handle of his umbrella, looked deep into my eyes, and said that, if I did not believe him, I could find it written in plain language in the Talmud, in the tractate of Bava Batra.

6.

My mother was not unaware of Leder's necrophiliac tendencies. This I learned to my surprise that same summer day, on the eve of the new moon of Elul, when the two of us traveled to Jerusalem to visit the new tombstones on the graves of my brother and my father's first wife.

As we crossed the Kidron bridge on our way into the Old City through the Lion's Gate, my mother stopped by a mound of stones erected by a paratrooper brigade in memory of its comrades who had fallen there during the Six Day War. She murmured the dead soldiers' names under her breath as though fearing to find among them the son of some former customer, then casually asked me whether I still often woke in the middle of the night from bad dreams about the Yom Kippur war.

During the fighting I had been attached to a burial unit in the north, which spent most its time trying to identify the bodies of ten young soldiers killed on the second day of hostilities when an Iraqi bomber crashed into their camp. Smoke and flames were still rising from the large black crater when we arrived on the scene, and fragments of metal stuck up from the bed of ashes made by the Tupolev 16 in its fiery skid across the eucalyptus copse into which it had plunged. The bodies of both the Iraqi crew and the Israeli soldiers were charred past recognition, and it took days to sort them out and determine who was who.

I had never told my mother about this nor been asked by her where I was in the war. Yet now, after our long, hot walk, her thirst and fatigue overcame her discretion and she announced that, even if I wanted to keep it from her, a mother's heart was not easily fooled. In fact, she could read me like an open book.

"Now that I'm sure that you know a lot more about life than I do," she said, "it's time that you, who have a son of your own, understand why it gave me goose pimples to see you with Leder."

She had told no one, she said, what she was about to tell me now, not since the night she had heard it from her brother Yisra'el, might God avenge his blood (so she always referred to my uncle, who was killed by an Arab sniper in downtown Jerusalem during the War of Independence), a few hours after the terrible bomb explosion on Ben-Yehuda Street during the last days of the British Mandate. That winter night in 1948, his face a greenish color and his eyes spinning in their sockets, her brother had knocked on our door and asked my father to walk him home. My father hurried to bring him a glass of cognac and, while my mother fanned his face that was sweaty from fear, my uncle, who served in the Civil Defense, told of the heartbreaking sight he had just come from seeing in the courtyard of Bikkur Holim Hospital, where the bodies of some fifty people killed in the explosion were lying in the open like offal because there was no room for them in the morgue. And, while the whole city was tearing its hair with grief, he had seen Leder walking among the corpses and fondling them.

As we slowly climbed the steep grade toward the Lion's Gate, which towered above us, a weight seemed to have dropped from my mother's chest. At the base of a grave to the left of the street, quite close to the stone wall forming the southern border of the Moslem graveyard below the east wall of the Old City, a broad-leaved century plant was growing. A tall, thick, pole-shaped spike, bearing thousands of yellow, funnel-like flowers at its tip, rose from the fleshy spears.

"I wonder where I'll be when it flowers again eight years from now," Mother mused. And she added resignedly, "When I'm gone, at least try to see to it that your own children stay clear of people like Leder."

7.

A light breeze blew through the cypress and eucalyptus trees around Mamilla Pool, spraying the drops of rain that had clung to them since morning. Despite its iron logic, Leder declared, Mathus' population law led nowhere, since there was not a single silver lining in its cloud. No theory that failed to contain the slightest ray of hope could be considered genuine or even close to the truth.

He plucked at a caper plant growing out of the grave on which we sat and asked if I had read the book on Popper-Lynkeus that he had lent me the other day in the Café Vienna.

Unfortunately, I replied, my studies took up so much time that I hadn't gotten around to it yet.

The fact was that I had leafed through it and had even read a whole chapter. Yet its contents were beyond me, and the only part of it to hold my interest was that telling of Popper-Lynkeus' first invention, which almost cost him his life. I tried imagining the utopian with the high forehead and drooping mustache as he sprang from the depths of a steaming boiler (in which, for fear of its being stolen, he had installed his revolutionary device with his own hands), his cheeks flushed and his white, hairy hands covered with brown spots of rust, climbing the ladder for dear life and collapsing on the moist, smooth factory floor.

Far away, the school bell rang. Leder gave me a probing look and glanced at the Gothic-windowed building that was covered along its east wall by the fierce purple of a climbing bougainvillea.

"All right then," he dismissed me lamely. "Go back to your Cecilia Schlank, and this evening I'll visit you at home."

I ran, stopping now and then to look back. In the distance stood Leder, one hand resting on a solitary tree and the other grasping his umbrella, still contemplating the runes of eternity. The further away I got, the more the wild bushes obscured him.

The school gate was still open. The last straggling pupils, "the ragtag and bobtail," as Miss Schlank called them, were climbing slowly up the stairs. I looked back one more time at the park. Silence enveloped it and a light breeze shook the trees around the pool. Leder was gone.

High by feathery clouds in the sky, a lone bird, come from the desert to seek its prey, glided on motionless wings. Its long, strong pinions were spread to the sides, riding the air flow serenely, while only its head, bent slightly downward, bobbed back and forth like a pendulum. Suddenly its body folded and it began its rapid plunge toward the earth.

Chapter Four

1.

My mother stood in the sunshine, her head thrown back and one eye shut tight. In front of her other eye she cradled an egg, which she scrutinized in the light.

As always when I came home from school, she asked if I had found favor with God and man and remembered to inquire how I had done on the dictation test. Then, keeping an eye on the egg, she told me to tiptoe in softly. We had, she informed me, a distinguished guest, for whom she was poaching an egg. Who knew, she mused after a pause, whether his coming was not a heaven-sent opportunity to purge my father of the melancholy that had possessed him ever since the Rationing Bureau inspectors turned our house upside down.

This was Riklin's first visit to our home.

He was sitting at the head of the table, sliding back and forth on it a china conch shell that contained several apples and spinning his tall tales.

Afterward, when she could no longer abide him, my mother claimed that even then a discerning listener could make out the graveward thud of earth and stones in Reb Elya's every word. Yet as she stood in the kitchen doorway on that sunny winter day, waiting in her new emerald dress for the water to boil, she was moved to rapture by the old undertaker's yarns.

As I entered, I could hear Riklin saying that most mortals foolishly believed that dying was a gross and wormy business, but that he, who knew death inside out, could affirm that the soul's exit from the body was a most ethereal event.

As daintily as a worm himself he took an apple from the pink conch shell, held it up to his nose, and declared that a dying man's senses did not depart all at once but rather left him one by one—to which he added, as though letting us in on a professional secret, that the sense of smell, being the noblest and most refined of the five, lingered the longest.

He pushed up his glasses and remarked that the lawgiver Moses, might he rest in peace, had died smelling the aroma of an apple, which had been his soul's last pleasant memory of earth. "Like an apple among the trees of the forest," Riklin chanted to the melody of the Song of Songs, and for a moment his whole face shone. A shaft of light from outdoors struck his profile and raised hand before they lapsed again into shadow as my mother shut the front door and hurried back to the kitchen, the egg like a fledgling in her hand.

My father sat without a word.

He was a changed man since the Rationing Bureau raid, with atrophied powers of speech. So taciturn had he become that Binyamin Haris, Ahuva's husband, scolded him one Saturday night, as the Sabbath queen was departing, that civilized men refused to speak only in their sleep and in the interval between washing their hands before meals and saying the blessing over bread, when they were not supposed to talk anyway.

My mother, on the other hand, had taken to talking more and more in my father's presence, and sometimes even shouting at him as though he were a deaf man. Yet my father's lips remained sealed and his hands rested heavily on his knees.

Riklin, who passed most of his time in naturally uncommunicative company, was oblivious to all this. He replaced the apple in the conch shell and asked whether my father had ever noticed that human beings were born with their hands balled into fists but died with their fingers spread wide.

My mother, who had been listening to the old undertaker's spiel from the kitchen, hastened to stick her head through the door and answer on my father's behalf that, if her memory did not betray her, she had already heard something of the sort from Bolisa the midwife on the day that her sister Elka was born.

Riklin stroked his ruddy cheeks and affirmed that truth spoke from many mouths, but that neither he nor the old Sephardic midwife, who in her spare time also bathed the corpses of destitute women, was the first to notice the fact, which already had been observed and explained in the Midrash. There it said that infants were born with tight fists because they felt that the whole world belonged to them, whereas the hands of the deceased were outstretched as a sign that nothing was theirs anymore.

The words of the sages of the olden times, Reb Elya went on, looking down at his yellow shoes, were like a spyglass through which one could observe the secrets of life—secrets that would be readily apparent if only we were not so myopic.

He held out a spread hand toward my mother—"Like the pig in the fable," she recalled to me long afterward, "who shows his split hooves and claims to be kosher"—and asked if she knew that each of the fingers corresponded to one of the senses. He stuck his thumb in his mouth like a baby and said that the thumb, as was evident, belonged to the sense of taste, while the forefinger belonged to the nose, the middle finger to the skin, the ring finger to the eye, and the pinky to the ear.

My father absently began to scratch his throat with his middle finger, which made Riklin, who was watching him from the corner of his eye, observe with a grin that the words of Bahye ben Asher, the thirteenth-century kabbalist from Saragossa, had just been strikingly confirmed.

Much to my amazement, my father's face lit up with a smile. Turning to my mother in a tone of voice that had long not been heard in our house, he ordered her to leave the talk to the men and meanwhile, while the water was boiling, to serve Reb Elya some fruit. She disappeared into the kitchen and soon emerged with a thin, green porcelain saucer, the last remnant of the tableware inherited by my father from his first wife, and an ivory-handled knife with which she began to peel Riklin an apple.

"I never eat Rome Beauties," he announced sadly, laying his hand upon hers. And he began to tell us about his diabetes and the medical wonders of insulin.

2.

During the last winter of her life, which she spent upright in bed by the window, staring at the clouds traveling eastward on the wind toward the mountains of Jerusalem in whose earth she soon would rest, my mother kept insisting that the first time she felt death's sting was on that day when Riklin's hand had touched hers.

Among the medicine vials, the thermos bottle, and the photographs of her grandchildren on the night table by her bed stood a white mannequin's head made of styrofoam, on whose featureless face hung a silverish wig. Her own head, which chemotherapy had made bald as an eagle's, stuck out of her nightgown, while tufts of hair grew on her chin and along the jowls of her cheeks.

She was rapidly wasting away and had taken to wearing woolen sweaters with flannel shirts to protect herself from the cold. When the pain eased a bit, she dryly remarked that at last, toward the end of her days, she had attained the status of a high priest, who wore eight different layers of clothes as prescribed in the Bible. Sometimes she even hummed to herself the Yom Kippur prayer that begins, "Yea, how comely was the sight of the High Priest coming out of the Holy of Holies unscathed."

She hugged the hot water bottle like a priestly breastplate to her chest and declared, without taking her eyes off the mercurial sky, how she hoped that spring would arrive. All her life, she said, she had wanted to be buried on a sunny day so that the mourners should not have to slosh after her shrouds in the rain and mud of the graveyard.

"Shhh," she silenced me when I sought to change the gloomy subject by protesting that she still had many good years ahead of her. Sitting up in bed, she calmly observed with a jut of her chin that nobody lived forever, and that no one, not even I, would want to preserve her in aspic when she went. We should be thankful that her brain was unaffected and that her mental faculties were intact. "Don't ever forget," she concluded, "what Reb Simcha Zissel once told us when he came to pay a condolence call after your father's death."

Rabbi Simcha Zissel Lapin, who owned a small dry-goods store near our home, had been a student in his youth at the yeshiva of the famous Rabbi Yisra'el Meir Hacohen, the Hofetz-Haim, as he was called. One day while he was studying with the old man, he told my mother and me, the Hofetz Haim had been unable to explain a passage from his *Mishna Brurah* that he had written with his own holy hand. Only the arrival on the scene of his son-in-law, who quickly cleared up the difficulty, saved him from total embarrassment.

The days began to grow longer, yet my mother no longer spoke of the spring. Though an almond tree suddenly bloomed white in the courtyard opposite her window, she asked me not to open the blinds. She sat propped up on pillows in the darkness and took her meals in silence. For a while she still sought to get out of bed to wash her underclothes in the bathroom, yet after falling several times she gave up.

Most of the time she spent drowsing. When her eyes slowly opened, she asked me whether I remembered the great snow that had fallen on Jerusalem soon after the English had come. Once or twice I tried to correct her, pointing out that she of all persons should know that 1920 was long before my birth, but when she began to call me "Papa" I understood at last that she was slipping away to that unknown land that lies hidden in the chiaroscuro of childhood.

Her hands, which had once held the corner of her handkerchief to her mouth while she moistened it with saliva before wiping the remains of lunch from my small boy's face and knocking on the door of Ahuva Haris, now lay on top of the blanket, fragile and hemorrhaged from her treatment. Gone was the smell of her leather purse, mixed with the odor of her breath and the sweet scent of her lipstick, while a chill wave of alcohol and ice water rose from the wet cloth with which I wiped her pain-wracked face.

3.

One morning in early spring, after I had given her a sedative, she felt stronger and sat up again in bed. It was still early, and the hidden light of the morning outside shone into the gloom-ridden room. My mother spoke to me in Yiddish (the weaker she became, the more she reverted to the language of her childhood) and said that on the other side of St. Paul Street, in the shade of some cypress trees in the courtyard of the Rumanian church, a dead bird was buried beneath drifts of snow.

"*Ikh vil geyn tsum Shchemer Toyer, ikh vil geyn tsum Shchemer Toyer,*" she sobbed in a voice stripped of all anger before lapsing back into sleep.

The walk to the Damascus Gate that she was referring to, and that she had taken on a snowy day long ago with her father, was one of those distant memories she used to tell me about when I was a child myself and it was snowing in Jerusalem. She would wipe the frost from the window with the back of her hand, peer out at the yard of our neighbor, the philosopher Dr. Peled, and at its stairway coated in white, and muse that she never did manage to find out where they had been going that day, or why her father had taken a small child like herself out into the snowy wastes. Long afterward, though, he had told her of his surprise at having met the renowned Rabbi Haim Sonnefeld, who was struggling along by a high bank of snow. When asked why he was out in such perilous weather, the rabbi replied that he hated to miss a circumcision and was off to Me'ah She'arim to help induct one more Jew into the legions of the Lord. Yet from that entire walk my mother herself remembered only a clock whose hands had stopped near the hour of twelve—a clock with Roman numerals that stood on the window sill of a house en route to the Damascus Gate. She had wanted to stop and look at it, but her father had pulled her away and warned that she would go blind if she stared at it any longer.

Not until many years later, when she was older and studying needlepoint at the Shoshana Handicrafts School, did she see that window again. On the holiday of Tu b'Shvat, while out walking with her class near the city limits, she passed the house. A white lace curtain hung over the bay window sill, and next to the clock, whose hands still pointed to twelve, stood a half-full pitcher of water with an almond branch kept flowering and fresh by anonymous hands. In reply to her query, her arts-and-crafts teacher told her that the house belonged to some eccentric American evangelists, who had set the clock dials at midnight because the hour of judgment was nigh. That evening, when she told my grandfather about it, he declared that Jewish children must avoid missionaries like the plague and forbade her to return to the school.

"*Ikh vil geyn tsum Shchemer Toyer,*" Mother resumed whispering when she awoke once more several hours later. She no longer had the strength to eat her rice pap by herself, and I had to spoon food and drink into her mouth. Yet she seemed not to care anymore, and though she opened her mouth obediently as the spoon approached, I never could tell if she liked the food or when she had eaten enough.

As usual, I continued to bring her news of the world, to give her regards from well-wishers, and to read her the letters that she received from her sister, which arrived more frequently now—none of which, however, seemed to matter to her in the least.

The day before the Passover Seder, I made her bed with fresh sheets, spread a newly ironed white cloth on the table, and showed her the flowery house frock that I had brought her for the holiday. To cheer her up, I told her that she could wear it to the Seder. Her eyes shut and she seemed to drift back into sleep.

I crept out of the house. When I returned two hours later, her bed was empty. I found her in the kitchen, leaning exhaustedly against the sink with a box of matches in her hand. "Don't be angry at me, I didn't burn anything," she murmured as I carried her in my arms back to bed. Her palms were black with soot and her jawbones clattered. "Why, Mama?" I kept asking, as I gave her a hot drink. "Why?" She did not bother to answer. By the sewing machine in the bedroom, whose drawers had been emptied, bulging pillowcases and plastic bags lay in disorder. She had managed to stuff them in my absence with spools of thread, needles, embroidery yarn, felt patterns, knitting journals, balls of wool, fashion photographs, and newspaper clippings. All was packed as for a journey. On the marble sideboard in the kitchen dozens of candles neatly cut in two stood in a row, while carefully wrapped in newspaper in the sink, as though ready to be thrown out, were her wig, a girdle, an old kettle, some hair combs, a shoe heel, the medicine tray, and her new frock. Many matches, most of which had gone out as soon as they were lit, were scattered about. The edges of the newspapers were charred and sooty little flakes still floated in the room.

I tried to make some semblance of order, but with the last of her strength she raised a hand from the blanket to signal me to leave.

4.

That evening she lost consciousness. Four months later, on a sunstruck summer afternoon, I saw her again for the last time. Reb Mottes, who had been appointed head undertaker after Riklin's death, prodded me lightly into the ablution room in the back yard of Ziv Hospital. On the floor were puddles of water muddied by feet, while in a corner of the room, which was lit by a bare electric bulb, a pile of soaked, wrinkled hospital sheets lay next to several large tin containers that looked like milkcans. Surrounded by burning candles in the middle of the room, on a stainless steel table over the drain-

way, my mother lay dressed in shrouds.

Two women, one stout and the other tall and hefty—both, judging by appearances, from old Jerusalem families—stood on either side of her with their hands folded over their slack bellies. As I stepped up to the table, the tall one began to mumble that such was the way of all flesh, and that, if I tried to be a good Jew from now on, my mother, might she rest in peace, would intercede for me and my dear ones in heaven.

The stout woman hushed her and declared that she and my mother had been taught their prayers together as children by the wife of Rabbi Eliach. It pained her to see how terribly my mother had suffered at the end. "How many victims that cursed illness claims," she said, taking down from the shelf behind her a glass jar half-filled with clean sand. She told me to wash my hands well at the sink, to take a handful of sand, and to follow her instructions quickly and carefully for my mother's sake.

She lifted the corners of the shroud to reveal the skull and face. The mouth, which had hung open during my mother's last weeks in a sanitarium in Petach-Tikva, was stopped with a ball of fibered flax like that used for wrapping citrons on the Feast of Tabernacles, making it seem stuffed with the green fruit itself; yet apart from that, and from the color of her skin, which had turned even grayer, she was unchanged. The stout woman told me to shut my mother's eyes and scatter sand on them. Then the tall woman placed her hand over mine and, pressing it into my mother's cold flesh, which was both limp and rubbery at once, she told me to repeat what the two of them said. "For dust thou art and to dust thou wilt return," intoned the elderly couple. "And Joseph will lay his hand upon thine eyes." When the last word had been echoed back to them, they quickly covered my mother's face with the shroud and hurried me out of the room.

Reb Mottes was waiting for me in the vestibule outside, by the door to the refrigerated morgue. He slashed the lapel of my shirt with a short-bladed knife and told me to finish tearing it as far as the heart. The sound of the ripping fabric rent the silence, after which my mother's friends, who were pressed in a circle around me, burst into sobs, and Zahava Kahaner announced that she had lost her private Wailing Wall and would be more alone than ever from now on.

Not many people were assembled in the narrow, sloping yard, and most had already taken cover from the sun in the shade of a high stone wall. On a stool beneath a drooping pepper tree whose branches hung over the wall sat a gaunt woman by the side of a young man. Since neither of them was familiar to me, I assumed that they had come early and were waiting for the funeral after ours.

Yet they noticed my torn shirt and the woman hesitatingly asked me if I was the son of the departed. When I nodded she said that although we had never met, and her name could mean nothing to me, she had known my mother well. The young man, whom she introduced as her son, shook my hand and said that his name was Yeru'el. "Yeru'el Barzel?" I asked. The gaunt woman stopped adjusting her kerchief and exclaimed, stepping back in surprise, that she had been sure all these years that no one in my mother's family knew the first thing about her.

5.

As a matter of fact, she was right. If not for the unusual name of her son, which I came across by accident one day while my mother was away ministering at the sickbed of Ahuva Haris, who was never to rise from it again, I would have never known about them.

While poking about beneath a stack of carefully folded sheets in the linen closet, I found an envelope with a photograph of a six- or seven-year-old boy wearing a beret and carrying a schoolbag on his shoulder. He was waving hello from the bottom of a steep stairway, one foot still on the landing below and the other on the first step, his body inclined toward the camera. On the back of the snapshot was printed in an unpracticed hand:

"To my dear aunt, from Yeru'el Barzel, first grade."

My mother returned, looking flushed, from her best friend's house toward evening. She washed her hands with water and Lysol, changed her dress, and remarked as though to herself—Father was still at the store—that only now did she see how right Turgenev was to have said that while death was the oldest of all human games, it was new to each dying man.

She leaned against the bedroom doorway, holding the copy of *Fathers and Sons* that she had borrowed from the B'nai Brith Library and stayed up reading at night long after my father and I were asleep. In a weary voice she asked where I had spent the afternoon and whether I had eaten the zwieback and drunk the glass of milk left for me in the fridge. I nodded and, turning the pages of the textbook in which I was studying about the fourth commandment for a religion test the next day, produced the photograph of the boy in the beret and asked who he was.

My mother froze for a second, then snatched the picture away and said, without losing control of her voice, that a boy in a religious school should know that it was forbidden by Jewish law to pry into other people's possessions, and that everyone, even a mother, had a right to have her privacy respected.

Never again did the name Yeru'el Barzel cross my lips, though sometimes, when I watched my mother spreading clean linen on the beds, I thought of him and wondered what the great secret was.

6.

The gaunt woman glanced sideways at the ablution room and declared that she was absolved at last of her promise to my mother to tell no one that she had named her son after my dead brother.

"But my brother's name was Re'uven," I interrupted.

The woman smiled sadly, fumbled in her purse, and took out a little olivewood jewel box. In it, on a blue velvet pad, lay a thin gold chain and a heart-shaped gold brooch on which were engraved the words from Moses' blessing to the tribe of Reuben, "Re'uven shall live and not die." On the back of it was engraved my mother's name.

She took the piece back from me, brushed off the grains of sand that had clung to it from my fingers, handed it to her son, and declared that now the medallion was his to wear as he pleased.

Several hours after Yeru'el was born, she told me, she had her first visit from my mother. She had been totally alone in the world after her husband, the child's father, abandoned her in her pregnancy and went overseas. All the other beds in the maternity ward were surrounded by visitors and flowers, while hers stood as unheeded as a stone in a field.

To this day, said the gaunt woman, she could clearly picture the black-pinioned eagle hovering over its invisible young on the label of the bottle of malt beer that my mother placed on her hospital table. Sitting by her side, my mother had stroked her slumped shoulders and said that worry was bad for a nursing mother's milk and that she would take care of everything until the confined woman was strong enough to stand on her own feet.

Before my mother left, the woman told me, her face grew weary and lined and she falteringly announced that she had a request. She too, she said, had had a little boy and she wished to keep his memory alive. She wanted to know if the woman would consent to call her newborn son Yeru'el, a name composed of the first letters of the words of Moses' blessing to Reuben.

My mother rose to go without waiting for an answer and said that she knew that such things needed serious thought and that there was plenty of time until the circumcision. In any case, she would return the next day with Mrs. Hochstein, the secretary of the Maternal Aid Society. Until then the new mother must rest and eat well, since fate had decreed that she would be both the little infant's parents in one.

7.

The fondness mixed with admiration that my mother felt for Mrs. Hochstein dated from the time that Riklin fell from her good graces. In her quarrels with my father, which grew harsher and angrier from day to day, she took to citing Mrs. Hochstein, whom she respectfully ceased calling by her first name, as a model of love for one's fellow man. Far better, she observed, to lend a helping hand to those bringing new life into the world, as did that dear woman, than to be the crony of a man who spent all his days splashing in Stygian waters.

My mother began to give Riklin the cold shoulder. She no longer troubled to prepare artificially sweetened diabetic dishes for him, stopped setting the table especially in his honor, and kept her distance when he came to pass the time with my father.

One day I returned from school to find Riklin and my father sitting at the table as usual, while my mother was cloistered in the kitchen, cleaning lentils. She hugged me and asked me in a whisper to tell her the news from school.

I could hear Riklin holding forth in the next room. Just the other day, he was telling my father, he had been shown a letter sent to the head of the Etz Haim Yeshiva, the great Rabbi Isser Zalman Meltzer, by his son-in-law, Rabbi Steinman of Rehovot. In this epistle the

chief rabbi of Rehovot wrote that in the nearby farming settlement of Kfar Bilu, which was too young to have its own cemetery, a man killed several years before in an automobile accident had been impiously buried in an orange grove outside the village. Not long after that a second villager died too and was buried in the same grove, although at a distance from the first man. And now, wrote Rabbi Steinman, a dreadful thing had happened in the summer of this year. A small child, the daughter of the first dead man, had been killed in an automobile accident, in the same place, on the same day of the year, and at the exact same hour as her father.

At this point the alarmed villagers, beginning to suspect that burial was a spiritual matter better left to the proper authorities than to ignorant young persons like themselves, had the dead girl buried in Rehovot.

In his letter, Reb Elya related, Rabbi Steinman inquired whether the Law permitted the bodies in the grove to be exhumed and reinterred, and if so, whether the soil in which they had lain could now be used for other purposes. But it was not on account of this, Riklin stated, that he was telling my father about it. It was to prove to him that the will of the Almighty operated in all things. Who was to say that the poor run-over child had not been condemned to her fate precisely in order to teach the dissolute villagers a lesson in Jewish piety?

My mother's face curled in disgust. She banged her fist on the table, rocking the bowl of lentils, removed her apron, and announced that she could stand it no longer and refused to spend another minute under one roof with such a sepulchral scoundrel.

Accompanied by Riklin's dry laugh and my father's bewildered glance, we walked out into the sun-stricken afternoon street, hugging the walls of the houses that barely cast a line of thin shade on the ground. My mother wrapped her head and face in a transparent silk kerchief as though donning a bridal veil and told me how my grandmother's father, when he was a disciple in Pressburg of the illustrious Hatam Sofer, Rabbi Moshe Sofer-Schreiber, had once tried to imitate his master. On the eve of the mourning day of the

Ninth of Av, my mother said, during the pre-fast meal, her grandfather took a half-pint glass kiddush cup, wept into it until he had filled it with his tears, and began to quaff it as the Hatam Sofer himself was wont to do. He had gotten no further than the second sip, however, when he threw it up again, after which he took sick for many days. "But you can also cry whole cupfuls of tears with no one knowing," she said meaningfully as we stood at the top of a staircase, in a broad corridor floored with shiny ochre tiles, before the door to Mrs. Hochstein's apartment.

Although it was the middle of her afternoon rest hour, Mrs. Hochstein received us cordially, pronouncing my mother's name in the same softly loving tones that my grandmother had always used when she was in a particularly propitious mood. Stroking my head, she said that she had known my mother since she was a tot even smaller than I was, a wonderful little girl with a thin, dirty-blond braid and long, slender fingers. To this day—and more than forty years had gone by since—she could not forget the terrible sight of her and her older sisters gathering grains of barley fallen from the feedbags of the horses of the Turkish cavalry during the grim, foodless days of World War I.

It was pleasantly cool in the dim, spacious living room, in the middle of which stood a heavy round table covered by a velvet, wine-colored cloth. Mrs. Hochstein took my mother by the arm, offered me a bar of something whose lime-colored wrapper bore a picture of a golden bird's nest, and said that I could succor myself with Nestle's chocolate while the two of them conversed in the next room.

I walked about the room examining its contents, which had an air of tasteful wealth. There was a crystal vase with a single rose in it, an ornamental silver sweets box, and a pair of ornate East European candlesticks. On top of a large radio in the corner stood several photographs, of which two caught my attention in particular. The first showed a group of no-longer-young women, with broad-brimmed hats and purses in the fashion of the 1920s, standing around a decorated table on which a fancy cake bore the whipped-cream inscription, "Welcome to Lady Samuel from the Maternal Aid Society." In flowery script someone had written across the photo "Reception for our distinguished Hebrew sister, Miriam Beatrice Samuel," who was, I knew, the wife of the first British High Commissioner of Palestine. The second photograph was of a young man with a lock of straight hair falling over his forehead. He was bent over a violin with an expression of intense concentration on his face, his thin lips pressed together and his puffy eyes tightly shut.

"That's Yehudi Menuhin," said Mrs. Hochstein when she and my mother emerged to find me regarding the photograph, at the bottom of which a dedication had been hastily scrawled. She patted my mother's shoulder and remarked as she walked us to the door:

"Perhaps your own son will yet surprise you one day by being as famous as my nephew."

From then on my mother visited Mrs. Hochstein often and spent long, intimate hours with her in her office. Soon her behavior took a mysterious turn.

One morning, before I left for school, she took down my baby carriage from the attic where it had been gathering dust, cleaned it, polished it, and retouched the rust spots with aluminum paint. Then, from the depths of the closet, she extracted the bundle of diapers I had been swaddled in as a child and carefully washed them. Ahuva Haris, who happened to be passing by and saw them hanging on the clothesline in the yard, burst in astonishedly and cornered my mother at once.

"Another child?" guffawed my mother out loud. "You're out of your mind, Ahuva." But she offered no explanation of her own.

That evening, my father returned from the store to find her at one end of the sofa, patching old diapers torn by shrapnel while hung out to dry during the 1948 war. He said nothing, faithful to his boycott of her since the day she had yelled at him, during a quarrel after her first visit to Mrs. Hochstein, "From now on in this house it's each man and woman for himself."

Once or twice a week my mother would slip out after dark with two baskets in her hands. "She brought me and the child fresh butter, chicken, and eggs," Mrs. Barzel sobbed into her tear-soaked hands, reminding me that it was a time of rationing and shortages when even the most ordinary foods cost a fortune on the black market.

When Yeru'el was a year old, Mrs. Barzel told me, she found work as a cook in Haifa and moved there with her son. She rarely traveled and hardly ever came to Jerusalem, but every year, on Yeru'el's birthday, my mother remembered to send a greeting card and a present. When Yeru'el started first grade he received a schoolbag from her, and when he began vocational school, a kit of draftsman's tools.

This year, the gaunt woman said, nothing had arrived for the first time since Yeru'el was born. She was about to tell me how she had learned of my mother's illness when two young men in black emerged from the ablution room with wooden poles. Over these they assembled a collapsible metal bed, screwing the iron shafts into their sockets, after which my mother was carried out by three bearded men and set down on it. Reb Mottes smashed a piece of tile on the threshold. "The snare is broken and we have escaped," the mourners joined him in chanting the traditional verse from the Book of Psalms, and the small group began to ascend the steep hill toward the bustle of Prophets Street.

We moved slowly along the narrow street, weaving our way between vehicles. At the top of it some black-haired girls of ten or twelve, dressed in blue-and-white checkered dresses over baggy blue trousers, darted out behind an elderly nun from the gate of St. Joseph de l'Apparition. They passed in front of us two by two, keeping close to the walls of the building and taking care not to step off the narrow sidewalk while stealing glances at the slender frame bouncing in its shrouds on the metal bed.

The hearse was waiting at the corner by a white stone building that had once housed the San Remo Hotel. The bier was thrust quickly into it and laid on its platform while the men kept mumbling psalms. The red-headed driver started the motor and turned his unshaven face to look back at Reb Mottes, who jerked his head imperceptibly in the direction we were to go. When the car was climbing Strauss Street, the old undertaker leaned toward me across my mother's corpse and whispered that it was well known that departed souls liked to revisit their earthly abodes, and that it would surely make my mother happy if we were to pass our old house, in which the two of us had sat in mourning for my father and had continued to live until the day we left Jerusalem.

8.

Its two tall, twin windows were hidden behind closed iron shutters and the jasmine bush that was knee high when we left now twined upward to wreath in fresh green the reddish keystone of the doorway. Of all those present on that wintry afternoon when my mother, in her new emerald dress, had flitted back and forth from the kitchen, trying to make Riklin's first visit a pleasant one in the hope that it might help cure the melancholy that my father was stricken by when the avenging angels of the Rationing Board descended upon us, I alone remained.

The water was bubbling in the kitchen. My mother hurried to spread a white cloth on the table, served Riklin his egg, a sliced tomato, and some homemade rusks baked in a pressure cooker from the leftover Sabbath hallah, and urged our guest to wash his hands quickly before the egg cooled and lost its heavenly flavor.

Riklin took the wash cloth from my mother and thanked her for her trouble while remarking that he had already eaten lunch at Baumgarten's restaurant. My mother, however, made light of this and replied that greasy sesame bagels and food that had cooked all night on a smoky burner were no meal for a hungry workingman, especially since who knew if it hadn't been fried in paraffin?

When Riklin returned from washing his hands in the kitchen, he took a bite of a rusk and lifted the edge of the tablecloth with his still-wet fingers to bare the wood beneath it. Mother, who was hovering over him, perceived his intention at once and assured him that the egg was soft-boiled and that there was no need to spin it on the table to make sure. She knew as well as he that no self-respecting Jew ate hard-boiled eggs except at the Passover Seder or after a funeral.

Reb Elya smiled and said that a native of Jerusalem like herself should not be too quick to condemn hard-boiled eggs, since without them Rabbi Shmuel Salant could never have made peace between two quarreling partners.

Once, Riklin related, when he was sitting with two other members of the Burial Society in Rabbi Salant's office, one of the city's leading egg merchants burst into the narrow room in the courtyard of the Hurva Synagogue to complain that dozens of fresh eggs were being stolen every night from his store and that he suspected his partner of the crime. Rabbi Shmuel calmed him and declared that a rabbinical court took time to convene, and that meanwhile the merchant should hard-boil fifty eggs and leave them in the uppermost crates. The man could scarcely believe his ears, yet promised to do as much that same night.

The next day all Jerusalem was agog with the wisdom of the blind old sage. When they arrived in their store that morning, the two partners excitedly told their fellow worshipers in the Hurva Synagogue, they discovered a dead snake on the floor. The serpent, which was as thick as the beam of an olive press, had choked on the hard-boiled eggs.

Riklin emptied his egg into a glass bowl and crumbled half a rusk into it while continuing to talk about the wonders of death, that hermetic peephole through which one could catch a momentary glimpse of the mysteries of the universe.

Someone tapped lightly on the window pane. Between the two curtains appeared the face of Mr. Rachlevski, my classmate's father and the owner of the grocery store next to ours. Mother invited him to join us, saying that he had chosen a perfect time to arrive and would soon be served a glass of steaming-hot tea like that he had drunk as a young colt in Russia.

As he entered, the visitor announced that we had a new neighbor who—judging by the dozens of cartons of books that the moving men were carrying upstairs—must be at least the head of a yeshiva.

My mother laughed out loud and said that seeing was believing and that she had seen with her own eyes—news that made Mr. Rachlevski's face fall—the heads of Lenin and Stalin embossed in gold and silver on the bindings of the new neighbor's books.

Riklin cleared his mouth and chin with the corner of the tablecloth—"Like a man wiping his behind with his friend's shirt," my mother said years later, furiously remembering it—and remarked that on his way to our apartment he had met the moving men going up and down like the angels on Jacob's ladder and had even stopped to greet them, since they were his professional colleagues.

The Kurdish porters of Jerusalem, Reb Elya continued, enjoying our nonplused look, had acquired the concession on burying the members of the city's Russian colony. Every now and then, while passing through the Russian Compound on his way to Avihayil Hospital, he would see them in their black, brimmed caps, waiting in a truck parked in front of the Byzantine cathedral with its ten green domes. As soon as the bells ceased ringing and the church doors swung open, bearded Russian Orthodox priests emerged bearing icons, while behind them followed a coffin wrapped in black and adorned with white wax flowers, yet lacking all signs of a cross. Standing in a circle around it, the porters received it from the priests and transported it in their truck to the Russian cemetery in Ein-Karem.

Since they were God-fearing Jews, Reb Elya said, they pointedly refused to travel in the company of either crosses or priests, so that the latter, accompanied by their white-faced nuns, had to follow the Jewish truck in private cars.

Mr. Rachlevski clucked his tongue and said that all roads in Jerusalem led to the dead, and that he hoped and prayed that his Kurdish brothers, who toted dead Russian Christians on their shoulders, would live to bury the books of dead Russian atheists as well—which prayer was granted one day, although in slightly altered form, when he and my father used the books of our neighbor Dr. Peled to wrap cheese and olives with in their stores.

Mr. Rachlevski drank his tea in two or three gulps, then seized me and sat me on his knees. In a loud voice he sang the song of the Volga boatmen as they rowed their craft up the river, swinging me to the left and to the right with each stroke of their oars. Soon, however, he stopped, stood me on my feet, and declared that his rheumatic limbs could feel it was going to rain.

There was silence while we all looked out the window at the clear blue sky. Far in the west, over the mountains in whose white, chalky soil my mother would one day be put to rest, a little cloud was rising, the size of a man's hand, like that seen by the servant boy of the prophet Elijah rising out of the sea.

Chapter Five

1.

True to his word, Leder turned up that evening in our house.

He fluttered in like a great, hairy moth, banging into doorways and dropping his briefcase full of coin bags, receipt books, and tin alms boxes at the entrance while declaring that it was ages since he had last come to see us and to inspect our School for the Blind box. No one besides me even noticed him come in.

In the darkness, through the half-open door of the bedroom, my father could be seen sitting up in his sleep, a green glow from the fish-eyed radio playing eerily over his face, while in the kitchen Ahuva Haris was taking my mother to task, waving my arithmetic book in her face, and inquiring how she could possibly waltz around in a new dress adorned with Christian symbols when even the teachers in the state religious schools, whom nobody could accuse of excess piety, were careful to amputate the bottom of the plus sign in order to keep it from looking like a cross.

The little alms collector listened mockingly to their disputation, which mingled with the strains of the cantor Secunda singing on the radio, then strode toward the yellow collection box that hung by the electric meter on the wall. He opened the bung hole in the bottom of it, shook its contents out on the table, and announced that, even if my mother should step out of the kitchen and find him tête-à-tête with her precious son, she would never suspect him of anything as long as he was hunched over his shekels like a mouse.

"You should have looked at yourself in the mirror this morning," he said. "You were as pale as parchment." And he told me that, while we were discussing Malthus' Law of Population Growth in Mamilla Park that day, I had reminded him of someone listening to the fire-and-brimstone sermons of Reb Sholem Shvadron, the popular preacher, who, by the sputtering blue light of a kerosene lamp, drew aside the curtains of Hell and invited his audience to glimpse the inferno within, where the damned stood chin deep in great vats of boiling sperm and begged each other not to make waves.

Leder giggled and said that if I had never been to the crowded, humid hall of the Zichron Moshe Synagogue, I should visit it one Friday night and see for myself how right he was in saying that death and sex went together from the bridal bed to the funeral bier, and, even more importantly, how great was the human fear of death and disease.

"And it's not just our friend the preacher," he went on, "who must concoct such hideously saccharine stuff for his audience. It's anyone who wants to shake this world out of its complacent faith in its own illusory stage effects."

The heap of money on the table grew steadily smaller, while around it towers of coins were rising in a semicircle, stacked according to their worth. His conscience did not allow him, Leder said, to beat around the bush with me about the true reason for his coming this evening. For quite some time, he confided, he had been troubled by the thought that he too, the standard bearer of refined Lynkean humanism, might have to resort to such scare tactics in his battle with sheer human intractability. And yet though forced to concede that terror was an unavoidable necessity, he was also more convinced than ever that vegetarianism was the least possible evil.

"The least possible evil," he repeated once or twice, adding that though there was a world of difference between that quixotic spiritual vegetarianism that dreamed of building paradise on earth and of taming wild beasts to be gentle as lambs, and the down-to-earth realism of Lynkeus, who had knowledge of human limits and wished only to free the divinely created creature called man from unnecessary dependence and bondage, both movements were positive forces, so that he meant to enlist the former, too, in the common struggle.

Leder reached for the glass of milk and the saucer of jam that had been slated to be my supper until his sudden appearance, and announced that tonight he intended to test his theories on my parents. For if he could manage to convert both my mother, who was known for her stubborn determination, and my father, who prior to the Rationing Bureau raid was reputed to have been a staunch individualist indifferent to the sneers of his critics, Lynkeanism would have taken a giant step toward winning the hearts of the masses.

"All I ask of you is to keep cool," he whispered to me with a wink as he noisily began to sweep the towers of coins into an empty container in his lap. At once my mother and Ahuva came running to the kitchen door, from where they stared at us in alarm, while my father could be heard stumbling about the bedroom as he searched for his slippers.

"Flesh is for lions, cream is for calves!" thundered my mother's uninvited guest at her, demanding to know how a woman who cared for the health of her only child could permit me to drink an animal secretion that was unfit for human consumption, since our bodies, as was well known, lacked the necessary enzymes to break down the lactose it contained. "And why are you poisoning him with jam?" he pressed home the attack, waving aside her feeble protest that the doctors and nurses in the child-care clinic recommended it even for infants. Taking the plastic saucer full of plum preserves, he dumped it into the glass of milk and watched as the sticky substance floated for a moment on the thin surface of the liquid before being dragged down to the depths. The manufacturers, he declared, made such sickening goo from rotten fruit that no one cared to buy and doctored it with citric acid and artificial coloring to hide its nauseating taste, though these destroyed the lining of the intestines.

Leder tapped the emptied alms box with his indelible pencil and began to list the evils of canned foods, which were not only full of poisonous chemicals but absorbed the deadly acids given off by the tins in which they were packed; the perils of white bread and refined sugar, which turned as they were chewed into a viscous cud ideal for cancerous growths; and—last but not least—the foolhardiness of eating meat and other animal foods.

"Have you noticed how the human body is a bottomless barrel for cattle, chickens, and ducks?" he asked, spreading his net. At once he drew it tight again by declaring that if only human beings were not swept away by their own concupiscence they would be healthier in mind and body and free of the dread of hunger, war, and humiliation, a small taste of which had been administered to my father by the Rationing Bureau.

My mother, aghast, looked back and forth from my father to

Leder, unable to utter a word even when the alms collector handed her a green card showing a lamb, a lion cub, and a fatted calf frolicking at the feet of a small child who led them and assured her that vegetarianism was the only solution. Passing a smooth, sweaty finger over the tiny lines of print that accompanied the crude drawing, he announced that, in the bookbindery of Mr. Greenberg next door to the Kamenitz Hotel, brown sugar, wheat germ, and educational literature could be found that were a balm for the body and a rest for the weary soul.

Leder licked the tip of his pencil, wrote out a receipt, and asked if I could show him the way to our new neighbor, in whose house he wished to hang an alms box, too. Although my mother pinched my arm to warn me against going out into the dark with him, murmuring weakly that it was late and past my bedtime, the alms collector ignored her and pulled me behind him out the door.

2.

"Are you crazy?" Leder asked, as he restrained me from opening the gate that led to Dr. Peled's yard. "Who goes visiting people in the middle of the night?" He removed my hand from the rusty latch that was wet from the night dew and said he thought I had understood that this was just a pretext to get me away from my mother and her loud-mouthed friend who had sucked the blood of Haim Segal and Binyamin Haris, and would undoubtedly run through half a dozen more men before the angel with a thousand eyes squashed her beneath his heel like the black widow spider that she was.

"Did you see how frightened they were?" he crowed, his warm breath eddying over me. If I still had any doubts about his methods, he added, my mother's certain visit to Mr. Greenberg's vegetarian bindery the next day would set them to rest.

"That's enough!" my mother shouted into the night air. "Come home, it's late!"

Leder glanced up at the square patch of light in the window and at the angry woman standing in the center of it and remarked that I had seen tonight how easy it was to cow people and bend them to one's will. "And once a person has come around to vegetarianism, and has learned to distinguish between what is essential to human needs and what is not, he is already halfway to the Lynkean point of view—which is based, as you know, on controlled minimal consumption."

"Come on home!" my mother kept shouting into the dark. "You come on home now!" Leder plucked a trailing tendril from the passion-flower vine that covered the fence around Dr. Peled's yard and said that tonight he had shared with me one of the darkest tactical secrets of our movement, which made it my duty to report as soon as possible to the headquarters of the Nutrition Army that were temporarily housed in his apartment and to pledge allegiance there to future Lynkean states. "We still have a long, hard road ahead of us, my friend," he said and saluted me before being swallowed by the lacy filigree of the blue-black night.

A smell of DDT and rubbing alcohol greeted me when I reentered the house. My mother and Ahuva were circling the table, my mother spraying the seat on which Leder had put his hat while her loyal friend and helper scrubbed the chair he had sat in with a rag soaked in alcohol.

"Wait, don't come in yet," Ahuva called out, intercepting me in the doorway, where she ordered me first to take off my clothes and leave them outside overnight. Meanwhile my mother brought a bowl of water, threw some permanganate salts into it that left a fizzing trail like long scarlet threads as they fell, rolled up the sleeves of her dress, stirred the mixture until it turned beet-red, and told me to wash my hands in its cleansing solution and even to immerse my face, which might have been touched by a drop of Leder's unclean spittle. Ahuva watched from the side and whispered through lips drawn back with loathing that I should be put in quarantine for forty days.

My mother pulled my hand from the bowl and asked, shaking the water from it while sniffing my fingers, where they had gotten such a strong smell of rust from. Ahuva chortled that I must have touched one of the devil's chariot wheels and that the only hope for me now was to bathe in liquid fire.

A knowing smile passed between them. Their friendship, which had been near the breaking point earlier that evening over the great cross debate, had now been cemented more strongly than ever by Leder. Rather than stalk out with a theatrical slam of the door, vowing that she would never set foot in our home again (an oath that she would have predictably found some excuse for breaking within two or three weeks), Ahuva was now free to resume her reign of tyranny. She opened the windows wide to let the fresh air dispel the vapors of Leder's breath and threw Mr. Greenberg's green vegetarian card into the sink, where she dowsed it with alcohol and lit it. As the purplish-blue flames licked the sink bottom, curling back where little puddles of water halted their advance, my mother's friend wished on Leder what had never happened to her in her own worst dreams. Although two or three times Mother warned her to hush, since all curses returned to their source as a pigeon returned to its roost, Ahuva went on breathing fire until her departure at midnight. Anyone who valued his life, she declared, should take care to keep away not only from Leder but even from his house, lest the earth open up and swallow the whole street, in keeping with the words of the rabbis, "Woe to the evildoer and woe to whoever is near him."

3.

The fact was that I had been putting a healthy distance between myself and Leder's street for a long time. Ever since I had had my tonsils removed the previous winter in Bet-Hadegel Hospital at the street's upper end, I had thought of it often, possessed by the urge to return there, clamber up the crude stones of the hospital wall, and glimpse the patients looking out their windows at the pedestrians below, who were too busy with their petty affairs to realize what it meant to be sick. Yet at the same time, the idea nauseated me so that I carefully avoided the place, terror-stricken by the possibility that a capricious fate might one day find me there again, dressed in a worn terrycloth robe over my transparent skin and staring longingly at the children coming home from school. And then . . . yes, and then what?

Yet before long I broke the ban that both I and my mother's best friend had placed on the street, for soon after Leder's nocturnal visit, upon returning one afternoon from a class outing to Miss Carey's, I found myself there unexpectedly. The chartered bus had let us off right by Judge Mani's house, near the Alliance Israelite

School, so that like it or not, I was at the bottom of Yehiel Michel Pines Street, which I ran up as fast as I could, escaping from my giggling classmates who trailed behind me in a group while inhaling the grimly sickening smell of the ether that came from the building on my right. At the corner, Leder was waiting for me.

He was standing in the window of his apartment on David Yellin Street, where—wrapped in an army coat and wearing a visored cap as he reviewed the invisible legions of the Nutrition Army beneath him—he looked like the pictures I had often seen in the Russian magazine *Ogonyok*, which our neighbor Mrs. Rachlevski read on the sly, of the inscrutably frowning leaders of the Kremlin saluting the May Day parade in Red Square from the roof of Lenin's tomb. He waved his raised hand to me and signaled me to wait.

"The scholar's feet lead him to the study house," he quoted as he came puffing down the stairs to invite me up to his rooms. Tied with wire to the grillwork beneath the archway of the entrance were a pair of green-painted ox horns, which my host contemptuously informed me were the work of the landlord, who had hung them there against the Evil Eye.

"Welcome to the headquarters of the Nutrition Army," Leder declared, giving his voice a metallic ring as he opened the door of his apartment. A yellowish-brown light filled the hallway. The few rays of sun that managed to pierce the brown wrapping paper covering the windows fell on numerous suitcases trussed with belts and neckties on the floor, balls of dirty socks, and School for the Blind alms boxes. Nearby, on an equally untidy table, were some wilted leaves of red cabbage, a half-pinched-off loaf of bread, and several oranges that gave the room its cloying smell.

"Let us not linger in the tedious present's vale of tears," Leder said, rolling up an army blanket that had been draped like a curtain in the doorway of the next room. (Years later I was to be reminded of this sight in improvised war rooms in Sinai.) I had to stoop to pass under it. A strong light streamed through the windows into the large, immaculate chamber that was the nerve center of the Nutrition Army. Green benches were arranged in a square around the walls. Above a blackboard opposite the entrance hung a picture of Popper-Lynkeus, an enlargement of the photograph shown to me by Leder during our first meeting in front of the Russian bookstore.

Flanking it were two pennants of green fabric bearing inscription in white. One proclaimed, "Of What Avail is the Society in Which Even One Man Is Forced To Go Hungry?" while the other said "Urgent: A Guaranteed Minimal Existence for Each and Every One of Us!"

I took it in dizzily, my eyes running from one thing to the next, while Leder stood behind me waiting for my reaction and humming the words of the Stern Gang ballad that went,

We are the plainclothes soldiers
We march in the shadow of death
And from the ranks our one discharge
Will be our parting breath.

In a corner, on a tailor's dummy between two windows, hung a grass-green paramilitary shirt, on whose brown collar, epaulets, and cuffs white hemming thread still showed. I reached out to touch it and the green beret that was slung on the dummy's round top. A hand-drawn emblem of a sailboat, on whose mast was an eye with a pupil that streamed rays of light—the same drawing I had seen that day on Leder's lapel in the Café Vienna—was fastened to the beret with a safety pin. I put it on my head and about-faced.

Leder stopped humming and declared that the hat of the Nutrition Army fitted me perfectly. "For the moment we're still an underground force, an army in progress," he said. "But on the day we go public and call for a mass mobilization, the new recruits will have to have uniforms." Pointing to the mannikin, he stated that the clothes that I saw had been designed by him and executed by the gifted hands of Behira Schechter.

He adjusted the bench beneath the portrait of the elderly utopian philosopher and, telling me to sit, continued to pace back and forth in the room, twirling in one hand a thin, whiplike baton like the conductor of a brass band. Now and then he stopped to gaze out the window. Through it David Yellin Street, which I knew well from walking along it to synagogue each week with my father, appeared in a perspective more mysterious and subtle than I had ever known it to have. The old cypress trees flickered greenly beyond the slightly frosted pane, while the pinkish planes of the houses fronts reflected in the wet asphalt shimmered in a way I was not to see again until many years later, when by chance I came across Albert Marquet's impressionist painting, *Quai de Conti Sous la Pluie.*

Something cracked sharply though the air by my ear and Leder burst out laughing and remarked that I was a typical daydreaming Jerusalemite. He tapped the beret on my head with his baton and asked whether I had managed to figure out the meaning of the symbol that it bore. My conjecture that it was the trademark of the shipping company with which he had sailed to Europe only met with an outburst of derision. Ridiculing my education, Leder said that if only I had read Goethe's *Faust*, I would know that the name Lynkeus belonged to a hero of Greek mythology, the captain of the Argonauts. He reached for a shelf on which he had diligently assembled a working library for future Lynkeanists, took down a green volume, patted it gently to remove the dust, and told me that in 1899, when Josef Popper had finished writing the work most profoundly entitled by him *The Fantasies of a Realist*, he had chosen to publish it under a pseudonym borrowed from that eagle-eyed helmsman.

"This is the symbolic expression of the Lynkean vision," Leder said, carefully removing the beret from my head. He hung it back up on the tailor's dummy and remarked that he hoped human beings would be mature enough one day to dispense with external trappings and insignia. "But even the prophet, as you know, must talk in a language that can be understood"—and just as Moses realized that the rabble he took with him out of Egypt could not worship God without the aid of animal sacrifices, which were universal in antiquity, he himself was well aware that the present generation must be talked to as one talks to a child, with anthems, symbols, and flags.

"But we who know the real truth," Leder said, "must keep our minds on essentials. Human duty demands that we be prepared to soil our hands with blood and guts for our ultimate goal." Even now, he added, it was not too early to begin composing the code of our army and to decide how to organize it.

"Nobody, and certainly neither of us, can question the fact that the Nutrition Army's most important task will be the liberation of the human race from the threat of starvation," he said. Yet as times had changed since Popper-Lynkeus' death, it was up to us to determine whether the period of compulsory service should be twelve years for all males, from the age of eighteen to thirty, and seven years for all females, from eighteen to twenty-five, or whether we should accept the opinon of our founder's fellow utopian Atlanticus, who cited reliable statistics in his *The State of the Future* to support his contention that five years of labor per person were sufficient to meet everyone's needs.

"Anyone who has followed recent developments in production," Leder concluded, "will easily be convinced that even five years are more than is needed to supply us with the necessary minimum. After all, most labor in the civilized world today is employed in the manufacture of luxuries and armaments that are of absolutely no use to anyone."

4.

Leder went on discussing the theoretical pros and cons of extended service in the Nutrition Army, taking down book after book from his shelf while drawing graphs and parabolas, accompanied by complicated mathematical equations, on the blackboard. At last he testily broke a piece of chalk, threw its pieces on the table, and proclaimed that, despite disagreements about the proper age for demobilization, it was universally conceded that all young men and women should commence their army duty at the age of eighteen. Unlike Lynkeus, however, he was of the opinion that this should be preceded by a youth corps like the Komsomol, which would prepare future cadres of leaders and indoctrinate schoolchildren from an early age in the principles of mimimum consumption.

"The youth is our future!" he cried, then burst into loud peals of laughter. "*Du zeyst oys punkt vi a meydele*," he exclaimed, pointing at my red boots and observing that it behooved a future youth corps commander like me to dress in keeping with my station and not to let my mother doll me up so vulgarly.

A lump of shame swelled in my throat as I answered that my only pair of regular shoes had been cut open at the toes to provide room for my growing feet, and that if I hadn't agreed to wear the boots that my Aunt Elka had kindly sent in a care package from South Africa, my mother would never have allowed me to go on our class outing to Miss Cary's.

“Miss Cary,” intoned Leder, his voice growing dreamy. “So you were at Miss Cary’s today!” And, neglecting the piles of books and the unsolved equations on the blackboard, he began to tell me how, in the early 1940s, Miss Cary used to invite him for high tea. A romantic air had hung over the shady pine woods as the guests of the English recluse—Jews, Muslims, and Christians—sipped tea together from the elegant china in which they were served by their hostess, dressed in their honor in a golden robe like that of a desert prince’s. Then, breathing deeply of the hillside maquis with its overpowering fragrance of wild sage, and feeling magically drawn to the mountains that were abandoning themselves to the mercies of the fading light, they climbed at sunset to the cloister overlooking Ein-Karem at the top of Jebel-er-Rab, the Mount of the Almighty, where each of them communed with his Maker in one of the three small apses that Miss Cary had set aside for the three monotheistic faiths, or in a fourth apse reserved for freethinkers. Emerging, they lingered together among the pine trees and gazed westward toward the sinking sun, where a tiny strip of blue in the distance was the Mediterranean Sea, while Miss Cary spoke of her dream of uniting the world’s great religions.

“Is it as lovely there as ever?” Leder asked, his gaze still lost among the bare hilltops.

I did not answer. In the pine woods near the top of the hill, which was now called Mount Ora, many of the trees lay felled by gunfire, while others had burned to a crisp where they stood. Trenches dug during the War of Independence snaked among them to the crest of the mount, encircling the white stone church. The flagstone path leading up to the edifice had been torn up and iron mesh laid over it to keep vehicles from skidding. The windows facing the four cardinal points—east to Jerusalem, west to Rome, south to Mecca, and north to a godless infinity—were blocked with crumbling sandbags. Bullet holes pockmarked the finely dressed stones of the church dome. Inside, desolation reigned supreme. Gone were the thick rugs with their patterns of religious symbols that had covered the floors in Miss Carey’s days, their place taken by lumps of earth, empty ammunition crates, and rusted tin cans. A smell of urine was everywhere. With poles dipped in excrement, soldiers had scrawled declarations of love on the walls and drawn pictures of naked women cupping quivering breasts and spreading their huge legs before erect penises.

On our way back down the hill, our teacher, Miss Schlank, announced that we would take a short break. We sat on the rocks, our

sweatsuits absorbing the cool, stony dampness. Miss Schlank turned to gesture toward the hilltop behind us and urged us to remember what we had seen there for the rest of our lives, so that we might never be led astray by the lying dreams of false prophets.

To drive home her point, our sybilline teacher dramatically picked up an empty blue medicine bottle that had been lying among weeds by the side of the path, where it must have been cast by a medic during the Jewish conquest of the hill from Arab irregulars in 1948; poured water over it from her canteen; and held it up to the sunlight. Its ultramarine blue sparkled gorgeously like a deep, fierce star before she tossed it in a high arc into the ravine at our feet, where it smashed against a sharp rock.

Miss Schlank smoothed the pleats of her plaid skirt, opened and closed a large gold safety pin on her wrist, and declared that such was the fate of all manmade utopias, which burst on the hard ground of reality. We stared as she spoke at the great vault of the sky, still searching for the lost, starlike splendor. Only the terrible squeals of pigs being stuck in the courtyard of the Russian monastery in the valley below broke the silence.

"She's a dear soul," Leder said.

"Who?" I asked. "Miss Schlank?"

"Wake up, wake up, you're not in school now," he snapped, and added that Miss Carey's fatal weakness had been her tendency to romanticize. "Meditation, five o'clock teas with Dr. Magnes, Musa Alami, and Mother Tamara of the Russian convent in Tur-Malka, and gilded silk Bedouin gowns are not meant for today's cruel world," he declared, although in all fairness to Miss Carey, she had also built splendidly equipped dormitories for the disciples she expected to flock to her in order to help her achieve her ecumenical goal. "But buildings are a sideshow," Leder said. "If they were still left standing by the war, they will probably be taken over by the welfare department, which will turn them into a mental hospital or a girls' reformatory because of their distance from town, while the commanding height of the church itself will make a perfect radar base full of antennas for the army.

"No, buildings are a sideshow," he repeated, relishing the phrase. "If you want to create a utopia, it's not enough to sit home and wait for it to come to you. You have to go out and stalk souls." He pointed at some election posters of the Labor Party plastered across the wall of the building opposite us, and at their bold, simple lettering like that in a first-grader's notebook, and said that if Ben-Gurion had not gone stubbornly campaigning from town to town in Jewish Europe during the 1930s, the left-wing Zionists would never have swept the elections there.

He drew back a curtain, revealing a masonite board that seemed to make Popper-Lynkeus' eyes widen with pensive surprise. The words, "Group and Organizational Activities," were thumb tacked to the middle of it, whence threads led off in all directions to numerous colored pinheads stuck into carefully printed slips of paper. Leder's baton skipped from pin to pin as he read aloud: "The Laundry Operators' Cell"; "The Mizrachi Women's Club" ("Women," he observed matter-of-factly, "are your main purchasers of food, which makes them the key to everything"); "The Shirat Yisra'el Synagogue"; "The Co-op Restaurant"; "The Friedmann Appliance Factory"; and so on. When he reached the top pin, which occupied the place of the hour twelve on a clock face, he said: "The Vienna Circle."

5.

"Vienna is our movement's biggest gamble to date," Leder confessed, since objectively, as dissected by the cold scalpel of logic, there was little reason to believe that any good could come from the Viennese, who spent their time eating pastries and whistling waltzes. What could such people have in common with Lynkean theory, which was all for moderation and self-control? "Perhaps," he went on, as though debating with himself, "we should simply write them off from the start. And yet," he mused, "Vienna is sure to become the spiritual capital of Lynkeania, and a mecca for every serious Lynkeanist who wishes to relive the glory conferred on it by the noble founder of our philosophy.

"Vienna, after all," he continued in a distant voice, "was the stage for Popper-Lynkeus' career, the city in which he dwelt, developed his ideas, and shut his eyes for all eternity." And in Vienna, that wild, licentious place, Leder himself had been privileged to be a frequent visitor in the famous thinker's home. Many times he had come to the modest dwelling in Hitzing to bask in the presence of the old

semi-invalid, who had suffered so much and was all but confined to his armchair. There it had been his good fortune to meet other great figures too, such as Professor Einstein, who came to chat with the renowned utopian about physics, or the immortal thespian Alexander Moissi and the actress Ida Roland, who gave readings for Popper-Lynkeus of well-known plays. Most unforgettable of all, however, was the afternoon of December 21, 1921, on which Leder was one of the dozen or so guests at the wedding, presided over by Doctor Rabbi Feuchtwang, of Popper-Lynceus and his housekeeper, Anna Kraner. Annarel, as the old man called her, was a woman of about seventy at the time, a simple Catholic peasant from the Burgenland who had loyally attended her master for years. Tears welled in the eyes of the onlookers as the rabbi knelt before the old utopian's sickbed, from where he had decided to make sure that Anna, who underwent a Jewish conversion for the ceremony, would be his legal heir. The rabbi handed him the marriage contract to sign, while Maridel, Annarel's cousin, stood silently crossing herself in her best church-going clothes.

When visitors came again the next day, Leder continued, they found Popper-Lynkeus lifeless in bed, his head on a velvet pillow and his handsome eyes shut. Around him stood his faithful Professor Jerusalem and, of course, his two constant female companions. An air of pent-up sorrow lay heavily over the room as Professor Jerusalem's wife related how, when he was granted a lifelong pension by the city of Vienna upon reaching retirement age, the elderly philosopher had quipped that he still had one wish—to wit, that seven cities should vie for the honor of claiming him as once they had vied over Homer.

Outside in the street, Leder said, Vienna continued to go its merry way as if unaware of the great luminary that had been struck down in its skies. And yet it was inconceivable that the appearance and disappearance of such a giant should not have worked in mysterious ways on men's hearts, sewing seeds of love and esteem that might germinate years hence or even in the generations to come.

“Who knows if such a time has not arrived this very night?” Leder asked. “We must strike while the iron is hot!” It had begun to drizzle outside, fogging the windows; now, after pacing up and down in the room, he stepped up to trace his initials on their panes, declaring as he wrote that tonight he would chasten the uncircumcised hearts of the natives of Vienna and Jerusalem alike, invited by him on this extraordinary occasion to attend the Viennese Circle.

“Twice tonight will I refute the saying that a prophet has no honor in his own country,” Leder went on dreaming grandly. Not only would the Viennese among us be made to pay respect to Popper-Lynkeus at last, but the Jerusalemites too, of whom he, Mordecai Leder, was one, would acknowledge their native son’s true greatness. With his back to me he drew his initials on the windowpane and beneath them an eye streaming light. He whistled as he worked, the gray sky and the treetops appearing alternately clear and befogged through the glass. As he seemed to have forgotten me, I asked, to remind him of my presence, whether “the Viennese Circle” referred to the banquet that our neighbor the wigmaker, Mrs. Ringel, was giving that evening in honor of the who-knew-which anniversary of the emperor Franz Josef’s royal visit to the Holy Land.

“How could you have known?” Leder squeaked, indignantly taken aback, as though his best-kept secrets had fallen into the hands of the mob. All my efforts to reassure him that the Ringels were our next-door neighbors, and that I knew everything about them because I was often in their house, fell on deaf ears. Even my promise to breathe a word to no one under pain of terminating our friendship left him looking skeptical. “Come what may,” he avowed, “you’re going to pledge allegiance to the Nutrition Army right now.” And he wagged a threatening finger and warned that any further malingering on my part would meet with severe retribution from the army’s general staff.

6.

The swearing-in ceremony took place clandestinely, in the best romantic-revolutionary fashion.

Leder asked me to retreat to the outer room and to wait there until he was ready. Behind the lowered curtain I could hear him moving frantically about, pushing furniture back and forth and hastily opening and shutting windows. When I was summoned back in, the room was practically pitch dark and the blue-and-white enamel-shaded lamp that hung from the ceiling had been lowered close to the table, where its light fell on a small, bile-colored flag with the Lynkean symbol in its center, upon which lay an old book.

"This is our movement's Bible," Leder proclaimed, carefully opening the volume and pointing to several lines written on the flyleaf in the jagged, unsteady hand of an old man. He let me try to decipher the German script myself before informing me that he had received *The Right to Live and the Duty to Die*, with a personal dedication, from Popper-Lynkeus' own hands.

The high commander of the Nutrition Army ordered me to place my right hand on the book and to repeat the words of the oath.

"I pledge allegiance," he began, his voice remote and official in the darkness, "and even my life . . ." Yet suddenly he broke off and slipped away into the outer room, returning with a battered suitcase from which, after laying it on a bench and poking through it, he produced a shriveled phylactery bag.

"Let's start again," he said, placing the phylacteries on the German book. The initials D.L. were embroidered in frayed gold threat on the faded brown material. Quickly he recited the oath while I repeated it back to him.

"Great things have small beginnings," he announced emotionally when the ceremony was over, revealing to me that I was the first person besides himself to swear fealty to our army, whose ranks would soon be as the sands of the shore. Opening the blinds and shutters again, he apologized for the unplanned departure from customary procedure. As I undoubtedly understood myself, however, prudence demanded that every possible precaution be taken, and now that I had sworn on his father's phylacteries, he was sure I would never betray him.

He returned the book to its shelf, carefully folded the flag and tucked it for safekeeping into a drawer of the table, and turned to replace the phylactery bag in the suitcase in which, when he opened its lid lined with bluish checked paper, a golden coin glittered.

"Is that real gold?" I marveled.

Leder showed me the coin, which hung from a red-and-white ribbon like a pendulum, and said that his maternal grandfather had received this *Orden* from the Kaiser, at the end of the latter's tour of Palestine, as a token of gratitude for having guided the imperial party on its expedition to the Wilderness of Judea and the Mountains of Moab. Rays of light from the lamp glanced off the bald plate and shiny nose standing out in relief on the medal.

"I forgot that you were only a boy," smiled Leder, who was in a chipper mood after the ceremony. As for the suitcase, he said, I would find it a fascinating treasurehouse. "This is a picture of my father leaving Government House," he said, handing me a crumbling photograph of Reb Dovid Leder with Dr. De Haan and Haim Segal, Ahuva Haris' first husband, in the courtyard of the building on the Mount of Olives where Sir Herbert Samuel had his office.

"This we received from Emir Abdullah," Leder said, dusting off a gilded Arab headdress. His father, he told me, had been part of an ultra-Orthodox delegation that journeyed to Transjordan to pay its respects to Hussein ibn Ali, king of the Hejaz, and to renounce the infamous Balfour Declaration while proclaiming the solidarity of the God-fearing Jews of Jerusalem with their Moslem brethren.

At the bottom of the suitcase lay a pistol.

"Will this be the Nutrition Army's?" I asked.

"Don't be silly," Leder answered. "The Nutrition Army's only weapon will be its hands." The revolver, he explained, was given to his father for self-defense by the British police after Zionist agents had gunned down Dr. De Haan as he emerged from an evening prayer held in Sha'arei Tsedek Hospital.

"But all these things are mere trivia," Leder added, shutting the suitcase. On the lid was a label with broad blue margins, like the stickers pasted by schoolchildren in their notebooks, on which a graceful hand had written the word "Reliquia."

"Holy relics," explained Leder, translating the Latin for me. "Like a hair from Mohammed's beard, or the handkerchief that Veronica wiped Jesus' face with." It was only his understandable yet unforgivable human frailty, he added, which he had not yet been able to surmount, that prevented him from throwing the suitcase and all its contents into the trash.

"We still have a long, hard road ahead of us, my friend," he concluded, saluting me as usual in parting.

Chapter Six

1.

Leder helped me into my rubber poncho, let me out at the gate below, and asked whether I had been invited that evening to the banquet that Mrs. Ringel was giving in her Golgotha. He sketched a skull in the air with his hand and said amusedly that if, on her pilgrimage to the Holy Land in the quest of the True Cross, Queen Helena of Byzantium had come across our neighbor's yard and seen its wooden heads standing piked for use in the wigmaker's trade, she would have unhesitatingly sanctified the place on the spot and christened it the Sepulchre of Our Lady of the Hair.

Only a thin inner wall, in the middle of which was a knobless door that dated from the days when the two apartments were one, separated us from the Ringels. On Sabbaths, when it was forbidden to turn on the radio, my father would lean against this partition, straining to make out the news bulletins broadcast on its other side, which he then hastened with to his confreres in the synagogue who were waiting impatiently for his tidings. His greatest coup took place one wintry Saturday morning in the early 1950s, when he arrived just in time to refute the rumor, which was spreading like wildfire among the frightened worshipers, that the Egyptian fleet had landed in the middle of the night on the shores of Tel Aviv. All that had really happened, he informed the congregation, doing his best not to laugh, was that Egyptian warships had tried bombarding the Tel Aviv boardwalk from the sea and had been quickly chased off by a naval patrol boat. Reb Simcha Zissel, the synagogue's uncrowned rabbi, fell on my father's neck silently weeping verses of thanksgiving and, when he had sufficiently recovered, ordered the sextons to have a special prayer said for the brave sailors and to honor my father by calling him up to the Torah. Yet though my father owed his position as an eagerly awaited herald entirely to the Ringels, his relations with them were cool.

In the evenings, the shouts and sobs often coming from our neighbors' apartment would thoroughly alarm any visitor who might be in our house—any, that is, except Ahuva Haris, who assured us that there was no need to rouse the police, since such behavior was normal for the *daytsh mitn baytsh*, the whip-wielding Germans. Only after one of them had beaten his wife half to death, she confided, could he allow himself to kiss and embrace her, while she would purr back like an alley cat that likes nothing better than such treatment. Indeed, my mother would add, backing her friend, if you had never seen our neighbor, all decked out like a bride, flouncing out the morning after such fights to hang her paramour's clothes on the line in the yard, you didn't know what a shameful sight was.

Yet not long afterward, when my father vanished on his first expedition in search of the true willow, and my mother despairingly made up her mind to declare him a missing person at the police station, there was no choice but to knock for the first time in her life on the Ringels' door and to ask if they could shelter me until she returned.

"*Schamen macht einen Fleck!*" exclaimed Mrs. Ringel when she saw me hiding behind my mother's back. "Shame stains like oil," Mother freely translated the German-Jewish epigram for me when I stubbornly refused to enter our neighbors' house. If only I would allow her to tend to her business for a few minutes, she said, she was sure that Aunt Hela the beautician would agree to put me in her barber's chair and crank me up to the sky.

Throughout the following summer, whenever I slipped off to the Ringels to get away from my mother's savage moods, I was met by the same smell of women's hair singed with cigarette butts and the same fragrance of red and green perfume bottles that had wafted over me that first night. Mrs. Ringel would pinch my cheeks with her sticky, hair-smeared fingers, give me a honey candy to suck whose imprinted bee had already melted away from the heat, and announce that the best-looking models in London and Paris were doing nothing but waiting for me. The foreign-language fashion journals that helped her design her wigs were scattered on the floor by an armchair in the corner of the room, in which, half asleep, her husband sprawled with a curler in his lips.

Black velvet curtains shut out the street day and night, so that Mrs. Ringel, who was still blinded after all these years by the glare of the local sun, worked by the light of a lamp whose tall brass stand was shaped like one of the gothic spires of St. Stephen's Cathedral in Vienna. Like her husband, she rarely rose from her seat, at which she sustained herself by sipping coffee from a thermos and nibbling at a platter of little pancakes sprinkled with confectionery sugar.

A wooden skull like those in the yard was gripped by a vise on the table, over which was stretched a brown woven net fastened with long metal pins. Through this Mrs. Ringel drew and wove one by one the filaments of hair that she held in a bunch between her fore- and middle fingers. She was wonderfully dextrous at her work, which she performed while humming lively dance tunes. Once, when in particularly fine fettle, she declared to me that parents and educators in Palestine should stop stuffing our little heads with Hasidic legends and cantorial dirges like those of the Malavski sisters and start teaching us European music. If only Herr Ringel were half the man he should have been, he would demonstrate a waltz for me right here and now. Yet her husband went on sitting in his armchair, no part of him moving other than his eyes, which ran back and forth over the elegantly dressed men and women promenading with their parasols along a quai of the Danube in the blue-and-white china bowl that hung on the wall between the Ringels' apartment and ours.

Whenever she heard a hubbub of women's voices drifting up from the street below, Mrs. Ringel would rise, pull back the heavy curtain, and peer outside. In the small front yard of the building, surrounded by a flock of Orthodox women in black squawking like chickens in Hungarian-accented Yiddish, a frightened young thing would appear, her two hands held up to protect her hair that was gathered in a white silk cowl. Mrs. Ringel would sit down again, stub out her cigarette in the wash stand, and signal her husband to leave the room in a hurry. Mr. Ringel would rise unwillingly, grip me by the shoulder, and lead me off to the next room, the door to which he left open a crack, while telling me in a whisper that soon the sallow-skinned bride would arrive, and that, with a bit of luck, we might feast our eyes on her head being shorn of its nuptial tresses. As though deliberately to spite us, however, the bevy of women with their fatty red earlobes would hide the bride from our sight, while the pious sound of their chanting drowned out the snip of the scissors shaving off the victim's locks and her own sorrowful sobs of distress—to the sound of which, while picking his teeth with his hair curler, Mr. Ringel would say that, if nature got the better of me and I wished to sample the flavor of sin, he would secretly allow me to fondle the fallen locks before Mrs. Ringel wove them into one of her perukes that gave off an odor of death.

2.

This routine, which I had gotten used to since the spring, was interrupted one Sunday morning in early August when the wooden skulls vanished from the house front and a notice in a Germanized Yiddish appeared pinned to the door, apologizing to the distinguished clientele of the Vienna Salon that Mrs. Ringel was away on a vacation that would last until the 19th of the month.

I entered their apartment in silence. It was hardly recognizable. The barber chair, the washstands, and the large mirror had been removed, and Mrs. Ringel's work table, which was usually littered with curlers, wooden skulls, and human hair, was now covered with a moss-colored tablecloth edged by a pattern of antlered deer. In the middle of the table stood a tall vase that contained several greenish-gold peacock feathers glowing at the tips with purple-blue-brown eyes. The house had lost its characteristic odor and smelled strongly of metal polish.

From where she sat in the gloom of her kitchen, at the apartment's far end, Mrs. Ringel saw me come in. She rose to greet me, holding an oval copper plate in front of her like a shield. In a whisper she told me to lock the door behind me and added: "One can't be too careful."

I followed her to the kitchen while she continued to murmur that, though she and her husband were taking every measure not to waken the sleeping Bolshevik dogs, I, whose good nature and sagacity had become known to her in the course of our friendship, could be trusted with the knowledge that even now, when "that round little man from Plonsk," as she called Ben-Gurion, was playing the despot with his people, she and her Heinrich remained loyal to the House of Hapsburg.

She rested the copper shield against the ice box, drew back the curtain a bit, and let the sunlight play over the two-headed eagle engraved on the gleaming metal and the imperial crown above it.

"Preserve this vision, my dear child, in your heart of hearts!" implored Mrs. Ringel in a high and antique tone. She realized, she said, that this must be my first glimpse of the glorious seal of the Austro-Hungarian Empire.

I suppressed a smile. In a drawer of my grandmother's desk, among photographs of her grandchildren, a small vial of camphor that she believed to be an effective remedy for polio, and the letter sampler with whose aid she corresponded with her daughter Elka in Zud Afrika, there had lain for many years a packet of bluish-gray government bonds on which the two-headed eagle appeared in bright indigo. Each Passover eve my grandmother dusted it off by vigorously beating it against the window sill while lamenting that, if only her father had not been a blind devote of the Kaiser Froyim-Yosl, he would have put his money into Jerusalem real estate, the fruits of which they would be enjoying today and for generations to come, instead of sinking it into these colored bank notes that you could not even paper the walls with.

With a piece of absorbent cotton soaked in gray cleaning fluid Mrs. Ringel gently brushed the eagle's spread wings; its beak, gold talons and two red tongues; its right hand that held the burnished sword and scepter; and its left one that grasped the imperial orb. In a few days she informed me, on the 18th of August, she and her husband planned a private party in celebration of Franz Josef's birthday. Their happiness would know no bounds if only I, their small friend, would honor them with my presence and join them in toasting his Imperial Majesty.

3.

The commotion in the Ringel household did not, of course, escape the sharp eyes of my mother, who—despite the fact that she was not quite herself because of my father's frequent disappearances—could not restrain herself from asking whether the feverish preparations of my German friends portended the imminent return of their daughter Amalia, that giddy filly who had hung out with the British soldiers in the Ritz Café and in Cohen's restaurant near the Edison movie theater until hoisted by an Australian officer's petard and blown away Down Under.

It was true enough that, propped on the glass buffet in the Ringels' house, against a harp-shaped frame whose strings were yellow-handled cutting knives, was a photograph of a young woman strolling arm in arm with a blond man in the middle of a field of pineapples. Yet when once I had paused in front of this picture to ask my friend the wigmaker in a low voice where in the world such exotic plants could be found growing all the way to the horizon, Mrs. Ringel had hurried to hand me a new journal of coming fall fashions and to express her opinion that young people like me should spend more time thinking of the future and less harping pointlessly on the past.

About a week later, however, in the midst of the Kaiser's birthday party, she broke this conspiracy of silence by removing the photograph from its glass frame and declaring that, now our friendship had been made fast by shared secrets, there was no longer any reason to conceal from me the fact that this was indeed their only daughter, who was living with her husband and two small children in Sydney, Australia.

Life for her daughter in Palestine, Mrs. Ringel heatedly told me, had been unbearable; it was only to be expected that the child should have sought out the company of refined persons of civilized background and spurned both her fellow schoolmates, who made fun of her milk-white skin and long pianist's fingers, and her teachers, who had had the effrontery to change her name to Amalia, as though she were a cow in some kibbutz rather than the namesake of the emperor's wife, Elisabeth Emilie Eugenie.

Mrs. Ringel glanced at the picture of the imperial couple hanging on the wall to the right of the purple pennant of the monarchy, her gaze lingering on the beautiful empress in whose hair were braided white orchids. Not only, she practically whispered to me, had the Kaiser's wife been blessed with a rare, classical beauty, but, as I could see for myself, she was also a highly cultured woman with an uncommon knowledge of poetry from the ancient Greeks to Heine, a torch bearer of liberalism and progress in her land. Alas, Mrs. Ringel went on, fate was unkind to this noble soul, and from the day of her son Rudolf's tragic death she took little part in the life of the court and traveled incessantly until she was killed by a heartless Italian anarchist in the streets of Geneva.

"Heinrich," Mrs. Ringel said, turning to her husband, who was helping himself to another slice of chestnut pie topped with whipped

cream, "would you be so kind as to tell our young friend about the Villa Achilleion on Corfu?" And at once, as though passing from his waking state into a trance, Mr. Ringel strolled again among the hushed paths of the garden that were flanked by marble statues of the muses, stood on the roofed veranda overlooking the wounded Achilles, and wandered in and out of the rooms where the empress had sought refuge from the madding crowd before ascending slowly to the upper gardens that commanded a view of the Greek city below, surrounded by olive and citron groves with a blue patch of the Ionian Sea far beyond.

Among the chocolate snowballs, the chestnut pie, and the candied fruit on the table stood a convex bottle of wine in whose brownish glass the festively dim room, lit only by the candles in its many-branched brass chandelier, was reflected behind the oval, slightly flattened face of the boy listening raptly to the story of his friends' trip to the Greek islands. Suddenly a fist banged on the table and the candle flames cowered in the bottle and clashed with the boy's flushed face as the gruff song of soldiers out on a night run from a nearby army base burst through the heavy velvet curtains.

Mrs. Ringel's lips curled like sabers. The day was near, she snapped (a prediction that several years later came true), when the barbarous Greeks would lease Elisabeth Emilie's last refuge to greedy American millionaires, who would turn the place into a casino. Mr. Ringel solaced his wife with a few soft puffs of his breath, gripped the wine bottle between his knees, and—while declaring that it was time for the Tokay and asking why his pretty missus should grieve over things that were not in her power—popped the cork with a single vigorous motion.

When we sat down again after the toasts, Mr. Ringel noticed that my glass was still full. My explanations that we drank no alcohol at home, and that even on the Sabbath my father blessed grape juice rather than wine, were to no avail. Mr. Ringel insisted that I down the Tokay, for which he had paid a small fortune in one of the unrationed foreign-currency stores. I need not, he promised, fear getting drunk, since he himself had often as a child imbibed the same drink on this day of the year with no harmful consequences.

Imperial flags had flown on those distant holiday evenings in his native town and festive candles had glowed in the windows of the houses when the torchlight parade set out with its marching band from the Great Synagogue, on whose steps the president of the Jewish community led the prayer, *Er Wer Sieg verlht dem Konigen*, and old Rabbi Reinach preached on the significance of the day, retelling, as he did every year, how long ago, on his first visit to their town at the beginning of his reign, the Kaiser had kissed the Torah scrolls carried in their arms by the leaders of the congregation when they stepped forth to greet him while ignoring the crosses and icons brought forth from the churches by the priests. When they came home from the parade, Mr. Ringel concluded, the servant girl set the fête-day table while his father fetched from the wine cellar a sealed bottle of Tokay brought back from the Carpathian mountains by his mother on her return from their summer vacation.

Forgetting their little guest, who was beginning to grow drowsy, the Ringels waxed ecstatic over the bittersweet wine the color of the autumn sun, reminisced about the gold imperial coach that flew through the streets of Vienna drawn by white horses and flanked by Hussars in leopard skins, and lamented the ill-starred day in Sarajevo when Hell burst forth from its gates. All of a sudden an unfamiliar and intoxicating melody burst out in that sweetly scented room with its smell of the golden Tokay, of the mothballs in which the Ringels' formal dress had been stored, and of the incense of the fast-dwindling candles. I had never heard the distant, rousing words before:

O Lord, forsake not our land,
O Lord, hold firm our monarch's hand,
With faith in Thee and Thy salvation,
May he wisely rule the nation.

Then Mrs. Ringel and her husband were standing up and unintentionally fanning my sleepy face with their black-and-yellow pennants.

After silence had briefly reigned again, Mrs. Ringel switched on the lights and informed me that tonight they had sung the imperial hymn in Hebrew in my honor, as had been the custom in the Zionist club back home. She adjusted the beret on my head, walked me to the door, and begged me never to tell a soul about what I had seen that evening in their house.

4.

My monarchist friends did their best to steer clear of the authorities. Yet though they were sure that they were only enjoying a momentary respite and that the inevitable clash would come, neither of them had any notion that it would take place as soon as it did.

The next morning, when I entered their apartment, which had meanwhile been restored to its normal state, Mr. Ringel greeted me with a plateful of leftover pancakes from the imperial birthday party, while Mrs. Ringel looked up from the wooden skull that she was lancing once more with pins as long as knitting needles, rummaged through a drawer, and handed me a long airmail envelope edged with red and blue rhombuses. She pointed to its green stamps, which bore a picture of a tiny bear clutching at a tree trunk, and asked:

"Have you seen a koala bear, my dear boy?"

Seeing my look of wonderment, the wigmaker smiled with satisfaction at her husband and declared that there was no better school than postage stamps for children growing up in remote colonies. After I had left the night before, she went on, she had decided to give me all the stamps from her daughter's letters so that I might learn about Australia's wonderful fauna, such as the lyre bird, the emu, and the bandicoot, which even my teachers had no doubt never heard of, since they were nowhere mentioned in the Bible.

"And do you know what a boomerang is?" Mr. Ringel queried from the depths of his armchair. He lifted high above his head a wooden crescent that had been lying as a paperweight on some letters and emitted a blood-curling battle cry. Just then, however, Mrs. Ringel stiffened, told her husband to stop acting like a child, and hastened to the window. The noises coming from the street below, Mr. Ringel sought to assure her, must belong to the retinue of the eldest daughter of Reb Yom-Tov Sheynfield, whose day had come to be shorn. Yet Mrs. Ringel dismissed his surmise with a wave of her hand and declared, without taking her eyes off the street, that instead of sitting there like a brooding hen he should go downstairs himself to find out why so many people were gathered around the mailbox on the corner. Could it be that one of Mrs. Adler's boys had once again thrown a lit match into it and burned all the mail, including the letter she had written to her daughter that morning?

"War! This means war!" shouted Mr. Ringel when he burst back into the house from his mission. He ran wildly about the room, stopping now and then to glance at the street below. Mrs. Ringel let go of the locks of hair she was holding, which scattered all over the table, and asked in a frightened voice if the civil defense wardens were going to make them cut up more sheets and glue them in strips to the windows, which she had only finished scrubbing clean a few months ago.

Mr. Ringel's furor grew as he snarled that he was not one for playing practical jokes at a time when the agents of the Comintern were busy destroying the last traces of royal rule in the country. While Mrs. Ringel stared at the floor he related that a gang of workers with hammers, chisels, and welding equipment had gathered around the old Mandatory mailbox from which, to the cheers of a hand-clapping, foot-stomping rabble of children, it was mercilessly expunging the British crown and the initials of George V. When he had politely sought to protest such vandalism, the foreman aimed an acetylene torch at him and threatened, causing loud laughter among the onlookers, to solder his gold teeth together if he did not immediately make himself scarce.

Mrs. Ringel gathered up the hairs she had dropped and remarked that she was not in the least bit surprised, having never doubted since Sir Alan Cunningham's furling of the Union Jack and departure on a British warship from Haifa that the bitter day of reckoning would come. To be perfectly honest, however, she had not dreamt that it would come in times like these, when cheese was made with powdered milk, ground peanuts were drunk in place of coffee, and eggs had to be bought with special tickets.

She held out the thermos bottle to her husband, urging him to drink and regain his strength, and avowed that they would have to do some hard thinking, since whether they liked it or not, it was now up to them—and the sooner the better—to rally the royalist opposition to the present regime.

5.

In the days that followed the Ringels talked about nothing else. To escape the eye of the censor, they sent crypticaly worded letters to friends in France and Uruguay asking for help, and they frequently visited the German library on Hasolel Street to borrow books on modern history. One Saturday they even traveled to Haifa to seek the advice of their acquaintance, Dr. Benediktus Weil, who also observed the imperial birthday each year as his parents had done in Moravia.

On the Sunday of their return from there, Mrs. Ringel smilingly greeted me with the news that their plans were taking shape and soon stood to be crowned with success. In talking to Dr. Weil, she told me, they had learned that local esteem for the Kaiser was far greater than they had thought, being by no means restricted to Jewish emigrés from Prague and Vienna, since, during his brief visit to Palestina in the late 1860s, Franz Josef had left an indelible impression. True, none of those who had seen him pass through Jerusalem on his way to the inauguration of the Suez Canal remained alive today. Yet she was sure that the event still lived on in the hearts of their descendants, who must have ingested its glorious memory with their mother's milk.

It was hardly a secret, Mrs. Ringel confided, that she thought little of the Levantine character of the native Palestinian Jew, whose whining language was replete with Turkish words and Arab proverbs and whose mind was as devious as the Greek monks of the Holy Sepulchre. Still, it was a fact of life that no one starting a political movement could afford to be too choosy about who joined it.

Repeatedly, the Ringels reminded one another that, in order to link up with the ranks of hidden Hapsburg loyalists in the country, they must do everything in their power to locate one of those Jerusalem Jews who still kept alive in his heart the memory of the imperial visit. Unfortunately, however, they soon discovered the truth of what my mother had always insisted about them, namely, that in all their years in the Middle East they had not managed to make a single friend, the proof being that in the weeks between Passover and Shavu'ot, when Jewish law forbade festive happenings like weddings and no brides cut their hair, whole days went by with no one to cross their threshold but me and their cat.

During one of these discussions, Mr. Ringel suggested that perhaps the people they were looking for might be found among the female escorts of the brides brought to their house. My friend the wigmaker, however, dismissed this conjecture out of hand, explaining that her clientele was composed entirely of Hungarian and Bukovinian Jews who had not been in the country for long. The truly old Orthodox Jerusalem families, she said, did not frequent her salon, since they held that marriage wigs were sinful vanity and that wives should make do with kerchiefs on their shorn heads.

Nor did anything come of Mrs. Ringel's proposal that I visit the B'nai Brith lending library, to which I went anyway two or three times a week to trade books, and look for memoirs there by old Jerusalemites whose ancestors had met Franz Josef. In each and every one of the volumes given me by the librarian the Austrian monarch's tour of the Holy Land was overshadowed by that of the German Kaiser Wilhelm, who paid a call on Jerusalem some thirty years later, as the century was drawing to a close.

6.

And then, just when it had begun to appear that the Ringels were getting nowhere, and that they were having second thoughts about their scheme for a royalist revival, they stumbled by pure accident on Riklin.

In those days, before the old undertaker and my father had become friends, Riklin used to drop in on my parents' grocery once a week in order to pick up his egg ration. Appearing in the doorway in the splendid dark suit reserved by him for the evening hours when he rejoined the world of the living, he would survey the other customers through the thick lenses of his spectacles. A hush descended on them as they moved wordlessly aside to let him step up to the counter. There, while my mother picked out the largest and brownest eggs for him, and my father clipped the coupons from his rationing book, Reb Elya reviewed one by one the roster of the week's dead, dwelling for his horrified audience on all the gory details of their demise. When done, he put the eggs carefully into his shopping basket, wished my mother many long years in which she might continue to serve him—a far better arrangement, he avowed, than its

opposite—and went his way.

"A deus ex machina!" exclaimed Mrs. Ringel when she sought to describe the magical manner in which Riklin had appeared to solve their problem. And in no small measure, she added, the person to thank for the miracle was Haim Rachlevski.

It all happened during one of Riklin's visits to my parents' store. As he was approaching it, he happened to look hard at Haim, who was gathering piñon nuts with me from a pine tree overhead, and beckoned to him to come over.

"Tell me, *vilder yung*," Riklin asked, grabbing my friend by a forelock, "who Reb Moshe Yules was, you know?"

Haim's nod made Riklin sigh that the staunch right hand of the Seraph of Brisk would turn over in his grave to see his great-grandson running about bareheaded like some hoodlum.

Haim wriggled free of Riklin's grasp and, from a safe distance, replied that the chief undertaker had better take back what he said, since he had his skullcap with him and had only removed it as a sign of respect.

"I hope you don't think that I'm the Kaiser Franz Josef," Riklin answered in his shrill voice, "because you're not going to get a single kopeck out of me . . ."

He clapped his hands in dismay when he saw the blank looks on our faces. Woe to the eyes, he exclaimed in a crushed voice, that must behold the descendants of the old Jewish community of Jerusalem confessing such ignorance about their own pious forefathers when they knew the history of every cough, belch, and hiccup emitted by the infidels at their Zionist congresses in Basel and London. And he proceeded to tell us that his own grandfather and Haim's great-grandfather had been in the retinue that accompanied the Kaiser on his visit to the Tiferet Yisra'el Synagogue in the Jewish Quarter of the Old City. When the delegation halted before the unfinished building, and the emperor glanced up and asked where its roof was, the two men heard Rabbi Nisan Bak answer with cool inspiration that the synagogue had doffed its hat in the visitor's honor.

Highly pleased by the retort, Franz Josef donated a thousand francs to the building fund then and there.

"Ignoramuses!" Riklin reproached us, and turned to the busy store while I hurriedly left Haim and set out for our neighbors' apartment. As soon as Mr. Ringel, who was in the middle of shampooing his hair, heard my tale, he wrapped a towel around his head like an Indian fakir and rushed to the store. The customers, spellbound by Riklin's account of an elderly rabbi from Russia who had died in a hospital for chronic diseases when a careless medic washed him with boiling water, gaped as the turbaned figure burst into the store. Ignoring their stares, Mr. Ringel tapped Reb Elya on the shoulder and whispered something in his ear. Mother, bent over the cartons of eggs, straightened up in alarm and asked what had happened to Mrs. Ringel, who had seemed in such good health just that morning when she went out to hang wash in the yard. Riklin, however, cut her short with the remark that he had plenty of work as it was and would thank her not to find him any more.

7·

A new mood tinged the Ringels' home when I entered it that evening. The two of them were seated together on the couch, snipping equilateral triangles from black and yellow sheets of paper. "You see, *liebes Kind*," said Mrs. Ringel, in one motion lifting me up beside her on the couch, where I sat between her and her husband with my back to the wall, "let no man ever despair of the Lord's mercy." More than anything else, this recourse to rabbinic language testified to the change that had taken place in them since Riklin had accepted their unexpected invitation that afternoon and disappeared into their house till after dark.

Mrs. Ringel laid some scissors and a bowl of glue in my lap and, having shown me how to cut and paste the Hapsburg pennants, began to laud the lofty-minded Herr Riklin's perspicacity, which had finally opened their eyes to the truth.

In Riklin's opinion, Mrs. Ringel related, it was vital for them, if they wished to wield influence, to cast off their foreign garb and make themselves a truly local movement. And indeed, as a first step, they had already decided to shift the Kaiser's party from torrid midsummer to the chilly days of fall, and to celebrate it on the 13th of November, the day Franz Josef set foot in the Holy City, not only because many Jerusalemites quit their town in summertime for the cooler climate of Safed or the seashore of Tel Aviv, but even more crucially because, while the European date meant nothing to those living here, the memory of the Kaiser's Palestinian visit was still fresh in their hearts.

From now on, the Ringels devoted themselves single-mindedly to their preparations for the eightieth anniversary celebration of the Kaiser's journey to Jerusalem. Riklin gave them the full benefit of his aid and advice, dropping by after work two or three times a week to add new names to the guest list he had made and spicing his reports with new yarns.

He told the Ringels how Mikel Cohen, the editor of the Jerusalem periodical, *Ariel*, had gone in search of a printing press to Europe, where he received a letter of recommendation to the Kaiser from the scholar Dr. Jellinek. "From behind green curtains, his Majesty suddenly appeared," Riklin told Mrs. Ringel, who was wiping the tears from her eyes, "and asked Reb Mikel in a courteous voice what the policies of his journal would be. 'Progress and Enlightenment,'" exclaimed Riklin, "those were Reb Mikel's very words!" He also told about Reb Selig Hoyzdorf's meetings with high imperial advisers, and of Rabbi Haim Sonnenfeld's belief that Franz Josef was a reincarnation of the Roman emperor Antoninus Pius, the friend of Rabbi Judah the Prince, redactor of the Mishnah.

One evening not long before the night of the banquet , Riklin appeared with a large package, carefully wrapped in an army blanket, under his arm. He laid it on the couch, waved aside the razor that Mr. Ringel impatiently offered him, and unhurriedly began undoing the knots.

"Lo, our eyes have seen the king in all his glory," he declared, quoting Proverbs, as he unveiled the contents of the package.

"But it's the Kaiser!" exclaimed the Ringels excitedly, setting about at once to dust off the portrait with their clothes.

A sword girt on one hip and a feathered hat on his head, the old emperor regarded them from the cracked canvas. The oil painting that they were beholding, Riklin told the rapt couple, had been given to him especially for the banquet by the janitor of the Lemel

School, which laid claim to having been the first modern Jewish establishment of learning in the Holy Land. On occasion of the school's fiftieth anniversary, Graf Golochowski of the foreign ministry in Vienna had presented the portrait to its headmaster, Mr. Cohen Reiss, who hung it on the wall of his office, where it remained until the British victory in 1917, when the new military governor, Sir Ronald Storrs, ordered all enemy relics removed from sight.

Mrs. Ringel raised her eyebrows, exchanged glances with her husband, and interrupted Riklin to remind him that now, especially in the presence of a young child, it was pointless to re-open old wounds and revive ancient quarrels among the royal houses of Europe.

Preparations for the banquet reached their peak on the evening of November 12. The street outside had quieted down and lost the last of its pedestrians when a car belonging to the Burial Society drew up in front of our house and Riklin hurriedly unloaded from it several wooden boards, some rolls of cloth, and numerous iron table legs. The car sped away and, while Mr. Ringel strung the yellow-and-black pennants from the four corners of the room to the chandelier in the middle of the ceiling, the undertaker set up the tables and covered them with white cloth. None of the guests at the banquet, not even the hosts, ever guessed that they were feasting on the ablution boards of the Burial Society, spread with linen shrouds from Reb Elya's office.

It was getting late and my mother, who was far from pleased with my long visits to the neighbors, started angrily pounding on the joint wall.

"Our neighbor is summoning her pride and joy," Mrs. Ringel smirked to the two men, who were busily at work, and sent me home.

"You'll never be able to get up in the morning," grumbled my mother, who was waiting for me at the door. "Did you forget about your outing to Miss Carey's tomorrow?"

8.

Upon returning the following evening, as I have already related, from my class outing to Ein Karem and my visit to Leder's apartment, I fled, as I did every day at the same hour, to the Ringels.

Beneath a forest of flags nearly a dozen peroxided women, oozing sweet-and-sour perfumes, sat at the festively set tables next to their pinched, white-shirted husbands and craned to look at Riklin, who was singing cantorially from a tattered little booklet in his hands. The song, I shortly found out, was a hymn to Zion by the nineteenth-century Jerusalemite Yo'el Moshe Solomon, sung in honor of the Kaiser by the pupils of the Lemel School when they greeted him before the gates of Jerusalem. On the buffet behind Riklin, under a bower of peacock feathers, the old Kaiser himself listened deafly, while in a corner next to Behira Schechter, Leder sat in a withdrawn state, peeling labels from the liquor bottles and making disgusted faces at the operatics of the elderly undertaker. Indeed, although Riklin liked to sing, whenever, accompanied by the youth choir, he led the Sabbath services at the Ruhama Synagogue, the aesthetes in the audience hastened to the lobby, where they grumbled that he could make the *Marseillaise* sound like a funeral dirge.

Leder winked, signaled me with a finger behind the backs of the guests to join him, and squeezed over to make room for me between himself and Behira Schechter. While licking a label removed from a beer bottle and reappending it to a wine glass that he twirled in one hand, he whispered to me and his friend the seamstress that as soon as the aria—that is, Solomon's reformist ode—was over, we were sure to witness, in typical Jerusalem fashion, a shameless wallowing in nostalgia for the splendors of the past—splendors, needless to say, which no one present had had anything to do with.

And in fact, as soon as he had tucked the yellowing songbook into his inside jacket pocket and thanked the Ringels on behalf of all the guests for so hospitably inviting them to this banquet in commemoration of the anniversary of the monarch of Jerusalem's entry into his royal city, Riklin fell to relating how his mother's eldest brother never tired of talking about that late autumn morning when he and a score of young men of Austrian origin had ridden out on white horses to the western outskirts of town to welcome the Kaiser Franz Josef, who had camped in Kolonia—now the Jewish hamlet of Motsa—after a tiring journey by night.

Riklin brandished one arm, as if holding an invisible scimitar, and added that the Jewish youngsters, who wore swords on their hips and ribbons on their chests in the colors of the Austrian flag, had dismounted and bowed before the Kaiser, after which they leaped back into their saddles and circled repeatedly around him, accompanying the smiling emperor as far as his suite of honor near the Damascus Gate, while a hundred Bedouin rode before him on their camels, trained ships of the desert that had been taught on a single command to drop all at once to the ground on their forelegs.

The next speaker, Mrs. Zimbalist, related how her grandfather—who was none other than Reb Pinchas Prust, the secretary of the Austrian consulate whose job it was to address in his calligraphic hand, considered the finest in Jerusalem, all of Graf Kaboga's official mail—had written the parchment scroll of welcome presented to the Kaiser. Then Mrs. Jungreis informed us that it was her grandfather who had conceived the original ideal of covering the honorary canopy erected at the entrance of the city with whole branches of orange and lemon trees laden with fruit, and who had personally pulled down the spiderweb that blocked the path of the royal retinue as it filed through the ill-lit passageway connecting Ha-Tsaba'im and Habad Streets.

The guests' excitement reached its peak when Mr. Reises placed on the table an inlaid chest of ebony and mother-of-pearl and announced that it was the twin sister of the cabinet that his great-grandfather, the celebrated olivewood artisan Ya'akov Dov Jacob, had made to order for the Jews of Hungary Society—the very cabinet given by it to Franz Josef and later put on display in his private museum in Vienna among the other priceless articles donated to him by his subjects.

"Fetishists!" Leder snapped mockingly, sipping his wine, at the very moment that Behira Schechter, like a good many other guests, rose rapturously to touch the crumbling box that Mr. Reises held in his lap. When all were seated again, Mrs. Ringel broke her silence to remark that such a treasure belonged in the museum that would one day be established in memory of the Kaiser's visit, together with the oil painting of the emperor from the Lemel School and other historic objects that were undoubedly to be found in the houses of the old families of the city.

After the drinking of coffee—which, Mr. Ringel swore, was every bit as tasty as that served in the cafés of Karanterstrasse—Riklin rang his fork on the wine bottle in front of him and announced that he wished to give the floor to his dear friend and companion Mordecai Max Leder, a scion of immemorial Jerusalem stock with a limitless love for the Kaiser—who, unlike the other guests, had been fortunate enough to have spent several memorable years in unforgettable Vienna and to have seen its great palaces and showplaces that were the pinnacle of European genius.

It was due to all these attributes, of which he had made a single synthesis, that Leder, Riklin concluded, was the man to build a bridge of friendship between them, the old families of Jerusalem, and the Ringels, who had come in recent years.

9.

Leder began his epic casting of pearls before the swine—an epic that was prevented from being immortalized for posterity, he was convinced, only by my cowardly refusal to act as his amanuensis—by lauding his maternal grandfather, that intrepid young man whom the Kaiser wished to reward.

Reb Mikhele Schwartz, said Leder, was the unknown Jerusalemite mentioned in several contemporary accounts as the man who guided the imperial party on its secret expedition to the salt flats of Jericho and the mountains of Moab, and who served as its dragoman with the local inhabitants. As a prize for his deeds, Leder whispered, surveying the guests with eyes bloodshot from wine, his grandfather received a gold medal from the Kaiser, whose one side bore the grand imperial seal that noone present had ever set eyes on and whose other bore a portrait of the emperor. Even though he numbered it among his most precious possessions, he would not hesitate to part with it should the museum dreamed by Mrs. Ringel ever become a reality, so that all might see the two golden griffons holding the great shield with the petit seal of the empire on which were blazoned the emblems of state.

As a young man, Leder continued, pouring himself another glass of wine, he too had dreamed of the legendary splendor and conviviality of Vienna, as embodied for him in the person of the beneficent Kaiser smiling up at him from his grandfather's medal. By the time he entered its gates, however, Franz Josef was already in the grave and the city's fabled past lay moldering like a discarded stage set among the ruins of Europe's oldest empire, the silver and gold paint all but faded from its smashed and broken struts. And while thousands of native Viennese, among them public dignitaries and high officials, had roamed the streets in hunger and cut down their trees for firewood, an old man had sat at home far from the center of town spelling out his "minimum social program" that would one day redeem the human race from the curse of starvation and the horrors of the struggle for survival.

Not many people in those days, Leder said, continuing his lengthy oration, came to pay their respects to this solitary thinker and to the good, simple woman who kept house for him. It was only through making the acquaintance of Dr. Abraham Sonne, the refined Hebrew poet, and of Mendel Singer, editor of *Der Yiddisher Arbeter*, that the privilege came his way of visiting the great utopian, whose life was then drawing to a close.

"What did you say the professor's name was?" asked Mrs. Zimbalist.

Leder smiled and replied that although the inventor of the pneumatic condenser that had revolutionized European industry, a man considered by Robert Maier to be on a par with Tyndall and Liebig, two of the scientific giants of the nineteenth century, had been denied a position in the Polytechnicum because of his Jewish origins, the name of Josef Popper-Lynkeus, even without an academic degree, would shine eternally in the skies of European thought long after many a university professor was dead and forgotten. Riklin, noting the lassitude produced in the guests by Leder's tipsy, disorganized speech, interrupted him to say that the banqueters would be happy to hear him reminisce in closing about the encounters he must have had in Vienna with the ministers of the Kaiser's court.

This interruption, however, drove Leder into a frenzy. Snorting and spluttering, he shook a fist at the Kaiser's picture and screamed that it was time for sensible, grown-up people to get over their infatuation with that bare-chinned, side-whiskered, uncircumcised old man who, one summer in Bad Ischel, between riding to the hunt and stuffing himself with marzipan and rum cakes ordered especially from Zauner's bakery, had signed the declaration starting World War I.

Riklin put his arm around him and sought to calm him, but Leder, ignoring him, kept pounding on the table and shouting that Schwanz Josef was an incompetent old bungler acknowledged by everyone to be responsible for the deaths of millions of human beings—by everyone, that is, except for a handful of would-be Jerusalem innocents and a pair of *Ostjuden* from Galicia with big-city airs.

Mrs. Ringel, who had been staring at him glassy-eyed, suddenly roused herself, shook the pitcher of beer at him, and screamed that the guards would drag him away in chains.

Breaking into peals of drunken laughter, Leder reached out with a flaming candlestick to the peacock feathers draping the imperial portrait and scorched their glowing eyes.

Riklin and Behira Schechter rose quickly to their feet and dragged him out by the armpits to the small front yard of the building. Meanwhile Mr. Ringel fanned his top hat to drive the strong, horny odor of scorched feathers out of the house and, one by one, the handful of guests slipped away unseen.

Chapter Seven

I.

"They carried me out just like the Austrian prince," Leder guffawed as he sat the next morning in the Café Vienna, looking out the broad window at Zion Square. He puffed his cheeks, disdainfully blew out the air from them, and explained that he had read in Ben-Yehezkel's collection of Jewish folktales that when Crown Prince Rudolf, Franz Josef's pampered son, took his own life, it was rumored in the Jewish synagogues of Galicia that he had not been borne to his funeral in a coffin like a common mortal but had walked to it with springs attached to his legs, propped up by two attendants like a bridegroom by his best men.

One might have thought that the morning after, in the harsh light of hindsight, Leder would have felt embarrassed enough to stay home for several days until his misbehavior was forgotten, or, at least, to keep away from places where friends of the Ringels were likely to appear—none of which, however, proved to be the case.

As I walked to school that morning, swinging my lunch bag to dispel the lingering stench of scorched feathers (an odor that would again afflict the crowd gathered by Leder's house three years later, on the day he went crazy and was dragged away by two orderlies to an ambulance belonging to Ezrat Nashim Hospital), the baggy-eyed commander of the Nutrition Army intercepted me on the sidewalk in front of the café and declared:

"No, dear friend and comrade, we have not suffered a defeat. We have simply fought a battle that did not go as planned."

And steering me inside to a seat by the window, he added that soldiers in a war must not fear the smell of gunpowder.

A musty scent of cigarette butts and stale beer filled the crepuscular café, which had just opened its doors. The *Jerusalem Post* reporters and foreign newswire staff who were its steady customers had not yet arrived, and the frock-coated headwaiter—who was said to have once been the wine steward of the first Czechoslovakian president, Tomás Masaryk—was exploiting the lull to berate in rapid

Hungarian two disgruntled waitresses from the morning shift.

Seated in a corner beneath a large oil painting of a mountain stream that foamed past rocks and trees, Malkiel Grienwald was writing one of his outspoken circulars to fellow members of the National Religious Party that were to make headlines several years later when Dr. Yisra'el Kastner took him to court in the famous libel case regarding Kastner's wartime negotiations with Adolf Eichmann. Nearby sat two retired lawyers engrossed in a chess game that appeared to have been begun the day before. Neither they nor Grienwald paid attention to the boy whose schoolbag lay on the table as he listened in silence to the monologue of a bizarre adult.

"Politics," Leder proclaimed, licking his mouth with his tongue, "is the art of the real, not the ideal. Of course, all means must be tried, but from now on we shall avoid frontal attacks." Citing the case of King David, who waited to conquer Jerusalem, the nerve center of Canaan, until the rest of the country had fallen into his hands, and even then preferred to take it by ruse, Leder announced that Vienna must be left for the end of our campaign, when I, his trusty general, would climb the gutter, as the Book of Samuel had it, to smite the lame and blind—who were none other than the Viennese munchers of marzipan and lickers of the Kaiser's behind. Only then would we triumphantly enter the city's gates. "The celestial Vienna," he declared oracularly, burying his head meditatively in his hands, "awaits us among the folds of the future like a bride attired for her groom."

Before long, however, my grown-up friend snapped out of his trance and resumed his soliloquy with redoubled vigor. Gesturing with a dilapidated wooden rack, on which hung the morning paper that he had been reading, toward the billy-goated letter writer and the pair of ex-lawyers, he informed me that here, during the 1940s, in this very place where now sat the old muckraker and the two pawn-pushers, a chamber trio had sweetened the evening hours with *Musical Tales From the Viennese Woods.* As though tacking a sail, he swung the suspended newspaper, until it pointed to a window where waiters and cooks could be seen in heated discussion, while observing that the empty, dust-covered cabinet that I saw there had once been full of the best fruit tortes and *Kaiserschmarren* that Jerusalem could boast. Yet now the cellist, violinist, and pianist were scattered to the four winds, while a few malodorous peanut pies were all that the kitchen had to offer to the café's clientele.

"These are the first slight tremors of the seismograph that foretells the coming quake," Leder chastised me, wagging his finger. "But no one wants to acknowledge the signs or prepare for impending disaster. They would rather bury their heads in the sand and warm themselves with their own reassuring illusions.

"The earth," he went on, "is rapidly losing its fecundity. Yet instead of harboring its resources to grow bread for those who are hungry and cotton for those without clothes, an irresponsible Europe continues to exploit them for its own selfish pleasures without a thought for the generations to come. By the time the moment of truth arrives, which won't be long, and people have to eat seaweed to keep from starving, the oceans will be poisoned with petroleum wastes and with sewage full of detergents."

The café was filling up, yet Leder, still immersed in his own tragic vision, failed to notice the curious looks that were being cast our way. He did not even see that Mr. Reises, the owner of the souvenir shop down the street who had been at the Ringels' the night before, where he regaled the banqueters with his grandfather's olivewood boxes, had entered the café for his morning coffee. He surveyed the customers, looking for a familiar face; then, catching sight of us, he made for our table, stopped before Leder, bowed, touched the brim of his Borselino hat, and said in a perfect deadpan:

"Guten morgen, Herr Pfau."

Leder stared up at him, his harangue breaking in the middle like a hot glass dish touched by a piece of ice. Without a word, he rose and stalked out of the café, leaving me to trail after him.

2.

We walked in silence up Ben Yehuda Street, Leder's eyes staring glassily at the pedestrians and the show windows while he mumbled "*Guten morgen, Herr Pfau*" to himself. Across the street, in the doorway of the Carmel-Mizrachi wine store, stood the local branch manager, Mr. Sadomsky, in lively conversation with a broad-shouldered, crewcut man whose back was turned to us. Despite the chilly winter morning, Sadomsky was wearing his usual khaki shorts. On his head was a ten-gallon cowboy hat, while beneath his sheepskin vest a pistol was strapped to one hip. Nachum Sadomsky was known to be a fearless hunter, and on our way home from school we often gathered in the doorway of his store to cadge empty cartridges from him.

"Did Sadomsky really go hunting around Jericho and across the Jordan before the war?" I asked my companion. Leder roused himself, glanced at the wine store, and remarked without answering my question that I was about to see his thoughts come to life. Crossing to the other side of the street, he whispered to me to keep a sharp lookout.

A sour blast of wine greeted us from within the store, whose dark walls were stacked with crates full of bottles. The sidewalk in front of it was smeared and sticky with wine, and pieces of glass—remnants of the bottles that had fallen and smashed while being unloaded from the winery trucks—gleamed in the sun. While his listener nodded excitedly, Sadomsky reached up with both hands and told in a thick Russian accent of having to hack his way through brush as high as the sky.

"Was I right or not?" Leder snickered once we were out of earshot. "The perfect image of Franz Josef!"

"Who, Sadomsky?"

"What a moron," Leder grumbled. "Didn't I tell you to look sharp?" And he added that we would have to turn around and walk back in the hope that my moth-eaten eyes would see what they should have seen the first time.

Indeed, the shaven chin and long, imperial side-whiskers of the man Sadomsky was talking to made him look like the double of the royal portrait brought by Riklin from the Lemel School to the Ringels' banquet. Making a right turn into a narrow alleyway by the Atara Café, Leder looked over his shoulder to make sure that we were not being followed and declared that Gustav Herring, the worthless lout who owned the tobacco shop at the top of Melissanda Street, would make a fit king for my neighbor the wigmaker and her friend Mr. Reises, since he not only looked like the Austrian emperor but was a blood-sucking skirt chaser too. Both Froyim-Yosl and he grew their side-whiskers to tickle women's thighs, shaved their chins to nuzzle female bellies, and thought only of growing rich at other people's expense.

"*Guten morgen, Herr Pfau, guten morgen, Herr Pfau,*" Leder mimicked, waggling his rear end and spreading his hands out like a fan. The nerve of that filthy Reises, with his Parisian suits, his loud silk shirts, and the Borselino hats that he stepped out in before noon, to say nothing of his shameless dancing in public places, to have called him, Mordecai Leder, a model of Spartan living in the true Lynkean sense, "Mister Peacock"!

"But enough of that," Leder concluded, and said nothing more until we emerged from the houses of Nahalat Shiv'a and stood at the edge of Mamilla Park. There he leaned against a still-lit street lamp and declared that I had had my first taste this morning of the bitter cup that must be drunk by every utopian who descends from his ivory tower to implement his ideas among men.

He removed the Lynkean emblem from his lapel and, like a secret agent, repinned the sailboat with its eyed masthead streaming light to the inside of his jacket while explaining that, as long as the times were not ripe for the full wisdom of Popper-Lynkeus, our work must be done under cover.

"But you, little brother, be of good cheer. Excelsior!" Leder pointed to some tall eucalyptus trees standing by the entrance to the park and declared that anyone like me who had heard his own father reviled in the synagogue, where he was called "Calypta" for his daring nonconformism, would certainly not lose heart at hearing Mr. Reises call him, Leder, a peacock.

"You come from fine old stock," said Leder, laying a hand on my shoulder and reminding me that my great-grandfather had gone to look for Time in the mountains and that my grandfather had roamed as far as the Syrian seaport of Ladakia in search of true biblical blue.

"Of course, all the treasures that your ancestors were hunting were perfectly useless nonsense," Leder observed—and yet not even the most confirmed freethinker could help admiring their courage and determination to go their own way in the face of public ridicule. "You have their blood and are meant for great things," my utopian mentor prophesied. "Just don't take after your mother, who hates adulterous men and comes from a long line of frustrated Lithuanian Talmudists descended from the nitpicking students of the Gaon of Vilna."

3.

My mother did not even try to conceal her loathing for my father's family.

There wasn't an argument between them in which she didn't hasten to roast him over the hot coals of her tongue together with his ancestors, or to declare that she had never heard of another family in which so many men abandoned their wives to go gallivanting around the world—from which they returned like roosters only to breed, or to marry off, or circumcise some child. "Don't act so innocent," she would snap at him, asking why all husbands besides him managed to make themselves useful at home, even Judge Frumkin, who helped his wife with the shopping each Thursday, so that everyone in the Me'ah She'arim marketplace stood and gaped at him proudly carrying her baskets without the slightest loss of dignity. In our house alone everything was different.

Sometimes, when she lost her temper, which had happened especially when my father was engrossed in stalking the wild willow, my mother stormed down to the storeroom at the end of the yard and came back brandishing a large copper washbasin with a dent in its bottom—the same washbasin that had saved the life of Bobbe Hayka, Father's great-grandmother, when it fell on her head, warding off the avalanche of dirt and stones that showered down on her during the great Safed earthquake of 1837. Spitting in it, then throwing it on the floor, my mother would swear that if not for the damned basin her whole life would be different today.

"Why don't you say something?" she would scream at father.

"What do you want me to do, scream back at you?" he would answer. He made no effort to defend himself or his family, whose heroic feats were never mentioned for fear of my mother's sharp tongue. What little I knew about them I learned from Aunt Tsviya on the night she came to stay with us after my father's third disappearance on the tracks of his will-o'-the-wisp.

That day he failed to come home as usual from morning prayers at the synagogue. My mother tended the store by herself and acted as though her husband's absence were of no concern to her. In the slack between customers she hurriedly ate some farmer cheese, washed it down with a bottle of honey water, and said that she couldn't care less if he had been carried away by the plague. She wouldn't bother going to his funeral if he had been run over like a cat and was lying right now with his guts spilled over Jaffa Road! Yet when Mrs. Adler came in at noontime and inquired whether we had finished getting ready for the guest we were expecting that evening, explaining in response to my mother's startled look that on the way past the bus station that morning she had seen my father board a vehicle for Haifa, which could only mean that he had gone to welcome an important arrival in the port, my mother's indifference gave way to open wrath.

"Go on home!" she urged the curious customers before closing the store early and hurrying to the Me'ah She'arim post office, where she cabled an SOS to Aunt Tsviya in Hadera.

Aunt Tsviya, who was my father's older sister, was the only member of his family to wield any influence over his recalcitrant soul. Despite the years that had elapsed since she and her husband Tanhum Deitsh moved from Jerusalem to Hadera, she had continued to manage her family's affairs from the provinces. It was enough for her, she was fond of saying, to glance at the orange tree thrusting its leafy boughs at her kitchen window in order to know at once if anything was the matter in Jerusalem. And indeed, the truth was that when something went wrong there she generally turned up the same day, even before the telegram that went out to her had arrived.

Which was what happened this time, too.

4.

At that twilight hour of the evening when long ago, as we learned in our Mishnah class in school, the priests sat down in the Temple to partake of their tithes, the door to our apartment banged open and in the entrance stood my Aunt Tsviya. Father's sister did not exude sweet smells of frankincense as was her wont, nor did she hold in one hand the jar of citron jelly that she regularly brought on her visits.

She looked in bewilderment at my mother and me sitting among unmade beds and vases overflowing with willow and eucalyptus branches, and asked apprehensively if her premonition was right that something had happened to my father.

My mother shrugged derisively and said that the time had come for my aunt to stop worrying about her little brother and to show some concern for her sister-in-law and half-orphaned nephew, who were slowly wasting away from shame at my father's adolescent shenanigans. Only when Aunt Tsviya raised her eyebrows and demonstratively picked up her suitcase as though preparing to walk out did my mother, conscious of having gone too far, invite her to sit down and ask in amazement how the telegram sent that afternoon to Hadera had managed to reach her so soon.

"You sent me a dépèche?" marveled Tsviya. It had not come before her departure, which was rather prompted by two omens revealed to her that morning. Not only—as always in times of distress—had the leaves of the orange tree outside her kitchen window looked especially distraught, but when she had stopped to glance at my parents' wedding photograph that stood on the commode in the living room, she had seen large, round tears in my mother's eyes behind the bridal veil. The pretty young bride looked so sad, my aunt said, that she decided to leave a hot lunch for her Tanhum on the burner and to set out for Jerusalem at once.

"I'd forgotten that I was ever a pretty young bride," said my mother, biting her lips. Nevertheless, she went on, she did not believe in such auguries. The orange tree must have been stricken by the Mediterranean fruit fly, while the tears in the picture were no doubt drops of moisture trapped between it and the frame.

Aunt Tsviya sat down on the edge of the sofa where Mother had cleared a place for her amid wash taken down from the line, crossed an ankle over her thigh, rolled down an elastic stocking, baring a hairy leg (for which alone, Mother claimed, she deserved to be crowned Queen of Sheba—if, that is, one could rely on the rabbis' descriptions of King Solomon's feral visitor), rolled it up again, and remarked that perhaps in the world-to-come she would finally be granted a much-needed rest.

"Why don't you go visit the neighbors," my mother coaxed me, adding that Mrs. Ringel must certainly have gotten new stamps from

Australia. As I left I heard my aunt sigh that she no longer had the strength to go carrying her family's problems on her shoulders as she had been doing all her life.

Soon after his marriage to her, Tanhum Deitsh sought to tear his young wife away from her family's embrace and gladly accepted the offer of Reb Ben-Tsiyyon Yadler, the fiery preacher who served as the model for Rabbi Gronam Yekum-Purkan in Agnon's novel, *Yesteryear*, and to appoint him the rabbinical court of Jerusalem's chief inspector of agricultural tithes in the Jewish colonies of Samaria—an office that he abandoned, in my Uncle Tsodek's words, as soon as he discovered which side his bread was really buttered on. It was not long before he shaved off his beard and earlocks, cast away his gray-and-white-striped caftan, and went to work as a clerk for the health insurance fund of the Labor Party.

Aunt Tsviya opened a dry goods store in her house. Over the entrance to the front yard she hung a sign with a painted butterfly whose bright wings turned into cascading folds of colorful fabric, while inside she also gave lessons in pattern making and sewing. Uncle Tanhum was annoyed at his wife's initiative, which made a marketplace, he said, of his home. "How much money do two people need?" he grumbled on each of our annual visits on the day after the Feast of Pentecost. And in fact, since they were childless, Tanhum made more than enough to support them. Yet Aunt Tsviya did not wish to be at the mercy of her husband and his moods and refused to surrender her right to a private nest egg of her own.

Although half of Hadera, as she put it, was constantly in and out of her house, Aunt Tsviya complained bitterly about her loneliness. Each night she wet her bed with tears of longing for Jerusalem, to which her bags were packed to return the minute that Tanhum was pensioned off—until when, to quote her husband, she was a junior partner in the bus company, whose early morning Jerusalem express she boarded every two or three weeks. Once in her native city, she resumed management of her family's affairs, made peace between her brothers and sisters-in-law, paid calls on all her friends, and, if she still felt a weight on her heart, went to visit the graves of her loved ones.

Our home was always her last stop. She would appear toward evening with a jar of the citron jelly that I loved and a piece of leftover fabric for my mother, enough for a talented seamstress to make a blouse or even a skirt from, and entertain my father with stories of the new immigrants who descended on her store like locusts and snapped up pieces of satin and brocade that her steady customers would not even look at. Tsviya was not fond of these recent arrivals, whom she called "the noovos," and, cheered by the slices of canned pineapple that my mother broke out especially for her, she would tell us about the savages in the immigrant transit camps who smeared their hair with margarine as a substitute for brilliantine and went into town wearing over their exilic rags the shocking-pink, synthetic-silk undergarments given them by the immigration authorities.

When it was late, my mother would make my usual bed in the living room with fresh sheets for Aunt Tsviya. I slept with my father in the bedroom, while my mother sat in the armchair talking in the dark to my aunt until sleep seized them sometime before dawn.

5.

When I returned from my banishment to the neighbors, my mother informed me that tonight I would sleep in my own bed. Aunt Tsviya went to sleep in the bedroom in place of my father, who was no doubt bunking at this hour in some remote hamlet of the Galilee. I imagined my aunt's open eyes crisscrossing the ceiling, the blanket pulled up over her to hide her empty mouth whose false teeth lay in a glass of water beneath the bed, grinding away there like the jaws of a primeval whale. She waited until I turned out my light to resume talking, her voice different from its confident daytime tones.

Aunt Tsviya picked up the thread of the conversation where it had been interrupted by my return, that is, with my grandfather, her own and my father's father. The less he was home, she said, the less my grandmother got out of bed. On the hottest summer days my grandmother covered herself with a quilt and ran her hand back and forth over the white pillowcase, tracing a meandering path through an imagined wasteland of ice in a trek that often ended in tears. "My little girl," she sobbed, referring to her own hand, "has fallen into a snow pit." And she begged for ropes to be brought in order to save her.

“My mother peed in bed, too,” Aunt Tsviya said, pointing out that in those days my grandmother was not even as old as she and my mother were now. “She couldn’t have been more than forty, at the most forty-three,” she reckoned, bitterly recalling the fate that had condemned her, then in the flower of her youth, to sit home caring for a madwoman.

“And all because of a little blue slime,” mocked my mother. “Because of some smelly old seashells.”

“You mustn’t say that,” Aunt Tsviya chided. Her father, she said, was so learned a man that even such renowned contemporaries as Gershon Heinik Leiner, the Rabbi of Radzin, and Reb Yehiel Mikel Tokachinski sought his opinion of the lost biblical blue, on which he was considered the world’s greatest expert.

In her parents’ home, Aunt Tsviya related, had stood shelf upon shelf of glass jars, some transparent and others painted an amber color to keep out the sunlight. Here her father kept the aquatic snails that he brought back from his travels.

“Just like the willow and eucalyptus branches blooming in this little Garden of Eden of ours,” my mother snapped venemously. But Aunt Tsviya hushed her with the remark that the famous kabbalists and talmudists who were regular visitors in their house were overjoyed at what they saw there and proclaimed that on the Day of Redemption, when the Temple rose again, her father would be indispensable, since he alone knew how to make the ceremonial garments worn by the high priest.

One day, my aunt continued, talking on into the darkness, two elegant Frenchmen in smart suits turned up in her family’s threadbare home in the Orthodox quarter of Jerusalem. Nahum Aboushedeed, the French teacher from the Alliance School who accompanied them as their interpreter, introduced them as representatives of *La Fabrique de Gobelins de Paris*, the world’s most famous tapestry manufacturers. They had come especially from Europe, he said, because they had heard of her father’s discovery and wished to purchase the rights to it. The two Frenchmen stood nodding their heads in agreement. They were willing to pay any price for *l’indigo israélite*.

My grandfather nodded back and replied that, while he was indeed close to unmasking the secret of true biblical blue, its exact nature still eluded him. Yet in any case, he continued, his quest for it was for purely spiritual ends, so that his co-religionists might don prayer shawls and four-cornered fringes as prescribed by the Law of Moses—beyond which he was thinking of the future, of the time when his people's ancient glory would be restored and priests dressed in azure like the angels of heaven would once again offer sacrifices in the Temple of the Lord. It was for them that he had undertaken his perilous journeys to the ends of the earth, not for roués and high-society ladies who wished for finery as blue as the sky in which to soil themselves in the brothels and parlors of Paris.

Aboushedeed anxiously stammered out my grandfather's refusal in his Levantine French while the two Parisians stared in amazement at this stubborn descendant of Jews from Pressburg and at the invalid lying in bed by the window, talking to her hand as it plunged from the peaks of glacial pinnacles into bottomless crevasses of snow. Was it not possible, they suggested, that they had been sent to him by God, like the three angels to Abraham, in order to rescue him from his distress?

Her father, Aunt Tsviya said, answered the two Frenchmen with a smile and declared that, since it was clear from their words that they were familiar with Holy Writ, they would understand his saying that only fools sold their birthright for a mess of pottage.

"And he, of course, was nobody's fool," my mother sneered. Had not the rabbis warned against being too much of a saint? Who was to say that a consultation with the best French doctors could not have cured her mother-in-law? Surely if she hadn't died soon after that my grandfather would have abandoned her by rounding up the hundred rabbis needed to grant a bill of divorce in cases where one of the marriage partners is not of sound mind.

"That's enough, enough!" The bed creaked under Aunt Tsviya. "One mustn't speak ill of the dead."

For several more days, Aunt Tsviya went on, the representatives of the French factory kept calling on the obdurate man, casting longing eyes at his bottles teeming with marine life until at last they returned as they had come. Long afterward, she said, my grandfather still spoke angrily about the bothersome French visitors, though in his heart he was proud of their offer, which he took to be a vindication of his ways.

The next crucial turning point in my grandfather's scientific career took place entirely by accident when he went one day to Dr.

Mazya's clinic to ask the Jerusalem physician to come visit his sick wife. In the waiting room he met a Jew from the Galilee named Elyovitsh, who had found near Tel-Hai, in the far north of the country, a wild antidiarrhetic grass that he wanted the doctor to test. While conversing with my grandfather, whose fame had reached not only as far as Paris but to the Lower Galilee as well, the northerner remarked that once, noticing a wonderful blue tint in the waters of the Hula Swamp, he had found in it some snails that were secreting the color from special glands.

That very day my grandfather headed north, where he and Elyovitsh began looking for the snails. At one point they stumbled into quicksand in which, had it not been for some Bedouin who had come down to the water to pick reeds, they would have drowned. When my grandfather returned to Jerusalem, he had several new jars in his knapsack covered with cheesecloth and filled with greenish swamp water swimming with snails.

Energetically, he resumed his experiments. He boiled the new specimens in water, dyed strips of wool with the indigo-colored liquid when it cooled, and hung them up for display.

This breakthrough led to a fresh wave of visitors. Yet this time an unexpected dispute broke out within the rabbinical camp itself. The Lithuanian Talmudists invoked Maimonides, who held that the biblical mollusk was to be sought in saltwater, along the seacoast of the tribal lands of Zebulun, of which it said in Jacob's blessing, "Zebulun shall dwell on the shore of the sea and his border shall be at Sidon"—all of which categorically ruled out my grandfather's latest find. The kabbalists of the Bethel Synagogue, on the other hand, appealed to the authority of the holy Zohar, which stated that the true-blue shellfish dwelt in the sweet waters of the Sea of Galilee, by which lay hidden the staff of the Messiah, for there the Redemption would commence. As it was common knowledge that the Hula Swamp and the Sea of Galilee were really one body of water, the true biblical blue, they maintained, had been discovered at last, and all prayer shawls should be dyed with it at once to enhance their mystical power.

This argument, Aunt Tsviya told my mother, led her father to launch still another expedition along the Mediterranean coast. He worked his way up from Haifa to Sidon, and from there as far as Ladakia, digging in the sand all day long and bedding down at night among fishermen and old ruins. Once, as he was climbing the roller-coaster hills known as the Ladder of Tyre, he slipped and nearly fell into the sea. After three weeks on the road, he returned home empty-handed, muttering a passage from the tractate of Menahot that described how the biblical snail surfaced only once every seventy years. Evidently he had mistimed his trip.

He had mistimed his homecoming, too, for he arrived to find his sons unshaven and his daughters looking distraught. His wife, the bride of his youth, had died while he was gone.

"They have hearts of stone, all of them." My mother burst out crying. "There's no difference between the fathers and the sons." During my father's second disappearance two weeks ago, she added, she had nearly come to a similar end. She rose, turned out the light, and peeked into my room. I pretended to be asleep.

"The child has had a hard day," Aunt Tsviya said.

"The child has had a hard life," my mother rejoined, and continued talking to her sister-in-law in a whisper. Not until years later, when I was married myself, did I dare ask her what had happened the second time that my father ran off.

"You mean to tell me that you were awake that whole night that Tsviya and I stayed up talking?" she asked, a distant reproach creeping into her voice.

"Yes," I said.

"The evening after your father ran off again," my mother said, "I had a miscarriage."

6.

The end of the story of true biblical blue was told to me by my father in the middle of the night, on our way by foot to Mount Zion to bless the rising sun.

Once every twenty-eight years, according to the ancient astronomers, on a Wednesday morning in the month of Nisan, the sun completes its great cycle and returns to the exact spot in the heavens where it was first called into being on the fourth day of creation. Father had waited with growing excitement for the day to arrive. He had already, he told anybody willing to listen, seen the grand solstice twice in his life, once in his father's arms from the roof of the Hurva Synagogue in the Old City of Jerusalem at the age of three, and once standing with his friends on Mount Scopus, among the unfinished buildings of the new Hebrew University. Now, for the third time, he was about to see the sun reborn over the Judean wilderness.

"The fourth time," he murmured, "I'll be up there with it myself."

Father stayed up all night on Tuesday the fourteenth of Nisan, keeping himself awake with cigarettes and black coffee until it was time to set out. At two o'clock on Wednesday morning he turned on the lights, stroked my face gently, and said we would miss the sunrise if we didn't get a move on.

The greenish light of the street lamps, filtered through the drooping pine boughs, cast clear, needle-shaped shadows that flitted over the stone walls of the houses to the rhythm of the breeze. My father held my hand tightly and told me never to forget this night all my life. Some other night, he was sure, when I would be pacing up and down in an army greatcoat, a rifle on my shoulder and my eyes longing to shut, or aimlessly roving through desolate streets, driven by the worry that was every man's lot, the memory of it would return.

"By then I'll be gone," he said and fell silent.

As we passed the last house a cold wind whipped our faces. My father draped his jacket, which reached down to my ankles, around me, and said with a laugh that I needn't feel sorry for him, since the next time I saw the solar birthday, it would be I who gave my jacket to my son.

I had never felt so close to him before. He was in one of his moods that I remembered from the days before the Rationing Bureau raid. He joked like a boy, played hopscotch with the paving stones, and told me story after story.

When we crossed the bridge over the Valley of Ben-Hinnom and passed the dry Turkish fountain there, a chorus of barks arose from the ownerless dogs chained to their kennels in the pound below and I clutched at him in my fright.

"When is it time to say the morning prayer?" he asked, softly chanting the words from the Mishnah while his hand caressed my goose-fleshed skin. "When there is light enough to tell blue from white. Rabbi Akiva says, to tell a donkey from a wild ass. Rabbi Meir says, to tell a wolf from a dog."

Muffled by a milky mist that had settled over the bottom of the valley, the screams of the children who were burned alive there in the days of the Bible and offered up to the Molech licked like flames at my thoughts. Above us, at the southwest corner of the Old City wall, a Jordanian legionnaire stretched in his sentry box whose sandbags grew higher by the day, wondering at the lunatic Jews who had risen so early.

As we ascended the dirt path to Mount Zion, my father told me the rest of the story of true blue.

Having waited the required year after my grandmother's death, he related, my grandfather proceeded to fall into the clutches of a Jewess from Transylvania, the widow of a follower of the Satmer Rebbe, who poisoned her new husband's life with her insatiable lust for gold jewelry and satin tablecloths. One day, two years after their wedding, he was run over by a drunken English driver while crossing Princess Mary Street in a melancholy fit. As soon as the seven days of mourning were over, the woman threw out his snail collection, his samples of dyed wool, his manuscripts and notebooks, and his voluminous correspondence with rabbis and dye experts all over the world, hung on the bare wall a tapestry she had made of a sailboat casting anchor on a sandy shore strewn with seashells, and slammed the door in the face of the dead man's children, who had grown up inside.

We were on top of Mount Zion now, ascending to the roof of the Church of the Dormition by a narrow spiral staircase whose slippery stone walls, rubbed smooth by human hands, we grasped at in pitch darkness. Then, abruptly, the moldy warmth of the ancient Arab building was behind us and the sharp Jerusalem wind struck us again. A grayish, primeval light, like that which hovered over the face of the water on the first day of creation, outlined the men in prayer shawls who stood pressed together by the guardrail of the observation tower overlooking the Temple Mount, their eyes fixed on the eastern horizon.

Beneath us, right under our feet, in the eerily empty room of the Coenaculum, mythical pelicans carved on stone columns pecked away at their own breastplates, feeding their young with their blood as did the man from Nazareth who broke the bread and passed the cup to his disciples at the Last Supper, while in a catacomb still further down, underneath a stone sepulchre draped with a black curtain and watched by a drowsy guard whose job it was to keep an eye on the heavy silver crowns of the Torah scrolls, the unawakened Messiah, David king of Israel, slumbered on in his burial cave.

The skyline slowly crimsoned, darkening the hills that rimmed it as black paper grows blacker against red. My father stood silently gazing at the Mount of Olives and at its tombs desecrated by the Jordanians, still hidden by the shadows of the night, in which the eternal rest of his first wife and my brother Re'uven had been undisturbed. A teardrop glinted in his eye. And then the sun came up.

It was my first sunrise.

7.

On our way home again, as we walked through the streets of the city that was rising to greet a new day, my father heaved a heartfelt sigh and said that I still had to learn that time was a great dragon whose tail lay coiled in the infinite bogs of the past while its eyes ranged into the future as far as the End of Days. He glanced at me to see what impression this had made and added that today I had witnessed one more skirmish in man's eternal war with the Dragon of Time—a war whose only weapons were calendars and clocks, and whose only victories were the desperate scratches made in the great beast's hide and called by us days, months, and years.

"But I want you to know that my grandfather stalked that dragon in the mountains," my father said, gesturing with his right hand toward the distance. Not only, he declared, had his father's father not been afraid of Time, he had been convinced that, if only he managed to snare it in that twinkling of an eye between the last glimmer of night and the first rays of day, he could actually bend it to his will.

Every night, when the rest of the world was asleep, my father's grandfather had climbed the Mount of Olives together with his good friend Reb Hiyya Dovid Shpitzer, the author of the solar almanac, *Sefer ha-Nivreshet.* There, next to the Russian Church of the Ascension, in whose high tower had recently been installed the great bell Russian pilgrims had dragged by rope all the way from Jaffa port, they assumed a position facing east and recorded the exact second when the first sliver of sun appeared above the Mountains of Moab. Simultaneously, others did the same from the rooftop of the

Hurva Synagogue in the Old City, thus enabling them to calculate how long the sunrise in the city below was delayed by the barrier of the Mount of Olives.

Day in and day out, summer and winter, they undertook the hilly ascent, until at last they prepared a table for every day of the year, so that the pious Jews of Jerusalem could time their prayers with the sunrise, which was the holiest moment of the day. It was the hope of his grandfather's circle, my father told me, that if enough Jews could be found to pray for the Redemption at the fleeting instant of grace between light and darkness each morning, Time's chains might be broken at last. Yet the bonds of sleep, that strongest of all human passions, condemned to failure this daring attempt to subdue man's cruelest enemy.

"Now you know why I grieved so much over the burned sundial in Mahaneh Yehudah," my father concluded, finishing his tale of those far-off days with a squeeze of my hand.

As we passed the Terra Sancta building, where the Hebrew University was temporarily quartered after its exile from Mount Scopus, which remained an inaccessible enclave within Jordan after the 1948 war, Father looked up at its high windows and remarked how certain he felt that a boy with a lineage like mine would grow up to be a great scientist. Perhaps I might even be the man to find the cure for polio, the dread disease that had claimed so many thousands of children.

He saw the quick smirk on my lips and asked why, if Haim'ke Weizmann, the son of a poor woodcutter from Mottele, could save the mighty British Empire from defeat in World War I by discovering a method of manufacturing acetone for TNT from corn cobs and orange peels, I, the fourth-generation descendant of intrepid adventurers whose powers of imagination far outstripped quotidian reality, could not heal an ailing humanity, especially since the modern laboratories of the Hebrew University would be at my disposal.

"You'll win the Nobel Prize yet," he predicted with a distant look in his eyes. And when that happened, he added, and the Swedish king stood before me to hang the gold meal on my neck, I must not forget to think of my father, that man of indomitable willow-power mocked by heartless cynics in his day; of my true-blue grandfather; and of—first progenitor of us all—my great-grandfather, who rose in the night to wrestle until dawn with the Dragon of Time as Jacob wrestled with the angel.

"Had he been born in nineteenth-century London instead of Jerusalem," my father insisted, "my grandfather could have become chief astronomer of the Royal Observatory in Greenwich." Why, take the case of Dr. Pesach Hevroni, who played on my great-grandfather's knees as a child and received his first lessons from him! What better proof could there be of the heights attainable by a Jerusalem boy who dared venture into the world?

Father spoke admiringly of this mathematical prodigy, whose discoveries had met with worldwide recognition from Holland to Japan. Even Professor Einstein, during his visit to Palestine, had taken time out to converse with him. "For an hour and ten minutes," my father said pedantically, "Einstein sat talking in the B'nai B'rith Library with this modest young teacher from the Pedagogical Institute—and when they parted he announced that Hevroni was the only man in the world to have completely understood him."

After the world war, my father went on, Hevroni went to Vienna, where, for the next four years, the scientific world marveled at the new star risen from the East. Famous professors expected wonders of him, attractive women sought out his company—yet he shut himself up in his room with his books and mourned his beloved Stella, the Dutch beauty who had been head nurse of Sha'arei Hesed Hospital until she died in an epidemic of typhoid fever at the start of the war.

"Did Luba tell you that?" I asked.

"That's none of your business!" my father snapped at me, and asked whether Leder had told me about meeting his first wife in Vienna.

I nodded, saddened by the lost intimacy between us that had melted away like the morning mist. My father communed with his thoughts.

8.

We sat down on a bench facing the entrance to Mamilla Park and my father declared that, after a night without sleep, the soles of his feet felt like pincushions. He poured us both tea from the thermos bottle in his prayer-shawl bag and looked with interest at the lawn in front of us, where a bold raven was tormenting a little puppy-dog by diving at it over and over and thrashing it with its wings. In the distance, between the pine boughs, rose the pale facade of the

Schmidt School, and above it, the central post office and the Generali Building with its winged lion carved in stone on the roof. Down below, Mamilla Pool, the stage for many a meeting of mine with Leder, lay quietly surrounded by its Moslem graves.

"What do you see in him?" my father asked irritably.

"In who?" I answered innocently.

"In who? In Leder! What are you pretending for?" He was red with anger.

For years my parents had been at a loss to explain the spell cast over me by the little alms collector. Over and over they tested me to see if his germs were still in me.

I did the best I could to explain the principles of Lynkeanism to my father, who pooh-poohed them and asked what possible good to the human race could come from such quackery.

"A guaranteed minimum diet for all," I stammered, choking with humiliation.

My father burst out laughing and said that if a minimum diet was the problem, it could be supplied by our friend the pharmacist, Mr. Mordechovitz, in the form of a small bar of Ex-Lax.

"*Ex-Lax iz a gute zach, m'est a bisl, m'kakt a sach*," I heard him say in Yiddish through my tears, like a peddler crying his wares.

"You don't know what Ex-Lax is?" my father persisted. "It's a good thing." And he translated for me:

"A bar of Ex-Lax hits the spot, eat a little, crap a lot."

Chapter Eight

1.

After Leder's stinging reversal in the Viennese Circle, the Nutrition Army's forward command post was moved from the Café Vienna to Greenberg's Bookbindery, which stood opposite the Alliance School at the top of Jaffa Road. There it stayed for the next two years, until the day of the great demonstration against the German reparations agreement, when the army was forced to disband.

"Our movement is over the last of its childhood illnesses," Leder promised me as soon as the dust from his outburst at the Ringels' imperial banquet had settled. Instead of spreading ourselves thinly in a vain attempt to reach all sectors of the public, among them the cavalier subjects of Franz Josef, we must act like a mailed fist centered around a serious, ideologically motivated cadre that would prepare the platform of the future Lynkean state and act as its cabinet when the time came.

Leder surveyed me sternly while dodging a pothole in the street and declared that such a cadre already existed, waiting for us to make use of it. Unless my memory was as weak as a cat's, I surely remembered his mentioning, during his brief nighttime visit to my home, the organic food club gathered around Mr. Greenberg. He hesitated for a moment, then nonchalantly inquired whether my mother had started buying yet at Greenberg's store.

Thereafter I often went with him to the vegetarian discussion club that met daily at the Greenbergs' during the early hours of the afternoon. At that time of my life my father was busy raising the dead with Riklin, my mother was totally involved with the abandoned Mrs. Barzel and her son, and I was free to do as I pleased.

Leder and I would cross the empty lot on which the Hen movie theater was later built, enter a yard fenced round with rough stone, tiptoe down a path of smooth flagstone on either side of which lay

Mrs. Greenberg's carefully tended vegetable garden, and furtively bypass the sleepy bindery in which a young worker in a Bukharian skullcap phlegmatically passed a brush dipped in glue over bindings while Mrs. Greenberg sat behind him sewing pamphlets with a large, curved needle. Behind them, in the murky depths of the shop, loomed the silhouette of the paper-cutting machine, its round, heavy weight hanging threateningly in midair like a guillotine.

The discussion club met in a room at the rear of the bindery, near the Greenbergs' living quarters, which served during the morning hours as a health food store. A sourish smell of wheat germ mixed with the sweetness of brown sugar filled the tidy room, whose windows were screened against flies. On wooden footrests along the walls lay opened sacks of unpolished rice, bulghur, buckwheat, and barley grits, above which on blue shelves stood jars of dried apricots, figs, and apple rings.

Mr. Greenberg, the two volumes of *The Organic Food Book* on his right and a cup of shelled sunflower seeds on his left, would already be presiding when we arrived, dispensing wisdom to the several disciples seated around him. He welcomed my début with a handful of crumbling molasses scooped with his fingers from the sack of brown sugar, topped it with two cracked walnuts, and declared that in my honor the club would adjourn its theoretical discussion of the works of Voltaire and Rousseau in order to listen once more to a familiar but still powerful passage by the immortal Lev Nikolayevitch Tolstoy.

Colorful bookmarks lay, as though in a hymnal, among the pages of *The Organic Food Book*, so that it did not take Greenberg long to have us all gagging on the harsh smell of hot blood, the bleating of oxen, the slippery, shiny brown floors of the abbatoir, the raised blades of the axes, the jets of blood caught in basins by the butcher boys. While the club members plunged eagerly into the saintly novelist's description of his visit to a slaughterhouse, I kept my eyes fastened on the cover of the book, on which were amateurishly drawn—like the pictures of famous rabbis hung by pious Jews in their sukkahs on the Feast of Booths—the portraits of ten great vegetarians from Pythagoras and Buddha to Leonardo and Lord Byron. On the back cover was printed the publisher's colophon, the firm's name cloven in two by an apple.

As soon as Mr. Greenberg finished reading I was raked by the zealous eyes of Noah Lev-Tamim, whose rope sandals, wild, flowing beard, and linen sash around his waist made him look like Tolstoy's twin brother. If one felt sick to one's stomach from the great author's account, Lev-Tamim declared, the chances were that one would never touch meat again. In fact, he went on, there was much to be said for the view that if each of us personally had to slaughter the flesh he consumed, most human beings would cease their carnivorous ways.

Leder, who appeared to be less opinionated and sure of himself in the presence of the club members than in our own tête-à-têtes, kept looking about him. When Lev-Tamim paused for breath, the future ruler of Lynkeania sought to get a word in edgewise by relating how, that very morning, on his way down Ge'ulah Street, he had witnessed a sight like that seen by Tolstoy in Yasnaya-Polyana. From a large red van parked at the entrance to Ende's butcher shop, workers in rubber aprons smeared with blood were delivering sides of beef on their shoulders.

"Why mince words?" Lev-Tamim interrupted him. "Let's call a spade a spade. They were delivering corpses, carrion, dead bodies . . ."

Leder waited for the fiery Tolstoyan to pause to collect himself and affirmed that he was absolutely right, since the only choice facing us was vegetablism or cannibalism. The club members nodded, amazed that none of them had ever thought of putting it so cleverly, while Leder, plainly encouraged, added that witnessing the ghastly scene in Ge'ulah Street that morning, with the glassy upside-down eyes of the cows staring at him accusingly from the chopped-off heads tossed into the bloodstained hands of the delivery men, made him realize more than ever, to borrow a phrase from Stendhal, that modern man lived between *le rouge et le noir*; that is, between the meat van and the hearse.

"What about the white?" demanded Lev-Tamim, inquiring who of us present could count the multitude of carnivorous sufferers waiting in ambulances, hospitals, and sanatoriums to be released by death from their pain.

2.

More than once these club meetings turned into a battleground between two rival factions, the moderates and the militants. The difference between them, Leder once explained to me in a moment of jest, was that the moderates loved themselves, while the militants loved cows even more, so that while the former wore leather shoes, the latter went shod in canvas or rubber.

One of the harshest of these clashes took place one afternoon after Greenberg had finished reading Gibbon's gruesome description of the nomadic Tatars in his *Decline and Fall of the Roman Empire.* Among these shepherd tribes so gullibly depicted by the poets as a peaceful, pastoral folk, Greenberg said, all the barbarism concealed by the genteel manners of Europe emerged in its naked brutality, for a single hand fed the lamb, dispatched it, and tore apart at the feast its raw, bloody limbs still warm with life.

Lev-Tamim rapped on the table with his rough wooden staff and asked why Greenberg, who was an Orthodox Jew, had gone so far afield as the Tatars. "Wasn't your Temple a slaughterhouse, too?" demanded the thick-bearded militant. "As if throwing a poor innocent goat off some cliff outside Jerusalem for a sin-offering on the Day of Atonement were any less barbaric!"

Greenberg sought softly to sidestep the attack, yet Lev-Tamim persisted and asked what would happen if biblical prophecy came true and a third temple arose on the ruins of the former two. Would the bookbinder, a Levite by descent, stand chanting hymns of praise while young priests flashed their cutlasses at frightened flocks of cattle and sheep?

"The House of the Lord that shall stand firm upon the mountain will be a sanctuary for the spirit," Greenberg replied, rising to take a Bible from a drawer and leaf excitedly through it. Lev-Tamim, however, told him to put the book away, since everyone knew that no priest would agree to forego his fatty morsels of breast and thigh in exchange for lettuce leaves and kohlrabi.

"But why argue about the distant past or future?" he went on in a more amiable voice. "Let's stick to the present." No sooner had Greenberg sat down, though, than the bearded Tolstoyan began baiting him again. How could a religious Jew, Lev-Tamim asked, permit himself every day to put on phylacteries that were made from the hides of slaughtered beasts? "For my part you can use plastic," he chortled while a cloud of sadness descended on the bookbinder's face.

When we came again the next day, we found Greenberg at work in his garden, bent over rows of carrots he was weeding.

The Greenbergs grew all their own vegetables in wooden barrels, blue-and-white enamel basins, and oil cans sawed in half. Tomato plants, peppers, and eggplants were tied to supports by old shoelaces and discarded bits of twine, while the soil around them, which was manured with grayish-white bird droppings, had been hoed as though with a kitchen fork. Between the vegetable garden and the stone fence stood a row of fruit trees whose apples, peaches, and lemons were each wrapped in old newspaper to keep off the birds and avoid the use of poisonous spray. Near the house grew parsley and dill, above which rose sunflower and corn stalks. Over the seedbeds, to which Greenberg had now tranferred his labors, metal netting was stretched against pests.

When presently the bookbinder took us on a guided tour of his garden, we were astounded by his knowledge of the fine points of horticulture. Had he acquired it by reading books, Leder wanted to know, or had it come from a British correspondence course?

Greenberg laughed and replied that some things could not be learned in old age, certainly not from books. He paused, then informed us that he had spent his youth in a village near the Carmel.

"Now do you understand?" he asked, a mischievous glint in his eyes.

Leder, who had been regarding a piece of newspaper in which a lemon was wrapped, nodded and replied that our host must have grown up in Zichron Ya'akov.

"Wrong," Greenberg said.

"Perhaps Bat-Shlomo then," Leder tried again.

"You'll never guess," Greenberg said. "I'm from Argentina." He marveled that his heavy Spanish accent had not given him away.

"What does the Carmel have to do with Ar*hen*tina?" Leder asked in a hurt tone, mimicking the bookbinder's breathy "h."

Greenberg retied a pepper plant that had fallen against the side of a basin and remarked that several of Baron de Hirsch's Jewish colonies in Entre-Rios had borne Hebrew names like Kiryat-Arba, Rosh-Pinna, and Carmel.

From the vegetarian clubhouse came a muffled but steady thumping, like the sound made by the drummer who marched before the Sephardic chief rabbi of Jerusalem in official processions. Leder, who had had enough of walking up and down the rows of vegetables, declared that he would go to have a word with Lev-Tamim, who was dying of boredom among the sacks of sorghum and bulghur and had begun tapping out a distress call with his walking stick.

Greenberg waited for Leder to vanish among the peach trees before remarking that I, who attended a religious school, would surely understand that after yesterday's sacrilege, he could no longer have anything to do with Lev-Tamim, despite their common vegetarian views.

"In his heart the man is a butcher," Greenberg declared, plucking a little lady bug from a carrot leaf and releasing it on the other side of the fence. "But since intellectually he's not prepared to slit animals' throats, he takes it out on human beings."

He patted me on the head, adjusted the blue school skullcap that had slipped over my ear, and said that most people formed their opinions not from intellectual conviction but from exposure to humiliation or violence. Had the *administrador* of the Baron de Hirsch not forced him to eat the flesh of a pig slaughtered in front of the baron's own offices, he himself would never have given up meat.

"Violence is always counterproductive," Greenberg said, scanning the laden boughs of the fruit trees.

Over his shoulder I spied a short, elderly man making his way almost noiselessly through the empty lot between Greenberg's yard and Jaffa Road. The closer he came, the clearer grew the features of his ascetic, white-goateed face with its deep-socketed, visionary eyes.

"*Saluton, sinjoro Greenberg!*" he greeted the bookbinder when he reached the front gate.

Greenberg spun around and quickly returned the greeting. "*Saluton, sinjoro Havkin, kiel vi fartas?*"

He fondly laid a mud-caked hand on his visitor's shoulder and informed me that it was our pleasure today to play host to a great pioneer of Jewish vegetarianism, the distinguished Mr. Havkin, who for years had been putting utopian theory into practice on the farm he had built with his own two hands in the hills outside Jerusalem.

"*Kiu estas, tiu bela knabo?*" Mr. Havkin asked, pinching my cheek.

"I don't know Spanish," I replied.

"It's not Spanish, it's Esperanto," said the old man, asking whether I had learned in school about Dr. Ludwig Zamenhoff and the international tongue he had invented. After inquiring again of

Greenberg, this time in Hebrew, who the handsome young boy was, he assured me that it would be well worth my while to acquire a language that was certain to be the world's most widely spoken before long. And it would be best for me to do so immediately, while I was still young and quick to absorb.

For once the club discussion, which, needless to say, concerned Esperanto, was conducted in an atmosphere of calm.

Greenberg ceded his place at the head of the table to Mr. Havkin, while he himself sat on Havkin's right, ready to do the old man's bidding. Lev-Tamim, unnaturally preoccupied, whittled flowers on his walking stick, while Leder busily jotted down notes.

Havkin began by remarking that, since the day of its groundbreaking, the unfinished Tower of Babel had loomed at humanity's back and cast its menacing shadow. "Once and for all," he said, "we must overcome this ancient catastrophe by taking the line of 'One humanity, one language'—not in order to rebel against the gods, but on the contrary, to fructify the earth."

In great detail the venerable old man listed the advantages of the language of the future. Though it was easy to learn, its writing being phonetic and its grammar so simple that it could be mastered in a matter of hours, it was rich enough to express all human thoughts, and, last but not least, it was the only neutral tongue in the world, whose rival power blocs were engaged in a cold war that might flare up at any moment.

Havkin ended his address by quoting forty members of the French Academy, who concluded in a report published as far back as 1924 that Esperanto was a model of logical clarity. Once the vegetarian movement adopted it as its official language, he hoped, the day would be near when the rest of the human race would follow in its footsteps.

3.

The meeting with Havkin marked a turning point in the annals of the Lynkean movement.

When we left the vegetarian discussion club, Leder was back in fighting spirits. Though our movement, he confessed, had fallen on hard times, indeed had sunk into lethargy, we were about to make a fresh start.

"Esperanto opens undreamed-of horizons for us," he nearly shouted, affirming that we must translate into it at once *The Necessity for General Nutrition.*

"We'll break through the narrow barriers of national boundaries," he went on, "and comb the civilized world for those chosen few who would rather make do with a kerosene burner and an ice chest than have the luxury of a gas stove and a frigidaire."

As usual, he became engrossed at once in the fine points of his plan; the first thing in the morning, he announced, he was going to Ludwig Maier's bookstore to buy some Esperanto texts. Within a few weeks he would be ready to begin translating Popper-Lynkeus' great work into the international language of the future.

That Saturday afternoon we set out on foot for Havkin's farm in Giv'at Sha'ul.

Leder lost no time on the way and occupied himself with memorizing Esperanto sentences from a primer on whose cover was a white, six-sided star of David with a green, five-sided star inside it.

" *Mi lernas Esperanton, vi lernas Esperanton, li lernas Esperanton,*" he recited as we left the city behind. " *Esperanto, Esperanto, Esperanto,*" echoed the hills rising above us. On the terrace of the mental hospital overlooking the road in which he was soon to be locked up himself, the inmates ceased their antics for a moment, grasped the bars like monkeys, and stared at the odd pedestrian shouting meaningless phrases at the brutal sun while a hypnotized child strode beside him.

Havkin was sitting in the shade of a grape vine on his front porch, his face in an open book. So absorbed was he in his reading that he failed to notice the two strangers disturbing the Sabbath peace of the sleepy dirt path leading up to his house. Leder scrutinized the jacket of the book, his lips slowly spelling out its title. Our vegetarian acquaintance, he whispered to me, was presently in the bedroom of an incurably ill Ivan Ilyitch, helping the dying man's faithful servant to prop up his swollen feet against the pain.

"*Bonan Sabaton!*" called Leder, leaning against the fence. "But it still isn't *your* death, *sinjoro* Havkin," he added, quoting Tolstoy's unforgettable line.

"*What, what?*" cried out Havkin, the book slipping from his shaking hands, amazed to find the printed words take flight from the page and double back to him from the street.

Leder laughed naughtily and remarked that sorrow was forbidden on the Sabbath—besides which, though Tolstoy's novella was a fine story, why should a man of Havkin's age want to read a book that only undermined the will to live, especially as he must have other volumes in his library more edifying than this depressing work?

Havkin's hands were still shaking when he pointed, as we walked with him among his terraced plots, to the budding branches of the apricot trees and promised us that we could soon return to enjoy their fruit. Rolling back a white millstone from the cistern that he had hewn out of the rock with his own hands, he let us peer into its depths. Below, our reflected faces kept changing with the ripples of the water.

Leder did not broach the reason for our visit until we were standing in a cave dug by Havkin in which his neighbors had found shelter during the 1948 war. Proudly our host ran a hand over the damp walls and boasted of his natural inventiveness, which had showed him a way to carve out this space with the aid of a karstic fault in the rock. The quarried stones themselves, he went on, had been piled by him for future use, three groups according to size, as opposed to the ordinary, lazy way of leaving them all in a heap. Leder heard the old man out with uncharacteristic patience, then casually inquired whether he had ever heard of Popper-Lynkeus' inventions in the field of aeronautics. With a smile Havkin answered that not only was he familiar with the biography of that unhappy and disappointment-fraught Jewish-Viennese genius, he was also well versed in his social and economic views. Indeed, there had been a time when *The Necessity for General Nutrition* had never left his side.

"Don't you think it should be translated into Esperanto?" queried Leder, who had never dreamed of such luck.

"It's a book of the highest importance," Havkin agreed, "a must for any Esperanto library." Unfortunately, however, the Esperantists had been unable to find the right man for the job.

"*Ecce homo!*" Leder cried, pointing to himself with childish glee. Waving the green primer, he declared that he was now engaged in studying Esperanto from morning till night and was sure that he could finish a sample chapter from Popper-Lynkeus' great work in several weeks' time.

Havkin threw his arms around his guest in a comradely embrace. Did Leder's decision, he wondered, have anything to do with his own appearance at Greenberg's bookbindery earlier that week?

Afterward, while we sat on the concrete patio in front of Havkin's house looking at the mountain ridges falling away in waves to the coastal plain and cracking almonds from the old man's trees, Leder explained his proposal for a united front of Esperantists, vegetarians, and Lynkeans. The forces of good, he declared, should band together in the struggle for their goals, which were complementary rather than opposed.

"In the Lynkean state," Leder announced, "Esperanto will be the official language of the government, as well as of all schools and universities. The eating of meat and fish will be illegal. All slaughterhouses and butcher shops will be expropriated for the public good, and the slaughterers, butchers, and fishermen will be sent to special schools to be re-educated. Eggs and milk products will be sold only by special permit and will have to be eaten in private."

The old man listened intently, making a sour face when Leder enthusiastically proclaimed that the portraits of Josef Popper-Lynkeus and Esperanto's inventor Dr. Ludwig Zamenhoff, the two official state philosophers, would be hung in all public places.

"That reminds me too much of the pictures of Marx and Engels in the streets of Moscow," Havkin said. In any case, he remarked, he was too old by now for such things. Leder, he added after a moment's thought, could do worse than listen to someone like himself who had seen so many lofty ideals besmirched through their contact with politics. "Don't forget the story of Icarus, my young man. If they come too close to the glowing sun of political passion, both Lynkeanism and Esperantism will smash themselves to bits on the hard ground of reality."

"Politics have nothing to do with it," objected Leder, trying to point out Havkin's error. But our elderly host only replied that he did not wish to spoil his Sabbath rest by losing his temper unnecessarily. If we were not in any hurry, he went on, he would be happy to welcome us inside his house and show us the one pastime of his otherwise Spartan existence.

The walls of the little work room in which Havkin produced the blocks and printing plates that supported him were as ornate as a Persian rug. Arabesques of hearts, leaves, and geometrical shapes wove in and out on them, repeating themselves in infinite patterns like some wondrous vine in the unreachable forests of dreamland.

"You're looking at ornamography," Havkin told us. Since his graduation in 1900 from the Munich School of Industrial Art, he explained, he had devoted every spare hour to creating this original art style, whose name was his own invention, too.

"With the help of a special table that I have prepared," said our host, handing us a sweet-potato-colored brochure, "it is possible to produce, from squares and triangles alone, an infinite number of symmetrically decorative forms."

Leder restlessly let it be known that we were pressed for time and could not remain any longer. Yet Havkin, paying no attention to the growing impatience of his uninvited guest, launched into a story of how even the great Hermann Struck had praised his discovery, and turned to ask me how I liked his designs.

"You should take it up yourself," he said, and announced that he had a small surprise for me to take home—a game of cubes called "Sheep and Wolves," created by him as an ornamographical exercise.

4.

Despite the disappointing results of our visit to Havkin, Leder did not give up his plan.

"The three-ply cord is not easily undone," he quoted Ecclesiastes as we left Havkin's house, the setting sun casting long shadows before us. "We're still young and strong. We'd do best to let Havkin dawdle away the rest of his life and not bother him with questions of the future."

His plan was listened to attentively when presented to a plenary session of the vegetarian discussion club the next day. The first reaction was Mr. Greenberg's, who remarked that it was no more practical than the recommendation made by a fellow vegetarian from Tel Aviv, in a lecture given several months ago, to swallow a spoonful of dirt three times a day in order to add missing trace materials to their vegetarian diet. To this Leder replied that it was precisely the practicality of his program, which had already been double-checked, that would give their amiable discussion group, whose meetings among sacks of sorghum and bulghur resembled an amateur conspiracy, the political dimension it lacked.

"So you want to start a new party and sit in parliament at our expense?" snorted Pesach Yabrov, the ladies' clothes wholesaler from Hasolel Street who occasionally dropped in on Greenberg's club.

"Believe me," Leder snapped back, "I have better things to do than waste my time with a lot of M.P.s." His purpose, he explained, was not to join the establishment, but to lay the foundations for a new, more just, and perfect order.

Lev-Tamim, who as a rule looked down on the club members and their ideas, sat leaning silently on his walking stick, deep in thought. When, during the next few days, the group continued to debate Leder's proposal for a three-way front, he became its principal supporter. The two men dickered back and forth, comparing Popper-Lynkeus' platform with various other social creeds, such as the Beveridge Plan and the Atlantic Charter, until at last the crucial question came to the fore: Was the European welfare state a preliminary realization of the Lynkean vision, or was it rather a false pretender to the title whose actual policies were the opposite of the great utopian's?

These discussions left me bored and fatigued, and I did my best to slip away from them into the bindery, where I played with the colorful paper snakes that lay in drifts beneath the work tables and watched Mrs. Greenberg and her Bukharian man Friday at their jobs. They labored quietly, without a sound, only the swish of the guillotine and the back-and-forth movements of the glue brush breaking the silence.

On our way home Leder remarked that one day this place, which had formerly been the home of the Austrian vice-consul, Pascal the Armenian, and now looked so run-down, would be the official state museum of Lynkeania. Pilgrims and schoolchildren would flock to it from all over the world, just as they did to the table in the British Museum where Karl Marx had sat.

"We are doing vital work here," he said as we crossed Strauss

Street, "even if it may seem tedious and unnecessary to you. The deeper you dig the foundation," he went on, pointing at a temporary wooden fence hiding the large, menacing pit in which the new offices of the national trade union were about to go up, "the higher the building that can stand on it."

On the face of things, his relations with Lev-Tamim were good. Both men agreed that in preparing a new edition of *The Necessity for General Nutrition*, Popper-Lynkeus' views should be brought into line with contemporary social and economic conditions, and both busied themselves with its double translation into Hebrew and Esperanto, which would be published simultaneously by Greenberg's vegetarian press.

Yet beneath the surface, Leder was awash in ugly waves of anger at his partner—an anger he was careful to conceal. "I'll never let him be field marshal," he grumbled to me once, after a long, secretive session with the Tolstoyan zealot in Greenberg's shop.

"Who?" I asked.

Leder caught himself and replied that, unity being of the essence, he was not at liberty to talk.

5.

Nevertheless, he now began to consider turning to some world-famous figure and offering the Nutrition Army's high command to him. One day he plucked up the courage to lay this new idea before the members of the discussion club.

An injured twitch passed over Lev-Tamim's lips, then slipped away into his beard, leaving him looking as thoughtful as before.

The names of Professor Einstein, Martin Buber, and Bertrand Russell were suggested by the club members as those of possible candidates for the position. Leder, however, objected at once that physicists, mathematicians, and philosophers, no matter how decent and outstanding, were not men fit to run a state.

"We need someone like Ghandi!" he muttered half to himself before explaining out loud that only a figure like the Mahatma, who had set a personal example by living a life of utmost simplicity, trudging on foot from village to village, and spinning at the wheel half an hour each day to symbolize the freedom of self-sufficiency, deserved to occupy such an august post.

It was then that Yabrov suggested Dr. Albert Schweitzer.

"The best doctor is a dead doctor!" Fradkin burst out uncontrollably, much to everyone's surprise. The most taciturn of the club members, who never before had taken part in a single discussion, he now informed his fellow vegetarians that for years he had worked as an orderly in the English Hospital. He knew from personal experience that every physician, even if he were an angel of mercy, was responsible for a private little graveyard of his own.

Greenberg concurred with this and observed that, in his own opinion, the beatific halo hovering over the rumpled silver locks of Dr. Schweitzer was an optical illusion, a clever job of promotion perpetrated on the public by Scandinavian corporations. Powerful economic interests, he was convinced, were behind the myth of this latter-day St. Julien l'Hospitalier, which rested purely on the profit motive. In his name, though perhaps without his knowledge, they had collected millions of dollars all over the world, the lion's share of which had ended up in their own pockets.

"How many of you have ever heard of Dr. Noah Yarcho?" Greenberg asked. Without waiting for an answer from the club members, who were dumbstruck by the pious bookbinder's venomous aspersions, Greenberg proceeded to relate that in Entre Rios there had lived for many years a rare doctor who had abandoned a brilliant practice in Kiev and come to the desolate pampas of Argentina in order to minister to the sick in Baron de Hirsch's Jewish colonies. Not only did he build his infirmary with his own hands, personally supervise the kitchen and sanitary conditions, and tend to every patient who knocked on his door, he also did much to treat the social and spiritual ills of the settlers by founding a Zionist society and a Talmudic study group, even though the baron's officials in Buenos Aires only laughed at him and did their best to make his life difficult.

"Just like Dr. Schweitzer," Leder interrupted.

"Yes, but Dr. Yarcho was a truly modest man, the proof being that not one of you has ever heard of him," replied Greenberg. And unlike his Alsatian colleague, he added, who left his wife behind in Europe and no doubt betrothed himself to a different nurse each night,

Dr. Yarcho was accompanied by a young bride who followed him wherever he went.

Seeing that the resistance to Dr. Schweitzer was growing, so that, if he joined it, he could hardly be suspected of a personal vendetta against his friend and rival, Leder, Lev-Tamim now declared that,
just as he was against the Jewish clericalism of the rabbis, so he did not wish a Christian missionary to head any state that he belonged to.

Yet nothing could deter Leder from his plan.

He took to visiting the university library, where he indefatigably tracked down every book and article that might cast light on our future chief of state, bombarding me afterward with endless details from the life of the extraordinary physician, who had spent decades in the jungle fighting illness, indigence, and illiteracy out of a deep sense of personal mission.

Leder was particularly pleased with himself when he managed to rebut one of Greenberg's accusations. The fact, he claimed, that every biography of Schweitzer stated expressly that he was joined by his wife Helena on his first trip to Africa in 1913 was not only irrefutable proof of the falsehood of the Argentinian bookbinder's libelous charge of infidelity, it cast serious doubt on his other prevarications as well.

Schweitzer's gospel of the sacredness of life preoccupied Leder more and more, so that there was no end to his joy when he came across, in a travel journal published by Professor Charles Garland of Cambridge, an eyewitness account of the power of this belief, according to which all things, even dumb beasts, were holy and had the right to live.

"Before the astonished eyes of the African workers," Leder read, repeating for my benefit the words he had copied into his notebook from the *British Geographical Annual*, "the elderly doctor personally descended into a hole dug for the foundations of a new wing of his leper colony and freed a toad that was trapped there."

"Love—no less than hatred and sickness—is contagious," Leder observed, adding that ever since that day even the most primitive of Schweitzer's natives had sought to do only good to helpless animals.

The most stirring of all Leder's encounters with the African doctor, however, took place in Steimatzky's foreign-language bookstore, which he entered one day in order to empty the School for the

Blind alms box that stood by the cash register on the counter. As he was struggling with the recalcitrant lid, his glance fell on the cover of *Life* magazine, from which his medical friend was staring genially straight at him with a spare and pensive smile half-concealed by his bushy white mustache.

Leder would not permit me to touch the magazine lest I smudge it with my fingers. It contained a photographic essay on the white-haired doctor, showing him with a cork hat on his head and an apron around his waist as he puttered around his hospital on the Upper Ogoué; superintended the laying of a new tin roof on a finished bungalow; chatted with African women who had come to pay a call on a sick tribeswoman; and fed a kitten from his hand against a breathtaking view of the equatorial jungle.

The concluding photograph of the article was taken at night in Dr. Schweitzer's study. Across the right-hand side of the picture fell the shadow of the grand piano on which he played compositions by Bach; on a neatly made bed to the left lay his cork hat and white smock; while in the center, leaning over his rough wooden desk, the doctor was writing with a look of concentration. The great lover of mankind, said the caption, was in the habit of personally answering every single letter sent to him.

"You can see for yourself," my friend said, his voice trembling, "how much he cares for the feelings of others."

Leder carefully slipped the magazine into his briefcase and declared that he intended this very night to write Schweitzer a letter inviting him to be chief of state, a position that would undoubtedly be the crowning summit of his humanitarian career.

The next day, on our way back from the central post office, to which we had gone to prevent any mishaps in the letter's long voyage from Jerusalem to French Equatorial Africa, we stopped by Behira Schechter's to see the Nutrition Army's new uniforms, and there—as will be recalled—I met my mother.

Chapter Nine

1.

"The boy needs to be kept an eye on," declared Ahuva Haris, who, let in that same day on the secret of my ties with Leder, insisted I wear a small linen bag full of camphor balls around my neck. As oil repelled water, she promised my mother, so the sharp smell of the crystalline substance would ward off Leder and his evil likes. Meanwhile, under her eagle eye, her husband Binyamin, whom she had dragged from his sickbed to our house, inspected the mezuzahs in our doorways and found them wanting. With a whoop of triumph Ahuva pointed at the crumpled talismans of parchment lying on our kitchen table and declared that the absence of certain letters from their sacred formulae was the cause of all our aggravation.

"Just as a zeppelin has to crash once the hydrogen leaks out of it," she announced rhetorically, scolding Mother for her negligence, "so a house with faulty mezuzahs is asking for trouble."

Every evening of that week Ahuva turned up again with some new charm for me in her purse.

"I've brought the child a yarmulke that was once worn by the Hofetz-Hayim," she announced on one of her late-hour, emergency visits while whisking away my dark blue skullcap with the name of my school in light blue on it, which she declared was no more Jewish than the beanies worn by the Pope and his crowd of cardinals. Reverently she laid the decrepit, sweat-soaked covering on my head with a prayer that, from now on, mercy and peace might rest upon me.

My mother balked and sought to remove it, fearful that I might, God forbid, catch lice or ringworm but Ahuva lightly slapped her outstretched hand and remarked that the lice of the great Rabbi of Radin were worth all the soap and Lysol of the Zionists.

Another time she stormed into our apartment with an embroidered hallah cloth in which was wrapped a wrinkled scrap of old paper covered with a sinuous rabbinical hand that turned out to be the actual writing of the holy Rabbi Israel of Shklov, who had settled in Safed over a century ago. Ahuva had been lent it after much pleading by the granddaughter of Rabbi Israel's great-granddaughter, who lived in Jerusalem.

"Put it under his pillow while he sleeps," she whispered, confident that its curative powers would repair my addled brain.

"Leder is a direct descendent of the snake in the Garden of Eden," my mother's friend informed me that Saturday night after having totally ignored me for the five days. Her hands made serpentine motions in the direction of my throat. "A snake that grew legs!" Once, when she was a child, she related, she had descended into the basement of her house, where among the palm fronds and stored sukkah walls that were awaiting the Feast of Booths she discovered a ball of golden thread, all prettily aglitter like silk—and had it not been for her mother, who appeared just in the nick of time to spank her soundly, she would never have known that the seductive beauty she was playing with was in fact a viper's nest. It would be best, she told my mother, to transfer me from the school I attended to the truly pious Shiloh School or the Yavneh Talmud Torah, where I would be given a proper Jewish education.

My father, who had thus far suffered in silence our garrulous guest's intervention in the family's affairs, could control himself no longer. According to Jewish law, he said to my mother, in words meant for Ahuva, he alone was responsible for the education of his son, which was no one else's business.

"Ahuva is not no one," my mother struck back, mimicking my father's manner of speech. If she were him, she added, she would keep her mouth shut, since on the day he began hanging around with Riklin he lost all right to decide how his son should be raised.

"It's you who ran out on this house!" my father retorted. If my mother would only think of what she had done, she would realize that all the trouble I had gotten into—my worsening marks at school, my having stopped borrowing books from the B'nai Brith library, my friendship with Leder—had begun on the day she took to sneaking out after lunch with baskets full of goodies for Yeru'el Barzel's mother.

"I know you like the back of my hand," my Mother replied with mock sweetness. "In a minute you'll accuse me of stealing chicken livers and honey cakes for my lovers."

"Nothing would surprise me more," shouted my father, growing even angrier.

My mother turned away from him and declared that the very walls blushed with shame when he fawned on the young female shoppers in the grocery, picking out the best eggs for them and throwing another slice of cheese on the scale to get a pearly smile. She was spending, she remarked to Ahuva, what should have been the best years of her life helping her dear husband in the store while he treated her no better than a galley slave.

The quarrel heated up. The truth was, my father rejoined, that theirs was a marriage on paper only. For years he had not had a shirt ironed or a hot meal cooked for him, while he counted himself lucky to find his bed made once a month.

"Your father sold me a whole milk-cow," screamed my mother, "and I don't have a single glass of milk from it!"

Ahuva, who had been sitting huddled in her chair, careful to avoid getting hit by the missiles flying back and forth, now raised her head and announced that there was no need for a boy like me to hear such things, which belonged behind closed doors.

"Yes," my father snarled at her, "I know you're a great expert on raising children." Instead of wasting her time in friend's houses, he asked, why didn't she adopt some poor orphan and give it a proper home?

Ahuva's barrenness—or rather her inability to conceive, as Mother put it in her all-night conversations with Aunt Tsviya—was a sore point respected by all. Father's violation of the ban on mentioning it cast a strained hush over the room, which was broken only by his slamming the door and stalking out into the magic of the night. While my mother comfortingly stroked her shoulder, Ahuva burst into silent sobs and swore that never again would she set foot in our home unless my brute of a father was somewhere else.

2.

The family fracas was still raging the next day when Aunt Tsviya, having divined trouble with the aid of leaves and clouds, arrived on the scene to announce that if my parents did not wish me to become a prematurely old man whose high-flown language concealed infantile emotions and a birdlike brain, they should remove me as quickly as possible from the adult world in which I had stewed since I was a baby and send me off to an agricultural boarding school.

"The child will get some color in his cheeks," she promised, feeling my biceps and adding that if I spent some time in the sun and ate beef every day, my muscles would not be as flabby as a religious young bride's.

Ahuva Haris, who was standing tensely in the kitchen doorway, ready to exit via the back door the moment she saw my father's shadow, protested that the life of the soil was for Arabs and worms, not for a good Jewish boy.

"Shhhh, you're insulting Father Isaac," Tsviya scolded, quickly invoking half-a-dozen other patriarchs from the Bible as well to prove how great had been their love of tilling and reaping.

"Let Isaac rest in peace," my mother's best friend answered back. "Have you forgotten that the first farmer was Cain?" It was a crime, Ahuva said, to teach the twenty-four holy books of the Bible as though they were agricultural or geographical texts. Why, if my aunt would only study the mystical *Zohar*, or even attend the sermons of Reb Shulem Shvadron, instead of reading the daily goose-papers, she would realize how foolish it was to think that so pure a sin-offering as Father Isaac, who was identical with the fifth kabbalistic emanation of Gevurah and symbolized God's justice, would have wasted his time plowing and weeding in the fields of Gerar.

"Every verse in the Bible contains great and terrible secrets," continued Ahuva, her voice rising feverishly. Just then, however, my father's footsteps were heard in the yard, coming home from the store, and she ran for dear life without finishing.

"Who would imagine such fanatics still live in our midst," sighed Aunt Tsviya after her brother had arrived and had a chance to listen to her plan. Though he looked pleased with it he said nothing, since he knew that the slightest assent on his part would be the scheme's kiss of death with my mother—after which, as the Arab saying went, forty English men-of-war couldn't get it off the floor.

My mother, however, refused to hear of it and nipped Aunt Tsviya's proposal in the bud by swearing that not even a court order could get her to banish her son from her house. "Why should he have to run away from home so early?" she asked in a hurt tone of voice. I would get to taste exile soon enough in the army, and worse yet, when I took a wife of my own, to say nothing of my old age, when my children would serve it up to me on a platter.

"On that I can agree with your mother," my father said, seizing the opening. "Here, in this house, I'm an exile."

"Enough, enough," Tsviya begged, clapping a hand to her mouth. From now on, she said, the two of them must make sure that I came straight home from school every day instead of running loose in the streets, and, even more importantly, that I befriended boys my own age.

And so, by compromise agreement, I began going to Haim Rachlevski's each day while my mother watched from the window, tracking me as I went lest I make a false move and flee to the viper's nest.

3.

Haim's childhood and mine had been involved with each other ever since the day during the 1948 war when my mother and I sought shelter in the Rachlevskis' house from a sudden Arab bombardment. Together with a few other passers-by, we rushed pell-mell into the living room behind the Rachlevskis' grocery store, where we took cover under the beds from the enemy barrage. A deathly quiet pervaded the room, whose windows were sealed with sandbags, as we listened to the shells that whistled overhead and tried to guess where they would fall. Suddenly, from under another bed, I heard a voice full of wonder remark:

"Look at how many white ants I have."

Since that distant afternoon I spent untold hours with Haim Rachlevski. Yet whenever I think of him it is still of his figure muffled by darkness, in his cupped palm specks of plaster fallen from the ceiling.

Yet it was not for someone like Haim that my Aunt Tsviya had prayed when she urged my parents to find me a playmate my age.

Haim was a delicate, spoon-fed boy whose every step was guided by a strong sense of destiny inculcated in him by his parents, and especially by his mother, since the day he was born. When once we talked about it, on one of those winter days at the war's end when both of us were stationed across the Suez Canal, he candidly told me how three times a year, upon returning from school with a below-average report card, he had been reassured by his mother that his teachers were all hopeless dolts, which was why they failed to recognize his true worth. To prove her point she had reminded him of the prophecy of the old Yemenite palm reader, who not only foresaw all the misfortunes that were later to befall her in life, even though she was only a young woman at the time, but also told her that she would bear a son in middle age who would be a bringer of light to the world. And seeing Haim's skeptical smile, she added that, if he didn't believe her, he could ask Ada Kaleko, who had worked in those days as an obstetric nurse at Hadassah Hospital on Mount Scopus, whether the delivery room had not gleamed with a preternatural light the moment he was ushered into it.

Haim's biblical drawings—of the copper snake with which Moses healed the Children of Israel in the desert, of King Saul coming to the witch of En-Dor by night, of Job debating with his three friends, and so forth—papered the walls of our school lobby and were a source of great pride to our art teacher, who was sure that a new Jewish Rembrandt was coming of age in the Middle East. His greatest love, however, was the painstakingly precise resurrection of lost worlds, with which he more than once surprised us, stepping with his mother from a taxi that pulled up in the morning by the school gate and unloading with her a huge board draped with a blanket. During the ten o'clock break our pleased-as-punch principal would unveil the new creation, perhaps a little model of the Tabernacle made of cardboard, plywood, and painted gold, so perfect in all its details down to the last curtain, plank, pedestal, and vessel that the Bible and Jewish history teachers were still using it in their lessons years later. There it would stand for several months until another little mini-world arrived, this time perhaps a model of the Old City of Jerusalem with all its quarters, gates, and mosques, which would eventually be donated to the geography teacher for his classes.

Yet Haim felt loathing for ordinary rote learning, and gradually, as these took up the greater part of our time, he lost favor with our teachers and began to fall by the wayside. His former admirers now held him up as a sorry example of the popular witticism about wonder children, namely, that the wonder vanished when they grew up, leaving only the child. In class he sat staring out the window, his gaze roaming back and forth from the YMCA tower to the Generali Building, or else he spent the time drawing galloping horses and mustachioed sword-swallowers in the back pages of his notebooks. His high-school years—during which his "academic situation" had "grown still graver," to quote the revolting officialese of our teacher Mr. Grienfeld—were largely spent in exile in the kingdom of the school janitor and his helper. There, in a little alcove at one end of the yard, among gym mats, vaulting poles, bottles of Lysol, and kerosene heaters stored away during the summer, the three of them passed the days while the janitor made Turkish coffee in a beaker, poured it into little, gold-rimmed cups on whose china glaze was a picture of Dr. Herzl regarding the Rhein, and told Haim and his assistant tall tales about princesses turned into fish, the fabulous Jemmim found by Annah in the Bible while tending his father Zibeon's donkeys, and the shipwrecked rabbi from Morocco whose mat—the Arabic word for which was *hassira*—turned into a life raft, this being the origin of the famous Abu-Hatzira family. When the warning bell rang to remind them that classes were nearly over, the assistant would turn to "Haimon," as he affectionately called my friend, and advise him to learn a useful trade instead of wasting his time and parents' money in this manner. The janitor, though, would scold his helper and insist that Haim must get his diploma. "Look at him, he has the hands of a poet," he would say, pointing at my friend's long, refined fingers and almost feminine hands. Had Haim ever heard, he asked as he rose from his place, of a poet called Amichai? "Amichai, the one that's got all his poems in the papers now, he was once a student here, too. Believe me, that Ashkenazi bastard Grienfeld dumped on him a hundred times worse than on Haimon." If Haim did not believe him, he added before letting my friend press the electric bell that signaled recess, he could check for himself with the poet's niece Hannah, who was in his class.

We too, Haim's friends, grew slowly apart from him and learned to laugh at him like our teachers. Years later, when he and I were sitting one day in the Genifa, waiting on a hilltop spotted with flint stones as large and smooth as ostrich eggs for the truck that was to take us back to Fa'id with what was left of some Egyptian soldiers who had taken a direct hit on their missile emplacement, Haim reminisced with a lump in his throat about a picnic our class had held in the Rothschild Gardens in Rishon le'Tsiyyon. There, he recalled, while we were waiting to visit the Rothschild wine cellars, we split into groups beneath the shade of some palm trees and began to share the tins of food that we had brought for lunch, leaving him with nothing to eat but a can of sour pickles, too proud to ask for more.

He had sat there wanting to die, while in his fantasies he climbed the high ladder of the winery and plunged into the intoxicating abysses of the giant wine vats below.

4.

Only in his own home did his true worth go unquestioned.

At the time that I befriended him on my mother's orders, and with my father's blessing, Haim was into chemistry. The desk in his room, which was piled with Bunsen burners, test tubes, an alcohol lamp, and strips of asbestos and wire netting, resembled a laboratory and smelled like the nature room in school. His books had been moved from their shelves to the wide windowsills, while in their place stood jars and bottles filled with powders, bits of metal, and other odd-looking things. On each of these containers was a label with Latin letters and tiny numbers beneath them.

"Here on this shelf," Haim grandly said, "you see a row of different chemical substances, or as they are called these days, elements." Whereupon, as though rehearsing a lesson only recently learned, he launched into a lengthy, monotonous lecture strewn with foreign words and obscure formulae that were scrawled by him as he talked on slips of paper scattered among the test tubes.

Yet before long, despairing of my powers of comprehension, he pushed the slips of paper away.

"The chemical elements," he said, trying a different approach, "were the magic building blocks used by God to make the world." ("I felt like Dr. Weizmann trying to explain things to the chief rabbi," he recalled to me years later in those days after the war.) Just as the thousands of words in the Hebrew language, he went on, watching me to see if I was following, were formed out of the twenty-two letters of the Hebrew alphabet, so everything in the universe was composed of only a hundred or so elements.

Haim expounded his metaphor, astonished himself by the unexpected similarity between the two realms. The role played by the elements in chemical formulae, for example, was like that of the letters in the formation of words, while both groups had rare and common members, none of which was subdivisible.

"It's an endless, wonderful world," he confided in me, adding that he was now busy building a collection of all the elements known to man.

The piecing together of this collection was an adventure in itself—one that, when I think of it, makes me stand to this day in awe of Haim's resourcefulness. A misshapen gold crown, extracted from his mother's mouth by the dentist while preparing a new bridge, lay on the bottom of an empty mustard jar that bore on its serrated glass the label Au.; lead was represented by some old type face found by the entrance to Solomon's print shop on Rabbi Kook Street; aluminum was accounted for by the cover of a pot borrowed from the kitchen. Haim had gotten hold of mercury by breaking a thermometer, and had obtained neon—a rare and noble gas, so he knowledgeably instructed me, that was produced from liquified air—in a long, milky fluorescent bulb bought at the hardware store.

Thus, our friendship was born under the sign of a never-ending search for missing elements.

From a table drawn up by him with the help of encyclopedias, guidebooks, and above all, a high-school chemistry text lent him by the son of our neighbor, Dr. Amiram Peled, Haim knew that his collection still lacked more elements than it possessed. Daily he went through his index cards of absentees, wracking his brain how to find them.

On my third or fourth visit to his house, he brandished an index card and announced that it had suddenly dawned on him during arithmetic class where he might get obtain iridium. "Iridium," Haim read from the card, "whose name derives from the word 'iris,' meaning 'rainbow' in Greek, is so called because of its iridescent compounds. It is a very hard, grayish-white, heavy metal of the platinum group. Its extremely high melting point makes it a valuable alloy, especially in the manufacture of fountain-pen tips."

Haim wrote Ir. on a label, licked it once or twice before pasting it on the jar, and asked if I saw what he was getting at.

That same day found us knocking on the door of the little fountain-pen shop squeezed in beside the missionary bookshop at the bottom of Princess Mary Street. The bespectacled shop owner, his smock stained with ink, listened to my friend's learned introduction with a half-ironical, half-curious look and replied that, although he himself was no expert on the chemistry of the pen nibs that he sold and repaired, he did have a box full of broken ones and would be glad to contribute a Waterman, which was known for its hardness, to Haim's collection.

Already on our way home, emboldened by the pen man's friendly attitude, Haim had the idea of trying his luck next at the Teva Pharmaceutical Factory on the outskirts of town. Flushed with excitement, he returned from it to report that the manager had told him that he too had been a chemistry fiend as a child and had performed experiments in his parents' kitchen—here he showed Haim a burn scar on his forehead—that had almost cost him his sight. "Boys like you should be encouraged," said the man. "You're the future of our profession." Then he took Haim on a grand tour of his kingdom and showed him how medicines were made.

Haim's new trophies were waiting for me on a shelf. Carefully he picked up a corked-and-wired bottle and shook it so that its thick, reddish-brown liquid sloshed heavily back and forth.

"This is bromine," he said. "A highly toxic element with a noxious smell that is an important constituent in the pharmaceutical industry."

Next to the bromine was another smaller jar with the letter I. on its label, whose purplish-black crystals, I was now apprised, were iodine. In an open dish beside them lay some soft, orange, crumbly bits of sulfur.

Haim stretched out on the couch and contentedly regarded his new treasures that I was not allowed to approach. The manager of the factory, he told me, had warned him not to touch these toxic substances, not to inhale their vapors, and above all, to keep them away from strong heat.

One day, Haim ventured dreamily, he would be a chemist himself. Perhaps he might even discover a new element, one of those whose existence was guessed by Mendeleyev, who had even left empty spaces for them in his periodic table, though no one had yet been able to find them.

"The new element will be called 'vitalium,'" declared Haim, "after its finder"—for "vita," he informed me, which meant "life," was the Latin translation of Haim. Yet should the modesty expected of a great scientist prevent him from naming it thus, he would call it "jerusilium" after his native city, like the French chemist who had named the seventy-first element lutetium after the Roman name for Paris, or the Swedish professor who had called the sixty-seventh element holmium after his country's captial.

Haim was in high spirits in those days, his future already mapped out. He often cut classes and made fun of the nonsense taught in school, especially Talmud and religion, whose propagation he regarded as a clerical attempt to prolong a doomed way of life.

Yet without his noticing it at first, the skies above him were beginning to darken. Weeks went by without a single new addition to his collection, while the index cards of missing elements lay like damning evidence on his desk. He grew moody and impatient, and he stubbornly refused my advice.

One day, entering his room to find a new row of jars on a shelf, I imagined that the crisis was behind him. Quickly, however, he silenced my cries of joy by explaining that what I saw was only a stopgap solution, a dishonorable compromise that true scientists would dismiss as a childish attempt to circumvent obstacles.

He took a bottle of ammonia down from the shelf and informed me, embarrassment creeping into his voice, that for the time being this common compound would stand for the hydrogen and nitrogen that composed it, just as a saltshaker would have to do for sodium and chlorine, and a jar of sand for silicium. Yet the more he continued to read, the more frustrated he grew.

"Where are we going to find prometheum?" he mourned one day. Leafing through the new chemistry book he had bought in the Atid Bookstore on Hasolel Street, he told me that this element, which had been identified in the spectrum of one of the stars in Andromeda, was extremely rare on the planet Earth, being found in small concentrations chiefly in gadolonite, and that synthesizing it in the laboratory involved an atomic reaction.

Haim knew no more about atomic reactions than he did about spectrums in Andromeda, where the element named after the mythological thief of fire was first identified, but it could not be denied that the mysterious reaction now taking place inside him, which appeared to produce some new unstable isotope every day, was ultimately responsible for the realization that a long list of elements would never be found for his collection.

This sealed its fate.

Haim stopped spending time in his room, whose full shelves were mute witnesses to a dream shattered by nuclear bombardment, and the two of us took to roaming the streets, where we brought up the rear of the safaris led by Menasheh and Efraim Hatulov, the Bukharian identical twins who caught cats for hospital laboratories, and teased the trio of dwarfs who owned a workshop for the production of buttons, ribbons, and bows.

Pending its final disposition, Haim's collection was stored away in the attic, thus putting an end to the chemical phase of his life. Now, having cast off its spell, he paced up and down again in his room, which seemed suddenly to have grown larger, and explained how the desire to complete his collection at all costs had practically driven him out of his mind, so that only his failure to carry out his plan to break into the X-ray room of Hadassah Hospital had saved him, his parents, and all their neighbors from a lethal overdose of radioactivity.

"True possession is mental, not physical," Haim pronounced, expressing his disdain for all hoarders foolish enough to believe that their money could buy them not only material things but the incorporeal ideas that these stood for. "The real owner of a book," he went on, "is he who reads it, not whoever buys it for his bookshelf." Pointing at his own naked shelves and empty file cabinet, he added sorrowfully, though not without a hint of fatalistic acceptance, that no man could reach perfection in anything, not even in a field so restricted that its entire inventory included only one hundred and thirty items.

He discussed himself and his recent endeavors as one discusses a not especially well-liked stranger. The more he considered it, he said, the clearer it became to him that the confines of a chemical laboratory with its cramped territory of gross matter were not for someone like himself, to whom the boundless horizons of pure philosophical thought were now beckoning.

5.

I could hear the voice of Dr. Amiram Peled in Haim's words.

Haim was the only person I knew who failed to steer clear of our neighbor the philosopher. News of the discovery made by my mother, who had seen portraits of Lenin and Stalin on the bindings of our neighbor's books the day he moved in to his apartment, had quickly made the rounds. The neighborhood children were warned not to play with the children of the Communist, and housewives threw out with a shudder of disgust the cup of sugar or flour returned to them by Dr. Peled's wife in lieu of what she had borrowed when the grocery closed. It was even rumored that our neighbor's last name was a Hebrew translation of Stalin, which meant "steel" in Russian—this in spite of Mrs. Rachlevski's insistence that it was in fact a Hebraized version of the German name Eisen.

At the time of the trials in Communist Czeckslovakia, the whispering campaign against Dr. Peled turned into open warfare. An unseen hand drew a hammer and sickle with a swastika in red paint on the door of his apartment, while the neighborhood mailman regularly crossed out his name on all mail and wrote beneath it in red ink, "*Comrade* Slansky, Lubyanka Prison, Moscow." Several months later, when news broke of the trial in Moscow of the nine Jewish doctors, led by Professor Vofsy, who were accused of plotting to murder the Soviet leaders by medical means, the chorus of hate reached new heights. One day Dr. Peled's little daugher Inbal returned home in tears beccause the school nurse had refused to bandage a bleeding cut on her forehead and had told her to ask her father to take her to Professor Vofsy instead.

Haim's mother alone untiringly stood up for Dr. Peled. Not only, she claimed, should we stop behaving like animals toward a man simply because he had different views, we should be proud that someone like him had chosen to live among us. "Where else in the world," she asked, "can you find university professors moving in among garbage collectors and shopkeepers?" In her conversations with Mother she often said that our hatred for Dr. Peled had nothing to do with his Communist opinions but was rather the irrational dislike of common people for anyone more cultured than themselves—in support of which she cited the story in the Talmudic tractate of the Pesahim of how the great Rabbi Akiva, before becoming a scholar of the Law, boasted that if ever he met a truly learned man he would gnash him like a donkey.

To prove that she meant what she said, Mrs. Rachlevski took to inviting Dr. Peled's children to eat in her house and urged her son to visit them in theirs—where, she hoped, he might pick up their respect for knowledge, just as the servant girl in the rabbi's house, in the words of the old saying, grew to be an expert in the Law.

None of this met with the approval of her husband, who confided to my mother that his wife's contrariness, and her friendliness toward the red philosopher, stemmed more from her hatred of Mordecai than from her love of Haman—that is, that they were her way of subtly getting back at him, whose loathing of the Bolsheviks and their fellow-travelers was well-known, while concealing what a shrew she really was.

All this seething resentment, which fear of making a scene had caused to build up behind Mr. Rachlevski's mild and taciturn exterior, burst furiously forth on the day of Stalin's funeral.

From the moment the news that the generalissimo in the Kremlin had suffered a stroke and was in critical condition took the world by storm, our house became Rachlevski's second home. He posted himself beside our radio, which unlike his own had a long-distance antenna, tuned it to Moscow, and listened tensely to the distant Slavic voices that reached us via thunderstorms and snows.

Periodically, Moscow radio broke off its Red Army Choir music, and its reading of telegrams from the sixteen Soviet republics and sister Communist parties all over the world, all of which expressed the confident hope that the sun of Iosif Vissarionovitch would never set, for an expressionless, metallic-voiced announcer to read the latest medical bulletin issued by the ministry of health.

The mood of our neighbor—whose ear was slowly collapsing the speaker of our radio, much to the annoyance of my mother, who feared that our Phillips would be ruined well before the drama in Moscow was played out—swung back and forth like a pendulum with each of these reports.

The announcement that Stalin's blood pressure had improved caused Haim's father no little anxiety, and not until a later bulletin confirmed that his pulse rate was up and his heartbeat more irregular did Rachlevski quit our house in the dead of night and go home to sleep, still sorely troubled by the thought that the Georgian tyrant had lost consciousness and could therefore feel not even a fraction of the pain he deserved. Whenever my mother brought him a glass of steaming-hot tea ("Rachlevski," she kidded him fondly in response to his complaints that the drink was always too cold, "they must have nursed you with boiling tea straight from the samovar when you were born"), he would turn down the radio and reminisce about his two brothers, one of whom, a loyal Bolshevik since he was a boy, had been declared an enemy of the people in an early purge, sent to a camp beyond the Yenisei River, thrown into a cellarhole dug in the permafrost, and left to rot until dispatched by a pistol shot. The other brother was taken away in the middle of the night and never heard from again.

My father and mother, who had experienced nothing worse in their own lives than the famine toward the end of Turkish rule, listened wide-eyed as these embers of the past, which the vicissitudes of time should have banked into dead ashes, glowed again in Mr. Rachlevski's memory.

That Friday morning, before he and my father went to synagogue, Rachlevski silently entered our apartment, which still lay in auroral slumber, and turned on the radio. A sad, heroic melody came from far Moscow. He listened with furrowed brows, struggling to make it out, then jumped up and began clapping his hands and singing the song from the Passover Haggadah,

Cometh the day, cometh the day
Cometh the day of no night and no day.

My mother awoke in a fright, emerged in her nightgown, and demanded to know why, less than a week after Purim, Rachlevski was already celebrating the Seder.

"The dirty dog is dead! The dirty dog is dead!" our neighbor answered, laughing and crying in turn. My mother inquired anxiously whether he wasn't rejoicing prematurely, but Rachlevski reassured her that Moscow would never have dared play the *Eroica* if the tyrant were not already dead.

At exactly six o'clock the music faded and a choked voice spoke over the airwaves.

"That's Yuri Levitan," our neighbor said, recognizing Moscow Radio's senior Jewish announcer. "If they got him out of bed this early in the morning, it's a sure sign that it's over with."

On their way out of the house, after the two men had heard the official announcement of the death of Lenin's heir and comrade-in-arms, Rachlevski remarked to father that a special prayer should be said that day in synagogue.

"For his soul," grinned my father, and the two of them burst out laughing.

All day long, until the Sabbath set in with the warning blast of a siren from the nearby ritual bathhouse, our neighbor remained glued to the radio, reveling in the unending stream of condolence cables read aloud by weeping female broadcasters. On Saturday night, as soon as the Sabbath was over, he returned to his listening post to join the long line of women with infants in their arms, the workers, and the masses from the provinces who passed in front of the coffin displayed in the Hall of Columns. Each new description of the corpse in its military tunic festooned with medals on its chest, of the flower-scented air, and of the great human serpent snaking through the streets of Moscow in the bitter cold of early March, was music to his ears.

Outside, in the streets of Jerusalem, a light snow was falling, but Mr. Rachlevski kept wiping the sweat from his brow while declaring that the millions of Russians waiting in line to pass before the coffin, and to stare for a moment at the whiskered monster it decked out like a whore, simply wanted to make sure that the Angel of Death had really been to the Kremlin.

On Monday morning Rachlevski came again to attend the funeral.

It was a torrid day. The Jerusalem weather had turned and hot, dry winds were blowing from the desert. Yet cold winter blasts still whistled through our house, mingling with the chimes of the Kremlin bells and the boom of the cannon resounding in Red Square. When at last Malenkov rose to deliver the eulogy for the dead *vozhd*,our neighbor opened a Bible and chanted Isaiah's prophecy of the downfall of Lucifer, son of the dawn.

"*Yea, those who see you will stare at you and ponder over you,*" sang Mr. Rachlevski. "*Is this the man who made the earth tremble, who shook kingdoms, who made the world like a desert and overthrew its cities, who did not let his prisoners go home?*" He intoned the ancient verses as though from the prayer podium and declared that, though the fulfillment of Isaiah's prophecy had taken time, now that the first part of it had come true, so would the second.

"*But you shall be cast out from your sepulchre like a loathed, untimely birth*," he continued, "*like a dead body trodden underfoot.*" And he avowed to my mother that the day was not far off when Stalin's heirs would throw his painted, powdered, and embalmed corpse out of the mausoleum in which it lay.

The party pooper was Mrs. Rachlevski, who burst suddenly into our house. Throwing a pile of bills at her husband she announced that she had no idea how much to pay the noodle man. Then she turned to my mother and complained that for a whole week Haim's father had done nothing but read newspapers and listen to the radio, leaving her swamped with work in the store.

"Soon you'll have another funeral on your hands—mine!" she shouted and demanded that he return at once to work.

He silenced her with a wave of his hand and asked to be allowed to listen to Beria in peace.

"Beria? You'll have to bury *me!*" Mrs. Rachlevski screamed. "You listen to your own dear wife, who's been slaving away like a jackass!" She began to pull at his sleeve.

He broke free of her grasp, shoved her toward the door, and asked whether she wanted him in the store so that she might bring a hot meal to Dr. Peled, who was undoubtedly sitting at home in mourning. "Do you have the hard-boiled eggs ready for him?" he snapped bitterly.

"Avram, rejoice not when thine enemy falleth," Mrs. Rachlevski chided him like a mother scolding a wayward child. Despite his politics, she said, Dr. Peled was a friendly, cultured man who wouldn't hurt a fly. Why blame him for Stalin's crimes?

"You stupid Jerusalem ninny!" Rachlevski silenced her. "What do you know about anything?" To my mother he declared that to this day it gave him goosepimples to think of some of the friendly, cultured people who wouldn't hurt a fly that he had known in Russia. "One of them once dropped in on us in Kiev," he said, telling her how one night, a few weeks before he himself escaped from Russia by the skin of his teeth, a young man wearing a fur hat and leather coat had knocked on their door at three o'clock in the morning. It was Vladimir Kogen, the son of the head of the yeshiva in Obrych, Rachlevski's native town. Behind the pleasant facade of this ex-rabbinical student lurked the brutal, inhuman stare of a Cheka interrogator.

"But why must you be as stubborn as a mule? It was probably the only way he had of warning you that you were under surveillance," Mrs. Rachlevski said to her husband for what must have been the hundredth time.

"I know them like I know I my own hand," he retorted. "Of all the devil's henchmen, none are as cruel and cunning as Jews." Pointing toward the house of our neighbor the philosopher, which was screened by a tangled passion-flower vine, he asserted that if, God forbid, the Red Army should conquer Israel someday, Dr. Peled would be the first to inform on him.

"*Paskudnyak!*" Mrs. Rachlevski exclaimed, flinging one of her husband's favorite words at him. At her wits' end, she stood with the noodle bills in her hand.

Rachlevski was about to drift happily back to the sound of the artillery salutes heard over the strains of Chopin's funeral march that were coming from Moscow when suddenly, through the front door that had been left open because of the unseasonable heat, he spied Dr. Peled, spotlessly groomed and with a red carnation in the buttonhole of his shirt, slipping out of his yard on his way to the Rachlevskis' grocery.

"Go back to the store, the Commie spy is looking for you," he snapped at his wife. "He must want to buy a memorial candle."

Four years later, pursued by the hostile glances of the neighbors and the maledictions of Mrs. Adler, Dr. Peled went down the same street again and entered the Rachlevskis' grocery. He waited there, so Haim's father told us, until the last customers had departed, then hesitantly inquired whether Mr. Rachlevski had any need of wrapping paper. That same day he and his son piled cartons full of dusty books and journals in the back yard of the grocery. Toward evening, when Rachlevski finally had time to bring them into the store, he was astonished to see that our neighbor the philosopher had thrown out the collected works of Lenin and Stalin, as well as all his articles about them.

"The Communist paper must have finally gotten around to printing the text of Khrushchev's secret Twentieth-Congress speech," Rachlevski gloated to his wife. Or was she still, he wanted to know, as naive as ever?

"Only morons never change their minds," she rejoined, slamming the door as she stalked out of the store, which resembled the warehouse of a remote Russian kolkhoz in which a new shipment of books for the collective's library had just been received from the provincial capital.

All night, behind closed shutters, Mr. Rachlevski sat up in his store. First he cut the pages loose from their bindings, whose sharp rip pierced the quiet night, and then he wrathfully tore out and shredded into strips the colored pictures of Stalin riding on a tank, holding a pink-cheeked little girl in his arms, and studiously sitting at Lenin's feet. For months to come, on the backs of their pencilled bills, customers who looked could make out stubs of mustaches, hard hands grasping pipes, and rows of military buttons—the sole remains of the late Iosif Vissarionovich Dzugashvili.

Next morning Mr. Rachlevski divided the paper among all the neighborhood groceries. Rolled into a funnel, it made a handy container for pickles and olives.

"*Chort vazmi*," he would mutter to himself, staring hypnotically at the brine-soaked Cyrillic letters washing off the soggy pages. And to Haim, who was helping out in the store, he added:

"Those Soviets can't even make decent paper."

Leder's prophecy, made during our first meeting in front of the Russian bookstore, which took place two weeks before Dr. Peled moved into our neighborhood, had finally come to pass, though he himself hadn't lived to see the day.

6.

Leder loathed anything that was even a little bit pink.

Once, when we happened to pass the trade union building on the First of May just as the strains of "Arise, ye wretched of starvation" were drifting out of it, he made a face and said that if anyone should be called wretched it was the Communists who brought Hitler to power in Germany, since, had they joined the other parties of the Left after the death of Abrett rather than run their own spoiler candidate in the 1925 elections, Hindenburg would never have been chosen president and the Nazi takeover might have been thwarted.

He spat at the red flags flying from the long balcony overhead and added that in all the rumpus over Stalingrad this crime of Stalin's had been forgotten, as even more unforgiveably had been his opening of the Kremlin gates to Von Ribbentrop and his signing of the infamous pact with the Nazis that, more than anything else, was the prelude to World War II with its murder of millions of Jews.

My objection that it was barking up the wrong tree to blame the Israeli trade unions for World War II made him furious. Pounding on the window of the Co-op Restaurant, which was closed because of the international worker's holiday, he declared that, my youth notwithstanding, my brain had already been poisoned by left-wing propaganda, whose claim that there was a difference between socialism and Communism I was foolish enough to believe.

"It's the exact same lady, she just looks less shady," Leder said angrily, adding that already in Vienna he had seen the Social-Democrats' true face. Describing once more the May Day parade he had witnessed there, in which—as has been related—my teacher Miss Schlank took part, he informed me that several years later during the July 1927 uprising, not a few of the Social-Democratic soldiers and policemen who had worn red flowers in their lapels and saluted the marchers streaming down Roussoir Boulevard opened fire on the same people.

"Only red cows like your Cecilia can go around mooing that the workers of all nations are brothers," Leder declared, pointing out how obvious it was that the forces of antisemitism were far stronger than the varnish of proletarian solidarity, even though, after the Schutzbund and the Austrian Left fell apart more quickly than could have been imagined, their members, who deserted by the thousands to the illegal Nazi movement, defended their betrayal of their Jewish ex-comrades as stemming from their hatred for the reactionary bourgeoisie of the *Heimwehr*.

A truck piled high with baled hay and sheaved wheat, and carrying young kibbutzniks in embroidered white blouses who stood beating tambourines and daredevilishly swinging their arms and legs, passed noisily down the street like a motorized threshing floor on its way to the assembly point of the parade that was to march through the city toward evening.

Leder looked disappointedly at my rapt stare and remarked that Jewish education in the country was already fulfilling the Internationale's vision of "Yesterday—nowhere, tomorrow—the world" . . .

by which he meant that nobody wanted to hear about the past anymore. The proof was my blank stare when he had tried telling me about recent historical events that would influence my own future and that of the generations to come.

"Everything in this country of yours is *mañana,*" shouted Leder. "You don't want to solve a thing today that can be put off till tomorrow." He stared at the truck disappearing in the distance and observed that, unlike the Socialists and Communists, who analyzed social problems with the help of complicated theories, apparently in the hope of putting off dealing with them forever, Popper-Lynkeus had sought speedy solutions independent of specific schools of thought, since not ideologies, but people and the need to save them, were his concern.

"I want you to know," Leder said to me, trampling underfoot one of the leaflets handed out on the street by a member of the leftist Young Guards, "that the Communists hate Popper-Lynkeus because of the irrefutable attacks on Marx in his work."

I took up this grave charge with Dr. Peled one day when I broke my promise to my mother and accompanied Haim on a visit to our neighbor the philosopher's apartment.

Despite what my mother had said about his study, neither the red flag nor portraits of the founding fathers of Communism adorned its walls lined with bookshelves, in the spaces between which hung several drawings and sketches. In one corner stood a plain desk on which a green glass vase containing a branch of acacia had been placed, while on the rug in the center of the room lay Dr. Peled, bleating like a lamb at his baby daughter, who sat straddling his chest.

The talk flowed pleasantly enough until I got up the courage to ask him:

"Tell me, Amiram,"—for he did not allow us to call him Dr. Peled—"is it true that you hate Popper-Lynkeus?"

"Whom do you mean by 'you'?"

"The Communists," I said, sorry that I had begun.

"What makes you think I'm a Communist?"

He sensed my discomfort and, without waiting for an answer, said that, if ever I visited the Museum of the Revolution in Moscow, I would see that an entire room there had been dedicated to Popper-

Lynkeus. There could be no more fitting gesture of appreciation for the famous thinker, whom neither Austria, his native land, nor Israel, the homeland of the Jews, had honored in this manner.

"The Soviet Union considers Popper-Lynkeus to be one of the great forerunners of the collectivist approach to human needs," proclaimed Dr. Amiram Peled, as though lecturing to a classroom. Then, realizing the absurdity of the scene, he rose, put the baby in its crib, sat behind his desk, and inquired, while toying with the ball-like yellow flowers of acacia, which he blew on before the open window, what made a boy my age so interested in Popper-Lyneus.

When afterward I asked Leder about the honor bestowed upon our great teacher by Moscow, he nodded and said that he had once read something of the sort in the newspapers. This, he went on, was nothing to be surprised at, since the Communists were more than happy to claim Popper-Lynkeus for themselves once he was dead, just as they claimed Spartacus and the Gracchi. Yet a moment later my friend reversed himself and declared that this was just another lie spread by *Pravda* in order to confuse the humanist opposition that had rejected from the outset the idea of the dictatorship of the proletariat and the violence employed in its name. "It's the world's most widely *red* newspaper," Leder punned while glancing around to make sure that my mother or Ahuva Haris was not hot on our tracks.

7.

Ever since our banned friendship went underground, the reading room of the B'nai Brith library on Ethiopia Street had served as our secret meeting place. There, while waiting impatiently for Dr. Schweitzer's response to the presidential offer made him, Leder had not been idly biding his time. Surrounded by texts on history and economics, he was—or at least, so he claimed—busily writing, clause by clause, a first draft of the constitution of Lynkeania. Each time I arrived at the library for one of our hurried encounters, I found him nibbling at the tip of his Parker pen while deep in the pages of some book. He would signal me to keep a safe distance so that no one might think we were together, and I would sit down two chairs away from him and pretend to be studying.

With its thick stone walls, the long reading room was pleasantly cool even on hot summer days. Bookcases lined it to the ceiling and a wooden ladder so heavy that two people were needed to move it stood propped in the corner. Between the rows of books rose tall windows whose artful lattices let in the softened light, while in the middle of the room was a long table flanked on either side by heavy, high-backed wooden chairs. Here a few teenagers generally sat, talking and giggling in whispers as they did their homework. No one bothered to silence them, since the sole librarian was changing books in the outer room for the young secretaries who, after a day's work in one of the offices on Jaffa Road, were looking for some fat, romantic novel to get them through the boredom of the oncoming night. Leder and I took advantage of the commotion to occupy ourselves with our plans.

Although usually he began with some observation about the Magna Carta or the American Constitution, sooner or later his thoughts drifted back to Dr. Schweitzer's still unreceived reply. By the time a month and a half had gone by from the day his letter was placed on the green marble counter of the central post office, Leder's eager anticipation had given way to a despair that alternated between fits of self-anger and outbursts of hatred for the world. At times he blamed his own penny-foolishness for not sending the letter, which had probably been consigned forever to the belly of a crocodile in some swamp of the Upper Ogoué, by registered mail; at times he regretted having allowed the postal clerk to stick on it a colorful stamp of Jerusalem, perched high among the mountains, that had undoubtedly been coveted by some pygmy warrior for his headdress, whereas had he had the sense to use ordinary stamps it would have arrived long ago; at still other times he suspected Dr. Schweitzer's African staff of plotting to hide it from its master.

Like the true believer who blames all evil on the devil, fallen angels, or an unregenerate mankind, but never on God himself, so it failed to occur to Leder that perhaps Dr. Schweitzer had simply not bothered to answer. Each time, having vented his spleen on everyone but the famous physician, he concluded by lauding his hero to the skies. Among missionaries, he told me, there often were exceptional persons. To this day he remembered fondly the two Catholic nuns who had arrived in Jerusalem toward the end of World War I and cured cases of trachoma with traditional Chinese methods of healing. After a moment's thought he added that the two of them were the first people he knew who had treated him with the courtesy and respect due a fellow human being, unlike the inhabitants of

Jerusalem, who either fawned all over you or mocked you to your face. It was they who had opened his eyes to the world and made him want to explore it.

Four months after Leder's letter was posted to Lembarané, Dr. Schweitzer's answer arrived.

I turned up that day at the library to find Leder looking glum. The books that were usually piled all around him were nowhere to be seen, and the only subject on the bare table before him was a long, bluish airmail envelope.

"Did it come?" I asked hesitantly.

"Here." He handed me the envelope. Some crook-necked herons nesting in the African jungle peered at me from the green-blue-and-black stamp in one corner. Carefully I took out the letter, which was written in a tiny, closely spaced hand on paper of nearly transparent thinness. In the upper right-hand corner appeared Albert Schweitzer's name and address, while further down on the left-hand side were Leder's. I could make out no more than the brief salutation, which said:

Lieber Herr Leder.

Leder took the letter and translated it for me line by line.

Dr. Schweitzer began by apologizing for his delayed reply. The river boat that delivered mail sacks from Libreville, he wrote, had brought with it a large group of Africans ill with sleeping sickness. "As you know," he continued, "treatment of this tropical disease is a long, slow, and arduous process, so for six straight weeks I was busy day and night with these unfortunate natives. Only now that they have recovered do I have the time to write to you."

Dr. Schweitzer spoke highly of Popper-Lynkeus and pointed out that Sigmund Freud, a man far from lavish with his praise, had considered the old utopian, whom he called the best, least deceitful and most unrepressed person he ever had met, to be one of his intellectual precursors. In addition the Alsatian doctor commended the splendid idea of founding a Nutrition Army, especially in Jerusalem, a city that had already given mankind one savior. And yet, he concluded, having lived for so long, like an ancient Jewish sage of whom the rabbi of Strassbourg once told him, within a narrow circle he had drawn around himself, he could not possibly leave it to accept Leder's alluring offer now that his life was drawing to a close, all the more so since this would mean abandoning his poor patients, who so desperately needed his help in their clearing between the jungle and the sea.

Leder folded the letter and stuck it in his pocket, his gloom growing thicker.

8.

Leder's depression colored the days that followed. He read only newspapers and frequently attacked the medical profession, which if left to its own devices, he claimed, would soon fill the world with hospitals chock-full of human vegetables in flower pots. All that would be left for the Nutrition Army to do would be to supply the fertilizer for these curious plants. As for Dr. Schweitzer, his name was mentioned no more.

Before long, however, the insult inflicted by the famous physician's refusal—an insult that threatened, so it seemed, to torpedo Leder's vision and submerge his human uniqueness—turned out to be a liberating force. It made him a new man, free of old burdens and obligations, and at liberty to adopt a fresh point of view that would finally, he was convinced, put the Lynkean movement on the map.

Once more he buzzed with activity and surrounded himself with books, the millenarian glow back in his eyes.

"Neither vegetarianism, nor Esperanto, nor celebrities," crowed Leder, rejoicing in his newly found freedom. "Enough of such childishness!" At last he realized, he said, that his program until now had been so much empty prattle, and that his fatal weakness for ceremony had no place in today's cruel, dog-eat-dog world.

"How could I have been so stupid," he went on musing out loud, "to have imagined that we could overturn the old regime while the vested interests facing us across the barricades—the ice cream manufacturers, the fancy dressmakers, the tobacco merchants, and all the rest of that unholy syndicate—would pinch our cheeks and look on with an indulgent smile?" Rummaging through a stack of books on the table, he handed me a slim, white volume on whose cover was a portrait of a smooth-cheeked young man dressed in an overly wide robe. Something about his thin, crafty lips and cold, cruel, little mouselike eyes, so obviously adept at well-timed subterfuge, sent shivers down my spine.

"Read Machiavelli," Leder demanded. "He's a must for people like us."

Two girls—who, judging by the open atlas in front of them, were doing their geography homework—looked at us curiously, but Leder tipped my chin back to him and reminded me that our work was cut out for us.

"Don't worry, Popper-Lynkeus read *The Prince* too," he said, opening another book, blue-bound and Latin-charactered, that lay before him. He showed me the flowery signature on its flyleaf and told me that this English translation of Machiavelli's classic came from Popper-Lynkeus' private collection, which had been donated by his heirs to the National Library in Jerusalem—whose first beginnings, as I no doubt knew, had been right here in this reading room.

Having set my mind to rest on this point, he thrust out his jaw and declared, gazing at the space above my head, that, whether we liked it or not, we must resort to violence to break out of the debilitating impasse caused by the ridicule and rejection met by the Lynkean idea.

He had spent long, sleepless nights, Leder revealed to me, wrestling with his doubts about taking such a new tack. And yet the more he thought about it, the more certain he became that unless forced to acknowledge us, society would simply sink further into its decadent state of eat, drink, and be merry, with consequences that could not be foreseen.

"You needn't worry about a thing," he repeated, as though this were the keynote of our meeting. "We're talking about a temporary, transitional stage until our movement has laid the groundwork for the Lynkean state and the need for general nutrition is accepted by all citizens of the land."

The relation of ends to means, and of personal to political morality—in a word, that problematic complex that historians have called the demonic dialectic of power—did not trouble Leder for long. When we met again a week-and-a-half later the will to power had gotten the better of his idealistic nature and he was engrossed in pressing practical problems.

"We must learn how to use weapons," he informed me as I entered the library while signaling me not to approach. Lying open on the table in front of him was a light arms manual issued by the Jewish underground in 1938, at the time of the Arab uprising. Over it was a sheet of tracing paper on which he was laboriously copying an illustration of a pistol while jotting down in his notebook the instructions for its use.

He seemed nervous and kept shifting his eyes back and forth from the tracing paper, on which he had so far managed to draw the gun's barrel and drum, to the illustration beneath it, checking his accuracy before proceeding to the trigger and its guard.

"We need cash, lots of cash," he muttered. Suddenly he started, as though he had given away a dark secret.

"Go away," he pleaded. I should wipe this meeting from my memory, he begged, and swear never to mention it to a soul.

I tiptoed out of the room. In the doorway I turned to look again at Leder, who was still tracing the stout lines of the pistol, and at the two girls, whose fingers were trekking through the sun-parched expanses of the Sahara as though looking for a lost oasis.

I never imagined that this would be my last private meeting with him, or that the dream of Lynkeania would be rudely shattered in a week, when rioters would rampage in the streets on the day of the German reparations debate in the Knesset.

Chapter Ten

1.

Already that morning my mother feared the worst.

"You're not leaving the house today," she stated categorically the minute I opened my eyes. The world wouldn't come to an end, she insisted, if I missed a day of school. My school was near the Knesset building, and my mother, who did not believe in looking for trouble, especially if trouble was already looking for you, feared the morning of Reparations Day.

The debate over the reparations negotiations conducted by the Israeli and German governments had naturally reached my parents' grocery, which became a miniature parliament in those days, the shouts of whose delegates often brought curious bypassers in from the street. That morning, however, when my father opened the store at five a.m. for his early-bird customers, the arguments soon turned into fisticuffs. Mr. Kipper, the night watchman who lived alone and stopped off each morning on his way home from the cold storage plant in Tel Arza where he worked for a pack of cigarettes and a glance at the headlines of the newspapers stacked in the corner, emptied a milk can over Ada Kaleko, a prominent figure in the nurses' union, and declared that never in his darkest dreams in Buchenwald had he imagined that one day the rulers of a Jewish state would sit down to make a deal with Hitler's heirs. In the ensuing fracas Ben-Avram, who worked in the warehouse of the co-op dairy, broke an egg on the head of Rabbi Shisha, whose son had been killed while fighting in the ranks of the Irgun. Only fascist hooligans, he shouted, supported Mr. Begin, who had organized the antigovernment demonstrations and deserved to be exiled to Kenya as his terrorist comrades had been by the British, where he could rot in the jungle with the blacks.

My father stood by helplessly as his store began to resemble our house after the Rationing Bureau raid. My mother, however, had the presence of mind quickly to turn out the lights, plunging the skirmishers into the darkness of the foggy, rainy winter morning. Soon they trooped embarrassedly outside, where Kipper continued to conduct a rear-guard action on the sidewalk.

All morning long, her mouth grim with worry, my mother watched the trucks and command cars full of helmeted policemen armed with billy clubs, and the fire engines with their menacing hoses, racing past the store.

"The Tenth of Tevet is only tomorrow," several customers tried to humor her, referring to the fast day that commemorates the start of Nebuchadnezzar's siege of Jerusalem.

"But the siege of Jerusalem has already begun," my mother smiled back. It was because of such jests, she observed, that King Solomon had said in his book of proverbs, "Even in laughter the heart is sad."

At noon the quickly thinning streets were blasted by the loudspeakers of a billboarded pickup truck calling the masses to a rally in Zion Square at four o'clock at which Menachem Begin and Professor Klausner would speak out against the satanic alliance with Evil. My mother hurried to close the store and stopped by Rachlevski's on her way home to tell him that civil war was imminent and that by evening we would be able to boast that Jews too could make a pogrom. If he was smart, she advised him, he would stay home like her and not re-open after the noonday break.

"Blessed are they who dwell in thy house," she announced in the words of the Psalmist when she got home. From now until tomorrow morning, she proclaimed, none of us would set foot out-of-doors. She had already bolted the door behind her when she discovered to her dismay that Riklin was in the house with my father, and that she had just condemned herself to an indefinite stay in his presence, from which he alone could release her.

The two men sat at the table, which was littered as usual with rolled up maps, registers of the Burial Society, and issues of "The Lawgiver's Plot" in their crumbling paper bindings. Father's attention was riveted on Riklin, who had been bringing him news of the world and was now telling him about the scandal that took place at the funeral of Reb Itchele Glazer, the stout little tutor from the Etz Haim Yeshiva who had died in Sha'arei Tsedek Hospital the night before. As the funeral procession set out, Reb Elya said, the sexton read aloud the ancient prohibition, immemorially obeyed by the God-fearing folk of Jerusalem, against the children of the deceased accompanying him to his grave. The dead man's son, however, a high army officer who had changed his name from Glazer to the more Hebrew-sounding Gal, insisted on going to the cemetery. The beadles, Riklin related, sought to persuade him to obey the age-old custom that was stamped with the approval of great pillars of learning and to spare his dead father's soul, which was still hovering over the empty sheath of its body, the mortification of seeing its issue defy the rabbinical ban. Yet the officer put his hand on the revolver strapped to his hip and threatened then and there to shoot the members of the Burial Society—parasitical whited sepulchres, as he called them, who spent their lives mining gold in the teeth of the dead—if they dared stand in his way. He then strode after the bier of his saintly father with two girl soldiers in tow.

"While the archangels Gabriel and Michael waited to welcome Reb Itchele to Paradise," Riklin mocked, "his son came to see him off with Gabriella and Michaella on each arm." The major may have been a great expert on guns, bombs, and things that went bang, yet had he known anything about the deeper mysteries of life, he would have understood that the ban, instituted two hundred years ago by Rabbi Shmuel Molcho, was aimed not at a man's earthly offspring but at the goblins and she-devils born from his nocturnal emissions, who thronged obscenely around his grave to thwart his return to his heavenly home.

"You can wipe that ignorant smile off your face," Reb Elya chided me when he saw my derisive look. If ever I studied a drop of sperm through a microscope, he said, I would be horrified to see a host of perfectly shaped little homunculi swimming vigorously about in it. He took a sip of his tea and observed that at present the most powerful microscopes had a magnification of only 18,000; yet as soon as 100,000 was reached, it would be possible to see how each little sperm-child resembled its parent exactly. What father would not gnash his teeth then at the thought of the many children of Satan he had brought into the world and hasten to perform the spiritual penances prescribed to destroy them and to restore to their divine abode the holy sparks trapped in their devilish forms, as set forth in the holy books?

"There is no greater sin than Onan's," Riklin shrilled. The prophet Isaiah was referring to its practitioners when he inveighed, "O ye who slay your children in the riverbeds," the rivers being rivers of sperm and the beds being beds of self-abuse.

My mother, who had been listening to every word from the bathroom, began to carol part of the High Holy Day service in a loud cantorial voice in order to drown Riklin out—which only, however, made Reb Elya chuckle to my father that, if she were to practice her scales every day and drink raw eggs with honey, she might develop a baritone as smooth as Goldaleh Malevski's and land a job as the *Hochkantor* of Temple Emanuel in New York.

". . . Who shall live and who shall die . . . who by fire and who by water . . ." my mother sang even louder while surveying the carp swimming back and forth in the half-filled bathtub and leaving a slimy trail of excrement in their wake. Twice a week we regularly refrained from bathing while the enamel tub on its four leonine legs was converted into an aquarium. Although I liked to feed the fish bread crumbs and wet my hands in pursuit of their slippery shapes, my father was annoyed by my mother's willingness to sacrifice even personal cleanliness on the sacred altar of fresh food. Now the carps' time was up. My mother pulled out the stopper and let the water drain from the tub while watching them flipflop against its smooth sides, then gathered them up in the folds of her apron and carried them to the kitchen, where she wrapped them in a towel and beat them with a knife butt until they stopped writhing.

She must have been out of her mind, she grieved to me while delivering the coup de grace, ever to have let my father befriend Riklin in the first place. To think that she had not only let him come and go in our house like one of the family but had actually been crazy enough to prepare special dishes of sugar-free kasha, baked apples, and saccharine-sweetened desserts for him—in place of foods that diabetics must avoid . . . for which he had thanked her by acting the ingrate and biting the hand that fed him.

"For what he did to me that Sabbath after Rosh Hashanah," my mother said, digging her fingers into the gutted belly of a fish in order to yank out the entrails, "I'll never forgive him, not even when I'm in the next world."

2.

That Sabbath Riklin had stopped off at our house on his way to hear Rabbi Sachs give his sermon in the Great Synagogue of Zichron Moshe.

As usual my mother greeted him with a smile, set the table royally in his honor, and stood by his side to wait on him. Reb Elya, his spirits buoyed by my mother's diabetic dishes and her sugarless stewed quinces, brought my parents up to date on goings-on in the world. He told them about Reb Yisra'el Bar-Zakkai, who still led the High Holy Day prayers as sweetly as he used to in the days when he was cantor of the Hurva Synagogue in the Old City, and about Velvete Tiktin, who blew the ram's horn so powerfully that Satan fled from its blasts as they winged to the Mercy Seat. Then—while downing and praising the last of the quinces, tastiest *kompot* he had ever eaten in his life—he asked whether we had heard of the death of Nochem Rubin.

Riklin stuck a finger in his mouth to adjust his false teeth and related that the shlimazel had choked to death on the first night of Rosh Hashanah while sucking the bones of his wife's gefillte fish. As was the custom in Jerusalem, the funeral took place that same night; but since it was forbidden to ride because of the holiday, the heavy corpse had to be carried on the undertakers' shoulders all the way to the cemetery in Giv'at Sha'ul, where they waited for an Arab from Beit-Safafa to dig the grave by the dying light of the oil lamps they had brought. It was early morning by the time they returned, trooping back through the deserted streets of the city and telling tall tales to keep each other awake.

As they walked up Rashi Street, past the house of a newly wed young novice in the Burial Society, a prankish mood overcame them and they decided to play a practical joke. Riklin and all but two of his colleagues hurried on to the ritual bathhouse, while the pair of undertakers knocked on the young novice's bedroom window and called, "*Boruch, Boruch, shtey oyf, a levaye,*" "Boruch, get up, there's a funeral." His young wife, the two later told their fellow mischief makers, pulled the blankets over her head while sobbing that even on the day of the New Year the dead refused to let her live and begged her husband to have pity and not leave her alone in the empty house. Boruch, however, hurriedly dressed and dutifully joined the two undertakers waiting for him in the street, where the light of the morning star brushed the sleep from his face. On their way, the two men told him that, while going to the ritual bath in the middle of the night, the Talmud teacher from the synagogue of the Wolhynian Hasidim had died of a stroke, and that Rabbi Vinograd had ruled that the funeral could not be postponed until morning, since then those attending it would miss hearing the ram's horn blown in the synagogue. The young man walked silently alongside them, preoccupied with his thoughts, and held his peace even when the two began to argue whether it was a good or bad omen for a man to die in the middle of the High Holy Days, when the divine ledger lay open and mankind passed before it to be judged.

They reached the bathhouse to find the narrow, musty room lit with a few candles, whose flames, reflected in the black water below, cast their shadows. On the ablution board in a corner, covered by a white sheet, lay the corpse of the stricken Talmud teacher. Reb Boruch washed his hands, mumbled the prescribed verses from the Song of Songs, and began to lift up the sheet—when suddenly the dead man, who was none other than Reb Elya himself, sat bolt upright and stuck out his tongue. Yet to the amazement of all present, the young novice refused to take fright. He pushed Riklin back down again, dowsed his head with water, and began washing his hair while reminding him that the dead knew perfectly well that they were not supposed to move. If the dead man, he stated, would be so kind as to stretch out his legs like any decent corpse, the proceedings might be gotten on with.

My father laughed at the young novice's courage and said that we would yet hear from him some day. My mother, however, aghast at the morticians' sense of fun, sat stunned in her seat, eating slice after slice of hard, dry honey cake.

"Stop stuffing yourself," Reb Elya scolded her, taking the cake tray away. If she gained too much weight, he warned her, she might give him and his friends a rupture when her time came. "Therefore my bowels are troubled," Riklin chanted from Jeremiah, adding that thus far a hernia was the one illness he had been spared.

My mother rose without a word from the table, the tears choking her throat, and shut herself up in the bedroom. Only after Riklin had left did her wounded feelings flood the house. Never in her life, she sobbed, had anyone wished her such things—and worse yet, at the beginning of a new year!

That was the end of my mother's romance with Riklin. She cooked no more diabetic meals for him and tried in vain to persuade my father not to let the death's-head, as she called him now, into our house again.

3.

Now, unable to leave as she always did when Riklin came to visit, my mother found herself the prisoner of her own curfew. The wail of the sirens, and the metallic blast of the loudspeakers urging the public to come demonstrate against the politicians who wanted to sell the blood of Jewish children for a few miserable German Marks, pierced the lowered blinds. Yet the commotion outside did not seem in the least to bother Riklin, who kept regaling my father with story after story, the hero of all of which was Death.

"That's enough funerals for you for one day," my mother told me, handing me a bowl of silvery air bladders taken from the fish. While she lay down to nap, she advised, I could make balloons out of them in the kitchen and then do my homework—or anything else that kept me away from Riklin's ghost stories.

Yet like Leontius the son of Agleion, whose curiosity upon seeing the corpses of men put to death got the better of his disgust, so that he ran to them crying out, "Behold your desire, O my poor eyes," I could not tear myself away from Reb Elya's soliloquy.

"It was like an atomic stink bomb," he was saying. Putting two fingers to his nose, he told my father how, when the temporary war graves in the neighborhood of Sheikh Badr were opened for reburial, white maggots as big as a man's thumb crawled out of the bubbling, brown batter that once had been human bellies and over the shoes and pants cuffs of the undertakers.

"Man cometh from dust and returneth to dust," Reb Elya crooned knowingly, continuing the same High Holy Day prayer that my mother had begun. Between dust and dust, he observed, human beings amused themselves with food and drink; yet long ago, when

God's face was not yet hidden and all was clear and unclouded as burnished glass between sun and shade, not only did righteous men receive their just deserts in the world of truth, they were rewarded in this earthly existence too with bodies uncorruptible by worms such as those whose horrid dance he had seen in the ghastly, seething cauldron of guts spewed up from the netherworld of Sheikh Badr.

A glitter of lightning shot through the closed slats, illuminating the room, and my father staring hypnotically in its blinding flash at his guest. Reb Elya waited for the ensuing clap of thunder to fade away and avowed that he himself could vouch for as much. The summer after he was married, he related, he and his wife, might she rest in peace, vacationed in Hebron, where they went to enjoy the cool air and the city's famous late-summer grapes. One day, as they were sitting down to lunch at Shneirson's Inn, a young Sephardi from the Sdei Hemed Yeshiva burst into the dining room and announced in a shaken voice that he had just come from the cemetery, where he was shocked to discover that the grave of his late master, Rabbi Haim Hizkiyahu Medini, had been opened. The whole town, Riklin too, rushed to see the vile deed. The grave, whose tombstones were displaced, had indeed been dug up, and the saintly rabbi's body had been moved, as indicated by the bent position of its knees. Yet the miscreants had abandoned their monstrous crime in the middle, leaving behind, in its still-spotless white shrouds, the one-and-a-half-year-old corpse, whose condition, the crowd could now see, was as pristine as on the day of its burial. An investigation carried out by the town notables revealed that some local Arabs, considering the rabbi with the knee-length beard to have been a holy man, had sought to reinter him in the courtyard of their mosque, only to flee midway through their task, frightened by the sight of his undecayed body.

"Don't make a comedy out of everything people tell you," Reb Elya rebuked me. If I didn't believe him, he said, I could find the same story, written in plain letters, in the volume, *A Treasury of Israel.* "You're raising a little heretic," he warned Father.

Years later, coming across an article on Rabbi Medini in the old Encyclopedia Judaica, I found in it Riklin's story of the attempted grave robbing. No mention was made there, however, of the miraculous preservation of the rabbi's corpse.

An early darkness descended on the shuttered house. My mother had fallen into a deep sleep, while the two men went on sitting in the living room without turning on the lights. Reb Elya's voice, lit by the red flame of the kerosene heater that burned between the table and the couch, seemed to plumb the depths as he spoke.

4.

At seven p.m. a knock on the door disturbed the quiet apartment. My mother awoke in a fright and whispered at the top of her voice not to let anyone in. When the intruder identified himself as Rachlevski, however, she went to turn on the light and unbolt the door.

Wet and bare-headed, his lips swollen and bleeding, our neighbor stumbled in as though fresh from a war. "Why did you go near the Knesset today?" my mother cried. "You could have been killed like a mad dog!" Her eyes, still blinking in the sudden light, stared at Rachlevski's nude, silver-cropped head, which had never been seen by us unhatted before. As soon as she could see, she pulled up a chair for him and surveyed him thoroughly from his torn coat buttons to the swollen bruise on his forehead, her glance taking in his ripped collar, his bloodshot eyes, and the clotted blood on his mustache and chin. She would not, she announced, allow him to go home before she had put cold compresses on the horn growing out of his forehead, cleaned off the blood, and dried his coat by the stove. While rummaging in the medicine cabinet in the bathroom, she ordered me to bring him one of my father's hats, so that he should not have to look like the bare-skulled Ukrainian pilgrims to Jerusalem who, in the days before the October Revolution, used to assemble on Christmas eves in front of the Russian cathedral.

"The troubled heart feels better when it speaks," my father quoted, pouring his two guests some brandy. The old undertaker, cheated out of being the center of attention, took his drink with a wounded air and sat sipping it with a show of indifference to the newcomer.

My mother placed a bowl of water on the table, added alcohol, soaked an old diaper in the mixture, and placed it on our neighbor's brow. Rachlevski leaned back in the easy chair, shut his eyes, and told us that he had missed by a hair being clubbed to smithereens, and then spending the night on the cold cement floor of the police lockup.

“You’re starting from the middle again,” scolded my mother, who only liked stories that had beginnings and ends. Without opening his eyes, Rachlevski began again, relating how he had gone for afternoon tea to the Spetanskis’, as was his custom every Monday since 1936, the year that he and they had disembarked together in Haifa from the ship that brought them from Odessa. Near the Nesher taxi stand, the street was blocked by rolls of barbed wire. A phalanx of policemen, whose job it was to guard the Knesset building, was staring tensely down Ben-Yehuda Street. At the lower end of the street, in Zion Square, a large crowd was listening to hoarse shrieks crackling from loudspeakers and answering them with its own surflike boom. A helmeted policeman with a metal shield pointed with his club to some leaflets flapping against the electric wires overhead and advised Rachlevski to move on before the frenzied crowd arrived and blood flowed like water. He continued along the top of Ben-Yehuda Street, passed the Bezalel Art School, and turned up Bet-Hama’alot Street, where his friends—who possessed, he claimed, the finest Tula samovar in Jerusalem—had their residence.

When evening came, Rabelevski rose to go despite Mrs. Spetanski’s insistence that he remain with them until the streets were calm. He was walking slowly through the drizzling rain, breathing the cold, almost European air deep into his lungs as he had done as a youth in Kiev, when suddenly, at the corner of Shmuel Hanagid and Ben-Yehuda Streets, a wave of demonstrators hidden behind the Kupat Holim building materialized out of the fog, throwing stones, smashing store windows, overturning cars, and sweeping everyone, Rachlevski too, before them on their way to the Knesset, which they sought to storm from the rear.

At the entrance to Be’eri Street they were ambushed by a fire engine, which blasted them with a powerful jet of water. A few of the mob, however, succeeded in clambering up to the driver’s cabin and pummeling the policeman at the wheel until he lost control of the vehicle, which skidded onto the sidewalk and crashed into a wall.

“Not one German cent / Down with the government,” chanted the mob as it sped down Be’eri Street while casting stones at the windows of the Knesset. Its vanguard had already managed to cross King George Street, overturning a Knesset member’s car parked in front of Robert’s Beauty Parlor on the corner, when policemen stationed on the roofs overhead let loose with a volley of smoke grenades, one of which landed in a puddle of gas spreading from the overturned car. In no time the whole street was lit by a red, hellish glare as far as the Eden Hotel.

He himself, Rachevski told us, was trapped between the policemen and the demonstrators like the dove in the Talmudic parable who, fleeing from the hawk, finds itself in the cleft of a rock facing a nesting snake. If he continued to advance, said our neighbor, there was the hissing snake, while if he attempted to turn back, there was the hawk. What did he do? He screeched and flapped his wings like the dove in the story, hoping that the owner of the dovecote would come to the rescue.

"The dovekeeper didn't come," Rachlevski smiled with swollen lips, adjusting the compress on his forehead. "He sent someone else in his place." He remembered a squad of policemen swooping down on him, and the next thing he knew he was lying on the rubbish-strewn, studded floor of a paddywagon. Someone next to him, a Polish Jew, to judge by the accent, was cursing Ben-Gurion—that little, troublemaking, left-wing nothing from Plonsk who was willing to shake the hand of Adenauer, might he roast in hell, to keep his nationalized businesses from going broke—and assuring his bludgeoned fellow prisoners that in Musrara and Bet-Yisra'el there were fresh reserves waiting to be thrown into the fray who would storm the Knesset that night and cut the traitors' filthy hands off. Every now and then the iron door opened and a new demonstrator was flung inside like a sack of potatoes. As soon as the wagon was full, it set out for the Russian Compound, escorted by the deafening wail of the police motorcycles.

The arrested men were unloaded at police headquarters under heavy guard and ushered into the detention room, where a group of officers checked them off against prepared lists of names. Luckily for Rachlevski, he was recognized by Sergeant Fishler, a regular customer in his store, who pointed him out to one of the patrolmen trailing behind the interrogators and ordered him brought into his office. As soon as the two men were alone, Fishler chided him gently, gave him some grapefruit juice and hardtack from his battle rations, and sent him home in a van. When Rachlevski saw himself in the rearview mirror, however, he decided first to recuperate with us, so that his wife should not have a stroke when she saw him.

We listened in shocked silence to our neighbor's story, at the end of which my father advised him to say a prayer of thanksgiving over the Torah in the synagogue. Rachlevski, though, replied that to someone like himself, who had been through the Petlura pogroms, a Jewish policeman's billy club felt like a caress. What really had frightened him, he said, was the demonstrators' violent attempt to force their minority views on the legislature. He sat up, removed the compress, and added that God only knew whether today, in the rock- and glass-strewn plaza of the Knesset, the fate of Israeli democracy had not been sealed.

Rachlevski tried on my father's hat, looked at himself in the mirror, and remarked that in fact Ben-Gurion was probaby right, since the reparations money would allow Jewish manufacturers to import modern machinery from Germany, Jewish farmers to plow with tractors instead of mules, Jewish children to eat fresh butter on their bread instead of the moldy stuff imported from Australia in barrels, and Jewish mothers to be spared the daily ordeal of force-feeding their babies cod-liver oil.

Riklin, who had not said a word since his rival's knock on the door, now stirred and declared that the only thing that should be imported from the unholy soil of Germany was the ashes of the Jewish martyrs who had died there.

"Remember Amalek!" shouted the elderly mortician. A jar of Jewish ashes, he avowed, should be interred in every public square in Israel, the names of the streets leading up to which should be changed to those of the perished Jewish communities of Europe.

"We have enough graveyards here already," Rachlevski interrupted. If he were Ben-Gurion, he said, not only would he forbid reburying Jabotinsky in Israel, as the right-wing parties were clamoring to do, he would refuse to admit the body of any dead Jew. "We need live Jews, not bones," said our neighbor, running a hand over his coat drying by the stove.

"And where do you suggest that we hold public prayers for the victims of the Holocaust?" Reb Elya challenged as though his livelihood were at stake. "By the soapdish in the bathtub?"

My mother, who as usual was the first to recover on such occasions, began to pelt Riklin with the maps of the Mount of Olives and the issues of "The Lawgiver's Plot." Shouting curses and abuse, she ordered the Nazi *merder* to leave her house at once and never to return again.

5.

By the time Ahuva Haris dropped in that evening the house had been purged of Riklin's sepulchral literature, which my father bundled into a sugar sack under my mother's watchful eyes and took down to the storeroom. There it would be at a safe remove until picked up by someone from the Burial Society.

My mother sat in her usual place, cross-patching a woolen sock stretched over a glass and waiting to hear the eight-thirty news, while my father, who went to bed every night with the roosters, as she put it, was already in the Land of Nod.

Ahuva had celebrated the news of Riklin's ouster with proud, conquistadorial reserve. Now she sat enjoying her triumph, her feet proprietarily propped upon the chair in which Reb Elya had liked to sit while she told Mother of the latest exploits of her Binyamin, who had dozed off again today while his milk-and-garlic was on the burner, causing the whole house to reek like a tannery.

The six beeps that signaled the news on the radio put an end to our guest's chatter. My mother listened carefully to the review of the day's events, murmuring that Jerusalem had already been destroyed once before because of needless brotherly strife. Yet when the newscaster quoted Knesset member Lavon as likening the rioting at the Knesset to an assault on the Temple itself, Ahuva could control herself no longer. Was it not bad enough, she exclaimed, that the Zionists, who knew and feared nothing in their shamelessly bareheaded skulls, were planning to spend Jewish blood money from Germany on profaning the Sabbath, opening more pork shops like the one that already disgraced the corner opposite their "Temple," and building brothels in which to keep their Midianite women, without their having to lay their hands, too, on the most sacred symbols of the Jewish people—symbols that had already been trampled in the dust by them in the days of Teddy Herzl and his Christianizing cronies in Basel? "Beware of Germans bearing gifts," Ahuva warned, turning down the radio.

The newscaster finished the headline stories and went on to the case of police officers Trifuss and Shvartzbard, who were suspected of taking bribes, and to the trial of the Englishman Robert Harson, who was accused of killing the Indian girl Majee Lassaree in Eilat. The two women pricked up their ears. The sensational murder perturbed them, and Ahuva declared that in this age of anything goes a respectable girl could trust no man, not even if he lay ten feet underground.

The crime news ended with a last-minute bulletin. Early that afternoon, it was reported, the augmented security forces patrolling the city had taken into custody a suspicious figure seen loitering at the top of Jaffa Road, in the vicinity of Barclay's Bank. A body search turned up a hidden firearm, and the suspect, Mordecai Leder, admitted under vigorous questioning that he had planned to hold up the bank. The police, said the announcer, were revealing nothing about the apprehended man's motives, but Israel Radio's crime reporter had it on good authority that startling disclosures, which would compel the guardians of the nation's democracy to take drastic measures in its defense, could be expected on the heels of the arrest. Within forty-eight hours, the newscaster concluded, shedding no further light on the enigma, the suspect would be arraigned in Jerusalem municipal court.

"Leder behind bars?"

"Leder in the clink?"

Mother and Ahuva stared at each other, uncertain whether they really had heard it or had dreamed it together in a single wishful trance.

"Why don't you ask your brother?" Ahuva proposed. Uncle Tsodek, who worked in the court building, had connections among the judges and policemen that could supply him with more details. My mother, however, who had been feuding with her brother ever since the death of my grandmother, replied that the morning papers, which were due to arrive at the grocery in a few hours, would enlighten us more than my uncle possibly could.

When she returned later that night from walking her friend partway home, she paused in the doorway and mused as though to herself that never could she have imagined that morning that the two men who boded ruin for our household would both disappear like a passing cloud before the day was out. She raised her eyes to the heavens, which were low with swollen rain clouds, and closed the front door behind her.

Chapter Eleven

1.

Two days later, forty-eight hours after Leder's arrest, I slipped away unnoticed from the packs of children streaming toward school and headed for the Russian Compound to see what would happen in court to the commander of the Nutrition Army.

In school all were busy with final preparations for our annual assembly in honor of Bialik's birthday. The fact was, of course, that our national poet had been born a day earlier, on the fast day of the Tenth of Tevet, but like all state religious schools we celebrated the event a day later because of the fast.

And so each year, as we stood in afternoon prayer, the martial strains of Bialik's "May Our Brothers' Hands Be Strengthened," sung by the "Red Army Chorus," as our teacher Miss Schlank called the student choir of the secular school across the street, whose windows faced our own, mingled with the lamentations of the fast day, as did the keening of our Talmud teacher Rabbi Vinshel, who tearfully petitioned "Answer us, Lord, O answer us on this day of our mortification, for we are in great distress" from his place beneath the folding cardboard prayer sign that hung on the east wall of the classroom. "Woe to the ears that must hear all this!" declared our principal annually when he came to shut the windows of our room. Surely a good Jew like Haim Nachman Bialik must be turning in his grave to see his poems used to desecrate a day set aside by the prophets of Israel to mourn the commencement of the Babylonian siege that spelled the destruction of Jerusalem.

Today, then, in our school auditorium—which once, toward the end of the last century, had served as the great guest hall of a wealthy Arab Christian tobacco trader, who drank coffee there with his visitors while his wives, concubines, and small children peered through the doorways of the surrounding chambers that were later turned into classrooms—the festive assembly would take place. At the front end of the hall, before a heavy iron portal that was always shut, a framed portrait of the poet, festooned with pine and cypress branches, would stand on a table spread with the Israeli flag, while beside it, in an empty sour-cream container, would be placed a bouquet of pale cyclamens freshly picked by our arts-and-crafts teacher on her way to school. In a semicircle around this altar, some opened and some closed, would be displayed the poet's books: his verses, his children's songs, his stories and essays, his two-volume anthology of Jewish legends, his translations of *Don Quixote* and *Wilhelm Tell*—all brought for the occasion from the locked bookcase in our principal's office.

The Bialik regarding us from the garlanded portrait wore a peaked cap above a broad, sleek-jowled face that could easily have belonged to a well-to-do grain merchant not averse to the pleasures of life. A more studious, hatless Bialik, seated with his co-anthologist Ravnitzky at a round living-room table covered with a fading cloth, looked out at us from the flyleaf of *The Book of Legends*. The two men were reading, on their heads black skullcaps inked in by our principal, who refused to have us believe that such eminences might be perusing holy books with their heads bare. Indeed, the Bialik who was taught to us in our childhood, as Haim Rachlevski observed to me years later, was still the youthful Talmud student from the Yeshiva of Volozhin who wore his black frock coat and his pious sidelocks long.

Each year the assembly began with Ruti Tsvebner playing Bialik's "I Have a Garden" on her flute. Next came Ya'el Solomon's moment of glory to rise and recite "Wouldst Thou But Know the Fount." While from the shadows of yesteryear she evoked the cobwebbed old study hall, in which "In some dim corner or by an old wood stove / A few last uncut human stalks still stand, Bare wraiths of what once was," the milky white globe of light hanging from the ceiling above her showered myriads of glittering kisses upon her red hair and spangled it with gold. As soon as Ya'el stepped down Ruti Tsvebner stood up again to the right of our national poet and piped "'Twixt the Tigris and Euphrates," after which our principal rose from his place among the troublemakers in the back, who might, if not carefully watched, break out at any moment into a rousing rendition of "Happy birthday, dear Bialik, / Happy birthday to you."

Globules of sweat formed beneath his armpits and trickled down his chest while he delivered his lengthy address on "Bialik and the Problems of Today" and then read aloud, through the thin film of tears hazing over his glasses, the text of "My Dear Departed Mother."

The elder statesman of our teachers, Rabbi Doktor Aharon Pflaum, annually concluded the assembly with reminiscences of Bad Gastein, the German spa where, in 1933, a year before the poet's death, he and Bialik spent long weeks together from the Sabbath after the Ninth of Av to the eve of the Jewish New Year. Year in and year out, anxiously humming the tune for us lest we forget it, priceless heritage that it was, and fail to pass it on to coming generations, Rabbi Pflaum described to us how Bialik, might his righteous memory be blessed, had bade farewell to the Sabbath queen at the Saturday night table with a melodic version of "The Lord Spoke to Jacob" learned as a boy in his grandfather's home in Zhitomir. When the meal was over the poet joined in saying the grace that he, Rabbi Pflaum, had the honor to lead, and, when they rose from the table, Reb Haim Nachman took our teacher's hand—which, well-manicured though stiff with age, the old man now held up for us to see—and said to him, "Well blessed, sir, well blessed."

"Bialik's birth-day-after party," as Miss Schlank called it, repeated itself so exactly year by year that one might almost have thought that time had ceased to flow, as it is generally assumed to do, and had come to an absolute standstill.

This year I would miss it, though I never doubted for a moment that no one would miss me.

2.

Near the Patt Café I left my friends trotting down Rabbi Kook Street on their way to school, turned left past the house of our family physician, Dr. Sigmund Muntner, who took my father's blood pressure while chatting with him about the medical writings of Maimonides, and passed the neglected show window of the stationary store on Prophets Street, littered with old magazines, out-of-fashion hairpins and canvas fabric for stitching home tapestries, where I sometimes stopped to stare at the colorful pairs of decorative stickers—angels with touching wings, young girls linked together like Siamese twins, and white-bearded dwarves standing head to head—that were pasted in sheets on the glass pane.

Near this store (which later became the studio of "the Falafel King" Mr. Elnatan, who would, when moved by the spirit, leave his snack stand at the end of Agrippas Street and come here to paint the apocalyptic visions that, propped by him against stone walls of the houses and sold for a song on the sidewalks, are now fought over by museums) I crossed to the other side of Prophets Street and found myself facing the Zion Missionary Bookstore on Monoboz Street.

This mysterious establishment with its glass-paneled doors that were always shut and made a hidden bell ring when opened; its ascetic-looking manager in a white polo shirt who sat in the back by the bluish-pink light of a table lamp reading a book from which he never looked up; and its exotic-sounding street name (which in those days, ignorant of the story Queen Helena of Adiabene, her son Monboz, and their love for the Jewish people, I assumed must belong to the occult history of the Crusades) was like a foretaste to me of the Russian Compound itself.

At this hour of the morning the compound was humming with officials going to work, barred police vans bringing prisoners to trial, and ordinary drifters drawn to the tumult of power. And yet on the fringes of all this activity, in untended courtyards hidden by ivy and jasmine vines that twined over rusting fences, the old Russian Orthodox *Nova Yeruselyma* continued to live its secret life. Little Russian babushkas moved slowly through the high weeds, laundering tattered clothing and hanging it out to dry on lines limply strung between rank ailanthus trees. Sometimes a heavy door with iron stripping opened to reveal a yellowish parlor with a peeling icon painted on the keystone of a second, inner door, from the invisible rooms beyond which came the smell of sour cabbage and bread.

Families of prisoners were gathered by the rear entrance of the court building, hoping to exchange a few words with the accused as they were transferred by armed guards from the vans into the building. I, however, made straight for the main entrance where the lawyers freely came and went, their books beneath one arm and their black robes draped over the other, while their stiletto-heeled clerks in pleated black skirts hurried to keep up with them.

"To Tsodek in the archives," I told the drowsy guard in his cubicle and climbed the broad stairs to the second story, pausing for a moment to admire the tall stained-glass windows before passing down a vaulted corridor with a slippery, stone-tiled floor. On my left were the doors of the courtrooms and judges' offices, while on my right, beyond the low casements at the windows' bottoms, an inner courtyard could be seen in which discarded old desks and chairs and broken oil stoves had been left to rot among abandoned lemon trees.

Uncle Tsodek sat in a corner between two female file clerks, his shirt-sleeves protected from ink stains by blue cotton sleevelets, deep in a pile of files.

"What on earth brings you here?" he asked in surprise when he saw me. In a loud voice meant for the file clerks he declared that it was his fate to be exposed to the seamy side of life, but that I, who was born with a silver spoon in my mouth and waited on hand and foot since I was an infant, might be expected to set foot in a place like this only as an advocate or judge. And indeed had not the Orthodox Community of Jerusalem already produced such distinguished jurists as Frumkin, Heshin, and Bar-Zakkai? Lowering his voice to a whisper, he asked whether, God forbid, I had gotten into trouble with the law and needed advice or assistance. "You know I won't breathe a word of it to your mother," he hastened to reassure me. Did I know that at the last memorial gathering at my grandmother's grave she hadn't even said hello to him?

He breathed a sigh of relief when I explained why I had come, leafed through some mimeographed papers that were fastened by a nail to the side of the door, and informed me that Leder's arraignment would take place in half an hour in Courtroom 8.

"The son takes after his maternal uncle," Uncle Tsodek quoted from the Talmud as we descended the "staff only" stairs. When he died, he confided, he planned to leave me his library, including those books of my grandfather's that he and my mother had been feuding about, it being already clear that I would grow up to be like him an incurable burrower in the local history of Jerusalem. He opened the door of the courtroom for me, patted my shoulder, and instructed me to return when the proceedings were over so that he could tell me things no ear had yet heard about the ancestry of the little alms collector for the School for the Blind.

3·

Only a few spectators were present in the long, narrow courtroom, which like all the ground-floor rooms had originally been used as storage space by the Russian pilgrims quartered above. All eyes were fixed on the small door at one end of the chamber from which the judge would enter to mount the dais. Already in the dock was an unshaven young man, who had been apprehended—so I heard a burly policeman inform his mournful-looking colleague sitting next to me—while catwalking on the drainpipe of Dr. Treu's residence on Prophets Street. When asked by the patrolmen who seized him what he was doing on the orthopedist's walls in the middle of the night, he replied that he had broken his arm and wanted the doctor to set it.

"In half an hour or less you'll be feeling as dizzy as in a New York subway," Uncle Tsodek had warned me as we walked down the corridor—and indeed, no sooner did the judge appear than the courtyard seemed to turn into a kind of rapid transit station. Suspects came and went, each accompanied by his guards, his lawyers with their clerks, and his family, which was generally composed of an old mother tearing her red, hennaed hair and several siblings cursing the police into their turned-up shirt collars for having picked on their innocent kid brother, whose only crime was to have fallen in with bad friends.

At nine-thirty Leder was led in.

He was flanked by policemen and his feet were in chains. Head bare, cheeks and chin streaked with gray stubble, he looked blankly at the judge and the courtroom. He was missing his glasses, which I had never seen him without, and had I passed him in the street I might not have recognized him. He, at any rate, failed to notice me.

The counsel for the police, a staff sergeant with a face as wrinkled as a citron in winter, declared that Mordecai Leder had been arrested under suspicious circumstances, in possession of a 38-caliber Webley revolver, in the vicinity of Barclay's Bank. The police had grounds to believe that he had intended to take advantage of the disorder created by the antireparations demonstrations in order to rob the bank for the purpose of financing the activities of a subversive organization. "The police are convinced," continued the sergeant, waving a sheet of paper at Leder, "that they have uncovered the existence of an illegal body like the National Front or the Zealots' Alliance, and that the suspect's release on bail at this time would imperil their chances of rounding up the remaining ring members and locating the arms caches that have undoubtedly been hidden somewhere in the capital."

The judge, who had been remanding burglars and small-time thieves in custody all morning, peered curiously over his glasses at the suspect—wondering, it appeared, whether this semblance of a grade-school teacher or office drudge could really be a political fanatic in disguise.

Leder's lawyer, sensing as much, began by stating that the court could see for itself that his client was not made of revolutionary stuff. Ever since the Zealots' Alliance was uncovered, he continued, the Jerusalem police force had hysterically suspected everyone in the old Orthodox community of belonging to some underground plot. He therefore requested the court to release his client on bail, or, failing that, to instruct the police to return his glasses, without which he was as blind as a bat.

At this juncture, the police counsel placed a folded note before the judge. He was, he confided, taking the liberty of providing the bench with top-secret evidence, confident that this would convince it to prolong the suspect's arrest. The judge studied the paper, on which the wrinkled counsel had hurriedly scrawled a few words, regarded Leder once more, and remarked to the lawyer in a mild tone of voice that, since the political history of the last century was checkered with revolutionary types whose external appearance belied their capacity for destruction, he was remanding Leder in custody for ten more days.

Leder's police guard—who all this time had been staring through the window, while twirling a set of handcuffs on his finger, at the cars and pedestrians moving on the visible bit of paved street outside—stiffened and winked to his colleague. At the bailiff's summons he rose to escort the suspect back to his cell, nearly pushing him out of the court. I hurried after them. Once in the corridor, the policeman slipped the cuffs back on Leder's hands and pointed him toward the exit. Leder was still exchanging disjointed phrases with his lawyer when he saw me and began to shout:

"Long live Lynkeania! Long live the Nutrition Army!"

Two plainclothes policemen pounced on him, gagged him with a scarf, and hustled him through the emergency exit.

4.

"Did you see enough, my good man?" grinned Uncle Tsodek when I returned to the archives. He looked at me and remarked that, now that it was clear from my frightened eyes that crime did not pay, the time had come to revive me with food and drink in the cafeteria. This small room by the stairway, the lower half of whose walls was painted gray up to a line exceeding human height, buzzed with a mixed crowd of lawyers, officials, and families of defendants whose conversation was all but drowned by the sputter of gas burners beneath giant kettles and the clink of dishes set down on counters and tabletops.

Uncle Tsodek stood in line and tried to catch the eye of the counterman, while I did as I was told and secured places for us at a small marble table in the corner, which was already occupied by the two file clerks I had seen before in the archives.

"The minute the movie began," the pudgier of the two was saying, neatly dissecting a honey bun with her fingernails, "Tsiyyon put his hand on my knee."

"He's disgusting, that Tsiyyon, just like his brother Ya'akov," replied her friend, whose oily hair was full of dandruff, while guzzling soda through a straw. "I swear to God, I'da given him such a pinch . . ."

"You don't know how I cried in the end," the pudgy clerk said, changing the intimate subject. "You tell me, Carmela, how could that filthy what's-his-name have left a wife as sweet as sugar . . ."

"Rhett Butler."

"Yeah, Rhett Butler. What a name! How could he have left her without even looking back?"

The two clerks continued to discuss the closing scene of *Gone With the Wind*, which was playing that week in Jerusalem, until the pudgy one, casting herself as Scarlett O'Hara staring from the front steps of her Southern mansion at her cad of a disappearing husband, leaped up and cried:

"Tomorrow is another day!"

"Cut it out, Levana, you're embarrassing me," Carmela whispered, noticing the mocking stares that two young lawyers were directing at them. "Sit down already."

Levana blushed and sat down quickly, while Carmela, who boasted of having seen the film twice, once with Moshe's sister Riki and once with Zehava Hayyun from the telegraph desk at the post office, announced that, though she hated Vivian Leigh, she had a crush on Clark Gable. "I'm crazy about him," she said dreamily. "What a man." She was still listing the irresistible features of the Hollywood heartbreaker—the smile beneath his sexy mustache, the dimple in his cheek, his wink made especially for her, Carmela from the archives—when Uncle Tsodek appeared with two plates of *burekas* and *haminados* and informed me that the coffee would be ready soon.

"Is this cutey-pie yours, Tsadok?" Carmela asked, patting my cheek and smoothing my unruly hair. Her fingers smelled of honey mixed with the intoxicating odor of Korrekt, the liquid eraser used for correcting stencils.

"This is my nephew," said Uncle Tsodek, introducing me to Levana and Carmela.

Tsodek knocked the *haminados* together, and their brown shells, boiled all night with onions, cracked open.

"Ermosa sure made some nice-looking eggs today," Levana said. Did we want to see, she asked, how her mother used to slice eggs? She yanked a hair from her head and, holding it between her two hands, sliced the peeled egg right down the middle.

"Neat," said Uncle Tsodek in the parlance of his two file clerks. "Now that's what I really call hairsplitting." It was, he went on, his second lesson that morning in what could be done with an egg, for while I was waiting for Leder in Courtroom 8, the serious trial buffs were gathered in Courtroom 7 for the arraignment of Dr. Caporella, the Italian physician accused of the attempted murder of an elderly patient in an old-age home. It had all begun last Yom Kippur when Caporella, as was his custom every year, paid a call on Reb Leibish Vechsler, the renowned former rabbi of Volkenik who now lived in Jerusalem.

"You and your Ashkenazim," Carmela mocked. "Every old fool of yours is a famous rabbi."

“And every famous rabbi of yours is an old fool,” retorted Uncle Tsodek. He ignored his file clerk’s stammered protests and continued that, since Reb Leibish’s age made it hard for him to fast, and Jewish law did not forbid non-oral nourishment on Yom Kippur, the

old rabbi had had the clever idea of paying Dr. Caporella to feed him a soft-boiled egg through the back door, an arrangement that became permanent with the years. This year, however, when the doctor came as usual on the morning after the fast to collect his fee, the patient refused to pay up and complained that, for the money being asked of him, he could have bought a whole crate of eggs. Dr. Caporella left Reb Leibish’s room in a fury, and some old folk seated on the terrace, where they were warming themselves in the September sun, heard him declare that he would get his revenge someday. Yesterday, on the fast of the Tenth of Tevet, when Vechsler summoned Caporella again, the day came. This time, Uncle Tsodek reported, the Italian used a hard-boiled egg. It took all the skill of the doctors in Sha’arei Hesed Hospital to extract it from the old man, who kept screaming that he was going to burst.

“I think I may have to puke,” choked Carmela. Levana, her face as green as her sweater, covered her mouth with one hand and dragged her friend from the table in the direction of the nearby lavatory.

“Alone at last,” Uncle Tsodek sighed with relief. He transferred the half-empty soda bottles left by his clerks to the next table and asked how two silly immigrant girls from Mesopotamia could possibly understand the labyrinth of Jerusalem life. And signaling Ermosa for the coffee, he declared that anyone with an interest in human behavior must make genealogy his first order of concern.

“Remember the days of old, consider the years of many generations,” Uncle Tsodek chanted, repeating Moses’ parting lines in the Bible, and asked me what I knew of Leder’s lineage.

5.

Uncle Tsodek was the uncrowned genealogist of the old Orthodox community of Jerusalem, the successor to Pinchas Greivsky and Nachum Dov Freimann. Yet unlike the latter, who, realizing that there is no better preservative than printer’s lead, took care to record and publish what they knew in journals and books, Uncle Tsodek, as my mother once said of him, wrote his vast learning on ice. And indeed, all his encyclopedic knowledge of the families of Jerusalem from the arrival early in the last century of the first ascetic disciples of the Gaon Elijah of Vilna early in the last century until the anarchic mingling of these proud old Lithuanian houses with the Russian hoi polloi who came a hundred years later—a knowledge freely dispensed to the kibitzers who gathered around him in the vaulted hallways of the Great Synagogue of Zichron Moshe—went with him to the grave.

A tiny fraction of what the man knew was jotted down by him over the years in the margins of his books. His enormous library, the original nucleus of which belonged to my grandfather, included many Jerusalem incunabula, such as the rare polemical tracts, "Truth and Justice" and "The Tears of the Oppressed," exchanged between Rabbi Shmuel Salant and his circle, on the one hand, and Rabbi Shmuel Binyamin Hacohen of Radishkov and his circle, on the other, in the course of the fierce and inextinguishable dispute that flared up between them over the purchase of a building plot for the Etz Haim Yeshiva. In Uncle Tsodek's possession, too, was the only known extant copy of "The Joy of Zion," the satirical broadside written against the suspected freethinker Rabbi Menachem Mendel Yerushalaymski—a poem that no other scholar, not even the omniscient A. R. Malachi or the indefatigable Shoshana Halevi, had ever set eyes on. And yet no sooner had my uncle's wife returned from the unveiling thirty days after his funeral than she ordered the barebellied Georgian porter Levi Trayger to rid her house of all her husband's "smelly papers," which were, she complained, only gathering dust and nourishing roaches and mice.

My mother actually cried with anger when she found out about this. Her worthless nothing of a sister-in-law, she raged, had paid my uncle in the exact same coin that my grandfather, my father's father, had been paid in by his Transylvanian widow, who threw out his writings on true biblical blue. What had her poor father done that his books, because of which a wall of enmity had risen between her and her brother, God rest his soul, should be thrown out like trash?

Thus, Uncle Tsodek's promise that I would inherit his library came to nothing. Not until years later, while browsing one day in

Sheinberger's bookstore opposite Sar-Shalom Daitsh's pharmacy on Me'ah She'arim Street, did I manage to lay hands on a few of his books.

Besides these several volumes that came my way by accident, my uncle's surviving library included some two dozen family trees that were scattered among various relatives. Whenever one of his male cousins or nephews reached Bar Mitzvah age, it was Uncle Tsodek's custom to issue him a certificate that contained a detailed genealogy going back as far as the two great Lurias, Rabbi Solomon and Rabbi Isaac, from whom we claimed descent. These books were in the form of small folders typed by my uncle on his secretaries' machine in the archives, bound by him in blue oaktag, and illustrated with a drawing of a many-branched tree on whose trunk were wound leather phylactery straps like the coils of the serpent that guarded the Tree of Knowledge. Above it, with the jots and tittles of a Torah scribe, Uncle Tsodek wrote in an elegant print the lines from the talmudic fable, "Tree, tree, with what shall I bless you? May your seedlings resemble yourself."

A second, larger family tree, painted in bright gouaches on a piece of plywood taken from an imported tea crate, was left by Uncle Tsodek, too. For years it hung in the sukkah of my cousin Shalom, until one year the winter rains came early and a sudden downpour washed it and its boughs away. Both my uncle's erudition and his artistry reached their consummation in this work. The tree itself was thick and gnarled with deep-reaching roots and nodules, on each of which was written the name of a distant progenitor. What made it special, though, was the beauty of its illustrations. The roots going down to Rabbi Solomon Luria, the author of the commentary "Solomon's Sea," were set in a copper basin resting on twelve oxen like the molten sea in King Solomon's Temple; those descending to Rabbi Isaac Luria, the great lion of the Kabbalah, ended in the raised tail of a king of beasts; and those tracing our family back to Rabbi Yisra'el of Shklov, the author of "The Corner of the Table," the distinguished supplement to Rabbi Joseph Caro's monumental "Table of the Law," grew out of the wonderfully crafted leg of a table set with scholarly books.

Now, too, as he sat narrating the history of the Leders in the court cafeteria, Uncle Tsodek resorted to graphic allegory as a way of explaining disembodied and difficult matters that had been rendered even more nebulous by the mists of the past.

6.

"But the flesh of the bull, and its skin, and its dung . . ." murmured Uncle Tsodek from the laws of priestly sacrifice while sketching in my Bible notebook the hide of an animal that resembled the blue and yellow drawings in the windows of the wholesale leather stores, humming in the late morning hours with shoemakers and pursemakers in Nahalat Shiv'ah. A smell of hard leather and pleasantly soft bolts of kid seemed to fill the cafeteria, in which I sat watching my uncle's quick pen strokes slice the hide into sections like a cutting knife. He wrote a different name in each of its four corners and said, punning on the Yiddish for "leather," that if I wanted to know the story of Leder I had better listen carefully and not ask too many foolish questions.

"I suppose you've heard of Rabbi Yosef Zondel Salant, the disciple of Rabbi Haim of Volozhin and Rabbi Akiva Eiger," my uncle began his chronicle. One distant day, four generations ago—that is, some time in the late 1850s, according to the Christian calendar—a young orphaned lad from Lithuania arrived in Jerusalem with a letter of recommendation to Rabbi Yosef Zondel. The orphan, it was said, had been sent to Rabbi Yosef by his student, Rabbi Yisra'el Salanter, the founder of the pietistic Musar movement. In his letter Rabbi Yisra'el wrote that Meir'l Leder's late father had been an outstanding pupil in his yeshiva in Kovno, but that after his death the orphan's uncle, his mother's brother, one of the town's most brazen freethinkers, had sought to make himself the young man's guardian and lead him down the primrose path. It was secretly decided, therefore, to smuggle him off to Jerusalem, where Meir'l grew up in Rabbi Yosef Zondel's home—which was in fact nothing more than a single, dark room belonging to the Ashkenazi religious council in the back of the Hurva Synagogue. Yet though Yosef Zondel and his wife barely eked out a living from the vinegar that the good woman made and sold, they raised the boy as though he were their own.

Half a year or so after Rabbi Yosef Zondel died, a terrible cholera epidemic broke out in Jerusalem. When neither the prayers that were said nor the incense that was burned seemed able to stop it, a local kabbalist decreed that the only way to end the plague was to marry off two orphans in the cemetery. And so, while fresh victims

were being interred there every day, and sacks of lime poured after them into the graves, a wedding canopy was erected on the tomb of the great mystic Rabbi Haim ben Atar, under which Meir'l Leder was wed to Bashe Goldschmid, whose parents and brothers had been carried off by the plague.

"You don't believe me?" marveled Uncle Tsodek. The next time I visited him at home, he promised me, he would show me the story as it appeared in print in an issue of the contemporary gazette, *Ha-Levanon*.

Meir'l Leder soon acquired a reputation as one of Jerusalem's leading pietists. The holy city buzzed with the knowledge that he could pronounce a dish properly koshered or not simply by looking at it and tell the number of goats in a flock at one glance. Once he even passed by a coffeeshop crowded with Arabs and guessed right away how many of them were inside. He was especially esteemed for his extreme punctiliousness in observing the commandments; he never donned a prayer shawl of silk, for example, lest in kissing it he touch with his lips the remnants of a cocoon spun by the unclean silkworm, and he refused to eat roast pigeon for fear that the bird might have swallowed a buttered breadcrumb prior to being slaughtered, thus violating the injunction against eating milk with meat. Moreover, it was said by those who claimed to know that, when alone, he ceaselessly made the sign of the Tetragrammaton with his fingers in the air in order to fulfill the verse, "I keep the name of the Lord always before me." Indeed, even while he was walking in the street or conversing with his fellow man, his fingers roamed back and forth, nor did they rest except on Sabbaths and the holidays, when writing belonged to one of the thirty-nine categories of forbidden activities, although even then his lips moved all the time.

Meir'l Leder's oldest son was Dovid Leder. The boy was a regular chip off the old block and was rumored to possess unusual powers like his father. Stories of his saintliness were widespread in Jerusalem, of which, it was said, he had drawn himself a map that would allow him to go from place to place without passing a single monastery or church—no easy task in a city full of such institutions—or walking down any alley so narrow that he might, God forbid, come too close to a window and infringe on a fellow Jew's privacy. At times, inspired by a spirit of zeal like that which moved Pinchas ben Eliezer to slay Zimri ben Salu and the Midianite woman in the book of Numbers, young Dovid fought the wars of the Lord by raiding Yeshayahu Refaelovitz's new photography studio outside of the Jaffa Gate, from which he confiscated the pictures of all the Jerusalemites who had dared violate the prohibition on making graven images and burned them with much ado in the Valley of Ben-Hinnom.

When Dovid Leder came of age and took a wife, he was given an apartment in Shtroys Court, that rectangle of buildings in the Musrara quarter that was inhabited by some of Jerusalem's most illustrious Musarniks, such as Rabbi Itchele Peterburg, Rabbi Yona Birzer, and the Gaon of Lublin, Shneour Zalman Fradkin. "Reb Dovid," Uncle Tsodek said, pointing to the haunches of the animal hide in my notebook, "was the youngest of the pious scholars to take up residence there."

The dwellers in the court looked fondly upon the young man, who burned the midnight oil over his studies and rapidly ascended the rungs of sacred learning. Yet late one night when, on his way home from the ritual bath, Reb Leib Milman stopped outside Leder's apartment to listen to him sweetly chanting the Talmud, he was aghast to hear Reb Dovid'l accompanying the familiar melody with an unexpected set of words. It was only because his memory failed him, Uncle Tsodek said, that he was no longer sure whether the heretical Hebrew novel that Leder had hidden behind his Talmud was Smolenskin's "The Donkey's Burial" or Mapu's "The Two-Faced Vulture."

Reb Leib Milman began to shadow Dovid'l and soon discovered that, while his map of Jerusalem indeed bypassed churches and alleys, the same could not be said of certain houses of ill-repute located in the American Colony. Moreover, it came to Reb Leib's attention that not all of the photographic plates removed by young Leder from Refaelovitz's studio had been burned in the Valley of Ben-Hinnom. Some of them had been taken to the darkroom of an Armenian photographer, where the faces of local women and young girls were mounted on the nude bodies of French models, after which they were blackmailed for money and more intimate favors.

One night shortly after Passover, when the holiday mood had

abated and life had gone back to normal, Reb Leib Milman invited Leder to his room. There he opened his Bible to the weekly Torah portion, which happened to be from Leviticus, and, sobbing helplessly as though at a funeral, read over and over the verse, "And if a leprosy shall break out abroad in the skin."

Reb Dovid cooed back as plaintively as a dove that he indeed deserved to be whipped, for there were times when his attention wandered from his studies and he thought of other things, and worse yet, still other times when he enjoyed his studies so much that he pursued them for their own sake and forgot that their sole purpose was the worship of God. Still weeping, however, Reb Leib proceeded to tell young Leder everything he knew. When Leder heatedly denied it, the pious rabbi assured him that he need not fear human retribution, since he only wished to reprove him before God and had not the slightest thought of defaming him in public.

And in fact Reb Leib Milman kept mum. Yet years later his wife, who had heard it all while eavesdropping behind the closed door, proved to have less self-control, so that when Reb Dovid'l's son Mordecai ran off to Vienna, she told the whole story to a friend. Moreover, she confided, when Dovid'l left by slamming the door and actually cursing her saintly husband to his face, Reb Leib lost his temper at last and shouted that if Leder did not repent of his sinful ways he would come to a bitter end. And so would his son Mordecai, who—since the little schoolboy no doubt already sensed in his childish way what the gross eyes of the adults around him failed to see—would grow up to be even more depraved than his father, a veritable serpent of Satan.

That same week Dovid Leder left the courtyard of the pietists and moved to the Neiten Houses, where he fell in with the ultra-Orthodox fanatics who later founded the anti-Zionist Neturei Karta and became their spokesman by virtue of the English picked up by him in the American Colony. Yet about this period in Leder senior's life, Uncle Tsodek declared, I must have already heard from Ahuva Haris, whose first husband, Haim Segal, was Reb Dovid's personal secretary, and he would not bother to tell me any more.

"But the flesh of the bull, and its skin, and its dung, thou shalt burn outside the camp, it is a sin-offering," Uncle Tsodek chanted, finishing the verse. He tore out the page from my notebook, put a lit match to it, and let it burn down in an ashtray.

"And thy camp shall be made pure," he chuckled, and asked if I had time for a short walk before he returned to his work in the archives.

7.

Although the sky was high and translucent, the rain that had fallen all morning and gathered in the crannies of the domes on the stone roof of the court building still dripped from the drainpipes onto the pavement, making its oval cobblestones that were shaped like infant head sparkle as though they were new.

From the enclosed space that linked the court building with Avihayil Hospital came a series of heart-rending shrieks. I tried peering down the mysterious hatch, several steps below street level, that led to the ablution room of the hospital, in front of which several Jewish women from North Africa were clawing their skin and pulling their hair. Off to one side, beneath a leafless mulberry tree, a huddled circle of husbands and sons conferred what to do. A black limousine rolled silently into the yard without slowing down, causing the circle to jump back in fright, along with an old man who had been in its center. Several Eastern Orthodox monks speaking a slurry Russian emerged from the vehicle, which bore diplomatic license plates, and disappeared through an iron door in a corner of the court building opposite the hospital morgue—within which, so it was said, was the seat of the Russian apostolic delegation and a magnificent chapel with a library of tens of thousands of volumes donated by Prince Constantine.

"You won't find what you're looking for here," my uncle chided me, dragging me away from the spot where, several years later, Riklin and his crew appeared with Leder's shroud. He led me down a paved footpath that led north toward Saint Paul Street and Musrara.

Old pine trees rose above us, their water-laden branches wetting the passersby with each gust of wind. Uncle Tsodek glanced at the raindrops glistening on the tips of the pine needles and said that sometimes, on winter days, when he stayed late at the office to finish his work, he saw great clouds of starlings descend on these trees to take up their roost for the night. With his arms and torso he tried mimicking the dizzying flight of the birds, how they fanned out like smoke and funneled back in steep columns before settling down on the pine boughs in thick clusters. Each time he witnessed this wonder of nature, my uncle said, he was reminded of the story in the *Zohar* of how, when the great Rabbi Shimon bar Yohai expired, the heavens shuddered so that the birds were shaken out of them and into the clefts of the sea.

To our right, by the deserted gazebo in the garden of the former Russian consulate, where ivy still climbed the tree trunks and wove green wreathes around them, a dry fountain waited for the cunningly wrought jets of water to tumble down on it again, bringing joy with their freshness to the hearts of the envoys from St. Petersburg here in the arid East. To our left, beyond the public washrooms, stood the grim old British prison, still surrounded by its rusty coils of barbed wire, in which the two Jewish freedom fighters, Barazani and Feinstein, had taken their own lives with a hand grenade.

At the top of St. Paul Street we caught a whiff of the zoological laboratories housed in the ex-consulate building, whose smell of frenzied guinea pigs and the moist sawdust floors of their cages, mixed with the indefinably erotic scent of the ailanthuses growing wild amid the barbed wire of the prison, accompanied us as we walked toward Musrara.

We strolled in silence, looking at the gleam of winter sunbeams on the wet tree trunks and stone walls, which gave off a fine haze. When we reached the wall surrounding the Italian school of the Salesian Sisters, Uncle Tsodek left the steep street and turned right.

"This is Shtroys Court," he said, entering an abandoned building whose roof was full of holes and whose walls collapsed in many places. In the courtyard, among sections of fallen wall and smashed roof tiles, nettles grew. A heavy stench of decay hung in the air. Uncle Tsodek climbed to the second floor up a rickety staircase covered with a metal mesh. I followed him down a ceilingless corridor, peering into rooms from which the door frames, the thresholds, and the window sashes had been pried out. Where the roof was gone the walls, slicked down by the recent rains, gleamed like the frescoes of Pompeii. Different layers of colored whitewash showed through in different places, leaving bright stains the color of bluing next to others of burnt sienna and still others of peach-blossom pink. Elsewhere the walls were all mildewed, suppurating with green or reddish ulcers like the skin of a leper.

"Here is where Leder was born," Uncle Tsodek said, skipping ahead of me to the end of the hallway. Suddenly he spat in disgust and hurriedly retreated down the stairs. In a corner of the last room, in a recess that had once held a closet, lay the bloated corpse of a stray dog. Worms scuttled over it and green flies of death buzzed around it in a cloud.

The street below pulsed with life. Housewives hurried to take advantage of the warm afternoon sunshine to stretch washlines supported by stilts across the street and hang their laundry on them.

The Jordanian border was just a few steps away.

Beyond the bare trees and the crumbling walls in the no-man's-land between Israel and Jordan we caught a glimpse of the Old City wall, gray and rain-washed. Cars honked within it, peddlers cried their wares, an invisible human throng went its way, so near and so far.

The untraveled-on pavement beneath us had turned pale from disuse. Cracks through which wild grass was coming up ran its entire length. Beyond the concrete cones of the antitank barriers, the barbed wire, and the yellow-and-red signs that warned of mines, a Jordanian legionnaire in a red headdress was looking at us.

"Now we are at the very tip of Israel," my uncle said, tearing me away with difficulty from the enchantment of land's end, "at the place where Israel is no more. Nothing can go on forever."

Chapter Twelve

1.

Leder's tracks vanished into thin air.

From the day I saw him dragged out of the courtroom and bundled through an emergency exit into a waiting van, I rose early every morning and made straight for the pile of newspapers in my parents' grocery. Yet I failed to find a single mention of his case.

"Stop reading all that newsprint," my mother said, worried that I might become addicted to the daily papers. "Believe me, you're wasting your time." For once I took her advice and decided to appease my curiosity with another visit to Uncle Tsodek, whose connections with the top brass in the police force, I thought, made him privy to all state secrets.

Yet this time my uncle was ill at ease and withdrawn. He glanced nervously at Carmela and Levana, who were both perched on ladders, looking for some lost files on the upper shelves; cleared his throat once or twice; and suggested that we go out for a breath of fresh air, since he had spent the whole day in a heated room with closed windows, choking on cigarette smoke. Once outside, in the little pine woods in front of the court building, he leaned against one of the concrete barriers that bordered the Russian Compound to the north—remnants of the anti-tank defenses thrown up against an expected invasion of Jewish Jerusalem by the Arab Legion during the 1948 war—and told me that, from hints dropped by the police, he gathered that Leder was suspected of grave crimes against national security. For all he knew, said my uncle, the man might be a Russian spy, and we would do best to mind our own business and leave him to rot in the dungeons of Israeli counterintellignce.

Two months passed before the curtain lifted again on Leder's mysterious disappearance. The morning after Purim, Sergeant Fishler, dressed in civilian clothes, appeared in the Rachlevskis' store, where he had been an honored guest since the day of the antireparations demonstration. When Haim's parents, who were used to seeing their hero in full regalia, asked whether he was still wearing his masquerade costume, Fishler replied that he had resigned from the police force because of disagreements with his superiors. Ever since Gleider was made precinct captain, he went on, the force had gotten loonier by the day. The case of Leder was a good example.

According to my friend Haim, who rushed over to tell me all this, Fishler related that not only had Leder been grilled day and night for a whole week without anyone suspecting from his incoherent answers that the man had a screw loose, but his revolver, which was taken from him at the time of his arrest, was kept in a safe at the station and never even sent for ballistic tests. Only when some veteran officers from Tel Aviv were assigned to the case was it discovered, as Fishler put it, that Leder "was out of his skull," and that his pistol was hopelessly rusted and lacking a firing pin, so that even a boy playing cowboy would not have been caught dead with it.

"He was a broken shell of a man," Fishler told Haim's parents, adding that as soon as the district psychiatrist examined him, he ordered him released from jail and transferred to a mental ward. Fishler himself only learned of this when he and the police doctor were detailed to escort Leder in an ambulance to the hospital in Nes-Tsiyyona. All the way there, he said, Leder never stopped babbling that if only they would let him go, he would appoint him, Fishler, minister of police, the doctor minister of health, and the driver minister of transportation in the soon-to-be-declared Lynkean state.

Apart from Fishler's story, which reached me secondhand and without further corroboration, I heard no more about Leder. "He's been swallowed up by the earth for his sins," Ahuva Haris periodically declared, expressing her amazement at the continued disappearance of the little alms collector for the School of the Blind, while my mother nodded and agreed that he had gotten his comeuppance. Indeed, had not the two of them regularly cited him as a horrible example of the most various and at times even contradictory vices, I might have slowly forgotten him and consigned his memory to oblivion, as we so often do to those who once accompanied us part of life's way.

Such was not the case, though. Three years after the doors of the police van closed upon Leder, he was cast into our life once more like a stone flung into a pond, whose placid waters it disturbs for a brief moment before sinking forever out of sight.

2.

That spring, during the afternoon siesta, the stubborn scream of a siren pierced the silence. I raced to the window to look out through the slats of the shutters, while Mother remarked that the east wind must have whipped up the embers of a bonfire left smoldering by some children and fired a field of thorns.

"You can make a million matches from a single tree and burn a million trees with a single match," she added, quoting one of the mottoes printed on the bottoms of the pages of our calendar before turning her face back to the wall and trying to fall asleep again. But the sirens kept wailing and soon, followed by a crowd of curious onlookers, two ambulances and several police cars sped past our house and up Ya'akov Meir Street.

"Curiosity killed the cat," my mother called after me as I ran out of the house. There was nothing I could do to help, she yelled, and if I had any sense I'd stay home.

A crowd had gathered by the building on the corner of David Yellin and Yehiel Michael Pines Streets that had for many years housed the headquarters of the Nutrition Army. It was staring up at the roof, at whose edge, on top of a barrel that had been dragged there to serve as a podium—one of those big-bellied tin drums once used by Jerusalemites to store rainwater for the summer dry season—stood a man dressed in a semimilitary chenille and wearing a green beret. Waving a green velvet flag on which was drawn a boat with an eye at the top of its mast, he addressed the crowd below.

It was Leder.

His face had grown more haggard and worn, perhaps because he had lost his false teeth, and a bushy mustache like Popper-Lynkeus' bristled above his upper lip. Although until now he had been speaking quietly in a proper Hebrew, almost as though to himself, he now began to harangue the crowd in a mixture of street invective and fragmentary verses from the Bible.

"If you would hearken unto me, Mr. Maidovnik," he screamed at a grocer standing bewilderedly in the doorway of his store, "and stop selling all those Portugese sardines, California canned fruit, English sucking candies, Swiss chocolates, and cans of Kiwi shoe polish, thy peace would be as the river's and thy strength as the waves of the sea." Next, turning to the owner of the local liquor store, he cried with Isaiah: "Thy wine is mixed with water, Mr. Shenker! You sell cigarettes to little children, you well-poisoning bastard!" Thus he savagely chastised all the storekeepers for luring their customers into overconsumption and addicting them and their families to fancy foods for which they had to work harder and harder while all spiritual concerns were deadened within them.

"The man's a dog," Maidovnik declared, wiping a knife still smeared with halvah on his greasy khaki pants.

"A person he lives by himself, all that loneliness she drive him crazy," said a heavily made-up woman with a Hungarian accent, who had been caught in the middle of her shopping by Leder's diatribe. Did Maidovnik have any idea, she asked, where that prematurely old-looking young man up there had been all these years?

"I don't run a missing persons bureau, Mrs. Laks," Maidovnik said, adding that it wasn't loneliness that drove people crazy, it was marriage. Just recently he had been told by Mrs. Poker, Leder's next-door neighbor, that over a year ago the little alms collector had married a dark-skinned Yemenite girl and gone to live with her in Rehovot, or maybe it was Nes-Tsiyyona.

"A man got so much culture with such a black animal," shuddered Mrs. Laks. Just then, however, the police, who had been trying to disperse the crowd in order to clear a path for a fire engine that had come tearing around the corner of Hagiz Street and was now extending its ladder toward the roof, swept me away from the two of them.

As soon as he noticed the tip of the ladder, Leder shouted to the firemen and policemen to keep off the roof if they didn't want him to jump. "And then, you sons-of-bitches, my blood will be on your heads!"

Next to the Ruhama Pharmacy—the first in a row of commerical shops beneath the apartment of Chief Rabbi Nissim—some police officers were quietly consulting with several doctors in white smocks. One of them left the group and climbed the stairs to the pharmacy. "He's going to telephone the loony-bin in Nes-Tsiyyona," an eavesdropper told the crowd. "They want more info on him."

"You bowed down to the golden calf in the desert!" Having run once around the roof to check that the ladder was gone, Leder was seized by the spirit of prophecy again. "And here you bow down to your latest love, *La vache qui rit!*"

He brandished a round box of the well-known French cheese and announced that the Children of Israel were no better than others when it came to worshipping the calf-idol of food, whose mother cow simply laughed at them from her label.

Leder's voice was getting hoarser. His pleas against overconsumption, and on behalf of the Nutrition Army and the Lynkean revolution, were getting so confused that even I, who knew all his theories by heart, could hardly make head or tail of them. "Behold your god, O Israel!" he cried huskily, dramatically removing a blanket from what had appeared to be a second water barrel. A giant doll in bovine shape, made of quilts and pillows strung and wired together, revealed itself to be the astonished eyes of the beholders. A daisy chain of sausages, cheese triangles, liquor bottles, and poppyseed rolls was draped around its neck in place of a bell.

Catcalls rose from the crowd. A few strapping Hasidim from the court of the Rabbi of Ger, young men who surrounded their master wherever he went like a wall of Cossacks, demanded that Leder cease his public blasphemy.

"Is it the sound of singing that I hear?" asked the man on the roof in the words of Moses descending Mount Sinai, cupping one hand to his ear. "Then be this a sign unto ye! " He lifted a jerry can above the huge pillow-doll. Drops of kerosene spattered down like rain on the spectators nearest the building, who shrunk quickly back. Leder gave the yearling calf a long look, as though loathe to part with it, then tossed a burning match on it.

Tongues of flame licked up, followed by billows of smoke. The pillowcases burned first, then the kerosene-soaked feathers and the quilts. A strong, horny smell, like that which stank up the Ringels' apartment five years before, filled the street.

The firemen abandoned the ladders and quickly unrolled their flat canvas hoses that swelled up like snakes when the water gushed through them. Aiming them at the roof, they awaited orders from a police captain whispering excitedly with the doctor who had telephoned Nes-Tsiyyona.

The doctor, a prominent psychiatrist, now shaded his eyes with one hand, made a funnel with the other, and looked up at Leder, who was still pouring kerosene over the burning doll. A rain of brown glass that had exploded from the heat, the shrapel of one of the liquor bottles garlanding the cow, showered down on the firemen.

"Mordecai, Mordecai, my friend! I want you to listen to me," the psychiatrist implored the madman, who capered unstoppably about his Olympian aerie. "I too have the greatest respect for Popper-Lynkeaus . . ."

Leder, however, while fanning with the greenish flag of the Nutrition Army the fire that was devouring the feathers and sausages, mocked the doctor's transparent attempt to find a way to his heart. In all this food-crazed land, he declared, he alone had remained true to the great visionary and his memory. "But you needn't worry, Doctor," he called out, seeking to calm the distraught physician. Now that he had warned the public of the catastrophes in store for it, he felt better and would come down from the roof of his own accord and go home.

He waved his flag one last time, saluted an imaginary reviewing stand, and disappeared behind the barrel. Just then the police captain flashed a signal to the firemen. A burst of water came from the hose, spraying the roof and wetting the bystanders below, while the captain made a dash for the stairs with a scrimmage of doctors, policemen, and hospital orderlies at his heels. Before long the entire entourage descended again, led by Leder in the grip of two burly men. In the doorway of the house he paused with manacled hands and bowed to the gathered throng, while on the lintel stone above him the green bull's horns hung by the Bukharian landlord continued to gore the thousands of sooty flakes and half-burnt feathers that drifted down from the sky on that hot, dry afternoon.

3.

About half a year later, on one of those October days when a first chill is in the air, there was a traffic jam on the same street. Once more it was on account of Leder, whose funeral procession, which had just set out for the cemetery from Avihayil Hospital, paused by his house for him to bid it a last farewell.

A small crowd of housewives, shopkeepers, and pedestrians gathered around the black hearse and looked curiously at the body inside under a prayer shawl. The morticians opened the car door but did not trouble to take out the corpse, while Reb Mottes chanted aloud the well-known saying in *Ethics of the Fathers* that a man must always keep three things in mind, the rancid drop that he has come from, the wormy earth that he is bound for, and the King of Kings who will judge him in the end. He passed quickly, as was the custom, over the first of these reminders and operatically drew out the last two. Then Riklin said a hasty mourner's kaddish and the group of men crowded back into the car.

I sat squeezed between Riklin and a young mortician, my feet bumping against the hoe and shovel that lay on the messy floor of the vehicle. The sour sweat-smell of the bearded men around me and the flaxen odor of the shrouds filled the cramped car as it drove through the noisy streets of Jerusalem. Yet when I tried opening a window, Reb Mottes, who was sitting across the corpse from me, grumbled that if he caught cold from the draft he would have the sniffles all winter.

All the way to the cemetery, the morticians droned prayers in unison, their eyes staring rigidly ahead as though at some point beyond death. I kept glancing at the corpse lying next to me like a baby in its crib, diapered with shrouds and wrapped in its prayer shawl. I tried thinking of Leder when he was alive. His body shifted with each jolt of the car, his thigh almost touching my knee on the turns, especially when we entered the old Roman road west of the cemetery. I had never been so close to death.

The stretcher was placed by the side of the open grave and Reb Mottes, Riklin's chief assistant, turned toward a memorial shaped like Rachel's Tomb that stood on the plot of the famous kabbalist Rabbi Yehuda Leib Ashlag and called out in Yiddish, "*A tsenter, Srulik-Osher!*"—that is, "Yisra'el-Asher, come to be the tenth man for prayer!" From the surrounding hills, the tribal lands of Benjamin that had in the days of Joshua been the home of the Gibeonites, came the rolling echo, "Kosher kosher kosher . . ." A young man dressed in a striped yellow caftan emerged from the stone structure and hurried toward us among the graves, hiking up the skirts of his robe as he ran to reveal the white knickers beneath them.

One of the undertakers handed Riklin a round tin snuff box, from which Reb Elya took several metal counters and placed them on Leder's stomach. Then his colleagues formed a circle about the corpse and, each seizing hold of the black cloth belt of the man on either side of him, began to revolve around it while mumbling psalms. Each time they came full circle Riklin, still grasped by his belt, picked up a counter, shrilled in a loud voice, "And to the sons of his concubines Abraham gave gifts and sent them away from Isaac his son while he lived, eastward unto the east country," and threw the pieces of metal as far as he could. Seven times the undertakers did their dance of death around Leder, banishing the ghoulish issue of his loins, while Riklin cast the counters to the four winds and the sunset whirled overhead in horror-stricken colors like the reds, blues, and scarlets above the screaming woman in the famous painting of Munck's that I was to see years later in a museum. When the seventh circle was completed Leder was let down into his grave.

For man is but vanity.

4.

On our way back into town, Reb Elya slapped my back and suggested that, before we went our separate ways, we have a glass of tea together at Nishel's to celebrate this day, the first on which I had seen a human life depart for its eternal abode.

The diner on Ge'ula Street was deserted except for a corner by the counter where Lapides, the crazy cantor, was chewing sauerkraut and paying for it by entertaining Mr. Nishel with Yossele Rosenblatt's rendition of U'v'nuho Yomar in a voice that rose at one moment to a volcanic crescendo and dwindled at the next to a pianissimo as frail as a violin's.

Mr. Nishel, keeping time to the aria by nodding his head and clucking his tongue admiringly, cut slices of lemon and leaned them against our glasses in their saucers.

Riklin interrupted the operatic cantor, who had thrown his arms wide in supplication, his Adam's apple bobbing up and down, and declared that there were, God be praised, greater pleasures in life than having to listen to such numbers.

"And what gives you pleasure in life, Reb Elya?" Nishel wondered as he served us our tea.

"On a Saturday night in midsummer, when the moon is full and the corpse is as light as a feather, there is no greater pleasure than an outing to the graveyard," Riklin giggled, stealing a glance at the tremor of fear that passed over Nishel's lips before they burst open in laughter.

Reb Elya was in high spirits, and I asked him a second time—the first having been while we stood in the courtyard of the hospital waiting for the corpse to be brought out—how Leder had died. This time, however, I pointedly inquired whether there was any truth to the rumor spread by Ahuva Haris that he had hung himself in the doorway of his hospital room when the orderlies were looking the other way.

Riklin ran a finger over the edge of his glass like a slaughterer testing his blade and remarked that a midrash in Bereshit Rabba commented on the verse, "For your lifeblood I will surely require a reckoning," by saying that it referred to the man who deliberately took his own life. Indeed, suicide was a greater sin than murder, since its perpetrator not only denied himself the absolution of his own death but openly confessed his disbelief in the immortality of the soul and the lordship of the Creator, blessed be He. And yet, even if there was substance to the gossip of those who claimed to know what went on in the back rooms of hospitals, there was no reason, Reb Elya concluded, to deprive Leder of a proper Jewish burial, as was the law with suicides, since being insane, he could not deliberately have done anything.

Lapides had resumed his ecstatic imitation of Yossele Rosenblatt and was now belting out the verse, "For I have given you good doctrine, forsake ye not My law."

"Mr. Nishel," Riklin rumbled at the proprietor, pointing at a pie dish in a glass case, "give the man some good pie, for God's sake, and tell him to forsake Yossele Rosenblatt." Although it was no secret, he added, that all cantors were men of little brain, perhaps if Lapides stepped outside for a moment, the divine air of the Holy Land might make him wiser.

I could get neither Leder's death, nor the last days of his life, of which I knew nothing, off my mind and asked Riklin if he knew whether my dead friend had left any children.

"What makes you think that?" asked Reb Elya, taking a cube of sugar and, holding it in one hand, sipping some spilled tea from his saucer.

I smiled secretively and replied that when Leder was carried out of the morgue, I had heard him, Reb Elya, announce that, by token of the age-old ban, none of the dead man's children were allowed to follow him to the grave.

Riklin looked at me and said that the fuzz on my cheeks and my tuft of a mustache bore witness to the fact that I was already a man, which meant that I must know what a nocturnal emission was. If I still remembered his discourse on the subject on the day that had ended with his banishment from our house by my irate mother, I also knew that the sons and daughters born to a man need not be of flesh and blood, and that there were disembodied spirits called night-demons who were created from drops of semen. After a man's death these offspring thronged around his bier, buzzing like stinging bees and wailing like banshees that they never would leave him again—which was why all children were barred from their father's funeral.

"You saw for yourself how we gave them gifts to make them go away," Reb Elya said, referring to the counters of the death dance. He sipped some more tea, still holding the sugar in his gesturing hand, and assured me that his warning had been purely routine and should not be interpreted as meaning that Leder had fathered real children.

And yet I could not help feeling that he was hiding something from me and tested him by asking whether he knew if it was true that Leder had married a Yemenite girl in Rehovot or Nes-Tsiyyona. The offices of the Burial Society, I said, must have a death certificate or passbook that listed the deceased's family status.

"The passbook is returned by us to the Ministry of the Interior," Riklin corrected me. "Aren't you the detective, though! How does a young man like you know so much?" And tisk-tisking at my astuteness, he remarked that a boy like myself who studied in a government school and had a modern woman who wore sleeveless dresses for a mother, undoubtedly knew more about contemporary life than he, a Jerusalem Jew of the old school, and should realize that some people were conjoined every night without the benefit of a rabbi or a wedding.

"'Chmiel," Riklin called to Mr. Nishel, who was tearfully standing in the kitchen grinding onions. "Leave the gefillte fish alone and come here." Why was it, he asked our host, that nonobservant Jews held gala bar mitzvahs for their sons and modest weddings for their daughters, while observant Jews did the opposite?

Mr. Nishel, his eyes riveted to Rikin's fingers, which grasped the cube of sugar yet never brought it to his lips when he drank, replied with a shrug that he had never given the matter any thought.

"You would know the answer if you went to hear Reb Shulem Shvadron's sermons instead of reading the newspaper every morning," Reb Elya rebuked him. And in the singsong of the preacher from Zichron Moshe, he told us that religious Jews made no fuss over the bar mitzvah, which merely marked the start of a boy's observing the same commandments that he would go on observing every day, whereas a wedding, which happened only once in a couple's life, was something special. With secular Jews, on the other hand, it was the other way around; their budding little soccer or basketball player put on his phylacteries just once and stuck them away in the closet, so that his bar mitzvah was truly an extraordinary occasion, but getting married was something that was done all the time and hardly deserved to be noticed.

Nishel doubled over, his teary eyes all but lost in his fleshy face that was rosy with laughter.

"We laugh through our tears, Chmiel, my friend, we laugh through our tears," Reb Elya said, and asked Nishel once more to make Lapides shut up. The crazy cantor was still crooning in his corner, while around him, on the table and floor, long strips of sauerkraut were scattered in a widening circle. Nishel took off his apron, peered out at the darkening street, and announced that by now even the alley cats were full, so that it was time to lock up and go home.

Yet after he had cleared our glasses and the sugar bowl from the table, he fluttered hesitantly around us for a moment before confessing to Riklin that he wished to ask him a question but was afraid to be deemed impolite.

"What is it, Reb Chmiel, what is your request?" answered Riklin in Ahasuerus' words to his queen and in the melody of the Book of Esther. "It shall be given you, even to the half of my kingdom."

“You needn’t worry,” Nishel laughed. “I don’t even want a tenth of your kingdom.” His question was, he said, that although his whole life had been spent in the presence of people eating and drinking, he had never come across anyone who drank tea like Riklin. “If you mean to use the sugar, why don’t you put it in your mouth?” he asked, shaking out the red-and-white checked tablecloth with gentle flaps. “And if you don’t, why hold it in your hand?”

Riklin flipped the sugar cube into the air and caught it as deftly as a dice player. Ever since he came down with diabetes, he replied, he had drunk tea in the manner of Rabbi Shlomo, the Hasidic master of Karlin. “One day Rabbi Shlomo’s son couldn’t stand it any longer and asked him, just like you did, why he drank the way he did.” Rabbi Shlomo—so Riklin had read in a Hasidic book—did not answer. When he had finished his tea, however, he gave his son the sugar to taste . . . and behold, it had lost all its sweetness. Ever after, when Rabbi Shlomo’s son told of his father, he boasted that the Master of Karlin could taste sugar with his hand the way other men did with their mouths.

“Has your sugar lost its sweetness, too?” I asked, reaching to take the white cube from Riklin.

“*Yunger man,*” Reb Elya said, “you’ve already asked one question too many today.” And he slipped the sugar into his pocket and rose to go while Mr. Nishel stacked the chairs upon the tables.

5.

Hardly a month had gone by since Leder’s death when a fresh breath of life could be detected in his old apartment. Bright curtains flapped in its second-story windows, which were opened to the breeze, and on the terrace, which in Leder’s day was a haven for all kinds of junk, a young woman stood hanging diapers and baby clothes on a line.

Each time I walked down David Yellin Street, something in me stirred at the resurrection of this dwelling that had languished so long in sterile solitude. I wondered, though I lacked the courage to introduce myself and ask, whether the new tenants knew anything about Leder’s heirs.

A suitable occasion soon presented itself.

In early December my classmates and I were asked to take part in a door-to-door-Hanukkah candle campaign whose proceeds were to go to the blind. My mother simply bit her lip when I told her about it, though later I overheard her complain to Ahuva that the schools nowadays taught children to be beggars from an early age and that thanks to the National Tuberculosis Society, the Israel League for the Blind, and the Committee for Deprived Youth, her son and his friends knew the ins and outs of Jerusalem better than those of the Talmud. Ahuva glanced at the stack of blue boxes of candles that I had brought home and remarked that before long I would follow in Leder's footsteps and collect alms for the School for the Blind.

Toward evening the next day, I stood before the door of the apartment in which my last and only visit had taken place long ago, on that distant winter afternoon when I returned from our class outing to Miss Carey's. The young woman I had seen hanging wash on the terrace answered my knock, looked at my basket full of candles, and asked me to wait a minute until she had finished diapering the baby.

A smell of soup cooking in the kitchen mingled with the sweet scent of Vaseline and the odor of baby poop. From the former command post of the Nutrition Army came a battle cry and a sound of falling chairs, whereupon the door swung savagely open and a boy of about five, sporting a gilded Arab *kaffia* on his head, ran past me into the kitchen. Hot on his heels charged his brother, who appeared to be a year or two older, wearing a green beret and an Austro-Hungarian medal pinned to his sweater, on one side of which was a bust of Franz Josef and on the other the imperial seal. "Hands up, you lousy Arab!" he shouted through a stuffed nose.

Leder's mementos.

"The kids can't wait for Purim," the woman apologized, returning with a baby in her arms. "What are you standing in the hallway for? Come into the living room." I must be tired, she guessed, from running up and down stairs all day long. "Are people nice to you?" she asked, offering to make me some cocoa.

A tapestry of a romantic couple boating on a lake in full moonlight hung on the wall in a heavy gold frame. On the buffet beneath it, between a bowl of oranges and a half-knit woolen pullover, stood a pink crepe-paper flower with a striped stem like a surveyor's rod held by a stylized green hand—the official symbol of the "Conquering the Desert" exhibition held at the Jerusalem trade center two years before.

"Amihai and Amikam, be quiet!" yelled the woman at the two boys in the kitchen while rocking the baby who had been awakened by their cries. She would buy two boxes of candles, she announced, one for herself and one for her mother-in-law.

She was rummaging in her purse for the money when the boy in the headdress burst into the living room sobbing that Amihai said he would cut off his wee-wee and stuff it in his mouth for being a dirty Arab.

"You're a good boy, not a dirty Arab," his mother calmed him, removing the gilded cloth from his head and toying with its velvet band.

I asked whether by any chance she had met the heirs of the former tenant.

"Are you a relation of his?" she inquired suspiciously, as though regretting having let me in. She let the headdress and its band slip to the floor and kicked them beneath the couch.

I assured her that Leder was no more than a casual acquaintance of my parents, and that we were simply curious to know if he had left family or friends behind.

She shook her head and related that the landlord, from whom they had rented the apartment for key money, had told them they could do what they wanted with the odds and ends in it, since the old tenant had died without heirs. On moving in, though, they were disappointed to find that the furniture was full of worms and all the clothing moth-eaten rags. It took her poor Albert three whole days, she informed me, looking lovingly at a photograph of a mustachioed soldier pasted to the inside of a soda bottle filled with patterns of colored sand from Eilat, to haul everything down the street.

"This is all that we kept." She pointed with the toe of her padded slipper to the fringes of the *kaffia* sticking out from under the couch. "This, the medal, and that army beret. Isn't that so, Anati?" She bounced the wailing baby in her arms and said that her sons had refused to part with these things, though she herself had been afraid that they might carry all kinds of diseases.

"What about his books?"

"Are you religious?" she asked, noting my skullcap. When they moved in, she said, they had found two shelves of books in the room that was now the children's, most of them not in Hebrew. After her father, a letter carrier who could read seven languages, had checked them all and found that none had God's name in it, Albert threw them out with the other junk in an empty field across from Bet-Hadegel Hospital.

6.

The field across from the hospital was a dumping grounds for broken utensils, rotting moving lifts, and abandoned heavy equipment. There, the next morning, next to Behira Schechter's black tailor's dummy whose leg was being tickled by weeds, I found a pile of Leder's books.

The heavy winter rains had ruined them. Their fancy cloth and leather bindings were waterlogged and cracked, and strips of Viennese newspapers from the turn of the century had peeled loose from their backings. The pages were stuck together in clumps as hard as bricks. I poked around in the pile like a hyena scavenging a dead lion. A brown manila envelope lay buried beneath the books. Its bottom had decayed into the soft, damp, verminous earth, but the black-bound notebooks inside it were unharmed, apart from a pinkening at their edges from the moisture. "The Constitution of Lynkeania" announced the title page of the topmost notebook in Leder's handwriting. Yet apart from Popper-Lynkeus' minimum social program copied out from one of his books, some attempted translations from Esperanto, and a few sketches of the Lynkean state seal, the notebooks had nothing in them.

Nearby, amid the soggy, rotting innards of a mattress, lay the photograph of Leder's father and Ahuva Haris' first husband emerging with Dr. De Haan from the British High Commissioner's. They were hardly distinguishable any more, and the snapshot, when brought to my eyes, had a fetid smell.

Next to it was the bluish airmail envelope from Dr. Schweitzer that I had seen on the massive wooden reading table of the B'nai

B'rith library. The names of the sender and addressee, once clearly legible in the old Alsatian physician's tiny but handsome script, had been washed away by the rain. Schweitzer's polite letter of refusal was missing, too. Perched high in their jungle treetops, the African egrets stared greedily at Behira Schecter's headless dummy, as though waiting to peck out its chest.

7.

Subsequently, on the wedding day of my cousin Shalom, Uncle Tsodek's son, I learned more about Leder's last days.

From the moment that Shalom was inducted into the army and sent to serve as a supervisor of the dietary laws in the kitchen of a transportation base between Safed and Tiberias, my uncle's face wore a look of dismay. To his son he kept repeating the ancient Jerusalem maxim, *Hit zikh fun fayer un fun vasser, fun Tveryer un fun Tsfasser,* "Watch out for fire, water, and Jews from Tiberias and Safed." To drive home the point he told him the story of the carload of goat cheese sold by an unscrupulous Safedian to a Jerusalem merchant, who did not discover until the shipment arrived that the sealed tins of "cheese" were filled with rocks.

In the end, my uncle's worst fears were confirmed and Shalom was caught in the snares of a young girl from Safed. At first Uncle Tsodek refused to hear about the match; then he began threatening to kill himself by swallowing fifty-nine pills of Luminel or jumping off the roof of the Generali Building, just so Jerusalem might know what his son had done to him; yet when the two love birds announced that, if he stood in their way, they would move to Australia, he resigned himself to his fate. No sooner had he done so, however, than he and his future in-laws fell to quarreling over where the wedding should take place. My uncle insisted that, since unlike his son he was still in his right senses, he had no intention of dragging himself to a distant dump like Safed, to which the parents of the bride replied that pilgrimages to Jerusalem had gone out of fashion with the destruction of the Temple. Only after arguing their case before a neutral rabbi from Haifa did they compromise on holding the ceremony halfway between the two cities, in Afula.

My mother, who had still not forgiven her brother for the episode of my grandfather's books, looked for some excuse to stay home—which was given her three days before the wedding by my coming down with the measles. Yet though my sickness seemed providential, my father insisted that she attend the ceremony nonetheless. "You and your brother can wash your dirty laundry here in Jerusalem," he declared, "but you're going to go to your nephew's wedding."

And so, in order to take out the waist of her regular wedding dress that had originally been made on the day that my friendship with Leder was discovered, my chagrined mother made her way to Behira Schechter's, from which she returned with the news that Miss Schechter would take care of me on the day of the wedding.

"He's a big boy already," mocked my father. "What does he need a baby-sitter for?" My grandfather, he added, already had two children of his own at my age, and if my mother was looking for a bride for me, she could certainly find someone younger and prettier than that stitched-out old maid.

Behira Schechter had been our seamstress for years. Two or three mornings a year I woke to find her flitting around my mother, who would be planted like a statue in the middle of the room, draped in pieces of roughly seamed fabric. Behira would hastily chalk some dashed lines on the material, gather it in at the waist, and pad the shoulders with triangles of lint while reminiscing with a mouth full of pins about Jackal Hole, which, lingering sensually over it, she called by its Arabic name of Hur el-Wawi, the place where she and her friends who came to Palestine had trained for life on a kibbutz. (From this brief period of pioneering in the swamps of the Hefer Valley, an episode soon ended by malaria, Behira had retained only the braids plaited in a circlet around her head and her militant disbelief in God.) Later, after we had finished eating lunch, she would brush off the threads that still clung to her blouse, take a sip from the mug resting on her sewing machine, and declare that religious Jews like ourselves didn't know what we were missing by not creaming our coffee after a good roast.

About a year after Leder's disappearance (no one but me, it seemed, noticed the timing of it) Behira removed the enamel seamstress's shingle from her door, curled her hair and dyed it platinum blond, and went to work in the kitchen of Fefferberg's restaurant on Jaffa Road. She now looked like an actress from the age of silent films, and sometimes, taking a shortcut on our way home from school through the back yards behind the restaurant and seeing her thick curls through a vaporous cloud as though they were the witch of En-Dor's, we stood by the kitchen window and caroled that Charlie Chaplin was waiting for her at the Edison Theater. After a while Mr. Fefferberg would come out in person to drive us away with a volley of curses or even a pail of cold water.

Wafted on a fragrance of eau-de-cologne, her neck and throat red from a long session with the hair dryer at the beauty parlor, Behira Schechter waltzed into our house to help me recover from the measles on my cousin's wedding day.

"Great, they're all gone already!" she rejoiced at finding the house empty. She shed her karakul coat, kicked off her snakeskin shoes, and came over to my bed.

"You poor darling! Can I have a look at your red little tummy?" She pulled up the blanket to see if I still had my rash. "And now a teeny-weeny kiss," she cajoled. I felt the velvety warmth of her lipstick barely brush my goosepimply skin.

She produced a pack of cards from a snakeskin purse that matched her shoes and asked if I knew how to play rummy. She dealt, laid the deck on the blanket, sat beside me in a chair, and propped her feet on the bed. Her toes, which were polished dark red, seemed to glow through her see-through silk stockings, wriggling inside their glossy net as though endowed with a life of their own.

"Do you have a girlfriend?" Behira asked casually, studying the cards in her hand. I felt the silky softness of her stockings and the warmth of her soles as her feet slid up my leg. "You go. What are you waiting for?" she pretended to scold as her toes slid toward my groin.

Mouth dry and head pounding, I looked blankly back and forth from the black clubs to the red hearts in my hand.

"You sweet thing, you," she teased in her husky voice, her head disappearing beneath the blanket, "let's look for our little joker. Maybe it's lost . . ."

The cards fell to the floor.

Afterward in the kitchen, over a supper prepared by my mother before setting out, Behira bemoaned her fate and spoke candidly of her relations with Leder.

"His fear of hunger drove him nuts," she said, peeling the red aluminum wrapper from a candy bar. "But he wasn't willing to move his ass enough to earn a decent living."

"But he collected alms for the School of the Blind," I objected.

She snickered and said that Mordecai never worked so much as an hour a day. "Anyway, what makes you think that he worked for the School for the Blind?" And Leder's ex-mistress revealed to me that what little money he fraudulently collected for poor sightless children went entirely into his own pocket.

"I put up with all his lunacy," she said, offering me a bite from the candy bar. Not only did she sew green shirts and pants for the moronic army of his dreams, she bought the material for them with her own money and even lent him her spare mannikin, which he never returned, though she kept asking for it, even when she desperately needed it.

"I washed his dirty underpants too," she said, adding that two or three times a week she cooked him special, high-protein vegetarian meals to keep up his strength, not to mention sharing his bed. "And don't think he was such a hot shot there, either," Behira declared, giving me a knowing look as she adjusted my mother's nightgown on her shoulders.

"He robbed me of my best years." The tears choked her throat.

I patted her wet, warm cheek.

"My love, my hero," she laughed through her tears. I would soon see the day, she predicted, when all the girls would chase after me. "But I'll be old and wrinkled then, if I'm still around."

"What did you need him for?" I asked to get her mind off old age and death.

"Mordecai? I wanted a child from him. But it was too late." All she wanted now was a decent man with a steady job who could make a respectable old woman of her. That was why she had quit sewing and gone to work at the restaurant, where she had hoped to meet an eligible widower or bachelor while waiting on his table. Yet despite her repeated requests, Mr. Fefferberg hard-heartedly insisted that she remain in the kitchen, which was ruining her health and skin.

"Do you hate Leder?" I asked.

“Hate a dead man?” she questioned, surprised.

But she had hated him, she admitted, when she heard of his marriage.

She had gone to visit him three times in Nes-Tsiyyona, wending her way on foot, among acadia hedges and lonely orange groves, from the main road to the top of the hill where, after the 1948 war, a mental hospital had been lodged in the former home of a a rich Arab effendi. Not once, however, did she get to see him. The first time she had arrived wet to the bones from a long walk in the rain to find him fast asleep after a heavy dose of sedatives. The second time he was out, and the receptionist told her that his condition had so improved that he was allowed to work during the day in a nearby village, watering and hoeing. The third time, Behira said, helpless anger creeping into her voice, some gaily shrieking female patients playing house under the shady canopy of the bus stop informed her that she had come a day late, since Motti-from-Jerusalem’s wedding had taken place in town the night before. The head doctor, whom she found in the occupational therapy room, confirmed the news, adding that Leder’s case was one of the few he had ever seen in which treatment was fully successful.

She had cried all the way back to the main road, ignoring the cars that stopped to offer her a ride to the junction and swearing that she would never lift a finger to help Leder again. Yet two years later, not long after his rooftop caper, she was visited one day by Mrs. Berliner, who worked as a volunteer in the mental ward of Ezrat Nashim Hospital. Leder, Mrs. Berliner told her, kept mentioning her name and apparently desired to see her. When the volunteer saw that Behira was cool to the idea, she added in a whisper that Leder’s condition, so the doctors had told her, was worse than hopeless. Behira went to the hospital.

From the moment Leder saw her, he did not stop talking and cursing his black worm of a wife who had ruined his life. He told Behira how she had thrown out sour milk that could have been made into cheese or yoghurt and dry bread that might have been baked into rusks or crumbled for frying; how she had laughed at him when, instead of putting out the garbage, he had tried turning it into compost according to directions received from a local vegetarian farmer; and how she had run away from home when he refused to buy another gas burner and insisted that she heat water for the wash over a fire of twigs in the yard.

"And that Yemenite hick actually had the nerve to call me more primitive than a caveman," Leder sobbed, and began to beat his head against the wall until an orderly came running.

On her next visit Leder told Behira, whispering to keep the staff from hearing, that although such a famine would break out within two months that people would drop like flies in the street, not only was Ben-Gurion doing nothing to prepare for it, he was actually ordering farmers to destroy fresh fruit and vegetables—"surplus agricultural produce," sneered Leder—in order to keep up prices. The most horrible sight he had ever seen in his life, he confided, had been in a grove near Nes-Tsiyyona where growers had dumped whole truckloads of citrus on the ground, gone over them with a steamroller, and then, to make sure that they could not be salvaged, poured kerosene over the orange pulp that was already mashed into the red clay soil.

"They'll be dying in the streets," Leder repeated his grim vision. And leading Behira into the yard of the hospital he showed her where, behind a row of cypresses, at the foot of the stone wall that hid the institution from the bustle of Jaffa Road, he had buried a cache with morsels of food saved from his daily meals. On her next visit, he requested, perhaps she might bring him several bags of walnuts and dates.

When she returned the following week, Leder had been moved to an isolation room and her conversation with him took place through a barred window in the door. They had, he informed her, found his buried treasure and burned it.

"They're mad," he moaned. "What will we do when the famine comes? What will we do when it comes?"

Two days later he was found hanging in his room.

Behira squashed an ant that was crossing the sugar bowl and declared that a man was worth no more than a bug.

"What you see of life is what there is," she said, stroking my cheek. "There's nothing else, no matter what anyone says. What you see is what there is!"

"But isn't it true that he had a son?" I asked, stupidly changing the subject back to Leder.

"It's true, my love, that what you see is what there is," she answered, mouthing her hard-earned knowledge of life once more into my ear while slipping her naked body out of my mother's nightgown. The nipples of her breasts grew hard again, brown and nubbly against her white skin. Her pubic hair was dark and cryptic.

"Would you mind another round of rummy?" Behira asked. And embracing my waist, she led me off to my parents' bed in the next room.

Chapter Thirteen

1.

The story I have told you was meant to end here.

Not only did Behira Schechter's visit cast new light on the last days of Leder, whose figure I have tried to portray in this book, it also officially sealed the story of my friendship with him and began another friendship that need not concern us.

Nevertheless, human relations, as my mother's good friend Ahuva Haris once described them, are like eczema: sometimes unrelenting, tormenting one day and night, and sometimes dormant in a state of remission that may last for years—yet even then, never totally gone. And so, the story of my friendship with Leder, which to all appearances was over somewhere in the late 1950s, was relived for a brief instant at the end of the Yom Kippur War, lit by that blinding lightning bolt of Jewish destiny, the low rumble of whose ensuing thunderclap accompanies this tale from start to finish.

2.

And so, some fifteen years after that voluptuous Jerusalem night, several of the characters in this book came together for a final epilogue, through which they stumbled like sleepwalkers in the yellowing landscape of the oases on the African side of the Suez Canal, carried unwittingly onward to a wondrous denouement that lent a kind of meaning to the chaotic events of long ago.

On my first day in Sinai, I ran into Haim Rachlevski. I had spent the entire month of the war in the western Negev, in a temporary military graveyard near Kibbutz Be'eri to which the dead were brought. Day and night, while heavily loaded trucks drove up from the south, we dug long rows of graves in the yellow loess. Once the trucks stopped coming, our commanding officer decided to send me and a soldier named Leibovitz across the canal to reinforce the front-line burial teams, which now, in the after-battle lull, were looking for the missing in action.

Toward evening, the two of us arrived at Absalom's Junction on the southern outskirts of the Gaza Strip. A long convoy of trucks, buses, and tankers was waiting to set out for various bases in Sinai. The bus to Tasa, to which an M.P. directed us, was as crowded as an opium den and littered with cigarette butts, orange peels, and newspapers thrown away by the passengers, reservists returning from brief furloughs, on their way down from up north. A hush descended on them as Leibovitz's huge beard and death-glutted eyes appeared in the door.

"Rabbi, come quick!" The silence was broken by a voice calling from the back in a Persian accent. "Moshe's dead between his legs."

A roar of laughter cleared the air and the soldiers went back to their noisy talk and playful bombardment of each other with the colorful woolen caps knit for them by their girlfriends and wives that had become their medals in those days. Soon, as the convoy set out and was swallowed up by the quickly falling desert night, they stopped talking and dozed off. The bus bounced and jolted along paved roads that were covered in places by sand dunes and that, as we traveled deeper into Sinai, grew pitted from Egyptian air raids. On the turns, sticking out of the sand that had already partly buried them, piles of shell cases, treads and turrets of wrecked tanks, and clusters of burned vehicles were trapped by the level beams of the headlights that briefly lit the sides of the road.

We reached Tasa in the middle of the night. Buttoning his pants, a sleepy sergeant from the chaplaincy emerged from the room of a female social worker and led us to an abandoned hut at the far end of the camp. In it, he told us, two men from another burial unit, who had come from the air base at Refidim, were already sleeping. Tomorrow, God willing, a car from Fa'id would take us across the Canal.

There was a masculine sleep-smell in the room, an odor of rifle oil and dirty, unchanged underwear. Leibovitz lit his pocket flashlight and arranged a bed for himself. By a masonite wall in one corner of the bare concrete room, the two men from Refidim lay curled up in their sleeping bags and army blankets. Leibovitz stepped outside to say his evening prayers, returned, and fell asleep. I, however, lay awake, as I had done night after night by the growing graveyard in Be'eri. The southern sky shone clear and frosty through the screened window, its stars in their grooved tracks accompanied by the stutter of a generator. Shortly before midnight the machine stopped and the silence was broken only by the distant drone of an army jet passing overhead, its red and green lights blinking on and off, and by the coughs of my roommates turning over in their sleep. Some time after the radiant hands of my watch had passed two, one of the men in the corner began talking in his sleep in the voice of a child calling its mother. A shiver ran down my spine. Hadn't I, I asked myself, heard that voice before—perhaps on that distant, blurry afternoon when my mother and I lay on the floor of the Rachlevskis' apartment, trapped by an unexpected bombardment, and I had heard Haim call his mother in the dark? The huge southern stars staggered drunkenly in the sky, and I told myself not to be foolish. Fatigue awakened old memories.

Toward morning we were woken by a scream and poked our heads out of our blankets in alarm. The owner of the child's voice was now tossing inside his sleeping bag, flailing with his hands and feet in his struggle to fight free of the Acrilac shrouds that encased him. Leibovitz, who was lying nearby, shook him and patted his head.

The sleeper opened his eyes, gave the unfamiliar men around him an anxious, embarassed look, and let his head drop back on the blanket that served as his pillow. Leibovitz took out a bottle of brandy from his knapsack, gave it to the awakened man, and told him to sponge his face with it. As he showed him how to do it, my thick-bearded friend looked like a bucolic satyr.

"Dreams aren't what they seem," he said, and told the awakened soldier that, after morning prayers, we would exorcise his nightmare.

The dreamer slipped out of his sleeping bag like a snake shedding its skin and swore that if he ever lost his mind some day it would be because of what he had seen in the great hangar of Refidim.

It was Haim Rachlevski.

After prayers, Leibowitz arranged three empty ammunition crates in a row and sat Haim on a fourth crate across from them. The three of us—he, I and the other reservist from the air base—sat down too and began the ceremony.

"*Helma taba hazit,*" recited Haim in Aramaic seven times. "I have seen a good dream."

"*Helma taba hazit,*" we all echoed after him.

Afterward, while Leibovitz evangelically went off to persuade some soldiers repairing a crippled tank to stop their work and put on phylacteries, Haim laughed and said that such foolish superstitions were as helpful as chicken soup for the dead. Ever since he had started laying out corpses in straight rows in the great hangar in Refidim, and covering them with blankets spattered with blood and bits of human brain, he told me he thought of nothing else all day and dreamed of nothing else all night. One nightmare in particular kept recurring, generally in the early hours of the morning.

In it our class was in the Maresha hills near Bet-Guvrin, walking between hedges of prickly pear heavy with fruit and dodging little Arab shepherds who prodded their flocks through fields of sceptered squills sticking up like bayonets from the earth. Our shoes had turned white from the chalky soil and our clothes were shot through with thorns. It was dusk. Street lamps, like those at busy intersections, threw an orange glow on hilltops crowned with abandoned Byzantine churches. Black birds that looked like little ravens were startled from the branches of the trees, their clipped, metallic cries piercing the stillness that stretched to the horizon. "Here come the jackdaws!" calls Miss Schlank, urging us to flee before night came. But the more we walked, the more of us kept disappearing, falling into narrow holes all around us. None of us stopped to help anyone. Suddenly, Haim continued, he, too, fell down one of these sinkholes into a cave whose floor was covered with a thick layer of campfire ash, dried bird droppings, and black and white feathers left from flocks of pigeons devoured by the jackals.

A moist, repellent slime coated the walls like fur. To his right, a conical shaft of light fell on a columbarium. Pigeonholes ran across a wall. In each was a glass jar. Haim strode toward them, knee-deep in dung. Curled up like fetuses in the jars, which reminded him of those he had once seen in a nature museum, were his friends, his father, his mother, and himself.

Haim and I waited until afternoon for the promised vehicle to take us across the Canal. Apart from a medic handing out anti-malaria pills, no one interefered with our reunion, our first since finishing school.

We sat in the open, under a camoflauge net strung between two troop carriers, drawing street maps in the sand and resurrecting houses and their inhabitants, our hearts full of longing for our parents who had left us to die and for the carpet of casuarina needles on which, in the shadow of Jerusalem's stone walls, we had taken our first earthly steps.

At about two p.m. a commandeered commercial vehicle, whose yolk-colored body with "Kodak" written on it in Hebrew and English barely showed through a heavy layer of sand, pulled up beside us with a savage squeal of brakes. An army rabbi with gleaming boots, a trim beard, and a smell of smoked sprats on his breath jumped out looking pleased with himself and demanded to know why we were not jumping in. He moved officiously about, destroying the houses and streets of Jerusalem without knowing it.

We took a last look at them as we climbed into the car. A black beetle that had appeared out of nowhere was crawling down what had recently been Ge'ula Street.

All the way the rabbi never stopped talking, telling us about the fighting that had taken place in the area.

"The code name for this road is Tirtur," he said knowingly, like a student put in charge of his class while the teacher has gone to see the principal. On Simhat Torah, he told us, he had braved a terrific bombardment not far from here in order to bring a Torah scroll to the soldiers of the engineering corps who were putting down the pontoon bridge on which our forces crossed the Canal. The engineers, the rabbi said, lay face down on the bridge as they built it, rolling a new float into the water every few minutes. The air was full of smoke and dust, visibility was practically nil, and even the xenon searchlights mounted on the tanks were unable to pierce the fog of battle.

"The Faith and the Glory to Thee, yea, to Thee," sang the rabbi as though dancing in a synagogue during the fete of the Rejoicing of the Law. With his right hand he pointed north, toward a cluster of buildings obscured by clouds of whirling dust, and asked if we had heard of "the Chinese Farm." This had in fact been, he informed us, a pilot agricultural project built for the Egyptians by the Japanese.

"The battle of the century took place there," he said. "Straight out of Hollywood."

Haim and I said nothing.

Soon after, we crossed the Canal.

We looked in amazement at the narrow strip of water. To think, Haim said, that the gutless wonders sitting by their top-floor windows in Tel Aviv had managed to brainwash us all these years into thinking that a goddamned sewage ditch was the best antitank line in the world.

"An impassable barrier," Haim said. "They can shove it up their ass."

The rabbi gave him a threatening look and warned that, if he did not watch his language, he would have him court-martialed. Did he want to go home when all this was over or to do time in an army jail?

3.

Mintz, who buried people in civilian life too, was in charge of searching for those missing in action from the battle for the Egyptian naval base at Fanara. Spreading some topographical maps in plastic cases before us, he ran a finger along the shore of the Great Bitter Lake, pointed to a number of red and blue squiggles made with a magic marker in the vicinity of the abandoned Egyptian base and the mine fields around it, and told us that, after talking at length with the men and officers who had fought there, he was fairly sure where the missing bodies must be.

At dawn the next day we went to see the lay of the land. When we returned toward evening, tired and tense from a long day in the mine fields, Haim and I invited Mintz to join us for a snack at the canteen.

"There are greater pleasures in life than to sit shooting the breeze and eating chocolate bars in that vaudeville hall," Mintz said, stroking his graying beard.

“The greatest must be on a Saturday night in midsummer, when the moon is full and the corpse is as light as a feather,” I teased him in the words of Riklin’s repartee in Nishel’s restaurant.

“You knew Reb Elya?” Mintz asked, surprised. “He was my father-in-law, Mina’s father.” Thus, newly bound to us by this mutual acquaintanceship, our commanding officer urged us to come with him to the synagogue instead. There, in a makeshift chapel housed in a former Egyptian armory, Mintz liked to discuss rabbinic fine points with the army chaplains who came to the base from their units west of the Canal, and with the Lubavitsher Hasidim who had descended on Fa’id, equipped with presses and photo-offset plates, in order to print a Land of Goshen edition of Rabbi Shneour Zalman of Ladi’s mystical *Tanya*, as per instructions received from the latter’s spiritual avatar, the Rabbi of Lubavitsh, via a hasty transoceanic phone call from New York.

Haim could not stand all these bearded young Jews who reeked of brandy and rabbinic wisdom. The blood of an observant Jew, he declared, was no redder than anyone else’s. Instead of running around this hellhole as though it were a Hasidic wedding, they might lend the other soldiers a hand and do something constructive.

And so, while Mintz spent his free time in the synagogue, lugging his field telephone with him to be on the safe side, Haim and I sat around the PX or went for long walks outside the camp, where we either wandered through the ruins of the ghost town of Fa’id, peering into empty yards behind crumbling mud houses and flocks of pigeons, that shot frighteningly up from their tower-shaped dovecotes with a stormy flutter of wings, or else strolled away from the destruction along the sweetwater canals. Long levers and bucket-wheels hung uselessly above the shallow wells and brackish water holes, whose only visitors were an infrequent swan or duck slipping out from the bushes. Time and again we were drawn to these withering oases, wondering when they would vanish at last like a mirage into the wilderness.

Upon returning in the evening to Fa’id, we shut ourselves up in our little room, where we kept warm during the cold desert nights by lighting dozens of unwanted Sabbath candles that the Hasidim had given out. While I made coffee, Haim rolled himself up in a blanket and told stories of the house he grew up in, a two-story, pink-stone Jerusalem building in which his childhood and youth were passed. He told me about his parents; about their neighbor, the old healer, who rose early in the morning to feed the pigeons bread crumbs dipped in milk and treated his patients with leeches and cupping glasses; about the unmarried brother and sister who quarreled in loud voices to scare off the municipal tax collector each time he came and hugged and kissed each other when he went away; and about the crazy boy above them who stuffed himself with shortbread and chocolate bonbons and peed off the terrace at people in the street below. Though there was not much depth to these vignettes, which were taken from his own lively observations and eventually published in the literary supplement of a newspaper under the title "My Parents' House," they were clever and amusing to listen to.

By ten o'clock Mintz would pound on the tin partition between us and shout that we were keeping him awake. Of the ten portions of idle talk that had been granted the world, he complained, nine had not been given, as the rabbis said, to womankind, but to us. Then Haim, who always restrained me from answering, blew out the candles, plunging the room into darkness as thick and mysterious as that of David's Tomb on Mount Zion, and we climbed into our ornate, captured Egyptian beds.

Before surrendering to sleep Haim liked to recite some favorite lines from a poem of David Fogel's that went:

This house
Will outlast me.
In it will live
Someone who won't know I was.
How tired we are, though.
Come, let us sleep.

4.

The days passed slowly that winter in Fa'id, tense and uneventful at one and the same time. Each morning the helicopters passed overhead, flying southwest to kilometer 101, where the disengagement talks with the Egyptians were being held. Above the Atka Mountains, smoke rising from great bonfires announced that the Israeli withdrawal had already begun. In the mine fields of Fanara one body was still missing. Every morning Mintz, who refused to give up, studied his maps and went over the testimony of battle once more, and every afternoon he took Haim or me and headed south. One

morning, while he was shuffling his papers, we were startled by the ring of the telephone. An excited voice asked us to come at once to the Fanara jetties. Mintz ran for our car, pulling me and a sapper from the engineering corps behind him, and declared that today we would surely lay the last of the dead in a Jewish grave.

We were greeted at the entrance to the Egyptian base by a frightened group of reservists, from whose confused shouts we were barely able to make out what had happened. Three soldiers, drivers of the big transports that were taking the equipment of the withdrawing units back north, had stopped that morning for a swim in the lake. A patrol warned them that bathing was strictly forbidden, since both the shore and the water were mined, but the drivers, paying no attention, stripped and plunged in. Suddenly there was a loud explosion. Two of the men stumbled out bleeding heavily, one of them minus a foot. The third was killed.

We passed the bombed-out train depot and walked to the end of the pipeline jetty.

"There!" cried a young first lieutenant, the commander of the patrol. He pointed to a thicket of reeds by the lake shore where a flock of storks was standing with outstretched necks. "The crazy bastards went in there."

The sapper went first, his mine detector in front of him. He was followed by Mintz, with the lieutenant and me bringing up the rear.

The storks, alarmed by our approach, took off with high-pitched screams and wheeled above us, beating their wings to an unseen destination.

Half-an-hour later, we fished the dead man from the water. His stomach and legs had been ripped apart, but his curly-locked, brown-skinned face was still lifelike.

It was evening when we got back to Fa'id. Haim was waiting in the doorway of our room, pacing excitedly as though he had news.

"Did you get leave?" I asked, wondering who could have given him a pass to go north.

“Do you remember Leder, the collector for the School for the Blind?” he asked.

“What on earth made you think of Leder?” I grumbled. I wanted to change my clothes, which were sour from blood.

“Did you know that he had a son?” And without waiting for an answer, Haim told us that in the mid-’50s Leder had fathered a son in Rehovot who was registered as Yosef Popper Leder but later changed his name to Yossi Shelach.

Mintz and I stared at him as though he were out of his mind. It was a fact, Mintz said—or so he had heard from his father-in-law, might he rest in peace—that Reb Dovid Leder had once sought to block the Suez Canal with sandbags for the Turks, but why bother us now with stories as old as the hills?

“You pulled him out of the lake today,” said Haim. And he handed us Yossi Shelach’s papers that were found by the military police in the cabin of his truck.

As with most human dreams, the end of this story lies shrouded in death.